Patrick Woodhead has been professionally exploring for the last eight years. He has scaled unclimbed mountains in Kyrgyzstan, Tibet and Antarctica, kayaked through the uncharted tributaries in the Amazon and skied over 4,000 km across Antarctica. He is also the founder of the first luxury safari company in Antarctica and divides his time between London and South Africa.

THE SECRET CHAMBER

A young English doctor disappears into the Ituri Forest in Northern Congo. No one who goes there ever comes back, so Luca Matthews, a brilliant climber, is tasked to find him. Mining troubleshooter Beatrice Makuru ventures into the same region. Coltan, the mineral essential for every laptop and mobile phone, is running dry. With its increased demand, the Congo is the key to the mystery. And whilst the new wave of Chinese demand grips Africa — the race is on for its mineral wealth. Meanwhile, in the depths of the forest, a plan takes shape which will rock the civilised world . . . With the world's eyes turned towards the Congo, Luca and Beatrice are embroiled in a mystery far more dangerous than a simple quest for a friend.

Books by Patrick Woodhead
Published by The House of Ulverscroft:

MISADVENTURES IN A WHITE DESERT
THE FORBIDDEN TEMPLE

PATRICK WOODHEAD

THE SECRET CHAMBER

Complete and Unabridged

CHARNWOOD
Leicester

First published in Great Britain in 2011 by
Arrow Books
The Random House Group Limited
London

First Charnwood Edition
published 2012
by arrangement with
The Random House Group Limited
London

British Library CIP Data

Woodhead, Patrick.
  The secret chamber.
  1. Congo (Democratic Republic)- -Fiction.
  2. Suspense fiction.
  3. Large type books.
  I. Title
  823.9′2–dc23

  ISBN 978–1–4448–1343–2

Published by
F. A. Thorpe (Publishing)
Anstey, Leicestershire

Set by Words & Graphics Ltd.
Anstey, Leicestershire
Printed and bound in Great Britain by
T. J. International Ltd., Padstow, Cornwall

To the farmers at the refuge camp.
May you find your way home.

1

The man was running, arms outstretched, fingers splayed, as if trying to feel the way.

It was early in the morning and the first of the sun's rays had just broken over the wide basin of the jungle. Despite the half-light coming down through the trees, the man's eyes burned as if exposed to it for the first time. Dark rings of exhaustion circled each eye, while his skin was ashen white. He squinted, trying to see a way through, but there was only the jungle.

He stopped by the low branches of an acacia tree, feeling his pulse beat at his throat and his lungs burn. Mud oozed up from between his bare toes and, for a moment, he simply stared at his feet, too tired to continue. After six hours of running, he had nothing left to give.

There was the sound of slapping leaves, then a high-pitched call. They had found him again.

Two hundred metres behind where he stood, three Congolese men moved with the skill of hunters born to the jungle. Their actions were fluid and self-assured, weapons held loosely in their left hand while their right was spread wide for balance. They were conserving energy, more jogging than running, being careful not to injure themselves on the treacherous ground.

All were naked except for a tasselled belt of twine wrapped around their waists and draped down between their thighs. The lead hunter was taller than the other two, with long, supple muscles that flexed across his back as he ran. His black skin gleamed with sweat; his nostrils flared wide as he drew the air deep into his lungs.

He looked up, recognising the acacia tree. They were nearing the river.

Quickening his pace, the lead hunter took one of the arrows from his fist and ran it across the shaft of his bow, finding the string without looking down. In almost a single movement, he jolted to a stop and loosed the arrow. It sliced through the broad leaves at waist height, missing its mark by a few inches and sinking into the bark of a narrow tree.

They were closer now, only twenty metres behind the man. Saplings still swayed as they passed them, while the hunters could hear the ragged sound of his breathing. As they crested a ridge they suddenly found themselves out in the open. There was the river, its waters brown and heavy in the heat. It wound through the jungle like the body of a giant snake, the only break in the canopy for hundreds of miles in each direction.

Raising his hand against the sun's glare, the lead hunter watched as ripples fanned out across the water. He waited, bow raised, for the man to surface. Then, almost a third of the way across, the water exploded with movement. They could see the man's head thrown back as he gasped for air, his body drifting sideways in the current.

For a moment, the hunters remained still, watching. Then, without a word, they retreated back into the jungle.

The man stared back in confusion before slowly swinging round towards the opposite bank. He swam with both arms clumsily slapping against the water, and with each stroke his face dipped further beneath its foul surface. He was tiring fast. Soon, he could do no more than keep himself afloat, coughing as the water seeped into his mouth. The river was pulling him down-stream towards a narrower stretch, its bed and banks strewn with huge granite boulders.

There were the hunters. Just standing there, bent low, waiting.

He tried to duck under the surface one last time and escape them, but sinewy fingers delved deep into the water, dragging him sideways on to the rocks. The man lay there, too tired even to raise his hands in self-defence, while the hunters bound his wrists with a thin twine cord, the fibres toughened from age. Dragging him to his feet, they looped a noose around his neck, pulling it tight into his throat. They pushed him back into the jungle, moving in single file and so close to him that he could smell the wood smoke on their skin.

'S'il vous plaît . . . ' Please, he begged, but they didn't respond.

The procession twisted one way then the next, not pausing, through the maze of trees and undergrowth, until finally they started to climb. The canopy grew thinner, with natural light pouring in through the gaps between the treetops with burning luminescence. Overhead, a vast column of black rock slowly appeared, dust swirling around its base in the breeze. Before they even reached it, the man could feel the heat of the volcano and smell the bitter stench of sulphur.

A wide crack ran down the rock face in front of him, funnelling back into the mountain. As he was pulled to a halt in front of it, he slowly sank to his knees, knowing only too well what lay in the shadows.

'*Libérez-le.*' The order to release him came from the darkness. There was the faint scraping sound of a boot, then a silhouette appeared just beyond the line of shadow.

'*Faites-le rapidement!*' Do it quickly.

The hunters hesitated a second more, not wanting to come closer. Then, snatching off the noose, they pushed the man forward, pitching him on to his hands and knees. Tears welled up in the corners of his eyes, mingling with the sweat running down his cheeks.

'Please,' he stammered, 'I never meant to . . . '

'Joshua . . . Joshua,' came the voice again. 'You have only to ask forgiveness. All I have ever wanted is that you should open your heart.'

The silhouette moved closer, its hands reaching out into the bright sunlight, gently pulling him closer.

'Come back to us, Joshua. Repent and you shall be forgiven.'

'I do. I do,' he blurted out, his voice choking with fear. In front of him, he saw the apparition slowly lower itself to its own knees. It was close now, almost touching him.

'See how easy it is,' the voice whispered. An arm reached forward to pat him on the back.

Joshua suddenly screamed as a knife was stabbed into the back of his right thigh. His mouth widened, the scream becoming high-pitched as the blade worked back and forth, severing his hamstring. A second later the knife was yanked free and Joshua was pushed back on to the hard rock.

'You may be forgiven,' came the voice one last time, 'but now you can never leave us.'

2

A low-pitched, mechanical noise bled out across the openness of the Kalahari Desert. It reverberated for a moment longer before being lost to the huge, still skies.

Three thousand feet above the scrubland and winding past the sporadic towers of brilliant white cloud, a Cessna 206 gradually made its way west. In the left hand seat of the low cockpit sat Beatrice Makuru, her long body hunched forward and one hand loosely gripping the control column. The side of her head was pressed against the perspex window as she idly watched the desert pass by beneath. It was hot inside the plane, the air stifling despite the vents being fully open, making her feel heavy and lethargic.

Every few seconds, her eyes flicked back to the instruments, instinctively scanning from left to right, the airspeed indicator, the DI and altimeter, before settling back upon the unchanging landscape beneath. She yawned, her wide, brown eyes blinking several times as she tried to force herself awake and find some sort of reference point outside the cockpit. But the desert was just too vast. It drifted past, endless and desolate, and she let her gaze blur in and out of focus. It seemed strangely peaceful out there, as if the sheer absence of people was something to be treasured. Ever since she could remember,

6

she had always preferred to be alone, the solitude matching a rare stillness in her character.

'Golf. Hotel. Juliet. Come in.'

The radio crackled to life and for a moment the sound washed over her. After a pause, she pulled her head clear of the window and sat up straight.

'Hotel. Juliet. What's up, Johnny?'

'Listen, Bear, we've just got word of some kind of explosion at the Bloemfontein mine. I don't have much more than that to tell you right now, but the labs might have been hit and there could be some contamination. Can you divert, over?'

'Stand by.'

Bear dragged her charts up from the seat behind, unfolding the first then pulling out the marker pen and slide rule from a clip in the sun visor. She quickly drew two tight green circles and, with the pen clamped to her mouth, measured the distance between them with the slide rule. She scrawled a quick fuel calculation, before pressing her thumb down on the comms switch.

'Affirm, I can divert. ETA twenty-five to thirty minutes. Any casualties?'

'Negative. Looks like they were lucky.'

'Wilco . . . ' Bear paused, the faint crackling of the radio echoing in her headset. 'And, Johnny, who's on the ground?'

'That's Wilhelm.'

'Copy that. Hotel. Juliet.'

Bear slowly shook her head, sliding the map off her lap and on to the empty seat beside her. She looked down at the smooth skin of her thighs and cursed herself for having worn such a tight skirt to the office that morning. She instinctively wriggled back in the seat, pulling it half an inch further down her legs, but knew it was useless. As she lifted her arm to check the DI against the compass for her new heading, she felt the shirt she was wearing cling to her skin in the heat. It outlined her cleavage perfectly. She shook her head once again.

That was all the excuse those testosteroned idiots at the mine would need. Stuck out in the middle of the Kalahari, they didn't see women for weeks on end. The only female contact most of them had was in the knocking shops in town. The proceeds of a month's work for a long weekend of boozing and whoring. Seemed like a high price to pay, given the looks of most of the women out in Bloemfontein.

This would have to be the one day she'd had to dress up for meetings. To make matters worse, the fitted jacket to match the skirt was hanging neatly on the back of her chair in the office. In the heat and the hurry to get back to Cape Town, she had managed to forget it.

Pulling her long, black hair into a tight ponytail, Bear looked down again to see the material of her white shirt clinging to the sides of her breasts.

'Shit,' she muttered, her French accent drawing out the 's' so that it reverberated into the radio mic. She buttoned the shirt a notch higher and pulled it away from her skin, trying to get some air beneath the fabric.

And Wilhelm too. That fat Boer bastard had

barely been able to stop himself from rubbing up against her when she'd been in overalls, let alone dressed like this. That leering grin of his always made her want to grab him by the balls and squeeze the look from his jowly face.

With another shake of her head, she angrily jerked the control column forward, sending the plane diving down in a steep banking turn. The noise of the wind increased with each turn of the altimeter and she held the column pressed forward, enjoying the feeling of really flying once again. Even an old boneshaker like a 206 could be fun if you knew how to push it.

Levelling out at only 100 feet, Bear rolled the wings on to her new heading and put in the power. Her eyes darted between the instruments and the horizon, while everything else seemed to fade into significance. It was always like this when she flew the way her father, Jean-Luc, had taught her. She was a gangly teenager with barely enough strength in her arms to pull out of a dive when she first started flying, yet even now she could remember his voice coming through softly on the mic. It was always calm, always precise. The instructions whispered, getting her to edge lower and lower, until the ground ripped past in such an adrenalin-fuelled blur that she could hardly breathe. It felt as if the termite mounds dotted across the red savannah would rip off the undercarriage, but still his voice told her everything was OK, that she could go lower, push it a bit more.

That was always the way it was with her father. It was one of his many hang ups from a life spent touring Africa as a mercenary. They'd ingrained it in him, and he, in turn, in her.

And here she was, the result of the most incompatible union imaginable. A single night spent by her father, the French mercenary, with a local woman from the Hema tribe in Eastern Congo. Back then her father had been a different man — a kind man with principles, despite the realities of his profession.

Eight years after that fateful night, when Bear's mother had abandoned her for some merchant trying to make it big in Lubumbashi, it was Jean-Luc who came looking for her. He'd found her at last on the streets in Bunia, her stomach swollen from malnutrition, her hair infested with lice, and wearing nothing but a ragged T-shirt and the beaded belly chain given to each girl from her tribe on the day of her birth.

With no paperwork or witnesses, Jean-Luc had smuggled her across the border into Rwanda. As the years passed, they travelled from Uganda to Liberia, then Angola to Sierra Leone; heading off into every war-torn, shit-hole on the planet where her father's mercenary unit could make some money. It became her life, became normality. She was just a little girl trying to do her homework amid the faded grandeur of the ex-colonial hotels with their pockmarked ceilings and incongruously smart waiters. She would hide under the piano, practising her English by listening to the BBC World Service.

In each new country she had to find her own space, construct her own little world amongst the chaos, while her father disappeared into the bush with his faithful unit, losing another part of his soul with every new war.

But it was Sierra Leone that really changed him. Something had happened out there while he was fighting the RUF. Even at the mention of Freetown, Jean-Luc's face would darken, his grey eyes clouding over with a terrifying blanknesss.

Then came the drinking. Drinking so hard that the weeks would blur and missions converge into a monotonous litany of atrocities. What little meaning there was to it became quickly lost amongst the spiralling complexity of feuding autocrats as he took one job, then the next. Her father became a stranger to her, showing sides of his character that she had never known existed, until finally he had become as amoral as the people he was fighting.

The others in the unit tried to hide it, of course; Laurent and Marcel the most. They'd apologise for him, tell her it was malaria or that her father wasn't feeling himself, but the excuses soon became hollow and repetitive. It was only when she got her scholarship to the University of Cape Town and actually broke away from it all that she realised how wrong it had all become, or had always been.

A few years later her father came to Cape Town to make amends, but instead of repairing their relationship, he spent the entire first day meeting an Englishman at Uitsig restaurant in the Cape winelands, getting increasingly drunk as lunch wore on. That evening, as they had all ventured off to one of the nightclubs on Long Street, Jean-Luc had screwed one of Bear's friends in the toilets before arguing with the coat check girl about his jacket. Bear had to drag her father off the bouncer he had beaten unconscious in the ensuing argument and walk him into one of the back alleys to try to calm him down. And as she stood there, barring him from returning to the club, all she could see were the wild eyes and bloodstained knuckles of a fighter and a drunkard. This wasn't her father any more.

She stared at his fists, clenching and unclenching in a constant rhythm, and felt a sickness well up inside her. In that moment, he seemed so disgusting, so absolutely wretched, it was as if the ugliness of all those African wars was seeping out of him.

Later, she realised that the Englishman had been Simon Mann and that her father had been involved in the attempted coup on Equatorial Guinea. Somehow, Jean-Luc had avoided the group arrests in Zimbabwe and had headed north to the Rwandan-Congo border. Now his unit was stationed there, flying helicopters in what was ostensibly a 'freighting' business, but with all the contraband coming out of the Eastern DRC each month, from diamonds to coltan, uranium to copper, it was all too obvious that he had become nothing more than a petty smuggler.

It was nine years since that night in Cape Town, the last time Bear had spoken to her father. She had a new life now; she was married with a two-year-old son. And, most importantly, her family was something that *he* had never been a part of. But even after all that had happened, and all that he had done, she would still sometimes imagine introducing her son Nathan to his grandfather. But even as she imagined it, the dream would start to collapse. Her father was too far gone now. Just another casualty of Africa's endless conflicts.

Through the cockpit of the plane, Bear caught the faint imprint of a settlement rising above the flat horizon. Pulling back the control column, she set the Cessna climbing in a steep arc, pushing Bear back into her seat from the positive G. As the speed bled off, she clicked down the first stage of flap, then the second, turning the plane in a tight, slow circle above the settlement. She could see movement outside the open-cast mine itself, with the conveyor belts fanning out like arteries from the northern entrance to the outlying buildings.

By flipping the plane on to its other axis, she was able to see the crater from the explosion. It had blown outwards in a massive but near-perfect circle. Reaching into her flying bag on the rear seat, she pulled out a small Lumix camera and took five shots in quick succession. From altitude, it looked like the lab complex had been just beyond the explosion's reach: It had been close.

Two hundred feet below the circling plane, three men stood beside a white Toyota pickup truck. All were dressed in khaki shirts with matching shorts and socks pulled up to just below their knees. Despite the scorching sun, none of them wore hats. They stood squinting into the cobalt blue sky, following the plane as it passed the windsock and came into land.

They heard the propeller speed change in pitch, then with a tiny spray of dust kicking up from the rear wheels, the plane touched down. A few seconds later, it came to a standstill on the far side of their truck.

The three men moved round the vehicle, their eyes fixed on the interior of the plane as Bear got out, trying to keep her knees as close together as possible.

'I don't believe it,' the largest of the men said to no one in particular, his voice thick with an Afrikaner accent and a lifetime of smoking. 'They've sent in that fucking kaffir woman again.'

He pulled himself to a halt, the others drawing up behind him, and crossed his forearms over his rotund belly. The natural scowl on his sun-damaged face deepened as his gaze moved upward from Bear's ankles and rested somewhere in the vicinity of her crotch. He nodded slowly, his tongue moving over his lips as if wetting the glue on a roll-up cigarette.

As Bear opened the rear door of the Cessna and pulled out a large canvas bag, Wilhelm squared off his shoulders a little more.

'You know we have this all under control, don't you?' he called out to her. 'Any idiot can see what happened. The compressors have gone. So you want to tell me why the hell head office have sent a little girl to inspect my mine?'

The man on his left gave a crooked smile,

14

taking a packet of reds from his breast pocket and tapping the filter a couple of times. Putting the cigarette in the corner of his mouth, he fished out a Zippo from his trouser pocket and went to click it open.

'Would you not do that?' Bear said, leaning her shoulder against the door of the plane to get the latch closed. The man eyed her disdainfully and, after a moment's hesitation, ignored her.

'It's just that you're standing a couple of feet away from the fuel overflow and, as nice as those tight shorts of yours are, you might not want to see them go up in flames.'

The man looked at the L-shaped pipe sitting under the wing of the plane and the single drop of fuel which had welled up on its end. He looked back at Bear, then gave a smile that didn't reach his eyes.

Wilhelm's bearish forearms flexed while he watched his colleague slowly lower the lighter.

'Now you listen to me,' he growled, his chin tilting upwards, 'we don't need some kaffir woman coming here and telling us how to run our own bloody mine. Why don't you climb on board your pretty plane and piss off back to the city?'

Bear swung the bag over her shoulder and stopped in front of him. Her eyes were fixed on Wilhelm, but her expression remained unreadable; neither confrontational nor compliant. His eyes met hers, then seemed to settle on her right eye. There was something strange about it . . . Only as he looked closer did he realise that there was a loss of pigmentation across the very

15

top of the iris, leaving a clear white fleck that made it appear as if the eye was constantly reflecting some distant light.

'Listen, Wilhelm, because I'm only going to say this once,' Bear said, her voice hardly more than a whisper. 'We both know I'm the only one here qualified to assess the damage. So instead of wasting everybody's time, why don't you just take me to those compressors?'

'I don't need you . . . '

'Just this once,' Bear cut in, 'try thinking with your head and not your balls. You've got a Cat-4 explosion on an open mine site. You could have all sorts of shit leaking out here.'

There was a pause while Wilhelm hesitated, torn between his pride and what he knew to be true. Without waiting for a response, Bear pushed past him and climbed on to the back of the pickup, throwing her bag into the corrugated well of the truck before settling herself on the edge with her knees clamped together.

'And by the way, I've got a Congolese mother and French father, but stick to 'kaffir' as I don't want to confuse you. So why don't you just get in and drive the fucking truck?'

Bear could see Wilhelm's entire frame quiver with rage. She knew only too well how proud the Afrikaners could be. She silently chastised herself for rising to the bait. Her job was to contain the site, not win a petty argument with a halfwit Boer. Turning her head away from Wilhelm's reddening face and looking out at the first of the prefabricated buildings, Bear

16

spoke again, her voice softer this time.

'Look, it's your mine, Wilhelm. I'm just trying to make it safe. That's all. Let's get this over with as soon as possible and all of us can go home.'

Wilhelm took a cigarette from the breast pocket of his shirt and lit it, closing the lid of his Zippo with a flick of his wrist. His eyes darted towards the fuel overflow pipe while he drew down on the cigarette, the paper crackling softly as it burned.

'Take her to the site then, but give her ten minutes. That's all,' he said, spitting a thick globule of phlegm on to the dry ground.

As they drove closer to the building complex, Bear saw that the explosion had ripped a near-perfect circle across the entire circumference of the mine. The sheer scale of the explosion was vast, and while she had heard of compressors exploding, she had never before seen anything like this.

Climbing down from the truck and unzipping her canvas bag, Bear quickly put on a rubberised protective suit, ignoring the stares from the men as she hoisted her skirt up to get her legs through the trousers. Zipping it up at the back like a wetsuit, she sealed in her elbow-length gloves with gaff tape and tightened the straps on her gas mask. With her tool bag under one arm, she slowly walked forward to the edge of the crater, listening to the gravelly intake of her breath as it passed through the mask's filters.

At the centre of the mine, slabs of the natural

red rock had been charred black, while loose piles of smouldering ash still smoked in crooked vertical lines. Amongst the debris were recognisable parts of what had been the compressor building; a corner join of the roof, metallic shelving units twisted in on themselves, and even lagging from pipes that had fed into the compressors.

To Bear's eyes, there was something about the shape of the crater that didn't seem right. The blast radius was strangely uniform, almost like a mortar shell's. The explosion had obviously emanated from a single point, instead of one compressor setting off the next in a chain reaction as it should have done. She shook her head slowly, wondering what the hell could have triggered it all.

Climbing down into the crater, Bear methodically moved through the wreckage, scooping up soil samples in one of the circular heat-proof dishes which she kept in a pouch on the trouser leg of her suit. As she reached the centre of the depression, she stopped. On the underside of one of the sections of broken piping was a thin, clear residue glinting in the bright sunshine. She lifted the piping into the air, feeling the warm glow of heat through her protective gloves. The residue had glazed into a hard film from the heat and she turned it slowly in the light, wondering what it could be.

Scratching a few shards into one of her dishes, she turned to see the two Afrikaners standing at the edge of the crater, signalling to her that her time was up. Bear ignored them, turning her back as her eyes traced once more over the line of rubble.

Whatever had triggered the explosion, there was one thing she was certain of. The compressors had had nothing to do with it.

3

The American stood with his back to the rest of the group, talking loudly on a satellite phone. His body was partially silhouetted by the evening light, framed on both sides by the steep lines of Himalayan mountains.

As the man adjusted his balance, his eyes switched across to the Nepalese porters arriving over the crest of the pathway. They huddled together in a group, neck muscles swollen from the massive loads strapped across their foreheads, as they waited for him to signal where he wanted the campsite to be built.

'You're not reading me,' the man said into the satellite phone, turning to gaze out over the view again and ignoring the porters. 'This ain't some Alpine trek. This is the Himalayas. It's us against the mountain out here.'

There was a pause as he waited for the journalist on the other end of the line to finish her question.

'Yeah, I guess there is always some fear,' he continued, nodding slowly to himself. 'But you have to conquer that fear, like you conquer the mountain. People back in civilisation can't understand what drives a man like me to be out here. It's more . . . '

He broke off, squinting down at the handset, and saw that the signal had dropped to zero. As he wondered how much of what he had said had got through, his shoulders slowly hunched.

'Bob, they want to know where you want the campsite fixed,' prompted a petite blonde woman standing at the edge of the pathway. She was dressed in the same bright yellow Gore-Tex jacket as the rest of the climbing team, but it looked a couple of sizes too big, bunching out over her hips.

Bob glanced up, then absent-mindedly waved his arm towards a wider section of grass directly behind him. As the sherpas gratefully dropped their loads and began unpacking the tents, he stalked across to the woman, waving the satellite phone in front of him as if that would somehow help with the signal.

'What is it with this goddamn' Iridium network, Sally?' he asked, his broad face creasing into a scowl. 'You get about two minutes before the satellite goes out of range. Why the hell didn't we use another system?'

Sally's head tilted downwards, her eyes dulling as Bob leaned in towards her.

'You know, if people are making mistakes like that down here, it's gotta make you think what's going to happen higher up.' He paused, his scowl deepening as if pained by his own premonition. 'You hear what I'm saying, Sally? And I'm saying this for the sake of the *team*.'

As he dragged the last word out, his gaze swung round towards the group of sherpas to where a sixteen-year-old boy had unclipped the Pelican case he had been carrying, and was uncoiling the thick computer wiring contained within.

'No touch!' Bob shouted, moving closer and waving his finger in front of the boy's nose with exaggerated slowness. 'No touch this!'

Sally watched, her cheeks flushing red with frustration, before turning away and staring out towards the lower reaches of the mountain. She let her eyes blur, exhaling deeply as she tried to force herself to relax. Why were the Wall Street set always so obnoxious? One minute they wanted to be a mountaineer, the next a goddamn' astronaut. She should have known it would be like this; every day a new reproach, a new reminder of her status as the newbie on the team, but she had taken the position anyway. Financing a Himalaya expedition was just too expensive to go it alone.

As Sally stared down the mountainside, she suddenly noticed a figure moving up the pathway towards their campsite. The man was moving fast despite the massive load he was carrying, more running up the zigzagging trail than walking.

A minute later, Luca Matthews climbed up the last remaining steps of the path and stopped. He stood for a moment, eyes passing over one person to the next in the group, before pulling off the thick rope strap across his forehead and deftly swinging his body out from beneath the enormous pack.

Sally stared at him, taking in his shoulder-length hair, matted by dirt and scraped back from his forehead by a faded brown rag. His face was deeply tanned, but his cheeks were hollow from the long hours of exercise and a meagre

22

daily diet. Across his jawline she could see a light beard, patchy from being trimmed without a mirror or care, and as he adjusted his balance and his face tilted a little bit further towards her, she caught sight of his pale blue eyes. They stared blankly ahead, almost mechanically, as if somewhere along the endless Himalaya paths, their light had been slowly snuffed out.

'Hi,' Sally began to say, when suddenly a chorus of 'Namaste!' erupted from behind her. Each of the Nepalese porters had their hands pressed together in the traditional greeting and raised towards Luca.

At the sudden commotion, Bob looked up. A disapproving scowl quickly darkened his face as he watched Luca drag his pack up from the ground and begin moving over to the other side of the campsite. Just as he drew level, Bob reached out a hand to stop him, but instead of gripping on to Luca's arm, his fingers slowly curled back into his own palm. Instead, he simply watched as Luca delved into the top of his pack and pulled out a battered hipflask. He took a massive swig and roughly wiped his mouth with the back of his hand, before passing the alcohol over to one of the other sherpas.

Bob clicked his fingers, signalling towards his head porter.

'Gygme, what the hell is this? Some other climber stays at my campsite and he doesn't even ask permission?'

Gygme smiled politely.

'But, sir, he is not a climber. He is one of my porters.'

Bob's nose wrinkled as if he had just caught wind of an unpleasant smell.

'Come again?'

'Luca is one of my porters, just the same as the rest of us. He has been part of my team for nearly six months and is proving to be a most fine worker.'

'But he's white,' Bob said, pointing at Luca as if the fact might have escaped Gygme's notice.

'He is indeed white,' the head sherpa agreed, the smile on his face thinning, 'but so far that has not proved too much of a disadvantage.'

★ ★ ★

As dawn broke over the far ridge of the mountains, Sally unzipped the fly-sheet of her tent and stepped out into the cold. The grass was hardened from frost. As she padded across it, there was a soft crunching sound underfoot.

Carefully picking her way around each tent, she stopped at the edge of the campsite and inhaled deeply, feeling the freezing air burn her lungs. She tilted her head up, marvelling at the immensity of the night sky. It felt somehow open and exposed, as if the cold had stripped it bare. The night's black was already turning a deep shade of blue, and over to the east the first flecks of dawn were backlighting the line of mountains like a halo.

Despite the lack of sleep and the headache from altitude, Sally suddenly felt an overwhelming sense of calm and majesty. The Himalayas were just spectacular.

24

She was about to turn back to her tent when there was a low groan from somewhere to her right. Turning in surprise, she saw Luca lying almost entirely outside his tent, with the main part of his torso resting on the hard ground and only a thin woollen rug loosely wrapped across his chest. His feet were shoved into an empty rucksack and frost had plastered the hair to the side of his face.

Crouching down, Sally found herself reaching out her hand as if to steady him, but before her fingers touched his chest, Luca's whole body suddenly jolted. His shoulders lifted off the ground, almost sending her toppling backwards in fright. Staring into his face, she could see his eyelids twitching in spasm. It looked like he was having some kind of seizure.

Then she realised it wasn't a seizure or even the cold. Luca was dreaming.

He jolted again, his expression twisting at some distant memory of pain before he let out another low groan and lay still. Sally watched him for a moment more before a voice suddenly rang out behind her.

'You mustn't worry about him, Miss Sally.'

She turned on her haunches to see Gygme standing outside his tent, arms reaching out to the heavens as he stretched out the night's stiffness. 'He always sleeps badly. Sometimes he even keeps the rest of us awake, but it's never stopped him from carrying his share in the morning. Come have some tea. He'll be all right.'

Sally straightened up. Dusting off some

25

imaginary dirt from the front of her jacket, she walked towards Gygme and the centre of the campsite. There were a few other rustling noises from within the tents as the other members of the climbing team slowly clambered out of their sleeping bags.

Soon, everyone was up and huddled around the smouldering remains of the campfire.

An hour later, the campsite had been packed up and the climbing team had gone on ahead under the direction of Bob, while the sherpas were strung out along the snaking pathway with their massive loads, following them up towards the snowline.

As the morning progressed, cloud moved across the sun, blanketing the summits from view. A heavy mist rolled up from the lower valleys, carried on a buffeting wind that soaked each man down to the bone. The sherpas had all stopped to wrap thin sheets of plastic across their bodies, tying them tight with pieces of rope, but it was little defence and soon water ran down their legs and into their broken shoes. They trudged on regardless, accepting the weather with hard-won equanimity.

The path soon rose up to the first of the glaciers. Patches of snow drifted together on either side of it, while further ahead Bob and the rest of the climbing team were huddled near a large rock, their brightly coloured jackets turned against the wind and rain. One by one the sherpas pulled up level with them.

'We set up camp one beyond that next ridge,' Bob shouted.

'Sir!' Gygme called out, blinking as the rain ran down across his forehead and into his eyes.

'OK, people, we're good to go,' Bob continued, not hearing his sherpa's note of protest, and then strode off purposefully. A few metres from the rock, Luca had dropped his pack on to the snow and was pulling out a few personal items before sealing it up again. Bob turned to see him readying himself to leave.

'What the hell is this?' he boomed, running back down the slope.

Luca didn't respond, just continuing to tie his few possessions into a bundle, while Gygme looked on. The head sherpa had both hands raised to the straps of his pack, trying to ease the strain.

'But, sir,' Gygme explained, 'we have been speaking about this in Kathmandu. I told you one of my porters was not crossing the snowline. This is why I asked for more men.'

'What do you mean, not crossing the snowline? We're climbing the Himalayas, for Christ's sake!'

Bob raised his hand and pointed at Gygme, his finger so close it almost caught one of the droplets of water running off the end of his nose.

'It's about money, isn't it?' he asked.

Gygme swung his body out from under his pack and slowly wiped his forehead. He stared at Bob, trying to control his voice.

'No, sir, it is not the money. It is always this way with Luca. He does not cross the snowline and we respect his wishes. I already agreed with him before starting that we will divide his share of the load.'

'You remember Gygme saying that at the hotel, Bob?' Sally interrupted, her face almost completely hidden under the hood of her Gore-Tex jacket. They could just see her eyes switching between them both. 'You know, when we had that meeting?'

'No, no, no,' Bob said, drawing out each word as he shook his head. 'It's about the money. It always goddamn' is.' Reaching into the front of his jacket, he then pulled out a Ziploc plastic bag. Thick bundles of rupee notes were rolled together inside.

'You!' Bob shouted down to Luca, pointing at him instead of Gygme. 'You can take your pay now, and I'll also give you an extra half each day if you man up and carry that pack beyond the snowline.'

'But that's not fair on the others,' Sally whispered.

'Why don't you just shut up for once in your goddamn' life?' Bob snapped, not bothering to turn towards her. He watched as Luca slowly turned towards him and reached out his hand.

'That's what I'm talking about,' Bob said, smiling as he hurriedly counted out the notes and pressed them into Luca's hand. 'Your name's Luca, right? Come on, man, I know you speak English, otherwise you wouldn't know I was offering you a better deal.' Bob smiled again, trying to see past the hair falling in front of Luca's eyes.

Luca counted through the money, folding the

notes into the fist of his left hand. A long scar ran back from his wrist, the red of the wound angry in the cold. After he had finished counting, he took six notes from the wad he had been given and handed them back to Bob. Without a word, he then turned to go back down the hill.

'Hey, what is this?' Bob protested, his eyes flicking between the notes and the back of Luca's head. 'We had a deal. Hey! Don't you walk away from me.'

Lunging forward, he grabbed hold of Luca's shoulder, swivelling his body round. As their eyes met, Bob saw anger flash across Luca's face before he reached up and wrapped his entire hand over Bob's, yanking it from his shoulder.

'The deal was to the snowline,' Luca said, his voice low but steady. There was an unshakable certainty in the way he spoke, as if there could never have been any other way. 'And you'd better pay the others their share, especially the boy, or I'll tell him how much those laptops he's carrying are worth.'

With that, Luca continued down the path, stopping for a moment next to the sixteen-year-old and tucking a few of the notes he had just received into his hand. The entire group simply watched as he then walked on, eventually becoming lost in the cloud rolling up the side of the mountain ridge.

Gygme was the first to break the silence, moving a few paces to his right until he was standing shoulder to shoulder with Bob.

'You must not take it too hard, sir. Mr

Matthews has always been his own man and I have never heard of him changing his mind for anyone. Especially when it comes to crossing the snowline.'

Bob's expression clouded over as Gygme's words resonated in his head.

'Matthews,' he repeated. 'You mean, Luca Matthews . . . the English climber? Jesus Christ, that's *Matthews?* But he's climbed every damn' route . . . '

Bob trailed off, lost in his own thoughts as Gygme slowly nodded.

'That is indeed Luca Matthews. One of my finest porters, but I don't believe he has ever been a climber. Apparently, it is mostly flat in his country. Only hills.'

Gygme then turned, hoisting his pack into a more comfortable position, and with the ambivalence of one born to the mountains, continued up towards the snow line.

4

It took Luca only three hours to descend to the nearest village. Without the load and travelling alone, he moved in a continuous flow, his feet instinctually finding a grip on the slippery path.

He arrived at the outskirts of the village and pulled himself to a halt just as the rain became heavier, descending in vertical sheets across the black sky. Rivulets of water channelled through the muddy ground, passing directly in front of a small collection of dilapidated huts built in a semi-circle on the edge of the mountainside. It was a desolate sight, the only sign of life coming from the smoke wafting up through the wooden roofs before it was beaten back down again by the rain.

Luca stood in the centre of the village, his sodden clothes steaming from his body heat. He tilted his head up and let the rain splatter down on his face. He could feel his heart pumping in his chest and, for the first time in as long as he could remember, he felt truly alive.

As he stood there, one of the doors creaked open and a huge bear-like man ducked his head under the low frame. He peered cautiously out, revealing thick black hair that melded into an equally thick beard. His eyes squinted at Luca, etching lines deeper across his craggy face, before a cigarette was raised to his lips and he inhaled deeply, drawing on it with such force that it looked as if he was trying to finish the entire thing in a single breath.

'I have heard the one about Englishmen and the midday sun, but I never knew they went out in the rain as well.'

Luca's eyes clicked open in disbelief, making him blink against the rain. His mouth opened too as he tried to speak, then he simply shook his head.

'René,' Luca breathed at last, a smile lighting up his face. 'What the hell are you doing here?'

René's face broke into an equally wide grin and he cast his eyes up to the sky.

'If you bother to get out of the pissing rain, I'll tell you. Or is this how you usually spend your days?'

Luca laughed, slowly shaking his head as he trudged over to the open door, his feet sinking into the soft mud. Before he had even had time to step up on to the porch, René grabbed him in his huge arms and hugged him.

'You always were a crazy bastard,' he said, pulling the younger man back a little so he could look into his eyes. Despite the layers of clothing, he could feel how wiry Luca had become, his hands gripping on to bands of pure muscle. There couldn't have been more than an ounce of fat on his whole body.

'You look well,' he lied, taking in Luca's hollow cheeks and faint beard. 'And you've been out here so long, you even smell like a mountain goat!'

Shepherding Luca inside the small hut, he helped him off with his coat and motioned for him to sit on a low wooden bench in the corner of the room. Luca sat heavily, resting his boots almost in the ash of the fire, and wiped his hair back from his face, sending a spray of water out behind him. As his eyes became accustomed to the gloom and smoke, he could see an old woman waiting at the back of the room, clutching a heavy pot of tea.

Without being asked she approached, balancing two small wooden cups on the top of a low stool, and poured. She handed one to each of them before smiling at Luca, revealing a mouth containing only three blackened teeth.

'Dhanyabaad,' Luca said, pressing his hands together. Thank you.

He took a few noisy slurps from the cup, enjoying the feeling of the steam rolling up his damp face, and then looked across at René. He was eyeing the viscous liquid suspiciously before his right hand went to the side pocket of his coat and fished inside. A moment later, he triumphantly pulled out a half-litre bottle of brandy and sloshed a heavy measure into both their teas.

'I've been in the Himalayas for over twelve years now and you want to know something?'

Luca nodded, knowing full well that conversations with René were rarely more than one-sided.

'I'd prefer to drink my own piss than yak butter tea. Every time I go into the bloody mountains it shocks me how horrible it is. You know what I say? Drown out the rancid taste with brandy. The problem is . . . the brandy here's not exactly much better.'

33

He raised his cup to Luca then took a heavy gulp from it, pulling his lips back across his gums as the cheap spirit burned his mouth. Luca drank his without flinching, holding the wooden cup in the palm of his hands as he let the warmth of the tea spread through his fingers. René looked on curiously as they sat facing each other over the fire. He could scarcely believe how much Luca had changed.

And it wasn't just the weight he had lost; his whole demeanour seemed to have changed as well. He had become shrunken and withdrawn, as if crushed by some invisible weight. The villagers had already told him that Luca refused to go past the snowline and that each day he volunteered for the longest treks and the heaviest packs. It was as if he hoped each minor act of suffering could help to alleviate his guilt; the punishment spread over a thousand of paces in the Himalayas.

Even as René stared at the reality before him, he still had a mental image of Luca visiting his restaurant all those years ago. He had been loud and outgoing then, even arrogant at times, with a mischievous grin to accompany each one of his mad-cap schemes. He had come looking for permits for a climbing expedition into one of the most remote regions of Tibet, and after only a few days together, René had found himself risking everything to help him. That's the way it always was with Luca. You got swept up by his energy.

But now, there was nothing left of the old Luca. There was only this tortured soul before him. It was like watching a cancer consume someone before his very eyes.

After a moment's pause, René took another cigarette from his pack and lit it with the end of one of the logs in the fire. He winced as the hairs on the back of his hand singed from the heat, sending a pungent smell into the air. Drawing on the cigarette, he looked across at Luca, his expression draining of joviality.

'I know it's been tough for you, Luca, but you could at least have responded to Jack's letters. It's been over three months now.'

Luca looked up from the fire.

'What are you talking about? I didn't get any letters.'

René raked his fingers through his beard and winced.

'Shit,' he breathed, exhaling a plume of smoke from somewhere deep within his lungs. 'I guess that makes some sense then. Look, Luca, Jack Milton has been trying to get hold of you for the last couple of months. When he didn't get any answer, he asked me to try and track you down. And you know how I hate leaving Lhasa and coming out to the mountains. It's three days just to get across the border and then those endless bloody trails . . . '

'The letter, René,' Luca interrupted, sitting forward attentively. 'Tell me what Jack wants?'

'Yes, yes, the letter. Well, it's not Jack that's in trouble. It's his nephew, Joshua. He went missing six months ago somewhere in the depths of the Congo. Nasty country, that. He was working for *Médecins Sans Frontières* and the truck he was on just disappeared. No one has been seen since.' René paused to take a sip from his cup, wincing again as the brandy went down. 'You know how resourceful Jack is, but he's tried everything — the UN, the consulate in Kigali, Amnesty International. You name it. He even thought about going to look for Joshua himself, but even he realises that he's just not up to it any more. I think the drink's finally caught up with him.'

Luca shook his head, his eyes resuming their blank stare. Jack Milton. He hadn't heard his name in over two years, but just the mere mention of it brought his childhood rushing back. It had been Jack, not his father, that had introduced him to climbing. From the very first day, he had recognised something special in Luca and had patiently encouraged it, spending hours with him at the climbing wall, the afternoons bleeding into evenings as they became absorbed in the next climb, then the next.

Somehow Jack always had enough time for Luca alongside his own nephew, Joshua. There was never a sense of competition between the two boys, but more a friendship that quickly developed into something deeper. They never thought of themselves as brothers, but to everyone else, that is exactly what they were. They were always together; in the same fights at school, chasing the same girls as teenagers. But their friendship had none of the jealousies or rivalry of family. Even when Jack presented Luca with his old climbing gear, including an entire sling full of expensive quickdraws and cams, Joshua didn't complain. Climbing was what Luca did. Period. And from the very beginning, it was something that Joshua had always understood.

Luca rubbed his hand across his face, wiping away the last of the rain. He hadn't spoken to Joshua in a couple of years, but he could still remember the stuttering phone conversation they had had. Joshua had been in Lahore, about to head off with one of the Pakistani relief teams into the Hindu Kush. He could still remember the excitement in his voice. It was his first proper assignment with MSF.

Luca looked up.

'How does Jack even know Josh is still alive?'

'They found some of his personal effects in the river. I don't know what exactly, but he certainly thinks there's a possibility.' René paused. 'I'm sorry, Luca. He told me you two were close.'

Luca nodded, his gaze turning back to the fire.

'Yeah, we grew up together. Went to the same schools and all that, but we lost contact when I started doing expeditions. Funny, Josh was always off trying to save the world, while I was only ever interested in trying to conquer it.'

The bitterness in Luca's voice made him almost spit out the words.

'Well, whatever the hell happened,' René said, levelling his eyes at him, 'we need your help. Joshua was last seen in the Eastern DRC outside a pissing little city called Goma. By all accounts, it's a sprawling mass of poverty, run by smugglers and gunrunners.' He reached across and slapped Luca's knee. 'I'm sure you're going to love it.'

Luca looked shocked. 'What do you mean, love it?'

'Are you deaf as well as wet?' René asked with a mock scowl. 'It's a mountainous part of the Congo, full of volcanoes and steep cliffs. No one can get in there because the terrain is so harsh. But you, you're one of the best damn' climbers in the world. Be a 'piece of cake', as you used to say.'

Luca raised his hands as if trying to push René away.

'I'm sorry, René, but I don't climb any more. You've got to find someone else.'

'For Christ's sake, Luca! I wouldn't have dragged my arse across the Himalayas if there was someone else. Do you have any idea how long it took to track you down?'

'I'm sorry,' he replied, avoiding his friend's gaze. 'Really, I am, but I have work to do here.'

'Work? You call this work! It's like the bloody labours of Sisyphus!' René flicked his cigarette into the fire in disgust. Then he paused for a second, his voice softening as he tried a new tack. 'Look, Luca, back in the day, I saw you climb things that I didn't think were even possible. There wasn't anyone around who could match you on a technical route. I know it's still inside you. You're just a bit out of practice, that's all.'

Luca stared into the embers of the fire. There was a long pause before he finally spoke.

'That's just not me any more.'

'But . . . Joshua?'

'Tell Jack I'm sorry. Tell him . . . tell him you couldn't track me down. Please, René, just tell him something, OK?'

With that, Luca swung himself off the bench and pulled his coat up from the floor, shoving one arm through the soaked sleeve. He was halfway to putting in his other arm when René stood up and moved in front of the door, grabbing his wrist. His colossal body filled the entire frame both lengthways and widthways. Luca tried to ignore him, forcing his arm forward, but it just jerked uselessly in René's bear-like grip.

Their eyes met and René leaned forward, squeezing Luca's arm a little harder.

'It's time for you to stop punishing yourself,' he whispered. 'You can't keep blaming yourself for Bill's death.'

Luca froze.

'Bill wouldn't want you to . . . ' René began, but fell silent as Luca's expression was wiped clear of any uncertainty or doubt. His eyes seemed to harden. Anger clouded his vision, making his whole body suddenly tense. René could see the vein on his neck pulse as a terrible rage built within him.

Gradually releasing his grip, René edged back a pace until his shoulders pressed against the wooden uprights of the doorframe. In that instant, he realised he had suddenly become an absolute stranger to Luca. He no longer had any idea what his old friend was capable of.

'Luca,' he whispered, trying to keep his voice level. 'You've got to let Bill go . . . '

'Stop saying his name!' Luca thundered, shunting René backward with his outstretched hands. Every fibre in his body seemed to combine with tremendous force, sending René crashing through the rickety wooden door and out into the rain outside. He staggered back on the wet porch, winded by the blow, his chest heaving as he tried to catch his breath. His right foot slipped off the step, sinking down into the mud and sending him spinning round on to his hands and knees.

At first, René stayed stock still, letting the rain run off the crown of his head and down his cheeks. Then, slowly, he tilted his head to one side, eyes widening as he stared back towards the hut. Luca was there, silhouetted in the doorway by the dull light of the fire. Violence simmered in his gaze, then with a jolt he seemed to regain his senses. Stumbling out of the hut, he grabbed René under the arms, forcing him up on to his feet once again.

'I'm so . . . sorry,' Luca stammered. 'I don't know what came over me. I just reacted.'

René held on to him, trying to pull himself up to his full height. A stabbing pain shot through his chest and he breathed out a long, winded gasp.

'I'm sorry,' Luca repeated. 'Forgive me, I just . . . '

René nodded, slowly regaining his breath. They looked at each for a moment before a pained smile passed across René's lips.

'Guess you're not as skinny as you look,' he said. Then he put his hand over Luca's shoulder and together they hobbled back to the shelter of the porch. With mud splattered over the palms of his hands, René signalled to Luca to pull out his cigarettes from the top pocket of his jacket and he quickly took one out, sliding it between René's lips as he patted his pockets for a lighter. They both stood hunched over, with their forearms resting against the porch rail and their heads just beyond reach of the rain. As René finally sparked the lighter, he looked down at the cigarette. It was already sodden, drooping in a crooked arc.

'About time I quit anyhow,' he said, spitting it out into the mud. 'One thing's for sure. The old lady isn't going to be too pleased about her door.'

Luca's eyes switched back to where the door swung loose on its hinges. Smoke from the fire curled out through the gap.

'She'll be OK. I know her from before and we can sort it in the morning. Listen, I am sorry about what happened. I didn't mean to hurt you.'

René nodded again, remaining silent for a moment before turning fully towards him.

'You do know that going to the Congo isn't just about saving Joshua, don't you?'

Luca stared, trying to guess his meaning, but René looked back towards the rain and avoided his gaze.

'This is about finding yourself again, Luca. And you know something? Sometimes life has a habit of finding you, no matter how hard you try and hide from it.'

Luca sighed heavily, his eyes fixed on the sodden cigarette resting on the mud.

'The truth is that I'm scared to go back. Out here, I never need to explain myself to anyone or justify what happened with Bill. Every day, I get up and I carry the loads. That's all anyone expects of me. Here, I just *am*.' Luca paused, letting his shoulders sag as the energy drained out of him. 'Now, suddenly, you're asking me to go back to it all. Go back to normality.'

René shook his head, a wolfish grin forming on his lips.

'You really are an idiot, aren't you? I'm asking you to go into one of the most war-torn, shit holes on earth . . . and you're talking about going back to 'normality'!'

He clasped his hand over Luca's shoulder, drawing him back into the hut.

'Normality!' he repeated, shaking his head again. 'I'll never understand what goes on in that thick head head of yours. Now come on, let's get out of this weather and talk more inside. There's still half a bottle of brandy left and we should drink it before the old lady serves any more of that filthy tea.'

5

The stretched outline of the Mercedes Maybach passed like a shadow beneath the raised security shutters and nudged its way into Beijing's traffic. As the 6-litre V12 engine powered forward, the car crossed Beihai Bridge, passing the tourists in their yellow paddleboats on the lake, and sped out towards the north-western suburb of Haidian.

General Jian sat in the white leather interior staring out through a rear window. His eyes held an identical sheen to the car's blackened glass, polished and opaque, concealing everything from the outside world. They lazily took in the chaos of China's greatest city while his mind reviewed each detail of the meeting he had just had. He could picture every movement, every feature of the three committee members from the People's Liberation Army, as he'd submitted his latest report on the progress of the satellite launches. For the last two years, his division of the PLA had been responsible for the implementation of the Beidou Navigation System — the Chinese military's new version of the American Global Positioning System, or GPS as it was more commonly called — and, as ever, the committee wanted to him to account for every last yuan spent.

But it wasn't the results of the meeting that stayed in his memory, more the minutiae of it. It had always been like that for him, every situation recalled in infinitesimal detail; the two scuff marks on the Vice-President's right shoe, the pale tan line on the Under-Secretary's third finger where he had recently removed his wedding ring, and the soft intake of breath from the President as he had scanned the accounts. The General could picture it all as if replaying it in slow motion, and he'd been correct in assuming that none of the committee suspected anything about his plans for the twentieth satellite launch. There had been not the slightest trace of suspicion.

Bringing his right hand up to his neck, Jian absentmindedly scratched a patch of dry skin poking out above the starched white of his collar. He couldn't remember when the itching had started, but felt sure that it must be connected with the resurgence of his headaches. They seemed to be an almost daily occurrence now; a low-level throbbing at his temples which never quite seemed to dissipate entirely before the next one set in.

Taking four paracetamol from the packet on the seat beside him, he washed the pills down with a sip of bottled water, before switching his gaze to the dark blue evening suit hanging over the opposite door. He could smell the subtle aroma of dry cleaning still pressed into its sleeves and, leaning forward in his seat, he unbuttoned his shirt and stripped off his trousers. He was about to pull a clean shirt over his shoulders when he caught sight of his own reflection in the darkened partition glass between the rear seats and the driver. For a moment he just stared at his large, ungainly body, studying it as if he were a surgeon about to make the first incision.

Despite their size, his arms lacked any definition, protruding from his shoulders in straight vertical lines like piping, while his stomach sagged slightly over the sides of his hips. Leaning forward so that his face was only a couple of inches from the mirrored partition, he ran his tongue against the sharp edges of his teeth, making a mental note to get them whitened again. He then surveyed his high cheekbones and wide-set jaw. There was only a smattering of Mongolian blood in his veins, but those bastards at the Guild never let him forget that he was not one of them, no matter how high in the ranks he climbed. But all that would soon be an irrelevance. Only a few weeks from now he would be rid of them once and for all.

Jian reached up and gently scratched the discoloration across the upper part of his neck. The skin was flaking off, revealing a darker patch just beneath the surface. For a moment he prodded at it, wondering what on earth could have caused it. He should have someone take a look at it, but right now there wasn't the time. Once the twentieth launch was complete and the money secured, he'd get it seen to.

A loud ringing echoed through the car and Jian pulled back from the glass, pressing the speaker button on the central seat bar.

'General, I have a message from Secretariat President Kai Long Pi.'

Jian inhaled deeply, always amazed by the

speed with which his movements seemed to be known to the Guild. He had only just left the building.

'The President has instructed me to inform you that Mr Xie will be visiting you today.'

'Mr Xie?'

'That is correct, sir. You will be updating Mr Xie on the Goma Project. He will be at your private residence in one hour's time.'

Jian's lips curled in disdain. He always despised the presumption in Kai's secretary's voice.

'I have an extremely important matter to attend to. I shall be there at 1400 hours.'

'But, General, Mr Xie . . . '

'Mr Xie can wait a couple of hours. I am quite certain such a busy man will have plenty of ways in which to occupy himself.'

There was a pause before the voice replied.

'Very well, General. I shall let him know of your delay.' The secretary signed off, putting extra emphasis on the word 'your'.

Jian slammed his finger down on the button, cutting the line. Every new contact with the Guild only seemed to enrage him further. It was the impotence of his own position that was so infuriating. They were financing the entire Goma Project, and rarely a day went by without his being reminded of that fact.

Nearly three hundred of China's most influential families were either directly or indirectly involved with the Guild, an organisation which tapped into every vein and artery of life in mainland China. They ranged from high-ranking PLA officers such as himself to Party members operating at Politburo level. Whatever it was, the Guild was there, its hand at work in every major undertaking since the overthrow of Mao in the 1970s.

But the Guild was a mercurial entity, multi-layered and complex. Families would align for a common purpose, only to find themselves competing against each another on a different matter. Alliances were tenuous and short-lived, the power struggles all part of a seemingly endless cycle. But there were times when the in-fighting had to stop. The scale of a project would reach such critical mass that it pulled the families together again to serve a single cause, one in which success would benefit all while failure would only destroy them.

The Goma Project was of such a size. They all knew it. The stakes were too high for any single family to opt out, and now each of them wanted to be sure of a return on their investment. The pressure was suffocating, the expectations unrelenting. For the last year and a half, Jian had been made to feel it every hour and minute of his life.

Turning away from the window, he curled his fingers into the leather necklace. His thumb rubbed over the blood-red stone hanging from it, finding the natural warmth of it strangely pleasing. The jewel was unlike anything he had ever seen before. Presented in a beautifully crafted, hardwood setting, it wasn't a diamond or gemstone but in fact a piece of the mineral they were buying in its purest form. His contact had called it the 'Heart of Fire', and it had been sent to him only one week ago. Since that time he had worn it every day, fascinated by the warm, mesmeric red of the substance so few people even knew existed.

The 'Heart of Fire' was a token of all that was to come. The fortunes of the Guild hinged around this one mineral, and the gift to Jian had served as a perfect reminder to the others that *he* was the one who had brokered the deal. He had been given this gift. No one else.

The car eased to a standstill and Jian heard the driver move around to the back. A second later, there was a gentle tap on the window and the door opened. As daylight flooded into the muted interior, a woman appeared, her long blonde hair flowing down past her shoulders. She paused, looking at Jian for approval before delicately easing herself into the seat next to him. He let his eyes run slowly over the elegant pointed lines of her shoes, up the length of her legs and over her close-fitting grey skirt. She carefully smoothed the fabric across her narrow hips before finally looking up at him.

She was younger than her clothes suggested, the skin perfectly smooth under her eyes and her lips still naturally full. The lipstick was a tone too garish for his tastes, but otherwise she had obviously paid heed to the instructions she had been given. She gave a well-practised smile that, despite her professionalism, succeeded in being charming, and twirled a finger through her white-blonde hair.

'My name's Imogene.'

Jian squinted at her, taking in every detail. Even the perfume she wore was the one he had asked for and his nostrils flared as he drank it in, marvelling at the way his preferred scent seemed to change against each new girl's skin.

'Beautiful,' Jian whispered, his voice deepening with anticipation. 'Just beautiful.'

6

Louis Bwalande stood on the runway smoking a cigarette.

Despite the sun's having set over an hour ago, he could still feel heat rising up from the tarmac and drew one arm across his forehead, wiping off the sweat on to the sleeve of his dirty uniform. He had been the airport manager at Goma for the last seven years, and was well accustomed to smuggling all types of contraband. But tonight was different. Every few seconds, he found himself glancing up towards the long row of white UN planes parked alongside the runway, and out towards the towering silhouette of the volcano.

The Frenchman should be here by now.

Louis inhaled deeply on his cigarette, trying to calm his nerves. The Frenchman should have been here twenty minutes ago. As he blew the smoke out, a bout of coughing shook through him, making him retch. He shook his head and stared down in disgust at the glowing red ember of his cigarette. He hated smoking and was terrible at it, but tonight he felt a compulsive need to do something. Waiting was always the hardest part.

Glancing down at his watch, Louis ran through a mental checklist. He had already chosen the hangar farthest away from the MONUC military base. It was the perfect place in which to avoid attention, partially hidden behind two moss-covered Boeing 727s that had been bulldozed off the runway a few years back and left to rot. There was nothing suspicious about that; scrap Boeings and Antonovs were as much a part of any Congolese runway as the tarmac itself. They lined every landing strip from Goma to Kinshasha, a legacy of five years' civil war. Like everything else that had once functioned in this country, they had been left to blur slowly into the landscape, like litter on the side of a road.

Louis turned as the lights from a convoy of 4 × 4s swung in a semi-circle around the airport terminal, before pulling to a halt by the runway's decrepit fenceline. He could see figures climbing out, waiting in the shadows. The client didn't trust the usual handlers and employed a Chinese crew from one of the nearby tin mines. Everything was arranged by the Chinese themselves and Louis was never given the slightest hint as to who the client actually was. The only thing he had deduced from all the military hardware involved was that the client must be part of the Chinese Army or, at the very least, well connected to it.

But, despite all their precautions, Louis had managed to get to one of the Chinese handlers. It had taken weeks, but finally money had won him round. Tonight was the first time they would actually go through with their plan, and as the moment drew closer Louis suddenly regretted the whole terrible idea. The *muzungos* watched everything like hawks and were as vindictive as

51

they were greedy. They would kill him without a second thought if they suspected he was skimming the deal.

For several minutes everybody waited in silence, with just the sound of the cicadas chirping in the background and the occasional beep of a car horn from somewhere deep within the city. Pacing along the side of the runway, Louis felt sweat beading under his shirt and pooling in the small of his back. What the hell had he been thinking, trying to double-cross the Frenchman in the first place? This was madness.

There was a roar of engines as a Russian Ilyushin 76 plane passed overhead. It switched on its landing lights, washing the dead space between the terminal and the beginning of the runway with a searing white light. Long black shadows sprang up across the dried grass, turning slowly with the trajectory of the plane, before the undercarriage touched down and the reverse thrusters thundered.

Gratefully screwing the cigarette into the ground with the toe of his boot, Louis waved towards the silent line of Chinese handlers, signalling for them to follow him. With a hiss of hydraulics, the ramp under the plane's enormous tailfin lowered, revealing eight Chinese Special Forces soldiers crouching within, rifles tight against their shoulders, eyes scanning the group of assembled men. Each was dressed in black fatigues with front webbing pouches stacked full of ammunition. Night-vision goggles were tilted up from their faces and only their eyes were visible through the balaclavas pulled tight over their heads. They eyed the handlers warily, making minute adjustments of the QBZ-95G assault rifles in their grip. It was obvious neither side was taking anything for granted.

In the dull red light of the plane's interior, Louis could see pallets stacked in neat rows throughout the entire length of the hold. It was the same every week. Each box had its identification marks scratched off, but despite the secrecy he already knew what they contained — standard issue AK-47 rifles. It was the most prolific weapon in Africa, and each week hundreds more were arriving at his airport. But guns had never interested him. It was the cargo they were being traded for that Louis was after.

As the plane's engines powered down, a new sound rose up from the north. Helicopters were flying towards them, snaking low over the lip of the volcano and hugging each contour of the vertiginous ground. The low thud of their rotors grew louder as they approached, before they began banking round in tight formation towards the edge of the runway. Everyone shielded their eyes from the downdraft as the bulbous frames of three Oryx Mk2 helicopters came into the light.

Each helicopter slowly turned on its axis, giving their door-mounted 7.62mm GMPG machine guns a perfect line of fire before finally touching down. Soldiers jumped out while a fourth helicopter continued circling, covering them from the air. As it passed a second time, the main body came into view, revealing the unmistakable stepped configuration of an AH2 Rooivalk attack helicopter. From the back of the plane, the Chinese soldiers cast glances at each other. They had never expected to see such firepower in a backwater like Goma. Aside from the missiles, the Rooivalk had a 20mm cannon under its chin that could cut an entire plane in two.

A man slowly clambered out of the leading Oryx and moved with no particular hurry towards the rear of the plane. As the crowd parted and he stepped into the red glow of the cargo bay's interior, they saw he was stocky, with a chest that stretched the fabric of his black T-shirt. A white kerchief was tied around his neck and his hair was longer than the usual military crop. He stood with one foot on the metal ramp, and then turned back towards his helicopters, signalling for them to begin unloading. As hardened plastic sacks were piled out on the ground to be swapped for the crates of AK-47s, the man kept his back turned towards the Chinese soldiers, seemingly oblivious to their presence.

Louis had recognised Jean-Luc as soon as he had stepped off the helicopter. There was just something about the way he moved. He exuded a cat-like confidence which succeeded in being both languid and unpredictable within the same pace. With his wide shoulders and thick-set forearms, he could easily have been mistaken for a bare-knuckle brawler if it weren't for the rugged squared-off jaw and intelligent, deep-set eyes.

Louis always dreaded Jean-Luc's arrival. Even when sober, there was a volatility to him which meant he could just as easily attack or hug you within the same breath. He would ignore direct questions, then moments later find something totally inconsequential hilarious. And trying to second-guess his moods was exhausting.

Looking out over the crowd of Chinese faces, Louis tried to spot his handler before the Frenchman suddenly swivelled round towards him.

'Louis,' Jean-Luc called, his gravelly voice cutting through the crowd. '*Comment vas-tu, mon ami?*'

The manager's cheeks immediately tightened in a smile.

'I am very well, Monsieur Étienne. Thank you so much for asking.'

Jean-Luc stepped off the ramp and placed one of his huge hands on Louis's shoulder, pressing down on it while slowly nodding to himself. It looked as if he had done something extremely agreeable but had now forgotten exactly what.

Louis's smile ratcheted a little tighter. He could smell the faint trace of aniseed on Jean-Luc's breath from the *pastis* and wondered if he might be resting against him for support, rather than out of any sense of goodwill.

'And how are you, sir?' Louis asked.

Jean-Luc's expression didn't alter, his smile set but vacuous. He swung his left arm up clumsily, waving for his men to bring over the cargo.

'Now, *mon ami*,' he said, whispering the words conspiratorially. 'Why don't we have a little chat about the rates you charge on my fuel? Surely we deserve a little discount?'

'But, Monsieur, it is not a question of deserving.'

Jean-Luc squeezed his shoulder playfully. 'But all the business I bring you. For an old friend, that's got to be worth something?'

Louis gently shook his head, turning his gaze towards the ground.

'Monsieur, it is the same for every person landing here. Even MONUC pay the same contract rates.'

Jean-Luc jerked his chin closer.

'Do I look like fucking MONUC?' he spat, sending tiny flecks of saliva into Louis's face. His eyes were glazed, the right one moving slightly out of sync with the left.

'Well, do I?'

Louis stayed motionless, surprised even now by the hostility in Jean-Luc's voice. In everything he said, there was a seething undercurrent that could boil over at any moment.

'I will see what I can do, sir.'

Jean-Luc patted his shoulder as if the deal had already been done. Then, without another word, he swung his arm around Louis until they were standing side by side like old comrades-in-arms. They watched while the Chinese soldiers fanned out from the back of the plane and on to the tarmac, taking up position silently with their rifles held at the ready. Then the handlers came into the cargo hold in single file, working quickly to unpack the wooden crates and run them over to the helicopters.

The whole process was completed in silence. Men passed crates to each other, keeping their eyes lowered and avoiding eye contact with the soldiers. Every few minutes the downdraft of the circling Rooivalk washed over them, its rotors deafeningly loud at such close range.

Once the crates of AK-47s had been packed on to the helicopters, the handlers carefully took the toughened plastic sacks and piled them in the centre of the cargo hold. Louis stared at each of the team as they passed him, desperately searching for his man, but the dull red lighting made their faces a blur. Then he suddenly saw him, almost directly in front of where they were standing. He was helping to straighten the crooked stack of cargo. Their eyes met, but there was not a flicker of recognition from the man. He simply stared ahead, while his hand surreptitiously dug into one of the plastic sacks and filled his right pocket with its contents.

Louis continued staring, mesmerised by how casually the man had done it, when suddenly he felt Jean-Luc turn towards him.

'Trust,' he said, breathing the words directly into his ear. 'That's what they say is the most important thing in life.'

Jean-Luc paused, letting the words hang between them, while Louis stayed absolutely rigid, his smile fading imperceptibly.

Swallowing several times, Louis tried to force some moisture back into his mouth, but he could feel the panic rising up inside him. It made him feel physically sick and he had to stop himself from reaching down to clutch his stomach. He could feel Jean-Luc's muscular arm resting across his shoulder and suddenly had a premonition that the Frenchman was simply going to curl it around his neck like some kind of snake and throttle him there and then.

'But these slitty-eyed bastards,' Jean-Luc continued, jerking his head towards the Chinese soldiers. 'They don't give a shit about loyalty or trust. They take as much as they can get from anyone who is selling. No questions asked.

'You know,' he continued, 'after all these years, it's not the guns, the dead civilians or even the pointlessness that gets to me. It's the hypocrisy. The West offers aid with one hand, then rapes the shit out of the country with the other. At least with the Chinese there is no pretence. They want minerals and will buy them from anyone who's selling. There's a beauty in that — a simplicity.'

Louis gave an enthusiastic nod.

'Yes, Monsieur Étienne. A simplicity.'

Louis felt his mind struggling to keep up. Was this another of the Frenchman's games or a genuine moment of reflection? He nodded again for good measure, wondering whether he was expected to add anything to the conversation, but his mind kept circling back to a single word Jean-Luc had said — 'minerals'.

In all the time that he had been managing these shipments, he had never discovered what it was exactly they were trading. There was too much for it to be diamonds and too little for gold. He had agreed to buy it blind from the handler, guessing from the high levels of security that the substance must be phenomenally precious. But now Jean-Luc had confirmed that it was a mineral. Which mineral was so valuable? Uranium ore?

When the last handlers clambered off the plane, the soldiers took their place, not lowering their rifles until the ramp was fully raised and the IL-76 engines had fired up once again.

'Until next week,' Jean-Luc shouted above the din. Leaving Louis standing mutely in the centre of the runway, he ran over to the nearest Oryx helicopter. As soon as he had perched on the edge of the cabin, the helicopter powered up, hovering a few feet above the ground. The others rose up one by one, forming an echelon port configuration, with the Rooivalk gunship continuing higher, until it was 1,500 feet above them and providing cover. They then dropped their noses and sped forward, banking round in a wide turn towards the pale orange glow of the volcano.

Louis stood still, just listening to the softening beat of the rotors. The nausea had quickly turned to exhaustion and he let his shoulders sag in relief now that the Frenchman was gone. Just as he was exhaling a long, deep breath, an arm suddenly grabbed him from behind. He was about to shout in protest, when he realised that one of the Chinese handlers was pulling him clear of the Ilyushin's engines. Side by side they scurried to the far side of the tarmac.

'Take attention, Mr Louis,' the handler shouted in broken English, gesticulating towards the plane. He then pointed again for extra emphasis. Louis could feel the weight of something being pressed into his open pocket, but resisted the temptation to look down.

'The money's under the rear seat of the first car,' he responded, through gritted teeth. The handler paused for a second as he tried to understand the meaning, then prodded into the air once again.

'Engine dangerous!' he said, and turned to rejoin his group.

Louis curled his fingers tight around his pocket, already trying to judge the weight of the substance. Whatever it was, he had the best middleman in town already lined up in Goma. All he had to do now was get to the Soleil Palace nightclub.

With a low-pitched roar of its engines, the plane departed, followed shortly by the 4x4s. Louis was suddenly alone once again. He looked over his shoulder, double-checking that no one was watching, then carefully pulled the packet from his coat. Rolling the substance through his fingers, the shards of rock felt brittle and flaky, but with a warmth to them that was somehow comforting.

He smiled. Strolling back to the terminal, he lit another cigarette and inhaled deeply on the rough tobacco. Whatever he had in his pocket, they had got away with it. And right under that bastard Frenchman's nose!

His smile broadened just as another bout of coughing shook him. Spitting the cigarette on to the ground in disgust, he wiped a trail of saliva from his chin with the back of his sleeve. Screw the *muzongos* and their damn' cigarettes. He needed a drink.

7

The Soleil Palace lay down one of the labyrinth of backstreets in downtown Goma. There was no sign to mark its existence, only two huge piles of black volcanic rock stacked outside the entrance, as if the nightclub had been carved out of the ground instead of being built on top of it. Inside, the lighting was equally subterranean with stubby candles on each table and a faintly neon-lit bar. At the end of an array of optics was an open stretch of concrete used as a dance floor, with towering speakers arranged around it in a semicircle. The music was already pumping. Friday night was always a big night in Goma.

Louis clasped the bouncer's hand, ignoring the rowdy queue outside, before swaggering through the entrance tunnel and past the pool tables to his right. Some local hookers were idly leaning against the cues, using each shot as a chance to hoist their skirts a little higher and tease the men at the bar. A couple of them glanced up as he passed, smiling suggestively but only half-heartedly.

Once through the heaving crowd, Louis approached one of the low tables on the edge of the dance floor. Fabrice was already there, wearing his trademark white suit and Gucci sunglasses. Seated to one side of him was his girlfriend, Marie, her long hair spilling halfway down her low-backed dress. She sipped her cocktail, shoulders twisted away from him and lips slanted in surly frustration. He was doing his best to ignore her and they sat there in silence, the aftermath of yet another argument. As Louis arrived, Fabrice leaped up from the table, overjoyed at the excuse to break the deadlock. He shook Louis's hand, twisting his palm round in the African style, then poured him a massive shot of vodka from the bottle chilling on the table in front of him.

'Hey, Marie, you remember my friend Louis,' he shouted, nodding towards their guest. The burn marks on the left side of Fabrice's face caught the light. They ran across the top part of his cheek and all the way back into his hairline.

Marie pulled a Swarovski-encrusted mobile from her handbag and pointed it at the centre of Fabrice's chest as though taking aim.

'You promised,' she said. 'No work tonight.'

'But, baby, you know how it is in the club. This is my office.'

Fabrice raised his palms imploringly, then winced as he caught Marie's smouldering glare.

'I'll see you later, dear,' she purred with mock affection. 'I'll be at the bar.'

'Baby, wait a second . . . ' Fabrice called, reaching out his hand, but she tossed her hair over her shoulders and stalked off.

Both men watched in silence as she moved through the throng of people, before Fabrice finally took a huge gulp of his drink, the ice clanking against his white teeth.

'She's too much,' he said, exhaling heavily. 'Every day she busts my balls about something else. I tell you, Louis, she talks more than your mama.'

Louis raised an eyebrow. 'If you're done with Marie, get yourself one of those big mamas down by the lake. You know, all booty and big love. Give them a bag of corn and they're nothing but grateful.'

Fabrice smacked his lips.

'Oh, yeah, got to love that big booty,' he said, thrusting his hips forward in time with one of the girls on the dance floor. 'None of this skinny-assed 'Why you working so much?' bullshit.' He pointed towards the bar, knowing full well Marie wasn't watching. ''Cos with me you get paid, girl. That's why!'

Thumping his chest a couple of times, he stared at the back of Marie's head defiantly, before adding 'Yeah' to no one in particular.

While Fabrice settled back in his seat and minutely adjusted his sunglasses, a couple of white men walked in at the far end of the nightclub. With their thick-set frames and cropped haircuts, they looked like off-duty MONUC forces. Fabrice caught the attention of one of the girls playing pool and, with a flick of his wrist, motioned towards the new arrivals. The girls immediately downed their cues and began scything through the crowd.

'Goddamn' UN,' Louis muttered. 'That's about the only thing they leave their compounds for. Screwing our women.'

'Should keep them busy, though,' Fabrice answered. Wiping the table with a few paper napkins, he motioned that they should get down to work. Louis dutifully placed the package on the table, carefully peeling back the edges.

'So they've been running this every week?' Fabrice said, taking a shard of the rock between his fingers and turning it under the candlelight.

'Every week. AKs come in. This goes out.'

Fabrice peered closer, lifting his sunglasses. He wrinkled his nose in concentration.

'And a helicopter?' he asked, over his shoulder.

'Not just a helicopter. They come in with four of them. Machine guns . . . Mercs. I told you, this is some big shit, Fabrice. There was a whole Chinese unit there and it wasn't easy to get that stuff out. I mean, I am taking a lot of risk here. We should talk about that.'

He looked across, keen to impress upon the middleman the difficulty he had had procuring the cargo, but as ever Fabrice was only half listening. He was turning the shard over and over in his hands, his expression darkening with each revolution.

'So where do they get it from?'

'North,' Louis answered, leaning back in his seat distractedly and catching the eye of one of the girls on the next table. He smiled at her, his eyes moving down from her face to her cleavage.

'North? What do you mean, north? Across the border?'

Louis shook his head. 'No. Not Sudan. I heard it's from somewhere inside the Ituri Forest. A place called Epulu.'

Fabrice's expression twisted in disbelief.

'The Ituri? Nothing comes out of the Ituri. No one ever goes past the river.' He paused for a moment, his mind racing while he wondered what could be so valuable that someone would risk going north. It was nothing short of suicide. Turning back to the shard, he shook his head once again. 'Jesus, it must be worth a fortune.'

Louis leaned forward eagerly.

'So come on, Fabrice. How much is it worth? I weighed it already. We got over a kilo here.'

'None of this makes any sense,' Fabrice answered, dropping the shard back on to the table so that it nearly rolled off the lip. Louis made a grab at it, catching it just in time. 'This isn't worth shit, Louis. It's plain old coltan.'

'Coltan?' Louis asked, his voice rising in shock.

'Yeah. You know, tantalite. The stuff they use in cell phones.' Fabrice waved his hand in disgust at the small pile of rocks. 'It's mined all over the place. What you got there is worth about fifteen dollars. Real 'big shit', Louis.'

'No, no,' he stuttered, shaking his head at the injustice. He grabbed the shard in his own hands and stared at it, holding the flame of the candle directly behind the rock, almost singeing it. 'I've seen the security they use. There's got to be something more.'

As Louis brought it closer to the light, Fabrice suddenly noticed a flash of red. Steadying Louis's wrist, he leaned forward. There was a thin vein of colour running the length of the shard. It was a smouldering, blood red colour, welling through the blackness of the rock.

'What the hell . . . ' he muttered, the words trailing off. He took the shard between his own fingers again and studied it more closely. The glow was soft and mesmeric, like lava cooling long after an eruption.

'What is it? Uranium?' Louis asked, craning his neck for a better view.

'I don't know, but I've traded everything there is and I've never seen anything like this before. One thing's for sure. If security is as tight as you say and it's coming out of the Ituri, then someone wants this stuff real bad.' Fabrice paused for a moment, distractedly scratching his left cheek. 'There is a guy I know who might be able to help. Works for one of the mining corps up here and he likes his women. He owes me.'

Fabrice signalled to one of his men, hidden by the shadow of the speakers. Louis watched him take the package, retreating towards the office at the rear of the club, and wondered if this would be the last time he would see it.

'Whatever it is, we're fifty-fifty, right?' he said, offering Fabrice his hand.

Fabrice ignored him, attention suddenly focused on the entrance to the club. He straightened his suit, tightening the jacket across his athletic shoulders, and adjusted his sunglasses once again.

'Hey, Fabrice, we're cool, right?'

Louis fell silent as he followed the direction of Fabrice's gaze. Four Chinese men were pushing their way through the noise and commotion of the club towards their table.

They had the same military bearing as the MONUC forces but these men were squatter, with jet black hair cropped so short the skin was visible underneath. Three of them were shunting couples out of the way on the dance floor, clearing a path for the man at the back. Only his silhouette was visible as he approached, but then the dance-floor lights turned full circle, washing his face with a searing white beam. He was much thinner than the others; his face long and gaunt, with hair receding from the crown of his head. As he came closer, they saw he walked with sharp, jerking movements as if his joints were fractionally too tight.

The three other men stood in a semi-circle in front of Fabrice's table, arms tightly folded across their chests. They all wore loose-fitting khaki jackets as if they had recently returned from a safari. They were armed and none too concerned about concealing it. A low stool was drawn up and the thinner man gingerly sat down, perching himself on the edge of the seat and crossing his legs. The movement was as slow as it was effete. The man's lips pursed as he finally raised his eyes.

'Give it to me,' he said, rocking his body in time with the words. His eyes were a pale shade of grey, almost translucent in the dimly lit club. They moved slowly, the watery pupils only just reaching up to Fabrice before sinking back down to the floor.

Fabrice beamed his wide smile.

'What do you want? Drugs? Girls?' he said, leaning back in the sofa seat and draping his arms over the backrest. 'You want girls, right?'

The man recoiled slightly.

'Do not play games. Give back what you took.'

Fabrice smiled like a naughty schoolboy and shrugged several times. The Chinese man seemed to try to restrain himself, then jerked open the breast pocket of his jacket and slid the contents across the table. Three images fanned out in front of them.

'The handler.'

Fabrice and Louis leaned forward to see a picture of a man lying face down by the side of the lake, the entire back of his skull caved in. The rocks and water surrounding him were tinged pink from blood and his right arm was twisted unnaturally behind his back.

'Sailing accident?' Fabrice asked facetiously, his forehead creasing as if in concern. 'Yeah, that's right. I heard the lake can be dangerous this time of year.' Then he leaned forward, peering over the tops of his sunglasses as his eyes suddenly drained of humour. 'You guys really should be more careful. Remember — you're in Africa now.'

At first, the man in front of them didn't react. Then he rocked forward again, hissing the words through clamped lips.

'You have no idea who you are dealing with,' he said. 'This is your last chance.' One of his men unfolded his arms, his right hand slipping inside the folds of his jacket.

'Wait, wait,' Fabrice called out, holding his palms up. 'You haven't heard my story yet.' He took off his sunglasses, pointing with them towards the assembled men, then cleared his throat theatrically. 'Trust me, you're going to love this.

'So, when all the Chinese miners came to the Congo a few years ago, aside from all the machinery and bulldozers, do you know what they brought with them?' Fabrice paused, waiting for suggestions, but the man in front only listened. 'Condoms! That's what they brought with them! Hundreds and thousands of condoms in their little silver wrappers. Can you imagine it? Rubbers everywhere. They must have been thinking that you boys would be pumping every Congolese girl from here to Lubumbashi.' Fabrice clapped his hands loudly together in rhythm, the noise cutting above the music. He smiled wider, so that the two gold fillings at the back of his mouth caught in the light. 'And we thought you guys were just here for the mining . . . '

'Enough of this,' the man opposite began, but Fabrice continued, wagging his finger as if chiding him.

'But, of course, your government didn't want you all getting infected, did they? All our girls are dirty, dirty. Not like you lovely clean Orientals. But as a gesture of goodwill, condoms were given to every tribe; the Lendo, Hema, Bantu, everybody got them. There was going to be no more AIDS thanks to our new Chinese friends. We were saved! But, you know, there was just one problem . . . '

Fabrice stood up and, widening his stance, pushed his hips forward and unzipped his fly. He reached inside to his crotch, casually pulling out his penis and letting it fall down one leg of his white trousers. The man in front flinched, pulling away from him with rare speed and losing his balance on the stool. As he half crouched on the floor, he stared up at Fabrice from waist-height, eyes wide with surprise and disgust.

'But the condoms were too small!' Fabrice exclaimed. 'We couldn't fit into your little Asian condoms!'

He pumped his hips, swinging his penis in time with the motion. The Chinese stared in mute fury, their faces already reddening. Without waiting for an order, the man closest to Fabrice pulled out the snub nose of a Glock 17 pistol from his shoulder holster, but before he could level it at him, there was the sound of shattering glass and chairs being overturned. Men sprang out from behind two of the nearby speakers and surged towards the table, AK-47 rifles held high.

The Chinese swivelled in surprise, the first still going for his pistol. Just as he brought his arm round to fire, one of Fabrice's men whipped the barrel of an AK across his jaw, sending him crashing down on to the low plastic table and spilling ice from the vodka bucket across the floor. After a few seconds, the man managed to pull himself back on to his knees. His right hand was clamped to his face, blood seeping out between his fingers.

There were shrieks at the sudden commotion, but Fabrice raised his hands for quiet and then signalled to the DJ to continue playing. As people warily returned to the dance floor, he zipped himself up, eyes still fixed on the thin Chinese man at his feet.

'You think you can scare us with your guns

and threats,' Fabrice said, crouching down so that his head was only a few inches away from the man's. 'Scare us? I saw my parents murdered when I was twelve years old. The Mai-Mai took their pangas and . . . chop-chop! They killed them. And what was their crime? They were from the Hema tribe, that is all. Then they took the rest of us into the long house and set it alight. They burned the whole village.' He raised his hands to his lips and blew softly through his finger. 'And just like that, everyone was gone.'

A bitter smile passed across his face as he pulled the Chinese man to his feet. Fabrice gently slapped his cheeks, as if he were an old friend.

'This is Africa, my friend. AFRICA.' He drew out the word, stretching each syllable. 'And out here, you got to remember one thing — you ain't the guys with the biggest dicks.'

8

The dull glow from a computer screen flickered across Bear Makuru's face. She yawned, stretching her back, and stared into the bottom of the cold cup of coffee wondering if she dared take a sip. An insipid brown film clung to the surface of the liquid and she swirled it around for a moment, before carefully balancing the cup back on the pile of food wrappers stacked at the corner of her desk.

Eight padded folders lay on top of one other in a crooked heap, with sheaves of paper poking out at different angles. Each was emblazoned with a heavy stamp reading 'Accident Report' and contained confidential information drawn from their mining archives. Bear had been steadily working through them all day, noting down details until the A4 pad perched on her thighs was a mass of scrawls and underlined words.

The files showed that two of the biggest coltan mines in Australia had suffered compressor explosions similar to their own. Another had been hit by a sudden contamination leak which had effectively halted all production since earlier that year, forcing Minecap, one of Australia's foremost mining companies, to turn to the government for a bridging loan.

As she trawled further through the archives, Bear found that there were others too — a coltan mine in Brazil, two in Canada, and finally a sketchy report from somewhere in northern Mozambique about an explosion in one of their mines.

Bear reached forward to her laptop, pulling up the coltan figures for the first two quarters. There had been an overall fall in production of twenty-three per cent, with only mines in China, the Congo and a smaller one in Indonesia remaining unaffected. Drawing a circle on her notepad around the number 23, she then drew a big arrow pointing downwards.

Getting up from her chair, Bear kicked off her high-heeled shoes and moaned softly as she stretched out her toes, splaying them against the threadbare office carpet. She twisted her thick hair around her fingers before piling it on top of her head and pinning it back with a well-chewed Biro. Gently massaging her neck, she felt the knots running deep into the muscle. She just wasn't cut out to be in an office all day. It always made her feel cramped and tired.

Pinned to the wall above her computer was a small Polaroid of her husband and their son, Nathan. She let her eyes linger on the boy's smile for a moment and sighed heavily, her shoulders finally relaxing. There was always something so uncomplicated in the way he smiled. Nathan lived every moment in the present, happy or sad, unburdened by the weight of life that seemed to suffocate so many people as they grew older.

Bear's gaze traced over his soft cheeks and the black, curling locks of his hair. Her husband, Jamie, always tried to get her to cut his hair

73

short, claiming that the other kids would tease him for looking like a girl, but she couldn't bring herself to do it yet. It was one of the greatest pleasures in her life, Nath drinking his bottle in bed with them each morning, his soft hair brushing against her neck as she cuddled him close. He was a perfect mixture of them both, not just the colour of his skin, which was lighter than Bear's and a few shades darker than Jamie's suntanned white, but in his eyes, the oval shape of his face, even his slightly misshapen big toes.

Bear looked at the wall clock and cursed out loud. It was 7.30 and she had promised Jamie she would be back in time to put Nathan to bed. Closing her eyes, she exhaled deeply, breathing out all the dry office air. It wasn't just the fact that she would miss Nath this evening, it was Jamie's inevitable disapproval. She could picture his face as she came through the front door, filled with unspoken disappointment. Nathan was always vaunted as the victim of her working late, used as camouflage for Jamie's own emotions. Guilt: that was the only thing she seemed to feel these days; guilt that she didn't spend enough time with her son, guilt that she apparently valued work over family, guilt that she had emasculated her husband by earning more than he did.

For so many months now, she and Jamie had led almost separate lives, speaking to each other but never really communicating. Their focus always seemed to be around the child, leaving unfinished business that exploded into arguments each time they had a moment to

74

themselves. Bear opened her eyes again and, after a moment, sat down and turned back towards the screen of her computer. If he was going to give her a guilt trip anyway, she might as well get a little more work done.

The phone rang and it took her several seconds to find it under the piles of paper.

'Madame Makuru,' came the voice of the security guard on the front desk. 'I've a Lieutenant William Cooper on the phone for you. Shall I put him through?'

'Yes, thanks, Sepo.'

Bear sat forward in her chair, instinctively reaching for the pen tucked into her hair.

'I got you working late, Coop?' she asked, smiling slightly. Lieutenant Cooper had been a friend of her father's in the early days, serving in the British army in Sierra Leone. He was one of the few English officers who had any time for mercenaries, and while Bear waited for her father to return from the bush, Cooper had been a regular at the Kimbima Hotel. In the old, vaulted dining room, he'd even spent some time helping her with her English. With three daughters of his own, Cooper had always had a soft spot for her.

'Listen, Bear, I need to know exactly where this stuff came from,' he said, dispensing with their usual chatter. Usually, Cooper was nothing but hi-jinks and gentle teasing. She had rarely heard him sound like this.

'It's like I told you. I got a sample of it, going through our coltan mine explosion. Why? What's happened?'

There was a long pause as Cooper hesitated.

'Eh! *Dis-moi!*' Bear protested. 'Come on, what have you found?'

'I've found something that definitely shouldn't be in a South African mine,' Cooper said slowly. 'It took me a while to pin it down, but after looking through the aerial footage you sent, I thought you might be right. The compressors didn't trigger the blast. They were part of a secondary explosion. So I started looking at a few different options.'

'So, what caused it? Was it something to do with that residue?'

'Yes, I am certain of it,' he replied, his voice dropping low. 'Its called diethylhexyl and I only picked it up after running it through some of the solvents. As far as I know, there's only one use for the stuff. It's the plasticiser in C-4.'

Bear went to note down what he was saying, but her pen paused above the paper.

'C-4?' she said. 'You mean, the explosive?'

'That is exactly what I am saying and it's not something you find that often in Africa. Too damn' expensive for most people's tastes.' He paused, thinking out loud. 'Listen, if you could find me a piece of the det cord or even a fragment of the actual trigger, I might be able tell you where it came from, otherwise it's all just guesswork, I'm afraid. But one thing's for certain, Bear, it's very unlikely that anyone other than the military could have it.'

'The military? You mean, the South African army?'

'Not bloody likely!' Cooper exclaimed, laughing slightly. 'They can barely afford boots these days and certainly aren't going to be using something as sophisticated as C-4 when some good old TNT would have done the trick.'

There was a pause and Bear could hear a faint scratching sound as Cooper raked his stubble.

'Off the top of my head, there are only a handful of countries that would use C-4 in this quantity: the Americans obviously, the British and French, and also the Israelis. Then, of course, there's India, Pakistan and China.'

'But why would any of those countries deliberately blow up a coltan mine?'

'You tell me. Maybe there's something specific about your particular mine?' Cooper suggested.

Bear's gaze drifted down to the pile of accident reports in front of her.

'*Putain*,' she swore. 'It's not just that particular mine. I have eight accident reports from mines all over the world. The details aren't the same for them all, but I think someone is trying to systematically take out coltan mines.'

'But why?'

Bear thought for a moment, her eyes panning through the cross-current of scrawled notes and figures on her A4 pad. They rested on the figure twenty-three per cent and the arrow pointing down from it.

'The explosions are reducing the coltan supply globally, right?' she said, her voice flat as she ran through the logic. 'So, what happens if you reduce supply? The price goes up.'

Cooper made a tutting noise as if scolding her.

'Come on, Bear, what you're suggesting sounds pretty unlikely. We're not talking about small amounts of C-4 that some terrorist group can get their hands on. To blow up that many mines, you'd need access to proper military stores, and I don't know about other countries, but in England they don't exactly hand out the keys.'

Bear tapped her pen on the desk.

'You said countries, right? Well, look at the only countries producing significant quantities of coltan that *haven't* been affected. That's the Congo and China. And somehow, I don't think the boys in Kinshasa can afford kilos of C-4.'

'Before you go gallivanting off on one of your hunches, have you stopped to suppose that maybe the Chinese are next on the list? Maybe next week you'll have another accident report on your desk about one of their mines.'

'Maybe,' Bear conceded, one eyebrow rising. 'But if they don't, then we *know* the Chinese military are involved. The PLA have their fingers in all sorts of civilian organisations. Maybe they're in bed with one of the major mining corps, trying to drive up the price.'

There was an exasperated sigh from the other end of the line.

'You know, I'd forgotten how willing you are to jump to assumptions. But listen, Bear, whatever is going on, if it does have something to do with the Chinese, then take it from me, let it drop. I know that on your assignments you can be as tenacious as a damn' pitbull, but even you don't want anything to do with them.'

Bear nodded her head slowly, a gentle smile forming on her lips. Cooper was always looking out for her, even now when she was a grown woman with a job that took her to some of the most dangerous places on the planet. If only her father had been anything like as concerned.

'Thanks so much for this, Coop. I owe you.'

'You don't owe me anything, except dinner with my girls when you're next over here. They miss you like hell, you know. And, Bear, just once in your life, listen to an old bugger like me and stay out of trouble.'

'I promise. *Merci beaucoup*,' Bear said, her smile widening as she put down the phone. Glancing up at the wall clock, she quickly got up from her chair, shoving her purse and mobile phone back into her handbag. Slipping on her shoes, she was turning to leave when out of the corner of her eye she noticed an email appear in her inbox. She was about to ignore it, but then changed her mind and clicked it open. It was a message sent through the company's secure intranet from one of their divisional branches in the Democratic Republic of Congo.

Beatrice,

We need some help here. Early this morning, we obtained a small quantity of a mineral I haven't seen before. The vendors couldn't tell me what it was either, only that it came out of a place north of here called the Ituri Forest. Anyway, Accounts aren't going to like this as we had to pay a small fortune for it, but it was worth the price. I think this might be something totally new.

We've been running tests all day and think it might be a concentrated derivative of tantalite. Can that be possible? What's strange is that usually tantalite is found alongside columbite, i.e. coltan, but this seems to be something else. And I can't find any references online.

Can you get up to Goma in the next couple of days? I want to keep this quiet and stay clear of sending anything via courier. Get Kimberly to approve and let me know your arrival times.

Pieter

Bear stared at the message, her body rigid. Someone had been systematically crippling coltan mines around the world and now this — a concentrated derivative of coltan discovered in the Congo. There had to be a connection.

Reading the message once again, she paused on the last sentence, feeling her stomach tighten. Goma. Why did it have to be Goma? That was the one place in the world she wanted to avoid — the place where her father was. And now, after all this time, it looked like she would be going back there.

9

General Jian sat hunched over a vast wooden desk, his face almost touching its surface. A single shard of light shone down from one of the high windows, its luminescence making his cotton shirt glow a brilliant white. Above him, dust motes hung in the beam, suspended in the perfectly still air. The room had a sense of undisturbed calm, like a long-forgotten store-room in the vaults of a museum.

In the centre of the table lay a large glass dome. The crystal was beautifully ornate, with a finely crafted handle on each side, shaped like the wings of an angel. Inside the dome were three large butterflies. They sat perfectly still, with their wings closed, revealing only the moss-coloured undersides of their bodies and their symmetrical 'eye' markings. Occasionally, one of them would slowly open its wings and a flash of iridescent blue would gleam in the light. The colour had a fierce metallic sheen which seemed to glow brighter as the wings parted.

Jian sat with the side of his head pressed against the table, waiting for the butterflies to reveal themselves. He didn't blink for several minutes.

'General. May I present Xie Zhaoguo?'

A man shuffled into the room, stopping only a few feet beyond the entrance. Slowly turning his head, he squinted, trying to adjust his eyes to the prevailing darkness. Shapes began to appear in the half-light and he soon realised that almost every inch of the walls was covered with wooden picture frames. There were hundreds of them, stretching high towards the domed ceiling.

'It is a pleasure to meet you, General,' Xie said, smiling awkwardly. There was no response from the man at the table. Only the back of Jian's head was visible as he bent forward, rapt in concentration. Xie waited, the seconds passing slowly. He coughed politely. 'And my apologies for disturbing your work.'

His voice was soft and light, with an air of sincerity which made Jian slowly turn away from the table. With the light directly behind him, his face remained in shadow, black eyes set deep in his skull.

'It is always a pleasure to receive a member of the Guild,' Jian intoned, his voice devoid of emotion.

Xie shuffled a little further towards the table. He moved slowly as if unsure he would be able to make the distance, and paused for a second just beyond the well of light. He waited, staring at Jian for several seconds before finally stepping forward to reveal a rounded face with dark rings visible under the eyes. Years of living with incurable insomnia had left Xie looking exhausted, with perpetually pallid, dry skin. Despite his relative youth, lines had already etched their way deep into the corners of his eyes, turning his expression into something approaching surprise.

'Butterflies,' he said, a faint smile appearing on

his lips. 'They call that entomology, right?'

Jian looked at the tired squint and dishevelled hair, wondering exactly how old Xie was. He could be anywhere from his mid-thirties to fifty.

'That's the generic term for the study of insects. For butterflies and moths, it is lepidopterology.'

'Lepidopterology,' Xie repeated, pronouncing the word slowly as though he were trying to commit it to memory. Jian watched him, detesting the idea of exchanging pleasantries with a Guild member. Usually, they got straight down to business, expecting him to account for every last yuan he'd spent on the satellite launches.

As Xie casually rested his hand on the table, Jian's eyes followed the movement. He took in every detail; the little finger on his left hand curling upwards, the knuckles pressing against the wood, whitening the skin over the bone.

'So what are these ones, then?' Xie said, raising his other hand. His forefinger pressed against the domed glass, leaving a small smear on the perfectly clean surface. Jian's eyes hardened.

'They're called Blue Morpho from South America,' he answered, his voice softening despite himself. He found even the names of these rare butterflies simply intoxicating. They had arrived only this morning from Colombia and were going to be the pride of his collection. As he spoke, one of the butterflies slowly peeled back its wings in a shimmering, electric blue burst, refracting the white light from the ceiling

83

like a mirage. The colour was rich and indulgent, broken only by delicate lace-like veins fanning out across the surface of the wing and blackening their tips.

'Beautiful,' Xie said, peering closer. As he said the word, Jian froze. He turned towards the butterflies, staring at them indulgently.

'Yes,' he breathed. 'Quite beautiful.'

The butterfly closed its wings, the blue suddenly replaced by drab green.

'They spend much of their time flying low through the canopy,' Jian said, his head tilting to one side. 'The contrasting colours make them look as if they appear, then disappear, with each beat of their wings, while the green perfectly camouflages them in the forest. It's how they confuse predators.'

'Is that right?'

'Yes,' Jian whispered. 'That is right.'

With his left hand, he pushed back the top of the glass dome, sliding his right hand underneath. His fingers inched towards the nearest of the three butterflies.

'But if you should so much as touch their wings, they would never be able to fly again. The natural oils on your fingers strip away the microscopic scales that produce the colour, and the wings are so finely balanced that if even a few scales are missing, it fatally disrupts their flight.'

As he spoke, Jian's black eyes narrowed in concentration and the tip of his tongue poked out. The butterfly went to move off, then paused for a second longer. Jian's hand skilfully slid out, pinching hold of its body between thumb and forefinger. The butterfly went rigid, then gradually its wings opened, quivering in reflex.

'You must partially break the exoskeleton, but take care not to crush the thorax,' Jian explained, his voice a hollow whisper. 'It paralyses the muscles that articulate the wings.'

Xie could hear Jian's breathing deepen. His usually blank expression had changed. There was a rare intensity to his eyes that glowed brighter as the life was gradually snuffed out of the butterfly.

'Wouldn't it be easier to use a killing jar?' Xie asked. 'Isn't that how it's normally done?'

'Ethyl acetate is for novices,' Jian replied, without looking up. 'This way you get to feel it.'

He then drew the dead butterfly out from under the glass dome and, with meticulous care, moved it across to the open wooden frame ready beside him. There was a space with the butterfly's genus and species already inscribed neatly beneath, but before laying it down Jian stared at the creature. After a long pause, he finally looked up.

'Beauty is so ephemeral,' he said. 'It exists only for a moment, a fleeting moment. That is why it is so difficult to capture.'

Xie stared at him curiously. 'But does beauty need to be captured?'

'Yes!' Jian exclaimed, as if he had been personally insulted. 'Otherwise how can you ever keep it?'

Xie remained silent. Not wanting to show his surprise, he looked up at the hundreds upon hundreds of frames displayed across the walls and wondered just how many butterflies they contained. It must have taken years to assemble such a collection. Whatever the General was, he certainly wasn't a standard product of the Chinese army.

Over the last year, certain factions within the Guild had alluded to some 'unusual' elements in Jian's behaviour. It had been decided it was up to Xie to determine the nature of these and, more importantly, whether they in any way compromised the Goma Project. He'd read all the reports and gone through the transcripts, but even now, after such a brief introduction, he already felt that the reports fell well short of accurately describing the man. Jian was clearly multi-faceted, and such types rarely played by the book.

Xie was about to say something to break the silence when Jian suddenly scraped back his chair and signalled for him to follow. Marching on ahead, he led Xie back along a corridor and out on to a wide veranda. A panorama of Beijing's northern suburbs fanned out before them, the rooftops bleeding into skyrises as they stretched away into the heart of the city. A table had been set with wine already chilling in a cooler.

As soon as they took their places, two servants glided on to the veranda, laying down delicate soufflés and pouring out the wine. Xie stared at the array of cutlery and decided to wait for Jian to start.

'So what exactly does the Secretariat President wish to know?' Jian began, dabbing the corner of his mouth with a napkin.

'It is actually more for my benefit, General. I was hoping you might be able to explain the Goma Project to me, as I've only recently been transferred to the Secretariat President's office.' Replacing his fork on his plate, Xie waved his hand casually. 'Mr Kai thought it would be better if I heard it directly from yourself. To get a better sense of it all.'

Jian's expression remained fixed. Did he really have to explain the minutiae of the Goma Project to some halfwit office junior just because Kai couldn't hand him a damn' file? He took a huge gulp of his wine, to wash away the dryness in his mouth. The powerful aftertaste of the Montrachet's Burgundy grape rose up in his throat and he shut his eyes briefly, revelling in the taste. What would the Guild think of next to waste his time?

'So how much do you know already?' he asked.

'Please, assume that I know nothing,' Xie said, his voice softening further in apology. If he was going to study Jian, he needed to hear him describe the project from the very beginning.

Jian swirled the wine in the well of the glass before taking another gulp. Pursing his lips, he drew in air through the liquid as he had once seen the sommelier do on a trip to France. The force of the alcohol hit him straight away and he quickly set the glass down on the table, wondering why on earth the Europeans practised such a bizarre ritual. Settling back in his chair, he began to speak.

'For many years now, the American military have owned and operated a Global Positioning System or GPS using low-earth-orbit satellites. From anywhere on the globe, these satellites can triangulate your position and tell you exactly where you are. But it is not just about navigation. Some of their basic missile systems use GPS for targeting, as do many of the UAVs.'

'UAVs?'

Jian's lips pursed tighter. 'Unmanned Aerial Vehicles — or drones, as they are more commonly known. The Americans are the only ones who have this system and can encrypt it or even switch it off any time they like. So, in response, other nations have been building rival systems, predominantly the Russians with GLONASS and the Europeans with Galileo. My division of the PLA was tasked with launching a Chinese version and, after two years of production, we are under a month away from the final launch of the BNS — the Beidou Navigation System. Almost all the satellites required have already been put into orbit by my team.'

'And the Americans know about this?' Xie asked.

'Of course,' Jian snapped. 'How do you hide a satellite launch?'

Xie nodded thoughtfully. 'But if this is a military operation, how is the Guild involved?'

'Money,' Jian said, rubbing his thumb against his fingers. 'A single satellite launch represents an outlay of nearly 150 million US dollars, which means the entire system will cost over 3 billion.

With the upgrade of the air force's J-11 strike fighters, budgets have been stretched across the board, and so we brokered a deal with the Guild to finance two-thirds of the satellite launches.'

Xie nodded again, but his expression made it clear he was struggling to keep up. Finally bringing the fork to his lips, he tasted the starter.

'This is delicious,' he said. 'What do you call it?'

Jian stared across the table, his frustration bubbling through into his voice. 'It's called soufflé. It's French.'

Xie took a huge forkful, gulping down the entire portion.

'Delicious,' he repeated, smacking his lips loudly.

'I'll have the chef send over the recipe.'

Xie leaned forward across the table, his forehead creasing like a man who has recently misplaced his car keys. 'So all of this because the Guild wants a GPS system?'

'No, not at all. It's a carefully guarded secret amongst the PLA's top brass that each launch contains *two* satellites. One for the BNS and another for a new mobile-phone network. They are designed to work concurrently and, with the expensive part of the operation being the launch of the actual satellite, both sides will be saving money. But, most importantly, the Guild wanted to launch their mobile network secretly.'

'And why would they want to do that?'

'Because what they are launching will do nothing less than revolutionise the entire communications industry. Every single phone will be a satellite phone, communicating directly with our BNS system.' Xie's expression didn't alter and Jian leaned forward in his seat, waving his arm for emphasis. 'Don't you get it? Every mobile phone will be usable from anywhere in the world; in the middle of the ocean, up a mountain, in downtown New York . . . anywhere. And with the same signal strength.'

'But aren't there already satellite phones?'

'They exist, but the handsets are huge and expensive. Ours will be just like a normal mobile phone but using high-frequency bursts to communicate with the satellites. Best of all, they will be only a fraction of the normal cost to operate. This . . . ' he paused, eyes fixed on Xie's ' . . . changes everything. And I'm not just talking about phones here. Imagine every laptop communicating at over 50 megabytes per second from anywhere in the world. There would be no more Wi-Fi, hotspots or routers. Your laptop would just beam directly to a satellite!'

Xie scratched his neck thoughtfully while Jian waited for his response. When none seemed forthcoming, he grabbed his wine glass, swirling the viscous liquid around with such force that he spilled a few drops. The servants quietly entered, swapping the dishes for the main course, and Jian stayed silent until they had left before continuing.

'Do you have any idea how much the communications industry is worth? Over two trillion dollars worldwide. And we conservatively estimate we'll corner fifteen per cent of that market in the first year. That's 300 billion US dollars in the first year alone.'

Jian paused to let the sheer scale of the project sink in.

'The only issue we face is actually making the handsets. Satellite phones are big and cumbersome, but by using a very rare mineral we have been able to miniaturise them to the size of a normal cell phone. At the same time, through some carefully planned military operations, we have been ensuring that the supply cost of regular cell phones is rising. Coltan is becoming more expensive.'

Jian leaned back, smiling smugly.

'Ultimately, we will control both sides of the coin — the handsets and the network — of an industry worth over two trillion dollars.' He raised his glass. 'This the largest endeavour the Guild has ever initiated, and now it is only a month away from completion.'

'It all seems very complicated to me,' Xie said, finally. 'But I am sure that's why the Guild entrusted their investment directly to you. And you said they invested how much in the project exactly? Two-thirds of three billion, yes? That's . . . ' He paused, eyes moving skyward. 'Well, that's . . . '

'Two billion dollars,' Jian said, staring at him incredulously.

'Yes, quite.'

Xie smiled, then glanced down at his watch, eyebrows rising in surprise. 'I didn't realise it was so late. I mustn't waste any more of your time. I am sure Mr Kai is most happy with each of the satellite launches and that the accounts are signed off.'

Jian absentmindedly touched his mouth with his right hand. He then seemed to register what he was doing and quickly brushed away some non-existent morsel of food from his lips. Xie watched the movement. It was a stereotypical response for someone being evasive. Settling back into his seat, Xie studied him closely.

'How many satellite launches did you say there were again?' he asked.

Jian stared at him over the rim of his glass, his black eyes appearing almost polished in the low light.

'I didn't. We have launched nineteen of the twenty-two satellites.'

'The next one must be soon, then?'

'Actually, tomorrow.'

Xie rubbed his eyes, bunching the loose skin across his cheeks. 'So close to completing the project,' he said. From the tone of his voice, it could have been a statement or a question. He then stood up and, placing his napkin on the chair, bowed politely.

'You have been most generous with your time.'

Jian nodded. Xie was about to leave when he suddenly turned back to the table.

'What was the name of those butterflies again?' he asked.

'Blue Morpho.'

'Blue Morpho, that's right.' Xie smiled, then raised a finger towards Jian. 'Lepidopterology,' he said triumphantly, and with the air of someone thoroughly pleased with himself, retreated back through the entrance to the veranda, followed by one of the waiting servants.

Jian didn't move until he heard the clunk of the heavy front door. Reaching into the pocket of his trousers, he pulled out a small plastic bottle of prescription painkillers. He unscrewed the cap and picked up his glass of wine with his left hand. Shaking six of the cylindrical blue pills into his mouth, he washed down the dose before bringing his fingers up to his temples and massaging them gingerly. He was now taking triple the amount of prescribed pills each day and even that wasn't enough. The headaches were getting worse, the throbbing so bad it felt as if it would split his forehead at any moment.

It was the stress he was under. It had to be. All he had to do was hold on until the money was out of the country, then in only a few weeks the share prices would be where he wanted them. The announcement was coming.

Jian thought about what Xie had said. Could the mention of the next satellite launch have been a coincidence? It had to be. How could the Guild possibly have found out what he was intending? The twentieth launch . . . That had always been the one.

Playing back every detail in his mind, he tried to think what Xie had been implying. He tried to focus, tried to pick through the intonation of each syllable, but the headache was clouding his vision, the pain absolutely maddening.

Jian took another gulp of wine and screwed his eyes shut with pain. What was he thinking? There were no coincidences. They must be on to him.

But the launch was prepped for tomorrow and an unexpected delay would raise more suspicion than going through with it. Jian's mouth went dry. For a moment, another sensation superseded the pain — fear. If the Guild ever found out what he was planning, he would have the three hundred most powerful families in China hunting him down.

10

Two 125cc motorbikes twisted round the potholes of Goma's high street. Despite their drivers being well used to traffic chaos, they were making slow progress. A long line of 4x4s stood idling, with the occasional blare of a car horn as, further ahead, the axle of a decrepit supply truck had sheared off, leaving the vehicle stranded across both lanes of traffic. The driver had already climbed down from the cabin and was gesticulating wildly at the gathering crowd. He shook his fist, scattering insults in every language he knew, while the crowd hungrily circled the grain sacks on the back.

Luca Matthews sat on the rear seat of the second motorbike, clinging to the waist of his driver, Emmanuel. The wind pushed his blond hair back from his face and he was leaning forward, trying to peer over Emmanuel's shoulder and second-guess their route along the potholed road.

Since they had left Nepal, he had shaved off his beard and, wearing a fresh white T-shirt and long, dark green shorts, looked almost clean-cut. His face was still deeply tanned, but in the heat his forearms and calves were exposed for the first time in many months and shone alabaster white. The pallor of his skin accentuated the bands of wiry muscle running down his legs and arms, making him look lithe and sprung with renewed energy. But despite his general appearance, his pale blue eyes still held the same blankness as before. Only when he and René discussed the task of finding Joshua did any trace of life return to them.

It had taken over a week for them to travel to the Congo in a succession of dusty vehicles and decrepit aircraft. During almost the entire journey, Luca had remained silent, lost in his own thoughts. Only at the mention of Joshua's name would he snap out of his trance, becoming animated and even, at times, emotional. He would talk for hours about Joshua as if no one else existed on the planet, then just as suddenly lapse back into silence. The duality was exhausting, and René found his initial doubts only worsening with each new hour they spent together. It was like travelling with a schizophrenic.

René had promised himself that he would keep a very close eye on Luca, but at that exact moment he was having problems of his own. Perched on top of the motorbike just ahead, he was trying to keep his balance as the entire bike listed backwards from his weight, forcing the driver to lean almost directly over the handlebars in order to steer. René had begun the journey by swearing loudly at each near collision, berating his driver and pointing out some of the more immediate dangers. Now, he had his eyes screwed shut and had somehow managed to light a cigarette, puffing away on it with almost otherworldly calm.

The two bikes sped further out of town, past

kilometres of shanty towns with their patchwork corrugated roofing and creaking wooden doors. The huts stretched for mile after mile, some broken and forgotten, as if their owners had left them only half-built, while others had people visible within, tending to cooking fires or minding children. Occasionally a figure sat curled against the wall outside, elbows and knees jutting out at angles. They were all simply there, waiting.

As they passed the last of the huts, they saw the still waters of Lake Kivu breaking through the foliage on their left-hand side. The lake looked sombre, with heavy cloud reaching all the way down to the surface of the water. Rain threatened with each soft roll of thunder. It hadn't started yet, but when it came the roads would be awash with mud and grit.

René's motorbike suddenly veered off the road and on to a dust track, with Emmanuel nimbly following, past a deep run of potholes. Several supply trucks were crawling along the road ahead of them, belching out great plumes of diesel, while beside them ran half-naked men, pushing rickety wooden scooters stacked high with bags of charcoal. The men's bodies were lithe and muscular, their black skin gleaming with sweat as they heaved their loads forward. They laboured without a break, only stopping to refit one of their plastic flip-flops when it caught in the tar-black mud.

As the motorbikes crested a rise, columns and columns of white canvas tents came into view. They stretched as far as the eye could see, fanning out across the hillside in every direction before eventually being lost under the distant cloud. As they drew closer, they could see the letters 'UNHCR' stamped boldly across each one, with old rope zigzagging across the top, weighted down by slabs of black volcanic rock.

'Kibati,' Emmanuel said, raising his hand from the throttle. Luca had heard of the refugee camp before. Jack Milton had said it was the last place Joshua had been working with *Médecins Sans Frontières* before he had headed north and disappeared.

There was a small hut at the entrance with a sign reading 'Gendarmes', but the door was firmly locked and no policeman was in sight. As Emmanuel and his companion went off to try and find one of the MSF doctors, Luca and René stood by the motorbikes, with René smiling awkwardly at the few people who bothered to notice them. A small child, dragging a filthy plastic tray, walked past them returning from some errand. He wore a ripped T-shirt and flip-flops of different sizes.

'*Bonbons? Stylo?*' he asked, raising a hand towards Luca. He looked to René for a translation.

'He wants a sweet or a pen,' René said, patting his pockets. He took out one of his cigarettes and gave it to the boy, gently rubbing the top of his head like a sympathetic father.

'René, for Christ's sake, he's about five years old,' Luca protested. 'He can't smoke that.'

'I don't have any sweets and he'll trade that smoke with one of the older kids. This is the

98

Congo, my boy, and here, everything is worth something.'

Pulling another from the pack and lighting it, he inhaled deeply, letting his eyes scan across the sea of faded white tarpaulin.

'You know, this is all a hangover from Rwanda,' he said softly. 'These camps were originally set up when all the Hutus came across the border after they'd massacred the Tutsis. There were nearly a million of them right here, all trying to escape RPF reprisals. Now, it's mainly displaced Congolese people, driven out of their farms by all these bloody warring militias.'

René exhaled a huge plume of smoke, eyes taking in the desolation afresh. 'It's just never-ending. All these different groups fighting each other ... until they forget the bloody reason for fighting in the first place. It's the biggest damn' mess on the planet and these are the people who suffer. Nearly six million dead in the last eight years and barely a person outside Africa knows anything about it.'

Luca followed his gaze towards a small group of men sheltering under an open-sided tent. The boy was already there, trading his cigarette. In the distance, there was a roll of thunder and the black skies looked full to bursting.

'You seem to know a lot about it,' he said.

René shrugged.

'You forget, I'm Belgian. This used to be one of our colonies, and I tell you, Luca, we were no better. Back then it was all rubber and ivory. The story of Africa — white man grabbing everything he could. Now, it's just a bit more complex. But one thing never changes — the number of dead.'

He paused, eyes glassing over as he scanned the innumerable rooftops of tents.

'First it was us, then thirty years of that bastard kleptomaniac Mobutu, and now an endless mess of militia groups slaughtering everything in sight. What you are looking at here, Luca, are people who have been fucked over for the better part of a century.' A grim smile appeared on René 's lips. 'It's like the devil came up to the Congo one day and decided he'd stay.'

There was a loud whistle; they turned to see Emmanuel gesturing at them. Leaving the bikes, they followed him down the lines of shoddy tents, picking their way carefully over guy ropes and across the rocky ground. Luca followed at the back of the procession, eyes glancing sideways and in at the open doors of the tents they passed. Occasionally people stared back, their eyes locking with his for the briefest of moments. Some were proud, some broken, some just old, but as he passed one after the other, he realised that they all told stories he could never truly understand.

They were led up to a central clearing with a huge medical tent dominating one side of it. A long line of people sheltered under a canvas awning as they patiently waited their turn to enter. By the entrance stood a white man smoking a cigarette. He wore a doctor's lab coat with a stethoscope around his neck, and stared into the middle distance with an air of exhausted indifference. René and Luca were standing almost directly in front of him before he seemed to register their presence.

'My name's René, and this is Luca. Have you got a minute?' the Belgian said, offering his hand.

'Doctor Sabian,' the man said automatically, more resting his hand in René's than shaking it. 'Christophe Sabian.' He looked towards Luca, who had his eyes turned towards the ground.

'And you have all of my attention . . . until I finish this cigarette,' Christophe continued, raising the half-smoked butt in front of his face. 'There was another massacre out by Bunia this morning. So my diary's kind of full.'

'I'm sorry to hear that,' René said.

'What the hell for? You didn't do it.'

'Look, I know this is a bad time . . . but we really need some information.' As René drew a small notepad from his pocket, Christophe's expression suddenly darkened.

'Great,' he hissed, 'more bloody reporters.' Before René could protest, he raised a finger towards him in warning. 'Just don't think you're going to start interviewing the women again. The last fucking story chaser from Reuters might as well have hung a sign out to the husbands as to which one of them had been raped.' Anger coloured his cheeks as he flicked the cigarette down into the mud. 'You know the men don't take them back again, don't you? Once they've been raped, I mean. The women are cast out of the camps and have to take their children with them.'

Nodding towards the dying glow of the

101

cigarette, Christophe shook his head in disgust.

'Time's up,' he said, but before he could take a step further, Luca suddenly pushed past René, grabbing the lapel of the doctor's white coat and shunting him back against the side of the tent.

'What the hell do you think . . . ' Christophe began, but as he looked into Luca's eyes for the first time, he fell silent.

'We're not reporters,' Luca hissed. 'We want information about a man named Kofi. Joshua Kofi.'

'Joshua? Why do you want to know about him?'

'We're looking for him.'

Christophe didn't respond for a moment, then a flicker of recognition passed across his face. 'Luca?' he asked. 'You're his friend from England, right?'

As Luca released the front of his coat and stepped back, Christophe stared into his eyes. 'Yeah, that's right. He mentioned you a few times. You're that climber.'

Luca didn't respond.

Christophe slowly straightened the front of his white coat, smoothing out the fabric. He shook his head.

'Look, I'm sorry to be the one to tell you this, but Josh is . . . gone.' He looked skyward for a second. 'Jesus, someone at the agency should have informed you. Why the hell they let you come all the way out here like this . . . Really, I'm sorry.'

Luca's jaw clenched. 'You knew him well?' he asked.

Christophe shrugged. 'Yes, I'd say quite well. We worked together for a couple of months right here in Kibati. But after that convoy got lost, he disappeared. Like all the rest of them.'

As he spoke, a huge Congolese man ducked his head under the entrance flap of the tent. He wore the same sort of stained white coat as Christophe, and had jet-black, pockmarked skin. Shoving the nearest of the line of patients out of his way with a rough swing of his arm, he stared up at the bruised sky for a moment before lighting a cigarette and turning towards them.

'Break's over, Sabian,' he said, in a thick French accent.

Luca turned to him, his eyes narrowing, but before he said anything, René quickly interjected.

'Could you give us a couple of minutes? This is important.'

The man's eyes turned towards him, looking tired and bloodshot, the residue of decades of exhaustion and low-level alcoholism. After a moment, with a single eyebrow raised, he said, 'There's a boy waiting inside with a machete wound so deep that it nearly cut off his whole leg. And he's the tenth child we've treated this morning.' He paused, sniffing the air. 'So I'm guessing what you've got to say must be pretty fucking important.'

He then gave a deep sigh. 'I said, move it, Sabian.'

Christophe nodded, but as he turned towards the entrance, he motioned for Luca and René to follow.

'We can talk more while I'm working.'

Following him into the medical tent, they passed a large area of low seating, packed with waiting people. They sat huddled together, their bodies pressed so close that their limbs seemed to meld together into a continuous line of broken forms. There was barely a movement from the entire group, as if a terrible apathy had infected every one of them.

Further back in the tent and stationed against one of the steel uprights was an operating table. On top of it lay a teenaged boy. He was rake-thin, with his shaved head bent low. His right hand clutched a bundle of gauze wrapped around his inner thigh, the fabric rust-coloured from dried blood.

'How much morphine has he had?' Christophe asked the assistant hovering outside the well of light.

'Two point five mils.'

Christophe's eyes widened in surprise. His assistant shrugged, both of them well aware of the lack of medical supplies. Donning a pair of plastic gloves, the doctor gently pushed the boy down flat on the table and peeled back the dirty bandages. A gaping wound ran right back into the underside of his leg. It was wide, the band of flesh raw and blotted with pools of new blood.

'Staples aren't going to work. We'll have to do it the old-fashioned way. Get me a needle and sutures.' As he started swabbing the grit and congealed blood out of the wound, the boy cried out in pain. His eyes were screwed shut as he tried to stifle his tears.

'They pack dirt into the cut as part of a traditional remedy,' Christophe explained, running his finger down the centre of the wound. 'Plays bloody havoc with infection.'

A sterilised needle was passed to him and Christophe paused for a moment.

'Désolé, mais ceci te fera grand mal,' he said. Sorry, but this will hurt a lot.

The boy only nodded, clenching his fists tight against the sides of the operating table.

'You need to understand something,' Christophe said over his shoulder, as he drew the needle through one side of the wound. 'Things are different now. Joshua disappeared north of the Congo River, somewhere in the Ituri Forest. Nowadays, no one goes anywhere near there. I mean, no one. Not even MONUC patrol that area.'

'So what's up there?' René asked. 'What's happening to everyone?'

'The LRA,' Christophe said, his voice flat.

'The what?' Luca asked.

'The Lord's Resistance Army,' René explained, scratching his stubble pensively. 'They're a nasty bunch from Northern Uganda, with one of the most murderous bastards in the world as their leader — Joseph Kony. I saw some photos of him once from this crazy war photographer who'd got in to interview him. They're famous for stealing children, forcing them to kill their parents before they pump them full of drugs and use them on the front line. Less of an incentive to escape, you see? The kids can never go home again after what they've done.'

Christophe briefly turned back from his work. 'You know your history.'

'Yeah, I am afraid I do. But the LRA have been around for years. What's suddenly changed now?'

'After they got pushed out of Uganda, the LRA tried to establish a new base on the Congolese side of the border. Kony was basically defeated and left with just a ragtag bunch of child soldiers and a few of his most loyal officers. They were broken and everyone thought the war was finally over.'

Christophe shook his head slowly, pausing for a moment.

'But then Kony himself was murdered. A new leader emerged and things began to change. They got worse. Much, much worse.'

'So who is this new leader?' Luca asked.

'No one from the outside knows anything about him apart from his name — Mordecai.'

At the mention of the name, the top half of the boy's body jerked upwards. His eyes stared at them, brimming with terror. He started shouting for his mother, tears running freely down his dirty cheeks. Christophe put his hand on his shoulder, pushing him back down.

'*Calme-toi*,' he soothed. 'It's OK. *Calme-toi*.'

The boy's whole body began to shake, the emotion breaking through in violent waves. He wailed again and again, his back arching and his legs kicking out across the operating table, ripping open two of the stitches in his leg. The flesh peeled open again with a globule of congealed blood oozing out on to the stainless-steel table.

He shouted louder, banging the back of his head against the table as he called his mother's name again and again.

'Jesus Christ!' Christophe shouted, clicking his fingers together at the assistant. 'More morphine. Now.'

He jabbed the syringe into the boy's upper arm, and his cries almost immediately began to fade. A few seconds passed before Christophe looked up at them.

'I've never heard a name inspire so much fear. It's on every villager's lips when they come in here. Some just repeat it over and over again.' He shook his head slightly as if not quite believing what he was saying. 'It's like he's the bloody devil himself.'

'Where did this guy come from?' René asked.

'Who knows? Some say he was one of Kony's officers, others that he came from southern Sudan. But whatever happened, the one thing I do know is that when he took over, the LRA suddenly became well financed, with someone supplying them with new, sophisticated weapons. They got stronger and stronger, defeating all the other militia groups, and eventually started herding up the villagers. Everyone just disappeared; men, women, children. Everyone. It was only a few months later that we started finding bodies washed up on the riverbanks. They all had this pronounced swelling on the side of the head, mainly around the temporal lobes. Christ knows what had caused it, but for each one of them it was the same.'

Christophe stared ahead, his eyes vacant in the light.

'I shouldn't have said *his* name in here,' he added, admonishing himself with a slow shake of his head. 'But now you both know it, I hope to God you never have to hear it again.'

Wiping the sweat from his forehead with the back of one forearm, he suddenly looked very tired.

'Listen, I'm going to be a while longer patching this one up and I am sure I am on report already for bringing you guys into the tent. Joshua was a good friend and I want to help you, but I already know where this will end.'

He turned to face Luca.

'There are only two choices. Either you accept what I have said — that Joshua is gone — and go home. Or somehow you find your way north . . . and never come back.' He paused, as if already knowing which way it would go. 'I sincerely hope you choose the first option, Luca. Any man who travels all the way to the Congo looking for someone must be a good friend.'

Turning to René, he nodded.

'Take care, René, and if you can't talk him out of it and need some help, then look up a guy in town called Fabrice. He runs the Soleil Palace and has his hooks into almost everything around here. I treated him once and he kind of owes me.'

'Is he someone we can trust?' René asked,

running his fingers through his thick black beard.

'For Christ's sake, no. Don't trust anyone out here.'

With a shake of his head, Christophe turned back to his patient and continued stitching, leaving Luca and René to file out of the tent in silence. As they reached the edge of the refugee camp once again both drivers were waiting patiently, leaning against their motorbikes with plastic tarpaulin wrapped over their shoulders against the onset of rain.

Luca trudged towards them, his face angled towards the ground. He didn't seem to notice the rain beating down upon him, and his shoulders were hunched in thought. René had seen that look many times before on their journey from Nepal. Just as they reached the bikes, he took hold of Luca's arm, pulling him to a standstill.

'I know I'm the one who got you to come here in the first place, but given all that the doctor said, you know no one would blame you for giving up now. Not even Jack.'

Luca slowly shook his head.

'Whatever is out there, I've got to try. I owe Joshua that.'

René exhaled heavily, raising his hand to shield his eyes from the rain. 'Well, I guess we'd better get hold of this guy Fabrice and see what he can come up with.'

Luca looked up into his eyes.

'It's you who doesn't have to do this, René,' he said. 'This was never your job. When we get back to Goma, I'll head off alone.'

René gave a snort.

'Still haven't learned anything, have you? Without me you can barely tell your arse from your elbow. Whatever happens, I'm going.'

Luca smiled, and in that single moment René suddenly saw a hint of his old self shining through. It seemed to wash away all the doubts he had been bottling up ever since they had left Nepal and a wave of optimism flooded through him. It was as if the rain dripping down their cheeks could wash away the past and somehow let them start anew.

Clambering on top of the nearest motorbike, René balanced his weight on it with some difficulty before the engine fired up with a plume of sooty smoke.

'It doesn't really matter either way,' he shouted. 'We've got another twenty kilometres before getting back to Goma. Chances are we'll be dead long before the LRA get around to killing us.'

11

Bear Makuru walked through the old formal gardens of the Ihusi Hotel towards the shorebanks of Lake Kivu. Despite the years of war and successive owners, the gardens still retained something of their former glory. By the water's edge, mauve wisteria hung in thick plumes, while the soft scent of honeysuckle drifted up on the shore breeze. Only the laurels seemed to have suffered from a lack of pruning, leaving long serpentine lines of hedges that appeared almost sinister in the evening light.

Bear stood still. Squinting out over the lilac-blue waters of the lake, she tried to relax. The rains had passed as quickly as they had come, and now the water looked serene and inviting, the perfect antidote to Goma's forty-degree heat and dusty streets. But it wasn't the heat that was getting to her, more the incessant string of bad luck she had encountered since arriving in the Congo.

After a two-day flight from South Africa to Goma, the plane's right-hand magneto had started running rough and it had taken her almost the entire day pressed against the searing hot tarmac to fix it. No sooner had she got the engine running cleanly than soldiers had arrived in two jeeps and surrounded her. For three hours she had sat in the MONUC Captain's stifling office, answering the same questions over again and again.

Only after the Captain had pushed her own flight plan across the table did she understand why they had impounded her plane. She had faxed it over to Pieter's office three days ago, and despite the words 'Strictly FYI' scrawled in bold red letters across the top, one of Pieter's more enthusiastic office juniors had sent it on to the officials at Goma airport, who in turn had informed MONUC. They had immediately questioned her motives for flying north into a region clearly demarcated as a military no-fly zone. With so much cross-border smuggling, any plane venturing into that airspace was immediately considered suspect.

Bear had eventually been discharged pending an enquiry, and simply watched as they drained the fuel from her plane's wings before towing it off into a restricted area. She was grounded, and all because of one of Pieter's idiot members of staff.

Turning away from the view, Bear pulled down the sleeves of her overalls and tied them in a knot around her waist. She looked filthy. Even the white vest she was wearing had become stained grey from working on the Cessna's engine, while her whole body reeked of aviation fuel. Despite the hotel's reputation as a bohemian hangout for war correspondents and UN workers, she wondered whether they would even let her in, dressed as she was.

Ignoring the sideways glances from some of the local girls, Bear stalked past the bar and drew up a chair by the water's edge. Gulping down a bottle of chilled Primus beer, she stared out at the still waters of the lake and tried to control her anger.

How could Pieter's staff be so damn' incompetent? All she'd needed was a few basic things and they'd even managed to screw those up.

At least he had arranged a meeting with the man called Fabrice, who was rumoured to be able to get his hands on just about anything this side of the border. Bear only hoped that twenty-four gallons of Avgas wouldn't be beyond his capabilities. She'd dealt with such types before. They were invariably the same: egomaniac pirates, as mendacious as they were resourceful. But all she needed from this guy was some fuel and a clear idea of where she was headed.

The food she had ordered arrived. As she cut into a fillet of grilled tilapia fish, her eyes idly passed over the other drinkers and diners, and connected with a man who had been staring at her ever since she first sat down. He wore a khaki hunter's vest and a sand-coloured shirt which clung damply to the swell of his belly. Thin wire glasses were perched on top of a red, aquiline nose, while his naturally fair skin was darkly freckled from years spent working in the tropics.

Bear broke his gaze, but the man was already getting to his feet.

'Hi, I just thought I should introduce myself,' he said, clutching a half-full beer glass. 'I'm Jeffrey Watkins, the Reuters correspondent out

113

here. Haven't seen you around.'

Bear gave a tight smile. 'Just arrived.'

'Well, that's great. Just great. More meat for the grinder, huh?' he said, giving a soft chortle. His free hand rested on the back of the chair opposite, knuckles squeezing against the plastic.

'You know, Goma's a fascinating place, just fascinating. Been in Africa for nearly a year now, so getting under its skin a little, eh?' He swung his body round again, bringing the beer up to his chest and clutching it tight like a preacher might a book of psalms. 'But don't worry, in time you'll get used to the madness. Be happy to show you around in the meantime.'

Bear put down her fork, picking a piece of fish from her teeth as unattractively as she could.

'I was born in Bunia, just north of here,' she said. Shaking her head, she reached one hand towards her stomach. 'Damn' fish gives me gas.'

Jeffrey watched, his smile loosing a little of its elasticity. 'Born here, huh? That's great. You know, I'm interviewing women from all the tribes for a global piece I'm doing. Actually, the story's going to be pretty big.' He jabbed his finger towards her. 'Don't tell me your tribe . . . Lendo, right?'

Bear sniffed loudly.

'Hema.'

'Of course. Perhaps I could interview you? You know, for my article. It'd be about getting your voice out there.'

'Uh-uh,' Bear said, grabbing the beer bottle and swilling it around a couple of times. She took an enormous gulp, her throat working up and down as she drained nearly half the beer before wiping her mouth with the back of her hand.

Jeffrey waited patiently.

'We could go out for dinner somewhere else,' he suggested. 'You know, make a night of it.'

Bear glanced up at him, then down at his belly. 'I don't think so.'

'Come on, what's the harm in a little dinner? You might like it. OK, just a drink, then. We . . . '

'*Mon Dieu, ça suffit!* My God, enough of this!' Bear snapped. 'What is it you don't understand? I don't want dinner because I am eating right now, and in case you missed it, I've been twirling my wedding ring around my finger since you first came over. Now, do yourself a favour, *Jeffrey*, and go crawl back to your table.'

Jeffrey's jaw clenched, accentuating the sunburn at the corners of his mouth.

'Bloody . . . hell . . . ' he managed before there was a loud burst of clapping from behind. They both turned to see an African man dressed in an immaculate white suit, with Gucci sunglasses carefully balanced on his nose. He rocked forward as he clapped, grinning so widely that each one of his white teeth were on display.

'Damn, Jeffrey, you are just a sucker for a beating,' he said, reaching forward to slap the journalist on the back. Beer swilled over the top of the journalist's glass, welling out over the front of Jeffrey's shirt. 'You're like some kind of fucked-up pitbull. Tenacious, but dumber than hell.'

He then stared down at Bear and, raising his

115

fists like a prizefighter, gave her a huge wink.

'And you! Wow, you gonna make a boy fall hard. I love that whole vest, grease-stained shit you got going on there. Ain't nothing sexier than a girl that knows her way round an engine.'

Fabrice smacked his lips together as he pulled back the chair Jeffrey had been pawing. He sat down, adjusting his sunglasses a little, and allowed the full wattage of his smile to shine on Bear.

Jeffrey coughed quietly. 'If you don't mind, Fabrice, I was . . . '

' . . . boring her to death. Why don't you try one of girls at the bar? I'm sure they'd love to hear all about that little article of yours. Just make sure you pay them their hourly rate.'

As Jeffrey slowly retreated to his own table, Fabrice shook his head.

'Gotta love journos like that. Barely left the city in nearly a year and wants to write about the *real* Africa. Damn' *muzungos* never get it. You want to get anything out here, you got to get out there and take it for yourself.' He paused, squeezing his fists together. 'You gotta have balls.'

'The trick is to have them. Not think with them,' Bear countered, folding her arms across her chest and pushing her cleavage up a little. Fabrice smiled again, trying to stop his eyes from flicking downwards. Taking one of the chips left over on Bear's plate in front, he pointed it at her.

'And while we're on the subject, that's exactly what I got you by. I am the only one around here that can get you the fuel you need to get into the

116

Ituri. Guess that makes me your new best friend.'

He chewed on the chip thoughtfully. 'And, girl, trust me when I say this: I ain't cheap.'

Bear's expression stayed fixed. Her eyes were drawn to the side of Fabrice's cheek, where burn marks rose up to his hairline. She knew that guys like this were a dime a dozen in the Congo; maybe not as slick or successful, but underneath they were always the same. They had seen too much war and horror to respond to threats, and universally seemed to follow only three passions in life: money, women, and a pathological hatred of MONUC.

Bear leaned across the table, releasing her hair with a sideways toss of her head.

'You know you'll get your money, so why don't you relax about that? But this isn't just about me getting what I want. You help me get that fuel and it'd be like sticking a finger up to MONUC. Screw everything else, wouldn't it just be fun to bust my plane out of the compound, right from under their damn' noses?'

Fabrice's eyes were masked behind the mirrored sheen of his sunglasses.

'Sounds like you're the kind of girl that likes to mix business with pleasure.'

'When it suits me.'

He slowly shook his head.

'Why do I get the feeling this is going to hurt?' He signalled to the waiter for a beer. 'I tell you what, you give me a thousand US a gallon and I'll get you all the fuel you need.' He paused, sniffing the air. 'That way you can use it for the plane instead of washing yourself in it.'

'Don't play me for a tourist, Fabrice. Two hundred a gallon, or I get it from someone else.'

'Where do you think are — JFK? There's only one airport round here and the manager's my boy.'

'Three hundred a gallon and I'll give the MONUC base the finger while I buzz the tower.'

Fabrice gave a deep laugh, clutching hold of his stomach as if it might crack. He banged the table a couple of times, making the bottles clank together, before finally offering her his hand.

'Five hundred and you take some cargo for me. And that's the last offer you're gonna hear.'

Bear held back, her eyebrows arching suspiciously.

'Cargo?'

'Yeah. A couple of *muzungos* are on some screwed-up mission to find a friend of theirs. They need to get into the Ituri and one of them's hell-bent on the idea. Damn' nearly started a riot in my bar when I told him it wasn't going to happen. Should have dumped the kid in the lake, but there was something about him . . . ' Fabrice paused, his expression clouding over as he remembered the same irreconcilable anger that he had carried for years after his parents had died. There was something about the Westerner that had reminded him so clearly of himself back then.

Bear waved her finger slowly in front of Fabrice's nose.

'Tell the tourists to take a hike. From what Pieter said, we need to get to a small village

118

called Epulu just over the river. Anything north of that point is LRA country and your boys aren't going to last five minutes on the ground.'

Fabrice took a sip of his beer.

'What makes you so sure you will?'

Bear's expression darkened. 'Just get me that fuel. The rest is my problem.'

'Look, Pieter told me you've done some impressive shit, but it's different here.'

'Spare me. This ain't my first time.'

Fabrice slowly took off his sunglasses, folding them carefully on the table. He stared at Bear with wide brown eyes tinged at the bottom with a rim of grey-blue. They looked somehow damaged, the irises textured with fine brown lines which laced out across the whites. Despite the smile still playing at his lips, there was not an ounce of levity in them.

'You look like the kind of person used to giving advice, not taking it. But let me tell you something from one Hema to another. We both know what it was like during the wars — neighbours, friends, everyone hunting us down until the roads were stained red with our blood. We've seen it all, right? But this . . . ' Fabrice's expression stayed absolutely fixed. 'This is like nothing the Congo has ever seen before. Something's shifted and no one, and I mean no one, who goes north comes back.'

He reached across the table, the palm of his hand open.

'I'll get you your fuel. Just be damn' sure you know what you're wishing for.'

Bear stared at him for a moment longer. What

could Fabrice hope to gain from such scaremongering? He was trying to push her out of the deal, not into it. Her eyes searched his before she reached forward and took his hand.

'OK. It's a deal. But I want the fuel and the Westerners at the plane by 4.30 a.m. sharp. We take off before dawn hits.'

Fabrice replaced his sunglasses and whistled softly between his teeth.

'Yes, ma'am.'

Standing up with her hands resting on the table, Bear stared down at him. His eyes ran up the length of her body before eventually meeting hers.

'And the money?' he asked. 'Or were you thinking of working it off another way?'

'The money will be waiting for you on the tarmac once we get our fuel. Until then, why don't you and Jeffrey cool off in the lake together? He looks like he could do with some company.'

12

The co-pilot of the Gulfstream 550 private jet undid his safety belt and squeezed his way past the pretty air stewardess into the main part of the cabin.

'My apologies for disturbing your lunch, gentlemen,' he said in English to the two men sitting facing each over an immaculate white tablecloth. 'A call has been diverted to the plane for a General Jian.'

The pilot's eyes moved from one man to the other, unsure to whom he should be speaking. Jian slowly dabbed the corners of his mouth with the napkin and looked down at the finely crafted hands of his Patek Philippe watch. The call was a few minutes later than he'd been expecting.

Moving round the seating area to the bureau at the back of the plane, he picked up the satellite phone. A few seconds later, he was shouting in Mandarin into the mouthpiece.

'This is an outrage!' he boomed. 'You will personally see to it that I get a full enquiry within two hours. You hear me, lieutenant? Two hours! I want to know how the satellite exploded and why.' There was a pause as he waited for the inevitable string of apologies. 'And when I get back, there are going to be some major shake ups. We are the PLA, lieutenant. We do not make this kind of mistake.'

Jian rang off, then paused before getting up

from his seat. He closed his eyes, systematically going over each detail in his head. He had deliberately used an unsecured line, certain that the Guild would be monitoring all communications from his office. The display of outrage had been for their benefit. Leaning back in the padded chair, he massaged his temples, rather pleased with his performance. But now they knew, and from this one single event, everything else would follow.

He already had a man in place to ensure the investigation team wouldn't find any evidence of the explosives they had used. By now, the wreckage would be strewn over a couple of miles and it would take them days to sift through it all. One thing, however, was vital — they had to believe the explosion had been caused by a technical fault and not the result of deliberate sabotage.

The truth was, there was no actual satellite in the launch. The rockets, fuel and guidance systems had been carrying little more than an empty shell into space before Jian's explosion had brought them all crashing back down again. Instead, they had manufactured a dummy satellite from low-grade aluminium which, when blown into a thousand pieces, should be more than enough to fool the investigating team.

He was taking a serious risk. It was too public and exposed for his taste, but it had been the only way he could hide the fact that only twenty satellites had been built, when the Guild had actually financed twenty-one. Thirty-six million dollars had remained unspent from the budget, which, after some careful reallocation, was more than enough to get him started.

From the very beginning, Jian had known that any joint venture between the PLA and the Guild would lead to a host of complications and, more importantly, miscommunications. Everything had to pass through circuitous chains of command and got bogged down in endless amounts of red tape. In the end, it had been a relatively simple task to feed in two conflicting orders to the construction company in Guangdong. With all the different prototypes and redesigns being built, they were soon unsure as to exactly how many satellites were in the final order.

General Jian had offered to intervene personally to clear up the confusion . . . and had succeeded in muddying the waters even further.

However, it had not been as easy to hide the accounting discrepancies nor to load the empty casing of the dummy satellite without any of the technicians realising that something was amiss. But, as with all high-level security matters, everything was compartmentalised, with each technician seeing only one small part of the jigsaw at any one time. Such protocols had left Jian just enough room for manoeuvre.

After eight months, he had finally succeeded in getting the money out of China. Using three separate export companies based in two different provinces, he had diverted small chunks of money every few weeks, eventually amassing the entire balance in a Lebanese account. The bankers out there were well accustomed to acting as intermediaries for the Saudis and were renowned for maintaining their clients' anonymity. The Lebanese were also natural-born traders. They couldn't care less where the money came from or how. Only their cut was important to them. As the saying went in downtown Beirut : morality was for the philosophers at Byblos.

Jian inhaled deeply, then slowly moved back to his seat. Settling himself against the tan leather upholstery, he stared at the man opposite, flashing him a brief smile that was meant to be pleasant.

'Everything all right, General?' his dining companion asked.

Jian nodded, faintly amused that Hao addressed him as 'General' despite their having known each other since university days, eighteen years earlier. Since then, Hao had pursued an unspectacular career in electronics, despite the industry's meteoric growth over the last decade. That mediocrity showed in his whole demeanour: in his sunken eyes, ringed with bags of tired skin; in his nose, reddened from drink.

They hadn't seen each other in over twelve years and ostensibly were still friends, but when Hao first clambered on board the plane in Beijing, Jian had been forced to mask his contempt. Hao's suit jacket had threadbare elbows and a greasy stain running up one sleeve. Here they were, flying on a $50 million jet, and the idiot hadn't even been able to find a decent suit to wear.

Jian soon discovered that Hao's drink problem was as bad as his research had suggested. Hao had gulped down a vodka and tonic shortly after take off and, although clearly desperate for another, had been too timid to ask. Instead, his right knee bounced up and down in nervous spasm and he shuffled continually in his seat, trying not to stare at the empty glass. Jian found almost every facet of the man utterly revolting.

'Do you think . . . we might have another drink?' Hao asked at last, smiling tightly.

'Sorry, my old friend,' Jian said, clicking his fingers towards the air stewardess. 'I thought you had given that stuff up.'

Hao shook his head good-naturedly, the relief of being offered something else to drink far outweighing his surprise that Jian had believed he was teetotal.

'General,' Hao began, pausing to take a deep pull of his drink, 'I'm flattered to be asked to accompany you on one of your trips, but when you called I wasn't sure what you actually needed.'

'Trust,' Jian said, his lips curving in a smile. He let the word hang in the air a moment longer before leaning forward conspiratorially in his seat.

'I need someone I can trust with an extremely important mission. This is a case of national security.'

Hao's eyes bulged. He was suddenly feeling decidedly anxious. For the last five years, he had been manoeuvred within his own company into a position which held almost no day-to-day responsibility. Now, the General was talking about national security.

'A mission?' Hao repeated, raising his drink slightly to attract the attention of the air stewardess. She came over quickly, loading it with another double shot.

'Yes, a mission, but I need someone outside the PLA for this ... outside the government even. This has got to stay completely off the radar, Hao. I am relying on you for that.'

Hao sat up straight, feeling a strange mix of surprise, inadequacy and pride that someone might actually need him to do something. He cast his eyes around the sumptuous interior of the Gulfstream, the whole design reeking of moneyed elegance. This was one of only two types of private jet which could fly from Beijing to London without refuelling. It was for the elite few, and here he was, sitting opposite a man who commanded that kind of lifestyle ... and that man was asking *him* for a favour.

'Of course, General. But what is it you need from me?'

'For you to be me,' Jian said, smiling inwardly at the irony of his request. He wondered whether the $4,000 suit and Rolex Daytona he had brought for Hao to wear would be enough to fool the bankers.

Hao was frowning heavily, while his jaw trembled very slightly.

'It's simple,' Jian continued, trying to sound reassuring. 'I have made a deposit at the Credit Libana Bank in downtown Beirut. I need you to access the funds and then short a list of eight telecom companies on the Stock Exchange.'

Hao's mouth opened as if Jian had asked him

126

to do something that was physically impossible.

'Short?' he stammered. 'It's not really my field . . . I mean, the whole stocks and shares thing.'

Jian smiled again, but his eyes had hardened. Suffering fools was one of his greatest pet hates.

'Shorting means that you promise to sell someone shares in the future at a certain price. For instance, in one month from now, you will agree to sell Vodafone shares for nine dollars each to a buyer. He'll take your shares, whatever happens, at that price. Now, if the market moves downwards and Vodafone shares drop in value, when you go to buy those shares, you can get them cheaper than nine dollars, right? You might buy them for, say, six dollars instead, but you are still selling them at nine dollars, because the buyer *guaranteed* you that price. You see?'

A knowing smile crept across Hao's face. 'Shorting,' he repeated, nodding vehemently. 'I thought that's what it was.' He leaned back in his seat a little, brushing an imaginary speck of dust off the tablecloth. 'So how much money are we talking about here?'

Jian stared at him. Despite every precaution, he still felt hesitant about disclosing such a detail, but there was nothing for it. Hao would find out soon enough when they arrived in Beirut.

'Using option contracts, we will leverage an initial investment of 36 million US dollars to nearly twenty times that sum.'

Jian had done his calculations and conservatively estimated that the stock market would initially drop five per cent with the announcement that their company, ChinaCell, was launching a standard-sized phone with global satellite capabilities. Once the full implications of this launch were felt across the board, all the top blue-chip companies, from Apple to Verizon, LG to Vodafone would come crashing down. Overnight, their iPhones, BlackBerries and Androids, once the pride of their R&D divisions, would be relegated to the past. The general feeling of the Guild was that they would become all but obsolete in less than two years.

If the market went as they predicted, on his initial investment of $36 million, Jian was set to net over half a billion dollars. In under one month, all that money would be his.

The announcement was coming soon.

'Thirty-six million dollars,' Hao repeated. The number was beyond anything he could comprehend. 'That's a lot,' he said vaguely. His forehead creased again. 'But I am still not sure where I fit in. Why am I being you, so to speak?'

'Because it's vital that my presence is not known to anyone in Beirut. I will be acting as *your* assistant under a different name.'

'You'll be my assistant?'

'That's correct.' Jian stared across at Hao. 'As you can imagine,' he began, his voice slowing as if speaking to a foreigner, 'my position as a general of the PLA has certain, shall we say, limitations while I am overseas. So the government has given me some different papers and I will go by the name of Chen. It's very important you remember to refer to me that way.'

'Chen?'

Jian stared across the table at him, wondering if he could actually entrust something so important to this imbecile. He had to reinforce the idea somehow. Just one mistake would be enough to blow his cover. Reaching inside the breast pocket of his suit, he pulled out his new passport and slid it across the table.

He watched as Hao cautiously picked it up, flipping through the fictitious visa stamps to the picture on the final page. They had done a good job; even the dark red cover had been faded and creased to make it look older than it was.

Over the last four days, Jian had grown a thin moustache and cut the sides of his jet-black hair extremely short. The effect was quite radical, lengthening his face. With some coloured contact lenses, he had dulled the black of his eyes to a lighter grey. He had been right to assume that Hao wouldn't notice the difference. Too much time had passed since they had last seen each other.

'And what about me?' Hao asked, slowly closing the passport.

'You will be travelling under your own name. All you have to do is treat me like your assistant and let me do the talking.'

'But don't I need some fake ID as well? And what if they should spot yours at Customs? What if something goes wrong . . . like . . . '

Hao slipped into silence, wetting his lips. He suddenly felt completely out of his depth. Fake passports and moving millions of dollars between accounts . . . Wasn't that spying? Surely, they could imprison them both without trial for that kind of thing. He'd heard what those Arabs could do.

'Look, General,' Hao said softly, 'I'm not sure about this. I'm not really cut out for . . . well, the whole spy thing.'

'No one is asking you to be a spy. Don't be so melodramatic.' Jian tried to smile, but succeeded only in showing his teeth. 'They can't touch a Chinese national in the Lebanon,' he lied. 'At the worst case, you'd be deported, and we're scheduled to fly back tomorrow anyway.'

'It's just that I'm really not too comfortable . . . '

'Trust me when I say you will be doing your country a great service. Remember — this is for the sake of national security. I will also use my influence to ensure you are recommended for a commendation after this.'

'A commendation,' Hao repeated. Despite himself, a glow appeared in his cheeks. Imagine what his wife and contemporaries would say to that! He stayed silent for a moment, mulling it over. As the General had said, the worst case was that he would be deported from a country he never intended to go back to anyway. After a minute more, Hao straightened in his chair, feeling his chest swell for the first time in years. Imagine coming home with a commendation!

'OK,' he said, nodding in a manner that suggested Jian had been right to bestow his trust on him. 'Let's do it.'

He reached across the table, smiling, one hand outstretched. Jian hesitated. Hao's teeth were a shade of dirty yellow with a gap between the front two, while his lips looked rouged and fat. The man was simply revolting, but he was necessary. As the fictitious assistant, it would be far easier for Jian to fade back into obscurity.

He shook hands.

'Good to be together again, huh?' Hao offered. 'Been a long time hasn't it? I was thinking of that time at university when we broke out of the campus together, right under the professor's nose!'

As he raised his glass to the air stewardess again, Jian suddenly reached forward, clasping his fingers around Hao's wrist.

'No more. You stay sober from now on.'

13

The white 7 Series BMW moved as sedately as it could through the utter anarchy of Beirut's main highway. Six lanes of traffic ran in both directions on the Hafez el Assad with cars swerving unpredictably from one lane to the next. A blacked-out Audi with Dubai plates veered inches away from the BMW's bumper, its engine revving loudly, as it tried to get past and beat a bikini-clad girl in a Porsche just in front.

Lining the searing hot tarmac were garish billboards offering cosmetic surgery, property deals and the chance to get your teeth whitened at a discount price. Behind them stood a multitude of white apartment blocks with views over the sparkling blue sea, that stretched all the way up to the outskirts of the city.

The BMW pushed through the traffic and finally into the downtown area. The entire central part of Beirut had been rebuilt after the war. After sixteen years of bitter conflict, only a handful of buildings were left standing, each pockmarked and gaping from mortar rounds and machine-gun fire. Amongst all the new construction and the prevailing air of opulence, a couple of these buildings had been left standing as a reminder to the hardliners that, despite the wealth pouring in, Beirut could easily succumb to troubled times again.

The towering minarets of Mohammad Al-Amin

Mosque with its domed turquoise roof came into view and the car slowly pulled round the back before arriving at the entrance to Credit Libana private bank. The roller shutters eased up to reveal heavily armed soldiers talking on a radio, before waving them through into the interior of the building.

They were led up a wide stone staircase and into an open-air courtyard. Protected from the noise and heat of the city by the building's heavy stone walls, the courtyard brimmed with Arabic refinement. Stunningly ornate mosaics ran from the floor into the arches of the vaulted ceiling, while water softly bubbled away in the central fountain. Cedarwood desks had been positioned to one side, while nearer to the fountain was a low seating area. Mint tea and pistachios arrived seconds later, followed by a rotund man wearing a tailored blue suit and sporting a well-groomed goatee. He had the soft, pleasant features of a man who had worked indoors his entire life, cocooned by money and privilege.

'*Ahlan wa sahlan, sharraftouna fi loubnan.*' Welcome, you honour us by coming to Lebanon, he said. Then in English, 'I am A'zam el Hussein.'

General Jian got to his feet and bowed courteously, before shaking his hand.

'I am Mr Hao's private secretary and will be translating for him on today's matters.'

A'zam nodded respectfully to Hao, who was fidgeting, his fingers drumming against the wooden armrest.

'We have already prepared the paperwork in

line with your request,' A'zam continued, 'but I wanted to speak to you privately, if you will permit?'

Jian nodded, reminding himself to play the role of assistant. He moved back a pace to allow A'zam to sit down.

'We understand you wish to invest in the following companies,' A'zam began, motioning with his fingers to a young assistant, clutching an embossed leather folder to her chest. A single page of A4 paper was presented to Jian. It listed the names of all the Western telecom companies he had stipulated and the amounts of each stock to be shorted. Jian ran his eyes down the list slowly, double-checking each amount.

'This is correct. It is in line with what Mr Hao has directed me to authorise.'

'As I am sure Mr Hao is aware, in each one of these cases you are betting against the market. In places, heavily. Telecom stocks have increased at an average of eight per cent over the last five years, with some of them doing considerably better.' A'zam paused, his expression sympathetic. 'I would not be doing my job if I did not caution you as to this fact and to the substantial losses you will incur if the market does not move as you hope.'

Leaning back in his chair a little, he raised his hands.

'As you can imagine, we here at Credit Libana handle many client portfolios and would be delighted to offer some advice.'

Jian turned back to Hao, speaking softly in Mandarin. A moment later he said to A'zam, 'Mr

134

Hao is aware of the situation and thanks you for your caution. If we could now settle the paperwork?'

Hao was presented with a gold Mont Blanc fountain pen with which to sign the necessary documents, with A'zam indicating that it was a small token of the bank's appreciation. Jian was handed another leather folder with the funds acknowledgement receipts tucked inside, and with that they were led back to their car.

Emerging into the hustle of the city once again, the BMW drove west towards the Beirut Marina Yacht Club, where a long line of dazzling white super yachts lay moored along the quayside. Crew members in matching outfits washed and fussed over each one, despite the fact that these millions of dollars' worth of ocean-going vessels rarely saw the outside of the harbour walls. Jian and Hao walked up the gangplank and settled down on the plush rear deck of a Princess 78 motor yacht, while a couple of crew members slipped the mooring. The deck crew stayed on the quayside as the yacht slowly glided out of the harbour and past the promenade, just as the sun began to set over Beirut's concrete skyline.

Jian opened a bottle of champagne, charged their glasses and peeled back the clingfilm from a silver tray of canapés resting on the table.

'You own this boat as well?' Hao asked, taking a deep slug of champagne. 'It's huge.'

'I'm chartering it,' Jian replied, watching him carefully. 'I thought you deserved the appropriate thanks for helping me.'

Hao smiled, raising his glass in a toast. 'I wasn't sure that I really did anything. But thank you.'

'Not at all, you played your part well.'

They watched the lights of the great city slowly recede as the yacht powered further out to sea. They followed the course of several large passenger ferries exiting Beirut's main port, the yacht bouncing up and down as they passed through the wakes.

Jian kept filling Hao's glass until he had worked his way through two bottles of champagne and was on to his fifth double vodka and tonic. His face was now flushed, his red nose shining, as he suggested they sing some of their old university songs together. He stood leaning against the stern rail, smiling cheerily, hair blown back into his face by the breeze.

'University . . . ' he slurred. 'Best bloody days of your life. Hope . . . that's what's missing from all this modernity. We need more . . . ' He got distracted, and stared down at the dregs in his glass. 'We need more vodka is what we need!'

Hao's eyes turned towards Jian, sitting quietly on the lounge deck. They were bloodshot, with tears from the strong breeze blurring the pupils. He hadn't noticed that Jian had stopped drinking over an hour ago.

'Can you pour me another drink?' Hao asked. Jian got up and poured him another huge measure of Smirnoff Black. At 50 per cent proof, it would probably be Hao's last before passing out. He took a couple of huge gulps, but the strength of the alcohol did not even register against his numb lips.

Jian was watching him now, following every movement. He reached into a small watertight bag that had been on the boat when they first arrived and began running a length of thin plastic cord through his hands. He did it over and over again, watching while Hao's movements became ever more erratic.

'What's that?' Hao asked. He raised his hand in the vague direction of the plastic cord.

'It's very special cord that dissolves in salt water,' Jian answered flatly. 'It's strong but only takes a couple of hours to disintegrate without a trace.'

Hao nodded his head slowly. 'Nice,' he mumbled, feeling his vision start to waver. He lurched forward, unsure whether it was him or if they had just passed through another ship's wake. Grabbing on to the railing with his left arm, he suddenly felt terribly hot. Reaching up, he found his brow damp with sweat, despite the sea breeze, and a wave of nausea washed over him. He shut his eyes, trying to block it out, but the whole boat seemed to roll again. His mouth felt dry despite all that he had drunk.

'I think I should . . . lie down for a second,' he whispered, staggering over to the wide sofa. 'Can one of the crew take me to my bed?'

He staggered forward a few more paces, then stopped. 'Actually, where the hell are the crew? Haven't seen anyone since we came on board.'

Jian didn't answer, just sat watching while Hao slumped down on to the sofa, his head lolling back as he tried to fight the drunkenness. He hiccupped several times before dry retching, with his hands over his mouth. He sat there for a minute, his jaw slack as his head gently swayed back and forth. A few minutes later he was curled up in the foetal position, his knees almost touching his chest. He snored loudly, with his cheek pressed into the upholstery and a line of spittle escaping from one corner of his mouth.

Jian got up and stood over him. He slapped Hao hard in the face with the palm of his hand, but Hao simply murmured and turned over in his sleep. He gave a loud snore, his feet curled on top of one other like a child's.

Jian wound the plastic cord around his ankles, tightening the knot with a sharp jerk. He then pulled Hao's hands behind his back and did the same again, taking his passport from the breast pocket of his suit jacket along with his wallet. He took the Rolex off his wrist. With hands under his armpits, Jian dragged him to the side rail without Hao even opening his eyes. Then Jian shunted him backwards so that he jack-knifed over the edge and into the black waters below. There was a faint splash and the imprint of his body against the silvery wake before it was quickly lost in the darkness. Jian didn't bother to look back but simply returned to his seat, wiping the palms of his hands.

The Lebanese skipper was the only other person on board and he had strict instructions to remain at the controls for the entire duration of the cruise. Jian cast his eyes towards the screen doors which led into the interior of the yacht. They were still firmly closed.

Two days later, the body of an unknown Chinese man washed up on Khalde Beach. There was a cursory examination by the pathologist, who quickly concluded that he must have fallen off the back of one of the many ferries which came into the harbour. It had happened a few times before with extremely drunk passengers. Without a single mark to identify it, the body was duly incinerated and a day later the file sent down to be archived.

14

Bear Makuru crouched down in the reed grass by the side of the runway. She squinted past the long line of stationary UN planes, their brilliant white fuselages grey in the moonlight, searching for the low wingtips of her Cessna 206. At last, she caught sight of the outline of the plane against a high mesh of barbed wire. It was parked right against the side of the MONUC compound and at the far end of the runway.

'You see it?' whispered Luca, squatting down next to her. Using the sleeve of his black V-neck T-shirt, he wiped his brow clear of sweat. He had a huge rucksack on his back and pressed into the long grass next to him were two oversized metal jerrycans, their caps still wet with Avgas.

'Yeah. The far corner, behind that old Antonov,' Bear replied.

'Shit. Right next to the compound.'

Bear turned as she heard René approaching through the long grass. He had two jerrycans clasped to his barrel-like chest, but was swaying with the effort of carrying them. He pulled up, dropping them on the grass in relief before resting his hands on his knees. His whole chest heaved up and down as the air whistled through his lungs, and in the heat of the night a line of sweat ran down from his forehead and beaded off the bridge of his nose.

Bear cast a sideways glance at Luca. 'Tell the

140

hippo to lower his breathing, or he'll get us all caught.'

René's forehead creased in pain.

'This wasn't exactly what I had in mind . . . ' he said, struggling to catch his breath ' . . . when we bought two seats on the plane from Fabrice. Kind of thought it might have fuel in it already.'

'So sue me.'

Bear hoisted another of the forty-kilogram jerrycan on top of her head, widening her stance as the weight pressed down on her neck.

'When we break cover, keep low and move fast.' She cast a glance back at René. 'Or whatever you can manage.'

The edge of the runway was worn through, with faded patches of tarmac broken up by virulent weeds growing almost waistheight. Bear picked her way through, careful not to lose her footing, with Luca following closely behind. They reached the massive tailfins of the UN planes, moving from shadow to shadow as they slowly made their way closer to the impounded Cessna. Bear could hear Luca grunting softly from the effort of carrying a 50-kilogram jerrycan in each hand. His shoulders were hunched over and his thighs crooked at the knee from strain, but the months spent carrying loads with the Sherpas had hardened his body.

They reached the undercarriage of an old Antonov cargo plane that had been bulldozed to one side somewhere in the distant past and left to rot. The outside was still charred black and caked in soot, while long vines had grown over the deflated tyres and up into the belly of the plane. Bear stopped, taking a moment to steady her breathing, and stared down the wall of barbed wire, searching for one of the manned lookout posts interspersed along its length. They had been lucky. The nearest was over a couple of hundred metres away.

'Let's go,' she whispered.

The Cessna looked dwarfed by the other planes. Bear swung one foot on to the step by the engine housing and pulled her whole body on to its wing. Twisting off the fuel cap with her left hand, she jammed in the funnel and began draining the Avgas, her arms straining to keep the jerrycan steady. Fuel sloshed into the tank, gurgling with a noise that seemed impossibly loud in the still night air. Scanning the line of barbed wire for the slightest movement, Luca passed up the next can, popping open the lid with a dull metallic clunk. Just as they had finished emptying the second one, René arrived, teeth gritted and nose flaring from the effort of controlling his breathing. He stood still for a moment before looking up at Bear.

'Get the plane ready. We'll finish these off.'

Sliding off the wing, she landed delicately on the ground and opened the door of the Cessna. She jumped into the left-hand seat, pushing down the master switch and roughly pulling the headset over her neck. The electrics gave a low whine as the flaps gradually lowered to 10 per cent. She jerked the control column sideways, flaring out the ailerons before checking on the rudder. With a soft clank, Luca laid the last of the jerrycans on its side and, piling his rucksack in the back of the plane alongside René, slid into the seat next to her.

'As soon as I crank this engine, all hell's going to break loose,' Bear said, her left hand resting on the key. Luca nodded, his eyes wide in the half-light. She looked across at him and could see pinpricks of sweat across the top of his cheeks.

'Do it,' he said.

There was a sudden clamour as the engine parts ground together. The propeller swung full circle then jerked to a standstill. As Bear tried again, turning the engine over and over, they heard sudden shouting in the distance and the long beam of a searchlight powered out across the open tarmac. It moved in long, sweeping arcs, jumping from plane to plane.

'Again,' Luca shouted, as Bear turned the key and pumped the throttle. The engine turned over, then again, but the propeller once more shuddered to a halt.

'Come on, you old bitch,' Bear shouted, while the beam of the searchlight traced towards them. She kept the key locked over, forcing the engine to turn and grinding the propeller round in a continuous circle. They could already hear the power in the battery starting to fade.

'Don't flood. Don't fucking flood,' Bear pleaded, jamming the throttle closed again. The propeller spun round once, then twice, then suddenly caught, roaring into life. Backwash from it made the open doors flap on their hinges as Bear quickly pulled her feet off the brakes, causing the plane to lurch forward. They were taxiing out towards the runway when the searchlight picked up the movement, swivelling round and hitting them full on. Searing white light filled every inch of the tiny cockpit, blinding them.

'I can't see shit,' Bear shouted, raising her hand to protect her eyes. She instinctively pulled back on the throttle, groping blindly at the controls.

'Just go!' Luca shouted. 'Go!'

Slamming the throttle back in, Bear grabbed hold of the control column to steady herself as the plane began to gather momentum. Then the beam suddenly disappeared, eclipsed by the wide hull of the Antonov, and they turned to see the Cessna's wingtip pass only a few feet from the undercarriage of one of the other UN planes. Luca saw it first and, before Bear had time to react, he kicked down the left rudder from his side of the plane, making them swerve out towards the main drag of the runway.

There was the sound of a siren, followed by engines. Then the main gates of the compound were thrown open and two military jeeps drove out towards them. They could only see the vehicles in momentary flashes as they passed each gap in the line of parked planes, but the silhouette of a soldier clutching a rear-mounted machine gun was all too clear. As the leading jeep accelerated, the engine dipping with each change of gear, the soldier swivelled the 7.62mm gun around.

Bear checked the air-speed indicator as the needle clawed its way up past 55 knots. She was nearly at rotation speed and heaved back on the control column, lifting the nose of the Cessna clear of the tarmac. The wheel drew up from the ground, then crashed back down again, pitching Luca and René forward in their seats with a brutal shunt. Bear swore, trying to hold the plane level with the rudder pedals as her hand held the throttle in tight.

'Too soon,' she said, cursing her own impatience. 'Come on, just a few more seconds.'

Slowly the plane eased up once again, airborne under its own momentum. Instead of pulling up and gaining altitude, Bear held them just a few feet above the ground, skimming under the long line of tailfins of the UN planes.

Taking up the flap, she skilfully balanced the sink, waiting for the needle to pass 100 knots before pulling the plane up in a steep banking turn in the opposite direction to the jeeps. They heard the thud of machine-gun fire and saw a fluorescent line of tracer rounds cut into the night sky just above them. Red sparks spat into the darkness, drawing a thin line of fire that swung in a tight arc towards the front of the Cessna. Bear angled the plane into an even steeper turn, swinging them wide across a dense area of scrubland and further into the night. The machine gun tried to follow their trajectory, thumping out rounds in a long, continuous burst, before the noise suddenly stopped. It was quickly replaced by the searchlight, the sharp beam criss-crossing the sky above them.

'Are we hit?' Luca shouted, turning towards Bear, but she had her head bent low and was looking past him out to the underside of each wing. She then cautiously tilted the ailerons, weaving the plane from side to side and double-checking that everything was functioning properly. Finally looking back at Luca, she exhaled slowly and shook her head. He went to say something more but she tapped her headset, indicating that they should put theirs on as well.

'You guys OK?' came her voice, crackling slightly over the intercom.

'Yeah,' said Luca slowly, his hand still gripping on to the grab handle above the window. There was a pause before René's voice suddenly boomed in over the mic.

'Bloody terrified!' he shouted. 'Always hated flying, let alone being shot at while doing it.' He then reached forward and lightly banged Bear's shoulder. 'But well done back there, girl. You were great.'

'It was close. Way too close. I can't believe they opened up on us like that.'

'They're bastards,' René said, fumbling in his pockets and lighting a cigarette. A plume of smoke billowed out into the cockpit and his face glowed red in the embers, a smile curving through his thick black beard. 'Just promise me you'll never do a turn like that last one again,' he added. 'My stomach damn' near went through my spine.'

Bear looked at the cigarette and the cloud of smoke encircling René. She began to say something, then turned back to the controls, pulling the air vents open a little further. Taking out a map from the side of her seat, she shone a small pencil torch across its laminated surface, checking their heading against the directional compass. She then adjusted the trim a little further and leaned back in her seat. A few moments passed before she turned towards Luca.

'So what's your story?' she said, finally breaking the silence. 'Fabrice didn't exactly say much about you.'

Luca was staring out of the window towards the open expanse of Lake Edward, directly beneath them. The water was translucent silver in the moonlight, stretching mile after mile towards the horizon.

'We're looking for a friend who disappeared about six months ago.'

'Six months? That's quite some time to be missing in a place like the Congo. What makes you think he is still alive?'

Luca shrugged.

'So what's your plan? Just to head into the Ituri and start looking?'

'Something like that.'

'It's a pretty big place and you don't seem to have packed much stuff. You don't think it's going to take a bit more than a rucksack and a few bottles of Deet?'

'We know where the truck was hit. That's all we need, to start with.'

'That's all?'

Luca nodded slowly.

'But you guys have experience of a place like this, right? You've been in the jungle before.'

'No. Not exactly.'

Bear paused, then she looked back at him.

'Look, don't take this the wrong way, but have you got any idea how crazy it sounds, going off into LRA country looking for some guy who disappeared six months ago? You sure you know what you're getting yourself into?'

'Just give us the lift. After that, we'll go our own way.'

'Damn' right you will! And you both need to understand one thing — the deal was to get you to Epulu. That's it. I don't give a shit what Fabrice told you because after we land out there, you guys are on your own.'

She glanced across at Luca, her voice hardening.

'And when things go bad, don't expect to be turning to me every five minutes for help. Out there, you're on your own.'

Luca's head snapped round and he stared at her, eyes shining with hostility. Bear returned his gaze, suddenly wondering what it was he was about to do. The change in him was immediate. She watched as his left hand reached down to the console and with a sharp tug yanked out the cables to his headset, killing the mic. He stared out into the night, the profile of his face lit by the dull glow of the cabin lights. She watched him a moment longer, recognising his anger and bitterness. She'd seen them both before, many years ago.

'He's not exactly talkative at the moment,' came René's voice over the intercom. 'But don't worry, he'll lighten up when we're on the ground. And, just for the record, we always knew it was only to Epulu. From then on, we'll make our own way.'

Bear nodded. 'Is he always this touchy?' she asked, knowing full well that without the headset she couldn't be heard above the noise of the engine.

'Luca?' There was a crackle on the mic as René exhaled heavily. 'No, he'd didn't used to be like this at all. Believe it or not, he was actually one of the top climbers in the world, a real genius. The boy could climb up rock as smooth as glass. Then something happened a few years back out in the Himalayas and he's never really got over it. Been eating away at him ever since.'

'Something?'

René paused, suddenly finding it hard to say the words.

'You really want to know?'

Bear didn't answer, only waiting.

'There was this big avalanche and then his best friend was murdered right in front of him. Shot between the eyes.'

'Jesus,' she muttered. There was silence again as she looked out towards the moon rising over the line of the water. It was already half up, drowning out the rest of the night sky. Bear stayed like that for some time, lost in her own thoughts, before glancing back towards René. Even in the dim light of the cockpit, he could see the intensity in her eyes.

'You know, I've been around a lot of wars and they affect everyone differently. Some people can't even speak when it's all over, some just get on with life again, and then there are others that

149

have this look — these blank, vacant eyes, with rage simmering just beneath. It's like this uncontrollable animal that bursts out of them.' She glanced back to the controls, her expression darkening. 'I guess it comes from just having seen too much. And out here, bad shit happens every day.'

'So what's your point?'

'The point is that these are damaged people, René. Really damaged. And people like that are dangerous to be around.' Her eyes involuntarily darted towards Luca.

René shook his head automatically.

'Come on, Luca's nothing like that. He's just going through a bad patch, that's all.'

'You sure about that? How well do you really know him?'

'From way back. Trust me, all he needs is a little more time to get over it. He'll be all right, you'll see.'

'Your call.'

René watched as Bear leaned forward in her seat and pulled the map on to her lap once again, systematically checking through each instrument and heading. He then pushed himself back against the uncomfortable rear seats of the plane and put out the last of the cigarette, wedging the butt into an old flip-down ashtray in the door.

He wondered how much of what she had said was true of Luca. Was he really that damaged? Had Bill's death broken him that much? There were these flashes, these brief moments, where the old Luca seemed to bubble through to the

150

surface, but just as quickly, he seemed to become lost in a bitterness of his own making. That rage she'd spoken of was there. He had already seen it up in the mountains. But René couldn't believe it was all there was left of Luca. There had to be something more.

René went to light another cigarette then stopped, his throat too dry for him to smoke it. He rubbed his hands together distractedly, feeling his palms go clammy with prickles of sweat. In a couple of hours they would be landing in one of the most dangerous places on the planet and Luca would be the only person in the world he could rely on.

15

René woke as the plane lurched downwards in a thermal. Everything jolted, the loose coins scattering to new positions on the carpet as Luca's rucksack slowly toppled sideways and on to his lap. René's hands shot out as he tried to steady himself. There was a terrible pain in his head, while a stale line of saliva ran from the corner of his mouth and across the line of his beard.

The morning sun streamed into the cockpit of the plane. The light was stark, with a fierce intensity to it that seemed to heighten the colours all around him, paining his eyes. He felt sickly hot and dehydrated, the cigarette he'd smoked a few hours ago still tainting his mouth.

The plane jolted again, then swung round in a steep banking turn that made René's stomach instantly cramp in on itself. Acid vomit rose into his mouth and he groaned softly as he gulped it back down again. He looked around the clutter of the rear seat for a bottle of water, but gave up after a few seconds of searching. His head was too painful for him to bend forward. Instead, he scraped up the headset and gingerly angled the mic towards his mouth.

'Where the hell are we?'

Luca's head snapped round. 'We've started the descent to Epulu. You've been out for a few hours.'

'Good,' René replied, nodding his head.

'How you feeling?' Luca asked, seeing the obvious strain on his face.

'Raring to go.'

Pressing his head against the window, he peered out. The canopy of the Ituri Forest stretched away in every direction. Millions upon millions of trees were densely packed together in one of the last great wildernesses on the planet. The trees formed a gigantic block of brilliant green, radiating colour against the harsh sun, while clouds hanging motionless in the sky above cast shadows on to the surface, like patches of spilled ink.

Meandering tributaries of brown water cut through the trees, heading towards some distant confluence with the main flow of the Congo River. They wound on for mile after mile, like tears across a seamless fabric.

'Phenomenal,' René breathed, forgetting the throbbing in his head for a moment.

'Quite something, isn't it?' Bear said over her shoulder. She leaned forward in her seat again, forehead creased in concentration as she brought the plane round in another wide banking turn.

'When Stanley crossed the width of Africa, this is what he called its 'black heart',' René said, almost to himself. 'Never thought I would get to see it.'

Bear glanced back at him.

'It's the real thing out there, that's for sure.'

Glancing back at the map, she checked their heading once again. They should be over the landing site by now, but there was nothing but trees. Slowing the plane to seventy knots, she lowered the flaps and flipped the Cessna on its axis, staring down through Luca's window as the ground seemed to spin round in a slow arc. Suddenly, she saw the dull grey of a thatched roof, then another. The village of Epulu was right below them, nestled in the shade of a group of wide bouma trees.

'I see the village,' Luca said, pressing his finger against the glass.

'Yeah, got it.'

Bear levelled out the wings and started prepping the plane for landing. As she ran through the checks, she spoke to them in the mic, her voice becoming matter-of-fact.

'At the last report, the LRA were seen about 30 clicks north of this village. They torched one of the pygmy settlements somewhere out in the forest, but after that we've heard nothing more. They seem to have gone silent.'

'Where's their main base?' René asked.

'No one knows. They haven't been able to pick them up with the satellites. They just seem to pop up anywhere from here to the Sudanese border, moving like goddamn' ghosts.'

Luca followed her gaze out to the horizon, understanding how easily an entire army could be concealed in such a vast expanse. Aside from a few settlements dotted close to the rivers, the Ituri was almost entirely unmapped, with only the major tributaries appearing on any of Bear's aerial charts. Gradually, he focused on a series of rocky outcrops rising in vertical pillars through the forest canopy. Giant slabs of red rock lay stacked up on top of each other, most of them covered by a net of vines with stunted bushes clinging precariously to their sides. The pillars ran away from them in a near-symmetrical line, like the knotted spine of a dinosaur.

'What are those?'

Bear craned her neck to see what he was pointing at. 'They call them inselbergs. They run from here all the way east to the rim of volcanoes on the Ugandan border. Right up to the Mountains of the Moon.'

Luca's gazed passed from one inselberg to the next, until out by the horizon he could just make out the ground bulging in a series of conical shapes. Traces of smoke hung lazily in the air above each one. These were the volcanoes, all of them active, with occasional spurts of lava spilling over the crater rims.

'How far do you think they . . . ' Luca began, when just in front of the plane the air exploded. The noise was incredible, sending massive shock waves shuddering through the plane and splintering the windscreen in long vertical cracks. Luca's door blew out, hanging limply by its lower hinge as air rushed into the cockpit. He could see the ground open up right beside him, blurred from the distance.

He turned, trying to understand what had just happened.

Everything went silent, muted by the intense ringing in his ears. The plane pitched upwards, then began to slow. Luca sat for several seconds, transfixed by how slowly they seemed to be moving, until a juddering motion rocked through the plane as the damaged air intakes of the engine began to starve the carburettors of oxygen. After a few muffled coughs the engine died, the propeller jerking to a halt just in front of him.

A sharp, high-pitched whine filled the cockpit, getting louder and louder as the stall warning went off. The noise grew louder still, shrieking, as the plane gradually listed to one side and fell like a deadweight.

Bear grabbed the controls as they dropped in a steep dive. She held the plane level with the rudder, desperately trying to keep them from spinning, while her eyes locked on the air-speed indicator. She watched the needle slowly creep up the dial as they gathered momentum and finally came out of the stall, but with each second that passed they had fallen five hundred feet closer to the ground, with the altimeter spinning full circle.

The ground seemed to fill the entire windscreen, looming up at them as they passed under three hundred feet. Luca could clearly see soldiers running out into the open in front of them, clutching rifles and pointing them towards the sky. They heard the clatter of machine-gun fire, then saw the smoke trail of a rocket-propelled grenade shoot past their starboard wing before exploding somewhere in the air behind them.

'Shit!' Bear screamed, as the plane rocked forward from the explosion. 'They've got RPGs.'

'Get us out of here!' Luca shouted as she heaved back on the control column, pulling the

156

plane out of the dive. The wingtips became lost in a blur of green and treetops as they skimmed across the canopy, the positive G-force forcing them back in their seats.

Just as they began to claw back some altitude, there was a sharp, metallic hammering against the portside wing. Bear turned to see the entire flap break off, twisting in the wind as it fell back towards the earth. Puncture marks from where the bullets had hit ran right across the underside of the wing in a long, curling trail.

'The bloody wing just . . . ' René shouted, eyes fixed on the gaping holes. Bear felt the plane list violently to one side as the damaged wing dragged them round. She jammed on full opposite rudder, levelling out their course, but without the engine they were already starting to lose the speed they had gained in the dive.

Grabbing Luca's hands, Bear pulled them towards the control column.

'Just hold this line,' she said, her voice level over the mic. He looked across at her before reaching forward, his forearms flexing as he squeezed the controls as tight as he could.

Bear grabbed the key with her left hand, checking one magneto, then the other. With her right hand, she pumped the throttle; desperately trying to kickstart the engine back to life. The engine ground round each time she slammed the key across in the ignition, but there was nothing.

Their speed was draining off fast, passing 70, then 60 knots. Luca instinctively eased back on the controls, trying to pull them further away from the ground.

'No, no,' Bear said, reaching forward to steady his hands. 'We'll stall again. Angle towards the ground.'

'But we're right over the trees.'

'Just do it.'

Luca pushed forward a little, easing the nose down and trading altitude for speed, while Bear turned the key again and again. There was still nothing from the engine. They could hear the sound of machine-gun fire once more, but it was distant now, almost irrelevant. In only a few seconds, they had flown far beyond the soldiers' reach and out towards a small tributary of the main river. In the heat of the morning, the brown waters looked placid and heavy.

The plane glided downwards, the speed dropping to 50 knots, then 40. Bear's hand brushed against Luca's on the steering column as she took control.

'We're going in,' she whispered. 'Tighten your belts.'

There was a pause as both René and Luca stared at her, as if not quite understanding what she had said. Then, in a flurry of movement, they grabbed the straps of their seat belts, yanking the webbing as tight as it would go. Luca held on to the handle above the window and wedged his left arm against the dashboard in front.

'We'll make it. We'll make it,' he repeated. 'Just land as close as you can to the riverbank.'

'Holy shit,' René breathed, his chest rising up and down as he stared past Bear's shoulder through the cracks in the windscreen. The trees rose up to meet them, suddenly looking enormous.

Bear reached forward, switching the transponder to 7800 and checking their position on the GPS.

'Mayday, Mayday, Mayday,' she called, her voice flat as she went through the protocol. 'This is Golf Hotel Juliet. 02.16.52 North 28.13.35 Easting. Engine failure. Three on board in a Cessna 206. Going down in a . . . '

She broke off, raising her thumb from the comms switch.

'What's the use?' she whispered to herself. 'No one's coming.'

The plane silently glided under a massive branch overhanging the river. She watched it pass over the top of them, her head tilting up in disbelief. They were only twenty feet above the water now, the river so close it looked as if it would rise up and touch their wingtips.

'This is it,' Luca shouted.

As they both braced themselves against the impact, René's voice came through on the intercom.

'Take care of each other,' he said, then his voice was suddenly drowned by the screech of the stall warning. There was a pause as the plane flared over the surface of the water, almost as if hovering above it, before the weight of the engine swung the nose down, pitching them into the river. The force of the impact smashed their bodies forward, the webbing of the seat belts cutting into their skin as a wall of water engulfed the entire frame of the aircraft. The windows instantly smashed in, the perspex banging against their arms and faces while a tide of brown water surged into the cockpit.

They felt the tailfin rise up behind them, twisting them vertical in their seats and arcing them over in a slow somersault. It crashed down flat against the water with a hollow thump, the momentum of the crash finally subsiding as the plane came to rest on its port side in the water, the cockpit already half-submerged.

Luca opened his eyes and slowly turned his head. He could see Bear's body pressed against the dashboard with her long hair matted across her cheeks and face. She was totally still. The whole of her seat had somehow broken free from the impact, slamming her body forward and into the controls of the plane.

Luca fumbled with the release clip of his seat belt, his fingers frantically working the metal clasp before finally managing to prise it open. He fell forward into the well of brown water at their feet and tried to steady himself. Water ran down into his eyes and as he raised his hand to wipe it away, he noticed his palm shone red. An open cut above his eye was pumping out blood.

He reached out, wiping back the strands of hair from Bear's face, leaving a trail of his own blood across her cheek. Her eyes were closed. He put his ear to her mouth, trying to hear her breathe. There was a soft moan, then her own hand slowly rose to her shoulder in reflex. Luca saw that the short shaft of the throttle handle had punctured her shoulder just above her left arm. The metal had broken off, and was bulging out through the skin on her back.

Unclipping her seatbelt, Luca took hold of her good shoulder and slowly pulled her back from the controls. Bear's mouth widened into an agonised scream as her damaged shoulder flexed from the motion. She screamed again, her jaw clenching tight, as he heaved her clear of the controls. Her body swung backwards, but her legs remained locked to the seat.

'Are your legs broken?' Luca asked, but Bear just stared at him. She looked totally disorientated.

'You're . . . bleeding,' she whispered, trying to raise her hand to point. 'There's blood.'

'I know. It's OK. Your legs. Can you move them?'

Bear's eyelids slowly sank down as she started to drift into unconsciousness. Luca smoothed her hair back from her cheeks.

'Bear, listen to me,' he said, raising his voice. 'Bear, you've got to concentrate. Can you feel your legs?'

Her eyes opened again, blinking as she tried to clear her vision. After a moment, she nodded.

'I can move . . . ' she breathed, her lips pursing together ' . . . move my feet.'

'OK,' Luca said. 'Just stay with me. Stay awake.'

He swung round to check on René. A huge split ran through the roof of the plane just behind the two front seats, flooding the interior with daylight. The splintered edges of the metal were peeled back, allowing water to lap through the lowest part, spilling down into the main part of the cabin. René lay with his head resting to one side, directly under the torn roof. His eyes were closed, the skin around them slack, while his lips were slightly parted beneath his beard. His massive frame was drenched with water, the black hair on his chest and arms glistening with moisture.

'René,' Luca called, twisting his body through the narrow gap between the front seats.

'Come on, René,' he called again, grabbing him by the lapel of his soaking cotton shirt. As he pulled René's head clear of the side wall it lolled back unnaturally, the weight unsupported by his neck. Luca let go in shock, staring in horror.

'No . . . no,' he breathed, feeling the panic rise inside him. He jabbed two fingers into the base of René's throat, feeling for a pulse, pressing down hard against the soft flesh by the side of his Adam's apple. He forced himself to stay absolutely still, his senses straining for the faintest beat or twitch. There was nothing.

'Come on, René,' Luca suddenly shouted, the sound of his voice reverberating around the tiny cockpit. 'Come on!'

Luca pressed lower on his friend's neck, waited a few seconds, then moved his fingers higher again, searching in vain for a pulse. He could feel the heat of René's body, the skin still clammy and glowing with sweat. He gently tilted the head forward and saw a deep-set bruise running all the way from his left shoulder blade up into the line of his hair. The skin was waxy and dull, bruised black at the centre and fading to a dull purple with blotched yellow patches lower down. Whatever had ripped through the wall of the plane had snapped René's neck with such force that it had nearly decapitated him.

Luca took René's cheeks in the palms of his hands, willing his friend's eyes to open, for his chest to rise and fall, for everything to be as it was. It was impossible for him to be gone, to die like this in the middle of a godforsaken jungle in Africa. René was a bear of a man; indestructible. He swore irreverently at every living, breathing thing and could make jokes when all seemed lost. How could this possibly have happened?

Luca felt a surge of heat rise up his throat and into his temples. His vision started to fade to black towards the edges. He widened his stance to try to keep his balance, but then suddenly gagged, convulsing at the unexpected reflex. Shutting his eyes, he let the tears stream down his face while the huge store of emotion, dulled and suppressed by those endless months in the Himalayas, came flooding out of him.

'Not this,' he gasped. 'Anything but this.'

'Luca!'

He stayed motionless, staring down into his friend's face.

'Luca!' Bear's voice was louder, a shrill scream that made him turn towards her. 'The water's getting worse. We're sinking.'

The angle of the plane had changed and now water streamed into the cockpit through the broken windows. Torrents of brown river water poured in, weighing down the front of the plane and plunging it further beneath the surface.

Luca turned, pushing his way back to Bear, and saw that the water level was already past her waist and steadily rising up the line of her stomach. He sniffed, wiping one arm across his eyes as he tried to focus. They had to get out.

'Over there,' she said, motioning towards the broken door. It was already peeled back on one hinge, facing down into the depths of the river. The water flooding through the gap was opaque and foreboding.

'What about yours?' Luca asked.

'Jammed.'

Bear rocked forward in her seat, wincing at the pain from her shoulder. She tried to pull herself out of the seat using her one good arm, but her legs were trapped by something below the waterline. Luca fumbled with the back of his belt, looking for the survival knife which was hooked into the leather. He drew out the dull blade with its serrated edge.

'I can force open the door with this.'

'There's no time. We're going to have to swim out underneath the plane.'

Luca grabbed her under her arms, his powerful fingers biting into her skin. He paused, knowing full well the pain he was about to inflict.

'Go,' she whispered. He wrenched her whole body sideways, using all the strength in his thighs. The veins on the sides of his neck bulged as he inched Bear free, her legs scraping against the crumpled control column and ripping the fabric of her trousers in a long snaking tear. Bear's shoulder hunched, pulled unnaturally high against the metal spike of the throttle. A horrid gurgling sound came from somewhere deep within her lungs as Luca heaved again, every muscle in his back straining with effort. Suddenly her legs came free, sending them both tumbling back against the other side of the plane.

Bear was pressed against him, her breathing shallow from the pain. She slowly opened her eyes and followed Luca's gaze to where the water was gushing through the open tear in the cockpit beside René. It poured down on to his massive head, flattening his thick crop of hair and filling his open mouth. It streamed down on to his face with such force that it seemed to blur his features, and Luca just stared, transfixed.

'We have to leave him,' Bear whispered. 'He's gone.'

Luca blinked. He knew she was right. But as the water rose past René's broad shoulders and up to his neck, he also knew this would be the last glimpse he would ever have of his friend. Suddenly, he felt a terrible urge to stay with him, as if to make amends somehow for it all.

'Come on, Luca!' Bear shouted, pulling him forward.

Grabbing her hand, he felt his fingers curl around hers, before he breathed in as deep as he could and plunged forward, into the foul water.

16

The rear wheels of the Mk2 Oryx helicopter touched down with a delicate bump. As the engines slowly powered down with a low-pitched whine, the downdraft from the rotors washed out across the searing hot tarmac, diffusing a mirage of heat waves.

Jean-Luc climbed out of the front passenger seat, slamming the door shut with a wide sweep of his arm. He stalked across the open tarmac of Kigali International Airport with his fist pressed against his forehead to shield his eyes from the glaring midday sun. It was 42 degrees in the shade and the fabric of his white T-shirt clung to his back and armpits.

Putting a cigarette to the corner of his mouth, he lit a match, recoiling sharply as the sulphur flared up more than usual. It sent a plume of smoke into his eyes, making him curse out loud all the way to the terminal building.

'Welcome to Rwanda, sir,' the young official said, raising his arm in salute. 'Your passport, please.'

Jean-Luc dug in the top pocket of his shirt and slammed his passport down on the counter. He stared at the official with undisguised annoyance, his chin jutting out dangerously. The official looked down at the passport and back to Jean-Luc's face. He began to speak, then picked up the well-thumbed booklet and let his forefingers delicately trace across the surface of the creased leather as if trying to decipher some kind of Braille.

'How long will you be . . . ' he hesitated, his eyes meeting the full wrath of Jean-Luc's stare ' . . . be staying . . . here in Kigali, I mean.'

Jean-Luc gave a slow shake of his head.

'Read the top of the damn' passport,' he said, his voice hissing out between nicotine-stained teeth. The official looked down again. The word 'Diplomat' was stamped in lettering so faded that he had somehow managed to miss it the first time round.

'That will be all, sir.'

Snatching back his passport, Jean-Luc crossed the marble floor to the rank of taxis neatly parked outside. He stood still for a moment and slowly shook his head. It was incredible how different from Goma this airport was, despite their proximity. Here, there were no hustling crowds fighting for a place on a bus, or fat officials eyeballing the passengers like cattle as they marched them through the turnstiles, looking for the easiest bribes. Rwanda had been reborn under President Kagame's iron fist and now even plastic bags had been outlawed, transforming the land of a thousand hills into a newly whitewashed tourist destination.

Jean-Luc signalled to the first taxi and was about to open the rear door when a white Toyota Land Cruiser pulled to a halt in front. It had the word 'UN' stamped in bold lettering across it. A man emerged from the driver's seat.

'Mr Étienne, if you will.'

As the engine fired to life and the Toyota pulled into the three lanes of bustling traffic, heading towards the city centre, Jean-Luc swivelled in his seat to face the other passenger.

'The CIA couldn't think of anything more original than a UN vehicle?'

'Oldies but goldies,' the man replied, giving a crooked smile that accentuated the crow's feet around his eyes. He had a slight accent from somewhere in the Deep South and a wholesome, all-American jawline faintly smudged by stubble. His blond hair had begun to grey at the temples and he had deep tan lines running across his forehead from a lifetime spent in the sun.

'Where are we going?' Jean-Luc asked.

'Does it matter?' the man replied.

Jean-Luc grunted, noting that the smile was still playing faintly around the other man's lips. It was as if he'd heard a joke several minutes ago but now couldn't quite remember the punchline.

They sat in silence while the Toyota wound through the lanes of traffic and pulled off on to a dust track towards the main market. Slowly bouncing down the potholed road in second gear, they passed lines of stalls made of thin wooden sticks bleached grey by the sun. Each was manned by a brightly clad woman selling piles of vegetables and waiting with the patience of stone for her next customer. They passed line after line of them, the mass of people growing denser as they drew closer to the main hub of the market.

Jean-Luc lit another cigarette. 'So, what do I call you, then?'

'Call me Devlin.'

'*Putain*,' Jean-Luc spat. 'Devlin? What, you think this is some kind of joke? What are you going to do? Kill this president as well.'

Devlin's smile widened a little.

'It wasn't us who killed Lumumba in the Congo. The Belgians did that one.'

'Sure they did.'

They entered the main entrance to the market, through two disused gates set back on their hinges. Devlin nudged the car to a halt by one of the roadside shebeens, where some locals were leaning out of the open shutters with bottles of beer clutched in their hands.

'Where I come from we only drink on weekends. We should make the most of this.' Devlin got out, slamming the car door shut. 'Although something tells me they won't have any of your *pastis* liquor here.'

There was a low table at the back of the shebeen, set slightly apart from the rest. They sat down and Devlin ordered two beers.

'You know,' he began, resting his hands lightly on the table, 'a couple of months back we had a message come through like yours, offering more information on this 'Mordecai'. Met the informant myself, hoping we might get to run someone within the LRA. Young guy, was one of the lieutenants turfed out of Uganda with Kony, but still part of Mordecai's inner circle.'

Once the beers were opened, Devlin waited for the barman to leave before continuing.

'He turned up dead a couple of weeks later with his arms and legs hacked off. He was all piled up in this big pine box.' He paused, forehead creasing in concentration. 'No, that ain't right. It wasn't pine. Oak, perhaps.'

'So?'

'Well, we were kinda thinking, if one of his own lieutenants can't get information through to us, what makes you think you can?'

Jean-Luc grabbed his beer and took a swig, wiping his mouth with the back of his hand.

'Because I'm not some idiot child soldier with a head pumped full of amphetamines. I've been running cargo for Mordecai for months now.'

'Cargo?'

'A mineral that everyone wants to keep quiet. Very quiet. Even the handlers are Chinese.'

Jean-Luc pushed a small plastic sack across the table, one end glued down to seal the contents inside. Devlin stared at it for several seconds before taking it off the table and resting it on the neighbouring seat.

'So what is it, this mystery cargo?'

'Just get your guys in the lab to take a look. It'll be worth the price.'

'It fucking better be, Étienne. You have any idea how much bullshit you have to go through to get that kind of money?'

Jean-Luc stared across the table. 'You asked for proof. There it is. So don't ever question me again.' He paused, inhaling on his cigarette. 'I can get through to Mordecai because I already have.'

'You've actually met him?' Devlin asked, trying to mask the surprise in his voice.

'No one from the outside has. But I know where he's hiding.'

Devlin exhaled deeply, running his fingers through his blond hair.

'OK, OK. This is good. I'm going to need to know what contact you've had with him. We know he's out in the Ituri but it's one hell of a big place and we've got some blanks that need filling.'

'Blanks? I'd say you guys haven't got the faintest fucking idea what's going on north of the river. You've been stationed out here in Kigali all this time, too scared shitless to do anything but file a report to Langley every couple of minutes.'

Devlin stared across at the table, the same distant smile returning to his lips.

'Langley do love their reports,' he said, seemingly oblivious to the affront. 'Look, the priority is the relationship with the Chinese. We know they're all over the Congo like a rash, but we wanna know what they're doing hanging around with this Mordecai. We need to get detailed reports of their movements, exact shipments and what the hell they are using this new mineral for. You get us that, and you got yourself a deal.'

Then he shrugged. 'As for the man himself, Mordecai's one of them tinpot militia leaders. Dime a dozen out here. We're only interested in him for his relationship with the Chinks. In the meantime, let him slaughter a few villagers up north, if that's what gets him off.'

Jean-Luc gave a grim smile, eyes dropping down to the table where the last of the cigarette he'd been smoking lay in the ashtray. It had burned down to the filter.

'You're underestimating him,' he said, dropping his voice. 'He's building an army that's a whole different animal from the Mai-Mai or FDLR. He's not here to skim a few diamond mines or get his hands on some gold deposits. Mordecai is looking at something bigger, much bigger.' Jean-Luc stared down at his hands, clenching the knuckles together with a soft crack. 'I've been a merc all my life, but I've never seen soldiers so fanatical. They do anything he says, even if the mission is suicide. A man with an army like that can do a lot in Africa.'

Devlin leaned back in the seat, folding his arms across his chest.

'Sounds like we've got the damn' bogeyman out there,' he said. 'If Mordecai wants to make a bigger play, we've still got contacts. Wouldn't take much for us to send over a few shipments to the Mai-Mai and get them to tie him up with a nice little war. But come on, Étienne. You wouldn't be hyping this up a bit just to get a better price, now would you?'

'You keep talking like that and I'll double my price,' Jean-Luc countered, leaning across the table, his eyes darkening.

'Well, here's the thing, *mon ami*. I did a little research of my own and figured that maybe you'd be wanting something else instead of money.' Devlin smiled, then put his hand out. 'Actually, you mind if I have one of them cigarettes? Gave up years ago, but can't seem to shake it.'

172

Jean-Luc pushed a dark blue packet across the table with some matches stacked on top. After a moment, Devlin drew down on the cigarette.

'Wow, these are strong. What are they?'

'The money,' Jean-Luc said flatly, a vein on the side of his neck pulsing with annoyance.

'Well, I did some checking and your name flagged up in an ICC investigation. Just a mention, of course, but no one wants the ICC on their tail, now do they?' Devlin inhaled again, nodding slightly to himself. 'I'll tell you how this deal's going to work. We pay you nothing, but you give us all the information you have on Mordecai and the Chinese. That happens and I'll personally see to it your name fades from the memory of the International Criminal Court.'

Devlin raised his glass in a toast. 'We got a deal? No sense letting something like that stay with you till the grave.'

Jean-Luc remained silent.

'Be nice to get back to France one day, wouldn't it? Get back while you still have a little lead in your pencil.' Devlin's eyes tilted up towards the cloud of smoke he'd just exhaled. 'You gotta remember something, Étienne, I know exactly what you did in Sierra Leone. I can have you arrested, just like that.'

Devlin clicked his fingers together then took a sip of his beer, resting the bottle against his lips while he stared across the table at Jean-Luc. His eyes sparkled with complicity, but failed to see Jean-Luc's right hand shooting upwards, slamming the bottle of beer hard into his mouth. It smashed against his teeth, the glass stem cracking off and clattering down noisily on to the tabletop. Blood spattered across Devlin's right cheek along with the splintered remains of one of his front incisors.

His hands flailed wide as he fell backwards in his seat, but Jean-Luc was already standing over him, left arm holding his head in a vice-like grip.

'Just relax,' he whispered into the American's ear. 'Take it easy and breathe.'

Devlin's eyes were screwed shut with pain. He moaned softly as Jean-Luc released his grip, grabbing a wad of cheap paper serviettes off the counter and thrusting them at him. Devlin pressed them against his mouth, feeling the blood welling out through the waxy paper and seeping down his throat. He stared at his assailant in disbelief, his expression blank with shock.

'Never mention that place again,' Jean-Luc said softly. 'It doesn't concern you.'

Taking a sip from his own beer, he eyed Devlin with casual interest.

'We were talking about a deal,' he prompted. 'You were about to offer me my money.'

'You just . . . fucking . . . ' Devlin stammered, spitting out blood between the folds of the serviettes ' . . . broke my . . . '

'Focus. Concentrate on the deal. You're going to go back to Langley right now and get me my money. You tell them that I am the go-between for the Chinese and Mordecai, and if they want to be a player in the Congo, they deal with me.'

Devlin's whole face flushed red. He pulled the serviettes away from his mouth and stared down at the blood as if not quite believing that it was his. Half a tooth lay in the centre with a piece of flesh from his gum still attached to it.

He felt a desperate need to escape from Jean-Luc. The man was a goddamn' animal.

'I'll tell them,' he managed, nodding quickly. 'I'll tell them you want the money . . . that you're the man to deal with.'

Jean-Luc reached across the table and slapped him playfully on his shoulder.

'*Bien, mon ami,*' he said, raising himself out of his chair. 'I will wait to hear from you.'

Turning to leave, he caught sight of the pack of cigarettes still lying on the table.

'You keep those. And they're *Gitanes Brunes*. The strongest cigarettes you can buy in France.' He gave Devlin a friendly wink. 'If you like them, I'll have my guy send some more over for you.'

17

Luca pulled Bear further into the forest. One hundred and fifty feet above their heads, the canopy of trees blotted out the sky, leaving only a dim half-light at ground level. It was dense and claustrophobic, the heat of the day trapped by the windless air. Between each mighty tree trunk innumerable bushes and saplings struggled for light, twisting and knotting over each other in the inexorable struggle.

Luca pushed his way up a slight incline, using his free hand to force his way through the wall of mapani bushes. Thin traces of a spider's web clung to his forehead, while a fine grey dust covered his face. The cut above his right eye had closed, leaving a red smear across his cheek and around the eye socket itself, ringing the white of his eye and making it seem unnaturally bright.

He stopped, looking from side to side for an easier way through, but the forest seemed the same in every direction. By his reckoning, they could only have gone a couple of kilometres from the river, yet he was already growing disorientated.

'Just keep moving,' Bear said, her right hand pressed against the wound in her shoulder. She was walking only a few inches behind Luca, trying to focus on his footsteps and keep pace. The pain in her shoulder made her feel weak, a sweaty sickness that only worsened with the growing heat of the day. She bent forward, resting one arm on her knee, and pulled up the bottom of her vest to wipe the sweat from her forehead. The white cotton was now a grimy brown, with a rust-coloured stain under her left armpit where blood had seeped down from her shoulder.

'We have to put as much distance as possible between us and the crash site,' she added. 'They'll know René wasn't the only one in the plane. They'll be looking for us.'

Luca seemed not to have heard and ploughed on, breaking the sapling branches as he passed. His movements were erratic and clumsy as he fought his way through the bush, the branches pulling at his hair and clothes, frustrating him more and more. He hadn't stopped for more than a couple of seconds in over four hours.

Bending one of the lower branches, Luca used the heel of his boot to kick it down into the mud. As he stepped over, there was a dull crack.

'Luca, stop leaving such a trail. They'll be tracking us.'

'In this?' he snarled, raising his arms as if to encompass the entire forest. 'I can't see my fucking hands in front of my face. How the hell can they track us in this?'

Grabbing a piece of dead wood off the ground, he hurled it at the bush in front. It bounced off the leaves and toppled back down to the ground, one end sinking into the soft mud.

'*Entends-moi,*' Listen to me, Bear said, taking hold of his arm. 'This is what the LRA do, Luca. They live here in the forest, every day of their

177

lives, and believe me, they can track us in this. Every broken branch or footprint is like a signpost for them.'

Luca turned to stare at her, his breath shallow from the effort and frustration. He started to say something more, then slowly his shoulders hunched and his whole body seemed to sag.

'Can't get his face out of my mind,' he whispered. 'The water running over it like that. And we just left him to rot in the damn' river . . . '

Bear gently squeezed his arm, feeling the soft trace of his pulse through the veins lacing his forearm.

'We've got to keep moving, Luca, and deal with this later.'

He stared ahead, his eyes filled with certainty. 'It's like there's something wrong with me. Some kind of fucking curse. Everyone but me seems to get hurt.'

'Wrong with you? Luca, it was his choice to get on the plane. *His* choice. Nobody forced him to do it, so you shouldn't have to feel this way.'

Luca suddenly yanked his arm free from her grip.

'Don't tell me how I should be feeling! You don't know the first damn' thing about me.'

Bear took a step back and counted down the seconds. Anger seemed to radiate from his entire body, his fists clenching and unclenching, accentuating the bands of muscle on his arms. Something triggered in Bear's memory but she couldn't place it. She looked back in the

178

direction they had come. They didn't have time for this.

'Luca, look at me,' she said softly. His face remained turned away from her. '*Eh, regarde-moi!*' Look at me!

As he slowly turned back to her, she tried to hide the impatience in her voice.

'You're not the first to feel this way.' She pointed to the ground at their feet. 'But we have to be thinking about here, Luca. Here! We've got to focus on getting as far away from those bastards as we can. Because if they catch us, make no mistake . . . they will kill us.'

Luca exhaled deeply, his hands resting on his hips. After a moment, he nodded slowly.

'OK,' he said, raising himself to his full height. He blinked, trying to compartmentalise his emotions as he had done so many times before in the Himalayas, but the same image of René kept flashing before him. He had to steady his breathing, had to focus on getting them out of this jungle.

'OK,' he said again, turning back towards Bear. A thin new trickle of blood had welled out of her shoulder.

'You're bleeding again.'

'I know. I'll have to take care of it when we stop to camp.'

★ ★ ★

The light grew fainter, dimming so slowly that night seemed to be on them without warning. Shapes that had once been varying shades of

179

grey had darkened to black and they found themselves stumbling forward, tripping on knee-high roots as branches slapped across their faces. Bear gently pulled Luca to a halt.

'I need to stop,' she said. He nodded. He had been breaking trail for the entire day and was exhausted, but it was only in the last hour that his movements had become tired and mechanical.

'I need some more water,' he said.

Bear pulled a Leatherman multi-tool from the pocket of her trousers and moved forward through the bushes, eyes scanning the dim silhouettes of the tree trunks. Luca trailed after her. About 100 metres further on, she reached up to one of the vines looping down from a branch and sawed it in half. Water oozed out and she drank deeply from it, gulping back the liquid before plugging it over with her thumb.

'Doesn't taste too good, but it'll do,' she said. As Luca took the vine from her grasp and drained it, Bear opened the side pocket on her trousers, pulling out two energy bars that she had tucked inside. She flung one across to him.

'Only got a couple more of these left. So enjoy it.'

After devouring the bar in just a couple of mouthfuls, Bear then sank down to the ground with her back resting against the tree, wincing as she felt her shoulder protest. The spike from the throttle handle was still there, bulging out of the skin on her back. She was sweating heavily now, eyes half-closed as she fought back the throbbing pain.

'I've got to take care of this,' she said. 'And we're going to need some light to do it. You got any matches?'

Luca shook his head, then suddenly stopped and pulled the survival knife from the back of his belt. He unscrewed the handle. Inside were four underwater matches, the long sulphur fuses carefully wrapped in cellophane.

'I'll try and find something dry to burn.'

'Wait,' Bear called, pulling out a small spray bottle of Deet from the thigh pocket of her trousers. She heaped a few twigs and some damp moss by the side of her outstretched legs and sprayed on the chemical. There was a whoosh as fire suddenly illuminated them with its yellowy-blue flame.

'No wonder the mosquitoes don't like it,' Bear said to herself, adding some more twigs to the heap and dousing them with a few more squirts. A grim smile played across her lips. 'Die of cancer from this shit or get caught by the LRA. Great choice.'

Sitting up a little higher against the tree, she gingerly pulled the vest over her shoulders, folding it several times before tucking the fabric under her arm. Luca could see her whole torso gleaming with sweat. Her black skin gleamed like oiled leather. Her hair had fallen either side of her shoulders, clinging to her skin and obscuring the wound. With a brush of her hand, she smoothed it away, peeling her left bra strap down over her shoulder to try to get a better view, but the wound was too close for her to be able to see it clearly.

181

'You're going to have to help. We've got to find the end of the metal and pull it out.' As Luca came and kneeled over her, she handed him the Leatherman, turning the handles round to reveal the pliers. Luca peered closer, gently dabbing the surface of the dried blood with his forefinger.

'I can't see the metal. Must be buried inside a little way.'

Bear nodded, her mouth wide as she breathed in heavily.

'I know. I hope to hell you're not squeamish, because you're going to have to dig it out.'

'You sure you want me to do this?'

'Do I have a choice?'

Luca didn't answer, but pressed his left palm against her shoulder to steady her. 'You want something to bite down on?'

'Just get the damn' thing out of me.'

She grabbed his wrist with her good hand. Her fingers gripped tight. 'Quickly, before I change my mind.'

Luca dug the tip of the pliers under the damp clot of blood, delving them deeper into the open wound. A mixture of clear pus and dark-red blood seeped out, running down her chest and into the fabric of the vest. Bear's body jerked away but Luca pushed down harder, pinning her back against the bark of the tree. He twisted the sharp ends of the pliers round, trying to find the metal spike buried inside her. As he forced the pliers wider, Bear groaned loudly, her legs kicking out in spasm.

'Wait!' she screamed, but he pushed deeper, the tips of the pliers finally connecting.

182

'Come on,' Luca hissed, his wrist turning the pliers as another gush of blood pulsed out of the wound. The tips caught hold of the metal again, but slipped off as he tried to pull backwards. Bear screamed again, her eyes boring into his as she pleaded for him to stop.

'No more,' she panted. 'Please, no more.'

Luca pulled the pliers out as cleanly as he could. As Bear's head collapsed against his chest, he held her tight, his right hand curling around the nape of her neck.

'*Salope!* Son of a bitch! That hurt.'

She opened her eyes, the pain dilating her pupils.

'You're going to have to use your knife to push it through from the other side.'

'Jesus Christ,' Luca whispered, staring at where the skin bulged out on her back. Even in the light of the fire, he could see the mauve discoloration around the swelling.

'On the count of three,' he said, trying to muster the courage. 'One . . . '

'Just do it!' Bear exploded, her whole body rigid with expectation. Luca brought the hilt of the knife thumping down on her rear deltoid, punching the metal spike out the other side. As Bear's whole frame recoiled, he grabbed the spike, drawing it out of her body.

Bear collapsed against the tree, lying absolutely still with her eyes screwed shut. Tears welled from the corners of her eyes, but gradually her breathing began to slow as the intensity of the pain faded. Luca crouched down next to her, waiting in silence for her to open her eyes again.

'I guess I should thank you,' she said eventually, 'but right now, I could kill you.'

Luca smiled, placing the stub of metal into the open palm of her hand. 'A souvenir.'

Bear looked down at it, before hurling it sideways into the undergrowth. She wiped the blood off her chest with the fabric of her vest, then carefully pulled it back down over her body. They sat side by side, staring at the low flame of the fire.

'You're going to have to watch that doesn't get infected out here,' Luca said, the tiredness creeping into his voice.

Bear nodded. 'There's stuff out here that I can put on it. Just got to keep my eyes open as we move through the bush tomorrow.'

A large moth flittered down from somewhere out of the bubble of light and circled closer to the flame. It was the size of a man's hand, with beautiful white-tipped eyes on the back of its brown wings. It came closer, hovering just beyond the lick of the flames, and danced in the light. They both stared, distracted by its movement.

Presently, Bear leaned forward slowly and with the heel of her boot snuffed out the small fire. It gave out a few dying sparks before succumbing to the darkness, leaving only the faint red glow of the embers to burn into the night. She and Luca were plunged into utter blackness, which magnified the sounds of the jungle all around them.

'Thought I'd better put it out before it attracted anything else.'

Luca grunted. He felt himself drifting into sleep almost immediately, his mind only half registering the warmth of Bear's shoulder pressed against his and the soft smell of her hair.

Bear listened while his breathing slowed, becoming deeper and more regular. She closed her own eyes, feeling the exhaustion take over and waited for sleep, but just then, a faint image of her father came to her. She could see his fists clenching and unclenching outside a nightclub in Cape Town years ago. The last night she'd seen him. It was what Luca had done that morning.

Turning sideways against the tree to protect her damaged shoulder, she found herself only inches from his sleeping face.

'You're wrong about not knowing you,' she whispered. 'I've known you my whole life.'

★   ★   ★

After what seemed like only a few minutes, Luca woke again. He shifted his weight, the tree bark digging into his back. He could hear the sound of Bear breathing right beside him. She had moved round during the night and her face was only an inch away from his cheek.

Moving onto his side, he tried to get comfortable, his eyes seeking the dull fluorescent glow of his watch. It was just after 2 a.m. and they had been asleep for several hours. Shutting his eyes again, Luca tried to blank his mind for sleep when gradually he realised what had woken

185

him. It was a noise, somewhere distant, as if on the other side of the jungle, but it was different from the other night sounds. It had a beat, steady and unrelenting, a bass note that pounded again and again and again. Luca stared into the darkness, trying to understand what it was he was hearing.

'Bear,' he whispered. 'Wake up.'

He reached across, shaking her knee. 'Hey, Bear, wake up.'

He felt her leg go stiff under his hand as she suddenly clicked out of sleep. She stayed absolutely still for a few seconds.

'*Putain*! Shit!' Bear hissed. 'Come on. Come on. Quickly!'

Luca stayed where he was, trying to discern her silhouette in the darkness.

'What the hell is going on? What is that?'

Bear was already on her feet, pulling her hair back from her face.

'They're drums, Luca.'

'Drums?'

'It's the LRA. They've found our trail. Come on, we need to get moving. Now!'

Luca quickly got to his feet, his hand moving round to check he'd put his survival knife back in its sheath.

'They can't track us at night, for Christ's sake. That's impossible.'

'You tell them that,' Bear said, grabbing hold of his hand and hauling him forwards. Luca stumbled for a few paces, groping with one hand stretched out in front of him to protect his face. His fingers brushed against the thick foliage, the

186

jungle alien to his touch. After a few seconds he stopped, and in the sudden silence they heard the slow beat of the drum once again.

'Bear, this is crazy. I can't even tell which direction we're going.'

She was right behind him, her hand clasped in his to stop them from getting separated.

'It doesn't matter now. Just go in the opposite direction from the drums. We have to keep ahead of them until dawn.'

There was a pause before Luca squeezed her hand in his.

'They won't catch us. I promise you that.'

18

As the first light of dawn rose over the basin of the Ituri Forest, Luca and Bear came out into the open. Amongst the endless trees and bushes, they had suddenly stumbled upon a wide area of rock jutting out from the top of a small hill. Staggering into the middle of it, they stood marvelling at the openness of the sky above. It finally felt as if they had been released from the clutches of the forest, if only for a moment.

Bear sat down on the red rock, drawing her knees up to her chest. She stared out across the grey landscape, watching the colour slowly return as daylight poured across the horizon. She blinked, trying to stop her eyes from closing with exhaustion.

All night, they had heard the drums. At first they had been distant, the beat just drifting above the hum of the forest, and they had had to stand stock-still, holding their breath, to hear them clearly. But as the night drew on, the beat grew louder, pounding relentlessly.

They pushed harder, redoubling their efforts as the noise grew louder, but whatever they did and no matter how much they hurried, the drums were always there, gaining on them. Only an hour ago, they had even heard voices. The shouts were deep-pitched, almost grunts, followed by howls which rose together in some kind of savage chorus.

Luca stalked over to the edge of the rock, squinting into the distance.

'We've got to figure out where the hell we are. And fast,' he said. 'That's the river we crashed in. It's got to be.'

Facing the rising sun, he got his bearings. 'So, that means we've been heading mainly west since then.'

Bear tried to concentrate. Calculations that normally came to her instinctively seemed to jam in her brain, the tiredness making even the simplest sum seem impossibly difficult.

'Come on,' she muttered to herself, trying to picture the contours of the aerial chart. After a couple of seconds, she looked up. 'We crashed seven and a half miles north, northeast of Epulu. That puts us exactly twelve miles from the nearest MONUC base. It should be about one hundred and sixty degrees from here, almost due south until we reach the other side of the river.'

'Twelve miles?' Luca asked, turning back from the view. Bear nodded, unable to meet his eye. They both knew that at the rate the LRA were gaining, they would be lucky to keep ahead of them for the rest of the morning, let alone cover twelve miles. With the words still hanging in the air, Luca reached out a hand to pull her to her feet.

Just as she stood up, they heard shouting again, the noise echoing out across the canopy, with parts of words even discernible above the beat of the drum.

'You understand what they're saying?' Luca asked.

Bear nodded slowly.

'What is it?'

'I'm not going to translate that. You'd never want to hear what they are saying.'

Luca could see her shiver, her skin breaking out in goose-bumps across the top of her arms. As he went to pull her forward once again, he noticed a gap in the bushes on the opposite side of the clearing. Sprinting over, he crouched down on the ground. There were scuff marks across the edge of the rock. He stared deeper into the forest. It was definitely some kind of path.

'Let's go!' he said, the energy returning to his limbs. Bear ran after him. She could see Luca twisting to left and right as the path wound through the bushes.

'It's a path!' he shouted over his shoulder. 'A bloody path! There'll be a village somewhere at the end of it.'

Bear struggled to keep up, raising her hand to fend off a swinging branch as it catapulted back towards her.

'Luca!' she called. 'It's an elephant track. They criss-cross through the forest.'

She ran full tilt, feeling her chest rise with the effort and the tiredness suddenly ebb away from the jolt of adrenalin. Just ahead of her, Luca had slowed slightly. They settled into a fast jog, running in unison, footfalls striking in time.

The minutes passed; ten, twenty and then thirty, with the pace not varying. Occasionally, they would have to jump over a fallen log, or weave sideways as the path turned around a

190

vine-covered boulder, but Luca always kept them running. Bear could feel her shoulder ache with every swing of her arm and, as the initial thrill of the discovery faded, so too did the adrenalin.

'Only elephants use this?' Luca said over his shoulder.

Bear grunted in response, too breathless to answer. She knew her shoulder was slowing her down a little, but even so, she had never met anyone as unrelenting as Luca. He just seemed to go on and on, continually breaking trail and barely even stopping to drink water. She had always prided herself on keeping extremely fit, but she was nothing by comparison.

An hour into the run, Luca suddenly jolted to a halt. He crouched down, pulling at a string of woven hessian that had snagged on a thorn bush by their feet. It was the mouldy remains of a piece of netting, hand-woven, with the thread worn rough around the edges.

'Someone's been here,' he said triumphantly. 'And I bet the LRA don't use this kind of stuff.'

Bear nodded, her nostrils flaring as she rested her hands on her hips.

'It's the . . . Maputi pygmies,' she said, trying to catch her breath. 'They net hunt along . . . these elephant tracks.'

'Well, they must be close.'

'Maybe. But that looks like it's been there a while.'

'OK. Let's go.'

They had just settled into the jog once again when the path forked. There was a toe print clearly marked in the mud on the left-hand one and Luca ran down it, ahead of Bear, to find himself in the middle of a small clearing with huts arranged in a semicircle under tall trees.

The huts were made of saplings bent round in a dome with broad, waxy leaves woven together and pinned through. Each hut was no more than chest height with entrances so small that a person would have to crawl on hands and knees just to squeeze through. Luca turned slowly, taking them in one by one while sunbeams pierced the canopy high above them, sending dappled light across the clearing.

'Pygmies?'

'Yeah,' Bear said, walking over to one of the huts and crouching down to peer inside. As her eyes adjusted to the dark, she could see the crude frame of a bed made from carefully whittled branches, knotted together with vine. There were a couple of metal pots neatly stacked to one side and a small bag of grain, tied close. She pointed down to the charred remains of a fire.

'This isn't right. Some of these huts have got fresh leaves, meaning that they must have repaired them recently. But pygmies never let their fires go out.' She stared at the other fires. The ash was dry and old. 'And if they were on a big hunt for a few days somewhere deeper in the forest, they would have left some of the younger children behind with one of the elders.'

Digging her fingertips deep into the ash, she felt for any trace of heat. It had been dead for days.

'There's no one here.'

Luca pushed his hair back from his eyes and stared blankly at the entrance to one of the huts. A mixture of disbelief and despair welled up inside him. The sudden rush of optimism he had felt at finding the village had already been replaced by the terrible certainty that *nothing* had changed. The LRA were still tracking them, and whatever he and Bear did they were there, gaining on them minute by minute.

He felt his chest tighten, as if the run had taken the wind out of him, but he already knew it was nothing to do with the exercise. They were being hunted down like animals through the bush and there was nothing he could do to prevent it. He tried to think what to do, but the echo of the drums seemed to beat in his head, ceaselessly pounding. It was the drums. They were driving him mad.

'You OK?' Bear asked, seeing his ashen colour. Luca looked as if he was about throw up at any moment.

'We'll just have to keep running as best we can,' he said flatly, hearing the hopelessness in his own voice. 'It's all we can do.'

Bear didn't answer immediately, turning her back to him and staring out into the bush. After a couple of seconds she raised her hands, palms open. She tilted her head back and shouted.

'*Jambo! Tunaleta madawa kwenye kabila lenu.*' Hello! We bring medicine for your tribe.

She shouted it again, turning slowly while her eyes scanned across the wall of bushes, so dense it was impossible to see more than a few feet into them. Suddenly, straight in front of her, there

193

was a rustle of branches and two boys simply stepped out into the open. They had been standing barely twenty feet away, absolutely motionless and perfectly concealed amongst the trees.

Both were naked except for knotted twine wrapped around their waists, which hung in a belt over their groin but left their buttocks bare. Their hair was shaved to the skin, while old white paint, cracked and faded around the edges, ran in a band across the tops of their arms and thighs in some kind of tribal marking. Each held a spear loosely in his right hand, with burn marks running down from the tip, while the second boy also had a bow and arrow hanging from a vine strap slung across his shoulder. A huge brown net, that had been carefully wound together, was balanced on the head of the nearest boy, its coils falling down his back to his waist.

'*Jambo,*' Bear said, her voice softening as she greeted the boys with a smile. It was hard to tell from their size, but she guessed both to be in their early teens. They stared at her, brown eyes wide, but not with fear or apprehension. They just stared, waiting.

'*Naitwa kina nani?*' What are your names?

The two boys exchanged glances before the first widened his stance and spoke. His voice was so soft it barely carried across the clearing.

'*Lanso,*' he whispered. He pointed with his spear to his brother. '*Abasi.*'

'*Na vijiji vyenu vingine viko wapi?*' And where is the rest of your village?

The boy's voice dropped even lower.

'*Yingi ni kwa moyo.*' Most are with the spirits.

'*Na wengine?*' And the others?

'*Ilienda kutoka hapa. Ni parefu.*' Gone from here. Long way.

Lanso blinked several times, before his gaze switched to Luca.

'*Tunawajua wazungu! Mwambie atupe dawa,*' Lanso said. We have seen white men before. Tell him to give us the medicine. '*Kaka yangu anahitaji pia!*' My brother needs some.

'*Tutakupatia dawa sasa hivi,*' We shall get your medicine now, Bear replied.

'You speak their dialect?' Luca asked.

'No, but a lot of the Maputies speak a kind of Swahili that's pretty close to what I grew up with.' She pushed back a loose strand of hair. 'He told me the rest of the village is either dead or gone.'

'So what happened to them? How come the boys are the only ones left?'

Bear turned back to them, speaking slowly while squatting down on her haunches, so that her head was just below the level of their chests. Lanso hesitated for several seconds, staring at her suspiciously, before taking a step closer. While Bear spoke, he seemed fascinated by her right eye where the loss of pigmentation had bleached the white speck across her iris.

After an exchange which seemed to go backwards and forwards for a couple of minutes, with Lanso getting bolder with each answer he gave, Bear turned back to Luca.

'OK, he basically says that they are here

195

because this is their village and they don't have anywhere else to go. As for the rest of them, the men were taken some time ago. I don't know how long ago because the Maputies only count up to seven, after that it's just 'a lot'. They followed the trail for a little while before they got scared and turned back.'

'And the women and children?'

Bear exhaled heavily. 'It doesn't look good.'

'You reckon this was the LRA?'

'Who else?'

Luca glanced back at the entrance to the village. 'We're wasting too much time,' he muttered, and when Bear went to speak further with the boys, motioned for her to be quiet. There was the drum again, the beat filtering through the tall trees and out across the clearing. As the boys caught the sound, they both went rigid.

'We've got to get them to guide us out of here,' Bear whispered, turning back to Lanso and gripping him by his shoulders. '*Unajua kituo cha MONUC? Kituo cha wazungu kusini mwa ha.*' Do you know the MONUC base? The white man's base south of here?

Luca shook his head. 'We shouldn't get them involved. We should just leave them and hope those bastards follow our tracks and not theirs.'

Bear stared up at him.

'We're not going to last another hour running like this! And these boys can show us a way out of this. What the hell are you talking about?'

'We could get them killed, trying to help us.'

'Are you crazy?' she shouted, turning to

196

confront him 'If they can get us out of here, then we go for it. Period.'

'Think about . . . ' Luca begun, but Bear raised her hand.

'*Assez!*' Enough, she shouted. 'There's no place for that bullshit out here. We survive. That's it.'

Both Lanso and Abasi were frightened by the sudden change in the foreigners. Lanso suddenly reached up, yanking Bear's hand to get her attention. He quickly muttered something in Swahili.

'They want to show us a place to hide,' she translated. 'Morality doesn't exist out here. You know as well as I do, it's our only chance.'

19

They scrambled down a steep hill to where a stream bubbled through the undergrowth, brimming out into clear pools of water before widening again. Luca could see flashes of colour through the bushes as Bear followed Lanso, sprinting upstream as fast as they could go. Water splashed up over his trousers and seeped through the stitching of his leather boots. At least the stream would hide their tracks.

Abasi was moving fast, ducking and flexing as he pivoted around the bushes and branches. His body was lithe and quick, while his size meant that he could duck under low branches with just a simple dip of his head or shoulders. His bare toes made nothing of the slippery mud and rocks, while behind him Luca crashed through the undergrowth, catching himself on the thorn bushes. It was as much as he could do to keep up, let alone see where they were going. And it was only at the last second that he noticed Abasi jump out of the stream and on to an outcrop of rock.

The boy was staring intently at something. As Luca pulled up next to him, he tried to see what it was.

Then, he saw it. Fingers of an upturned hand poked through the scattering of leaves. They were curved unnaturally back on themselves with the wrists bound together with old rope twine.

Just above the fingers, he could see the shape of an arm, then further up a bulge in the leaves where a head might have been.

Luca stared, transfixed by the body, then he realised there were more of them. The ground was covered in a twisted heap of limbs, the joints angular and tortured. Tens of bodies lay half-submerged in the mud and leaves. They faced in different directions as if carelessly discarded like so much rubbish. As he looked from one to the next, he saw a single hand clinging to the remains of a torn, once brightly coloured piece of fabric. It still clenched tight in death, the fingers pudgy, with tiny half-moon nails rimmed with dirt. It was a toddler who lay as he had died, clinging to the hem of his mother's skirt.

'Jesus,' Luca breathed, feeling his stomach clench as he caught wind of the stench. Flies feasted on the decaying bodies.

He gently put his hand on Abasi's shoulder.

'I'm so sorry,' he whispered. The boy stared at him, looking deep into Luca's eyes, before grabbing his forearm and pulling him forward after the others.

They continued over the rock, steadily climbing higher. A crude rope bridge had been erected by the pygmies at some point in the distant past, spanning a deep chasm between two of the larger outcrops. As he came to it, Luca hesitated for a second, staring at the old twine, weathered by the rain and sun. It had been built to accommodate people barely taller than five foot and less than half his weight. He wondered if it would support someone his size, but glancing back down the slope, it was clear there was no other option.

With Abasi just ahead of him, they worked their way along the bridge, gripping on to the sides as the structure swayed from side to side. Each thread and knot seemed to creak as Luca passed, with the bridge sagging deeper into the chasm under his weight. They clambered on, soon coming out in a wide, open area.

Here, the bushes had thinned, with only dwarf trees managing to gain any sort of purchase on the rough ground. Pools of stagnant water had collected naturally, scummed with algae, while higher up Luca could see the beginnings of a cliff rising up ahead of them. It rose about twenty metres in an almost smooth vertical stretch, like the base of a mighty pillar. At the very top it tapered off into a flat section covered in knotted vines and foliage. It had to be one of the inselbergs they had seen from the plane.

Bear and Lanso were waiting at the base of the cliff.

'Lanso says we'll be safe here,' Bear said, her eyes narrowing against the sun. 'It's one of the village's holy places and, at the very least, a good vantage point from which we can see them coming.'

After a moment, Luca shook his head.

'This isn't going to work, Bear,' he whispered. 'They tracked us the whole way through the night. And they didn't just track us, they gained on us. The stream and rocks are only going to fool them for so long.'

She exhaled heavily, letting her shoulders sag against the rock.

'There's nowhere left for us to go,' she said, turning to face him. 'And I can't keep running like this.'

He had his head tilted back, hands clenched in front of his mouth as if blowing on them for warmth. His gaze ran over every impression in the wall, and as it settled on the overhang, his right hand moved away from his body, fingers curling into position as if already touching the rock.

From this distance the route looked technical, but he knew he could work the crack running all the way up to the summit. Aside from the lack of ropes, there was the added danger of climbing 'on site', with no way of knowing how good the handholds were until he actually reached them. But despite all that, he knew he could make it. As a teenager, he had free climbed much harder routes in Chamonix, let alone the kind of competition pitches he had been used to before heading out to Tibet.

Bear pushed herself off the cliff.

'You can make it,' she whispered, following his gaze. 'It's perfect. They'd never find us up there.'

Luca continued staring towards the overhang.

'Just one more climb, Luca,' Bear breathed. 'One more, and you can save us all.'

Luca's eyes narrowed as he squinted into the distance. He then suddenly stepped away from the cliff.

'The overhang,' he whispered. 'I won't make it past the overhang.'

Bear reached out her hand, pressing her fingers against his shoulder. 'You can do it, Luca. René said you were one of the best climbers in the world. So, come on, let's do this.'

He stared out across the tops of the trees, fists clenched tight. She could see the skin had whitened along the bridge of his knuckles.

'No,' he said flatly. 'I'm not a climber anymore. Think of something else.'

Bear raised her arms towards the rock to either side of them. It hemmed them into a narrow gully and would mean they would have to descend all the way to the stream again if they wanted to try to work their way round to the other side of the inselberg.

'Something else?' she asked, the frustration causing her voice to raise. 'If we don't find a place to hide, they will kill us, Luca. Do you understand that? And they'll take their time with the boys for helping us. Make no mistake about that.'

Luca stared ahead.

'Come on, Luca!' she screamed. 'This is our only chance!'

She pushed his shoulder, shunting him forward a step. 'Stop being such a coward!'

Luca suddenly grabbed the front of her vest and pulled her whole body towards him. Bear was forced up on to the tips of her toes, as he almost lifted her clear of the ground.

'If you're in such a hurry to get up there,' he snarled, 'why don't you fucking climb it?'

Shunting her away, he shouted in frustration. Then he turned back to the cliff and began stalking along its length. All the while he muttered to himself, his gaze occasionally lifting as he followed the line of the crack running up the side of the inselberg. Twenty metres away from the others, he stopped. A series of thick vines clung to the rock, reaching up into a narrow gulley that led unbroken all the way to the summit. Luca yanked back on these several times, testing their strength, before his head slowly lowered again and he continued.

Lanso and Abasi were watching him carefully. A few seconds later, they followed Luca to the same spot, talking quickly to each other. Throwing down the coils of netting, Lanso immediately began clambering up the vine, his movements quick and well-practised. His bare toes curled into each indentation of the wiry stem, while his body was so light that within just a few seconds he had pulled himself nearly five metres off the ground. He stopped, shouting down to Bear, as a smile lit up his face.

'He says he can make it to the top,' Bear translated. 'He's saying it's no higher than some of the mapani trees near the village.'

Luca stared down at Lanso. 'He's sure about this?'

Bear nodded. 'But how the hell do we get up? There's no way that vine will support our weight.'

Drawing his survival knife from his belt, Luca crouched down, picking up Lanso's netting in his free hand. With a few turns of his wrist, he unravelled the coils on the bare rock, steadily working his knife down the netting.

'Cut it the same way on the other side,' he said, motioning to Bear. She unfolded her Leatherman, cutting similar strips, while he pulled the netting's fibres apart with sharp tugs of his hand. It had been woven tightly enough to trap an antelope running at full speed. It would be more than strong enough for them.

'Tie them off like this,' Luca said, knotting the ends together and offering one up to Lanso. 'And ask him if he can climb with this tied around his waist. When he gets to the top, he is going to have to secure the line to something.'

Without a moment's hesitation, Lanso started climbing. As he moved higher, hand over hand with his fingers curling into the vine stem, he shouted down between his legs to his brother. On the ground, Abasi had his head tilted back as a constant soundtrack played out between them. Before long, Lanso reached the end of the vine and began worming his body into the narrow gulley. He arched his back, managing to draw himself into the rock, and, using his elbows and knees, pressed his whole body against the side of the gully. Inch by inch, he worked his way higher.

Arriving at the overhang, they could see Lanso's arm flailing across the surface of the rock, trying to find something to grip on to.

'Careful,' Luca breathed, as the boy stretched too far, causing his right foot to slip as his balance shifted. He jolted downwards. Only a couple of inches, but it was enough to startle him.

They could see Lanso inhale several times in

quick succession, trying to steady his nerves, before he wedged his knees a little higher in the gulley. The extra height gave him enough reach and, with a final shout to his brother, he pulled himself over the rock and disappeared from view.

'*Incroyable*,' Incredible, Bear whispered.

Abasi shouted several times before gripping on to the trail of netting. As he swung himself above Bear's head, moving higher, she could see a nasty wound on the underside of his thigh. Dirt had been packed into it, while a thick band of swelling surrounded each edge. But despite the obvious pain he was in, Abasi climbed fast.

'You go now,' Luca said, holding out the netting to Bear. She stared at him, but he didn't return her gaze.

Bear climbed one move at a time, fighting the pain in her shoulder. Raising her right arm put pressure on the wound, sending an intense pain shooting into her neck. Gritting her teeth, she forced herself on, listening to the slow creak of the netting each time she shifted her weight. Seconds passed with just the sound of her breathing, her eyes locked on the sight of her own hands as she gripped hard on the knotted threads.

Finally drawing level with the overhang, she stared down between her legs to where she could see Luca far below. The cliff looked so much higher from this vantage point, while all around she could see the forest stretching off in every direction. Just over the summit, she could already hear the boys talking.

Bear dragged herself up on to the top of the

inselberg, and stopped. She was breathless from pain and exertion and stood hunched over, with her hands resting on her knees. Tilting her head up, she could see that the inselberg ran back surprisingly far. A whole ecosystem thrived on its summit with small trees vying for place amongst the tangle of vines, while the occasional rock pool appeared in between.

From here, she could see all the way to the crash site on the river, while further to the east the nearest of the volcanoes dominated the horizon. Its huge flanks rose up above the canopy, reaching to a hollow point at the summit. Smoke curled up in a single column, smudging the perfect, cobalt-blue sky.

Before Bear had managed to regain her breath, Lanso had joined her at the cliff edge, pointing towards the volcano as he spoke. He talked in an almost continuous flow, his voice soft, while his eyes squinted out towards the horizon. By the time he had finished, Luca was standing on the summit, curling up the last of the netting. He had his back to them.

'He says that all the villagers are gone,' Bear called across to him. 'Says that there's no one left in any of the settlements along the river.'

Luca didn't respond and Bear wondered if he was still bitter about the climb. Whatever happened, she had to try and keep him on side.

'And it's not just the Maputis that have been hit. There are other tribes as well.'

Luca turned.

'So why are they doing it?'

'He doesn't know, but it's only the men the

LRA are after. You've already seen what they do to the women and children.'

Bear stepped closer to him. 'Lanso said he heard the elders discussing it many times before. Everyone who went anywhere near the volcano just disappeared. Like they were swallowed up by the ground.'

'That's got to be the LRA base everyone's looking for. Over by the volcano, I mean.' Luca shook his head slowly. 'But what the hell are they doing with everyone?'

Bear paused. There was no reason why she shouldn't tell him her suspicions, but still she hesitated. Sharing information wasn't something she ever felt comfortable doing. But they were in the same boat. She could see that now. Although Luca didn't know it yet, they were looking for the same thing, if only for different reasons.

Reaching into the thigh pocket of her trousers, Bear pulled out a small Ziploc plastic bag and tossed it across to him.

'I think it's all about this.'

Inside was a small lump of dark grey rock. It looked like the charred remains of old volcanic lava, but as Luca brought it up to the light, he saw a blood-red streak running through its centre.

'The LRA are kidnapping people to mine this stuff out of the ground,' Bear continued.

'A mine? A mine for what exactly?'

'The locals call it fire coltan. We think it's some kind of highly concentrated form of tantalite.'

'Tantalite?'

Bear nodded. 'Yeah. Tantalite is used in every single computer and mobile phone on the planet. It's one of the few key components. That's how they get handsets to be so small. If it weren't for tantalite, we'd all be walking round with cell phones the size of bricks.' Bear raised a finger, pointing at the rock Luca was holding. 'But that stuff is different. It's some kind of purer, more powerful form. No one's ever seen anything like it.'

'So that's why you're here?' he asked, throwing the packet back to her in disdain.

'Fabrice told me the Chinese have been buying this stuff in massive quantities in return for weapons. I thought I could get into Epulu and ask around without being spotted.' She shrugged, exhaling heavily. 'But no one guessed the LRA were already so far south.'

Luca pushed his hair back from his face, switching his gaze to the volcano. 'Well, if that's where everyone has been taken, there's got to be a good chance Joshua's there too.'

He then pulled back from the edge of the overhang, resting his hand on Lanso's shoulder. 'Ask him if he knows the way to the volcano. Ask him if he's ever seen this mine.'

Bear spoke with Lanso for several minutes, the boy gesticulating towards the volcano with swift stabs of his hand.

'He says their hunters sometimes used to shelter in tunnels running around the side of the volcano, but they didn't like to do it much because of the smell. Aside from that, he doesn't know . . .'

Bear stopped mid-sentence. There were the drums again, reverberating up the rock in a slow pounding beat. All of them instinctively lay flat and a few seconds passed before Bear slowly edged her way to the overhang.

'Careful,' Luca breathed.

The drums grew louder, followed soon after by shouts. Through a gap in the trees, they saw the first signs of movement, figures frantically combing the ground, shouting as they worked their way through the bush. The noise grew louder, drums spurring them on like the beat of a boat's oars.

Luca slid up next to Bear, inching over the rock. There was a high-pitched call and the soldiers began to group together, beating their way through the undergrowth to a central clearing on the rock just below them. They looked dishevelled and exhausted, wearing a rag-bag mixture of clothing. Some wore military fatigues with red berets bleached pink by the sun, while others had ripped T-shirts with strings of bullets draped over old pictures of Bob Marley and wore ankle-high gumboots on their feet. One had a cream necktie knotted over his forehead, filthy brown from sweat, with the end trailing down over his narrow shoulders, and each clutched an AK-47 with an assortment of grenades and water bottles tied with bits of string around them. Most had the gangly look of children just into their teens, with young, smooth skin that gleamed with sweat.

A massive man with a shaved head and thick bulging arms stood in the middle of them. As he turned in the light, staring at each one of his patrol in turn, they could see his forehead was marked by V-shaped cutting scars running down from his hairline all the way to his eyes. They made the skin bulge out like the scales of a lizard. His skin was blacker than the others', almost blue-black, and he stood a foot taller than them as well, with the wide, powerful shoulders typical of Dinka tribesmen. When he spoke, his voice was deep and naturally raised in a shout, with his Sudanese accent drawing out the French words.

'*What are you doing?*' he hissed. '*Why can't you find me those fucking muzungos?*'

No one answered, each avoiding the Captain's gaze. He moved closer to one of the soldiers, sitting with his legs splayed flat in front of him, and slammed his boot down on the boy's shin, grinding his heel into the bone.

'*I said, what the hell are you doing? The tracks can't just disappear!*'

He moved to the other side of the circle, lumbering like a huge boar.

'*You weak Congolese bastards. You disgust me!*' he roared, turning as he spoke. '*You will find their trail again and you will bring them to me . . . or when we return, you will all be put in front of him. Every last one of you.*'

A few of the boys looked up, their faces blank with fatigue and desperation. They clambered to their feet, shuffling forward towards the Captain, hands outstretched.

'*Good boys,*' he said, his face breaking into an ugly smile. '*Good boys!*'

Reaching into the breast pouch of his front webbing, he pulled out a thick cellophane bag and poured a small amount of grey-coloured powder on to each boy's hand. They licked it out of their palm, hardly even wincing at the acerbic taste of the amphetamines. The patrol readied itself to leave. Now the drums started again, the noise gradually building into a frenzy as they pounded.

The soldiers had begun to peel off when the Captain suddenly shouted for them to wait. He pulled the heavy rubber earpiece of the radio set off his shoulder and wedged it to the side of his head. He nodded several times before speaking into the mic.

'The helicopters are coming. Release the smoke.'

A canister rolled out on to the rock, billowing thick red smoke which drifted across the sky with the faint breeze. A few minutes later, the heavy thump of rotors preceded three helicopters flying only 100 feet or so above the canopy. They moved in a tight tactical formation with a Rooivalk attack helicopter high above them, keeping watch. As the Oryx buzzed overhead, continuing their course, the Rooivalk suddenly pulled away from them and looped back in a tight turn towards the red smoke. It ploughed straight through it, the downdraught from its rotors dispersing the smoke like the sweep of a paintbrush.

The Rooivalk orbited overhead, taking orders from the Captain shouting into his headset below. It then lowered its nose, turning in widening circles, with both pilots craning forward in their seats, searching the impenetrable jungle below.

'Not good,' Luca whispered, quickly pulling back from the edge of the overhang. They led the boys into the relative shelter of the bushes, keeping their backs low as they ran. Jumping over the smaller trees and shunting back the vines, they worked their way deeper into the centre of the inselberg.

The bushes and undergrowth started to thin, leaving bare patches of rock exposed to the sky. As they darted across one of these, they suddenly heard the Rooivalk's engine rise up behind them, with the rear-seat gunner arming the nose-mounted 20mm cannon. The snub barrels swivelled as the helicopter bore down on the figures below.

The helicopter swung level. Luca reached out and grabbed hold of Abasi, trying to shield the boy with his body as he sprinted towards the far side of the inselberg. Around them, the vines and bushes were pushed flat by the downdraught of the helicopter, the noise of the rotors absolutely deafening.

Bear was a few metres further to Luca's left, running full tilt with her head bent low. They could see the far end of the inselberg ahead of them now, the top of the cliff level with the branches of some wide acacia trees. Just as Luca reached the edge, he suddenly realised that Lanso had stopped a few feet further back. The boy looked hopelessly small on the bare patch of rock and was staring up at the massive machine hovering just above his head. His left arm was raised to shield his eyes, while his right arm drew back his spear. He paused for a split second before taking aim. The spear flew upwards, looping below the belly of the Rooivalk before falling back down into the bush.

'Lanso!' Luca screamed, letting Abasi slide to the ground. He cupped his hands around his mouth against the deafening noise of the helicopter. 'Lanso! Run!'

Abasi was already sprinting forward towards his brother, bow clutched in his left hand, when the ground became a blaze of fire and sound. The 20mm cannon opened up, strafing a line of bullets across the rock and sawing Lanso in two. The ground shook as the cannon changed angle, sending bullets thudding into the rock next to Luca. He could see the tracer rounds glancing off in streaks of phosphorescent light, while around him clouds of dust exploded in the air, laced with splintered branches.

Luca doubled over as he instinctively tried to protect his face. He lost his footing and toppled forward over the edge of the cliff, raising his hands as a tree branch smashed into his stomach, driving the wind out of him. Leaves were whipping across his back and head as he landed square in a thick bush. There was a brittle snapping sound of branches, before finally he connected with the muddy ground below.

Luca lay still, listening to the shallow gasps of his own breathing as he tried to draw air into his lungs. His chest jerked in spasm, while above he was dimly aware of the beat of rotors somewhere much higher in the canopy. He squinted as light came flickering through the tree branches, watching it for a moment until the edges of his vision clouded over and everything went black.

20

Xie stood at the entrance to the aircraft hangar, dwarfed by the colossal sliding doors. He checked his watch, squinting as his eyes took in the endless criss-cross of beams supporting the hangar's roof. Everything had been painted a drab military green and the supports stretched for hundreds of metres, fading to darkness somewhere high in the distance.

Xie inhaled deeply, taking in the smell of engineering grease and the charred remains of the satellite wreckage. Over the last week, the wreckage had been laboriously sorted into piles, with angular piping and once expensive Space Age materials heaped together in carefully denoted type and order. A few lab-coated technicians now moved between the piles with clipboards and scanners.

One of the technicians finally glanced up from his work and immediately hurried over to where Xie stood, waiting patiently with an old leather briefcase gripped in one hand. He bowed low, ushering the visitor past the armed guards.

'I didn't see you, sir,' he apologised. 'It's not yet eleven o'clock and . . . well, I was just preparing some extra documentation . . . for you, sir.'

Xie gave a tired smile, the dry skin around his eyes creasing like old paper. 'It's OK, Captain. I arrived a little early.'

'Yes, indeed sir,' the Captain replied, surprised to be treated so cordially. He had only taken orders from General Jian before and had quickly learned that he was not a man to be left waiting. 'May I offer you some tea?'

Xie nodded gratefully. His brown linen suit was creased across the back and shoulders so that it looked as if he had woken up in it that morning, while his tie was twisted slightly to one side. He seemed to be in no hurry to begin.

He had in fact been awake almost the entire night, reading through the crash report submitted by Jian's investigation team. It had made for dry reading with a huge amount of technical detail which he didn't fully understand, but one thing had become apparent and that was the absence of some of the key materials used in building a satellite. When he compared it with the inventory of raw components he had procured direct from the manufacturers, there was a significant gap. He wondered if this was simply due to the fact that they hadn't managed to recover all the pieces from the crash site. With such an enormous explosion, presumably a lot of the satellite would have been permanently lost.

A few minutes later, Xie was clutching a small bowl of steaming tea, smiling distractedly as the aromatic vapour wafted under his nose. He took a sip, his smile widening as if it was the first cup of tea he had drunk in years.

'Captain,' he said softly, 'I understand you have done superb work in recovering the wreckage from the satellite.'

He paused, allowing the man time to enjoy the

compliment. 'Very detailed work, and it seems you have managed to recover nearly everything.'

The Captain nodded enthusiastically. 'Yes, sir. We believe we have recovered nearly ninety-five per cent of the original components. It was an exhaustive process, but we pride ourselves on being thorough.'

'Quite so.'

Xie looked at the young captain, with his smart bearing and open face. There was something naturally forthright about him. He had an obvious desire to please, coupled with a delight in the slightest hint of appreciation. Such people rarely told lies, unless by mistake, and Xie found himself almost warming to him. In his line of work, such types rarely crossed his path.

'Ninety-five per cent,' he repeated. 'Very impressive. But I noticed quite a few components were missing from the inventory lists. Could they still be lost out there?'

The Captain looked uneasy. 'I'm afraid you have to expect some missing items, sir. But we have already highlighted the items not yet accounted for in the report, and as I say, it's only five per cent of the total.'

'And you check through each item? You know what each part was originally?'

'I am afraid not, sir. Our remit was to find everything on the manufacturer's inventory. But it's a hugely detailed list, sir, and I can assure you, we've double-checked every item.'

'I don't doubt that for a second, but could you just let me have a copy of the list for my files?

Routine stuff, but someone has to wade through the red tape.'

The Captain nodded sympathetically. 'Please follow me.'

Once Xie had sipped the last of his tea, the Captain ushered him over to an enclave on the side of the hangar which had been set up as a temporary office. An array of high-tech scanners were positioned in neat rows next to a large set of weighing scales. Around them stood a collection of trestle tables arranged in a semicircle, with laptops open on each.

'Just here, sir,' the Captain offered. Xie perched on a swivel chair and took out the dossier sent direct to him by the manufacturers. He ran down the list while scrolling through the Captain's Excel file on the computer, comparing like with like.

'Tell me, Captain,' he said over his shoulder, 'how did the actual satellite launch go wrong? And use laymen's terms, please. I get a bit bewildered by technology.'

The Captain drew himself up to his full height.

'We believe that moments after the launch sequence was initiated, the right aft joint seal blew off, causing a combustion gas leak which in turn ruptured the integrity of the main tanks. The ensuing explosion moved . . . '

Xie raised his hand.

'And what caused the right aft joint seal to blow off in the first place?'

'I am afraid we are still working on that, sir. We haven't found the missing pieces, but the

218

General himself reached that conclusion.'

'General Jian came to this conclusion *personally?*'

'That is correct, sir. It was added to the report only yesterday.'

Xie smiled pensively. 'Yes, I remember him saying as much. The right aft joint seal.'

He turned back to the paper on the desk. He had already underlined twelve items that were totally absent from the list on the Captain's computer and, as he worked his way down, there were others. He paused, letting the graphite of the pencil gently rest against the computer screen.

Someone had deliberately doctored the investigation team's list. There were too many discrepancies for this to be some kind of clerical error. But what were they trying to hide?

Xie remained silent for a moment, his pencil hovering over a couple of items in particular.

'Tell me, Captain, did you ever come across any parts of the helical antenna or circuitry for the transponder systems?'

The Captain looked up, surprised. 'I don't believe we did, sir, but I am sure it would be listed here if there was anything.'

'And what about traces of lithium from the battery system? Would they have been picked up by the scanners?'

'They would indeed. But I don't believe we found any, sir.'

'Then where are these missing pieces?'

The Captain suddenly looked uncomfortable. His tongue darted over his lips several times before he actually responded. 'I am afraid that we have a very specific brief. It is not permitted to question matters outside our remit.'

'But didn't it strike you as odd that none of the components from the actual satellite was found amongst the wreckage?'

The Captain was well accustomed to the General's virulent temper and had been told to expect that a high-ranking Party member would ask for a personalised account of the situation. He was sure that such men didn't tolerate their questions going unanswered either. He waited for the inevitable outburst, but Xie only eased himself up from his seat, smiling amiably.

'I am sure I must have missed it in your report,' he said. 'No matter, Captain. I shall have another look. And in the meantime, do keep up the good work.'

⋆ ⋆ ⋆

The curved, gilt-edged roofs of the Yu Yuan Gardens teahouse cast a shadow over the surrounding lake. The water had long since turned phosphorescent green from the summer algae, offsetting the building's vibrant red woodwork and ornate stone carvings. Normally, the teahouse was the exclusive preserve of the Shanghai elite, with long waits for tables, even for those with contacts in the Party.

Today, the entire venue had been sealed off, with a hand-picked team of PLA Special Forces wearing civilian clothing discreetly positioned at either end of the lake's zigzagging walkway. The

General Secretary of the Party's Politburo, Kai Long Pi, was marrying off his third son to the Governor of Chengdu's illustrious daughter, Li Ling, and in doing so cementing yet another alliance within the Guild. It had been an open secret for some time now that the Governor was vying for Kai's position as head of the Guild, but with this match the hatchet was to be buried, and their feud finally put to rest.

Kai had come to realise that the Guild as a collective entity must not have its factions competing openly in the final stages of the Goma Project. There was just too much at stake. And so a marriage had been swiftly arranged. Marriage, and by extension family, was still the best way to seal an agreement.

Kai sat in his wheelchair at the head of the table, arms folded across his lap while he watched the newly-weds parade between the aisles of guests. His son, Qingshan, could not have hoped for a better arrangement and Kai stared hard at the Governor's daughter, his old eyes magnified by heavily rimmed glasses. She was indeed beautiful and her red silk wedding dress nothing less than the epitome of refinement and tradition. She looked very graceful, confidently chatting with each of the assembled guests, while Qingshan stood at her side, nodding vaguely, too shy to acknowledge his guests properly. It almost looked as if he were struggling to follow the formalities of the marriage ceremony.

A troop of Kai's grandchildren followed the bride and groom, ranked by age and all wearing matching silk outfits. Kai allowed himself a slight smile. His younger grandchildren were his one weakness in life. At seventy-five years old, after losing the use of his legs, he had taken stock of his life again. He now made a point of making time for them in his schedule each day. Only for five minutes, but it was enough.

As Qingshan sat down with a sigh of relief, Li Ling approached Kai's table and with a bow delicately poured a single cup of tea. She did it with the flowing ease of ritualised custom, her eyes lowered with due deference. Kai took the proffered cup, and with that formally accepted her into his family. But as he took his first sip, he glanced across the crowded room to see a man leaning against one of the heavy wooden pillars. The man's dishevelled appearance immediately singled him out. He looked as if he hadn't slept in a week. Kai knew Xie's hangdog face well, and with the slightest inclination of his head beckoned him closer.

Steadily working his way through the ranks of well-dressed guests, Xie approached discreetly, hovering beside one of the nearby annexes until Kai signalled for his wheelchair to be eased back from the table.

'Many congratulations on your son's marriage,' Xie said to him, bowing low and presenting him with a small red envelope held out in both hands. Kai's expression didn't change, but inwardly he was impressed. Too many of the youngsters ignored the old ways, sacrificing everything from the past for the sake of expediency. But Xie was different, even observing the old marriage rituals. It was one of the reasons why Kai trusted him to be his right-hand man.

'You said that you have discovered some discrepancies?' he prompted.

Xie nodded slowly, averting his eyes as he always did. He was conscious of towering over Kai and always tried to keep a respectful distance between them, but it was difficult within the confines of the teahouse. Even before he had to use the wheelchair, Kai had only ever been a moderately sized man, but now age seemed to have shrunk him further. He looked up at Xie, the lids of his eyes heavy and tired.

Xie coughed. 'We have gone through a number of files and it seems that the actual satellite is missing from the wreckage. The inventory the technicians were using was also doctored.'

Kai inhaled deeply.

'Has General Jian been informed of this?'

'Not yet, sir. I thought it best to come to you first.' Xie paused. 'It was actually Jian himself who declared the reason for the satellite crash. Not one of our technicians, as we were led to believe.'

'To what end?'

'We don't know yet, sir, but I am almost certain there was no satellite in the first place.'

Kai eyes narrowed. 'If he produced fewer satellites than were originally financed, he would have had to disguise the fact by sabotaging the launch. It would also leave a significant amount of money left over. Have you found any trace of it?'

Xie shook his head. 'Nothing unusual has passed through his accounts or those of any of his associates. We have gone through the budgets extensively, but can't find any inconsistencies. If he is moving money out, then it's being done extremely subtly.'

'And the surveillance?'

'Nothing, sir, but I am quite certain Jian would already have suspected that we would be following his movements. We do know his plane stopped en route to Europe in the Lebanon, but have yet to ascertain why.'

Kai stayed lost in thought, his thin arms resting against the sides of the wheelchair. He had always been slow to condemn a man, and the bloody years of the Cultural Revolution and the endless denunciations under Chairman Mao had made him even more circumspect. He knew all too well how whole lives could be swept away on the faintest suspicion, and was not about to make the same mistake again.

Neither was he prepared to throw the entire Goma Project into turmoil at this crucial stage on the basis of Xie's suspicions, however well founded they might prove. Too much was at stake to risk confronting Jian right now. If indeed he was guilty, then it was something that could be dealt with once the dust had settled, quietly and permanently.

'The alternative is that Jian is innocent,' Kai said eventually. 'And that others are responsible.'

Xie bowed his head. 'That is of course possible, sir.'

Kai looked over his shoulder to where his host was preparing the ramp to the platform for the wedding speeches. He would be expected to participate soon.

'The destruction of the satellite was highly embarrassing and I will hold Jian accountable for the loss of face I suffered in front of the other families. But until such time as you provide me with incontrovertible proof, he stays.'

'Yes, sir.'

Kai pulled back the sleeve of his suit and glanced down at his watch. Despite himself, he felt his pulse quicken. The announcement was due to be made in less than two hours. ChinaCell was going public on the new satellite handsets in a long series of worldwide press releases and interviews. The media storm would be frenetic, while the vast warehouses in Guangdong were steadily being depleted of the millions of handsets and laptops they had already produced. Nearly two-thirds of the entire production facilities in Shenzhen had been diverted to this single aim. Never before had China's equivalent of Silicon Valley been so monopolised.

The products had already left the warehouses, dispatched by a fleet of container ships to the European and American stores, and were due to arrive in three days' time. The world's telecommunications would be changed irreparably, and with the resultant sales the Guild would see their fortunes soar. It had been an enormous risk getting each family to invest so heavily, but here they were in the last stages of the Goma Project and everything was finally set.

Nothing could be allowed to disrupt it now.

'I believe that the General is personally overseeing the final payment in the Congo,' Kai said.

'That is correct, sir. He is leaving for Goma tonight and will make the payment there.'

Kai raised his head to stare at Xie through the thick lenses of his glasses.

'It is a very significant sum and the General is not to be trusted to make such a payment alone. You will go with him, to ensure everything is as it should be. And Xie . . . I want you to watch him like a hawk.'

'Go with him? To the Congo, you mean?' Xie replied, taken by surprise.

The old man didn't respond but instead jerked his head sideways, indicating that Xie should move out of his way. He then slowly wheeled himself forward towards the crowd. The assembled guests quickly got to their feet, applauding loudly as he was wheeled up on to the low platform.

Xie shifted his weight from one foot to the other. 'The Congo,' he said to himself, his mouth shaping the words. He had never even been to Africa, and now he was venturing into one of the most dangerous parts to oversee a general he was certain was double-crossing them.

As he looked around the room, he took in the pinnacle of Shanghai's society, complete with spectacular dresses and ritualised table settings, collections of jewellery and polite small talk. With just one sentence, Kai had changed everything. In a matter of hours, he would be stepping off the plane into Africa's black heart.

21

'Luca!'

Bear stood over him, both hands twisted into the neck of his T-shirt. Each time she screamed his name, she lifted his whole head off the ground, her mouth so close that it nearly touched his cheek. Letting his head drop back into the mud, she slapped him hard across the face, the force of the blow stinging her hand.

'Luca! Wake up!'

He moaned, blinking a couple of times as he slowly opened his eyes. Bear's face filled his entire vision. She was leaning right over him, cradling his head in her hands.

'Come on, Luca! Get to your feet.'

Tugging backwards with all her strength, she pulled Luca's torso clear of the ground, but his head lolled backwards. He raised his right hand, vaguely trying to fend her off, but Bear slapped him again.

'Luca!'

His eyes settled on hers, then slowly drifted closed again, the effort just too much. Bear lifted her face up towards the sky, shouting in frustration. She could see the helicopter hovering above them now, the wash from its rotors shaking the high branches of the canopy. Leaves slowly floated down from the sky, twirling in the beams of light before gently settling on the forest floor.

The helicopter banked round in a wide turn as it continued its search. Bear caught glimpses as it passed gaps in the canopy, but here the forest was too dense for the pilots to see anything clearly. For now, at least, they were safe.

She had been trying to wake Luca for over two minutes. Time seemed to drag in rhythm with each beat of the helicopter's rotors, the precious seconds wasting away while Luca lay unconscious on the ground. She stared into his eyes. His pupils were wide from concussion and it might take him hours to regain his senses fully. One more minute, she whispered to herself. One more minute, then she would have to leave him.

'Wake up!' Bear shouted again. 'You've got to get up and rescue Joshua. Remember Joshua!'

The name seemed to spark something in Luca's memory and he blinked again, trying to raise his head.

'That's it. Joshua,' Bear repeated. 'Get up and help him.'

Luca grabbed her arm, pulling himself up with surprising strength. He groaned, his right arm moving down to his ribcage.

'Where is . . . Joshua?' he murmured.

'He's this way,' she said, pointing away from the inselberg. 'But we have to hurry to catch him.'

Luca's eyes moved in the direction she was pointing, then he shuffled forward unsteadily. After only a couple of paces, he collapsed on to his knees. Bear rushed to him, stopping him from toppling all the way to the ground, but strained under his deadweight. After a moment, she managed to adjust her footing and get him up again. As Luca stood there swaying, she glanced back down at her watch. The minute was up. It was time to decide.

'Shit,' she breathed, her thighs straining from supporting his weight. She had to make a decision. And do it *now*. Every rational part of her brain screamed for her to duck out from under his arm and sprint off into the jungle, to put as much distance between her and the LRA as possible. But something held her back and she stood there, fighting every instinct to flee.

Just as she went to move, Luca's right fist pressed down on her shoulder, holding her still, as if he had sensed what she was thinking. He held her tight, the power of his grip unbelievably strong.

'You lead me,' he said. 'I can move if you lead me.'

★ ★ ★

They pressed on, the sounds of the helicopter receding with each minute that passed. Occasionally, they would hear the engine change pitch and the noise come closer, but then it dipped again, fading into the background hum of the forest. Luca was moving faster now. He still held on to Bear's shoulder, following her lead like a blind man, but his steps were less erratic and clumsy. She could hear his breath in her ear and feel the sweat on the palm of his hand. There was something almost comforting about his proximity, as if in all this chaos they were one entity, not two, trying to break free from the endless forest.

They had been going for about twenty minutes, forcing their way through acres of young saplings, when Luca suddenly spoke.

'The boys,' he said in a low voice. 'What happened to Abasi?'

Bear didn't turn her head. 'Neither of them made it.'

There was a pause, with just the slapping sound of their feet dragging through the undergrowth.

'What kind of people gun down a boy with a spear?' Luca whispered.

Bear felt him start to slow, lost to the horror. She ignored him, trying to force the last image of Abasi out of her mind. They had to be practical, work in numbers not emotions. She guessed that they would have at least two hours on the LRA patrol because they still had to descend all the way to the stream to get around the inselberg. It also sounded as if the helicopter had either given up or was too low on fuel to continue searching, and had returned to its base. They had a head start, but it wasn't much.

They trudged on for a few more paces, the undergrowth thinning as they began to climb a slight rise.

'He was just a kid,' Luca whispered again, slowing to a walk. 'What kind of people . . . '

'Stop it!' Bear screamed, swivelling round and pushing him back with the palms of her hands. 'Stop thinking that way!'

Luca stared at her.

'They're dead. You got it? *Dead.* We have to move on.'

'Can't I just have a moment . . . '

'No! No, you can't!' Bear shouted, shoving him once again and forcing him to take a step backwards.

'What's wrong with you?' she blazed, levelling a finger at his chest. 'Why don't you understand and harden the fuck up? This isn't the West. No more, 'I'm sorry for him . . . I'm sorry for her.' This is Africa, and no one gives a shit what you feel!'

Luca just stood there, too shocked to respond. Bear turned away from him, scraping her hair back from her face with such force that a few strands caught in the webbing of her fingers.

'Millions of people have died horrible deaths in the Congo,' she continued. 'Millions! And not a single other person cares. So why the hell should we?'

Luca glowered at her.

'Because that's the only thing that makes us different,' he snapped. 'Stop talking to me like I've never seen death before. Like I'm some kind of fucking tourist.'

'That's exactly what you are out here — a tourist. You know *nothing* about any of this.'

Luca's eyes grew cold as he stared at her.

'You think you know all about death just because you've seen it? Well, I've crossed that line.' His voice shook with anger. 'You don't just move on and forget the whole thing. It doesn't work that way. Their faces stay with you, staring at you above their open mouths . . . ' Luca fell

232

silent. He could see the avalanche again and the faces of the men he'd killed tumbling through the wall of snow and ice.

'So what is it with you?' he continued. 'Seen one too many wars to give a shit about a couple of kids?'

'Screw you,' Bear spat, folding her arms across her chest. 'You don't know anything about me.'

The wound on her shoulder had opened again, sending a trickle of blood down into her filthy vest. She didn't even notice.

'I care about surviving,' she said, her voice dropping to a hiss. 'That's it. I'm not here for you, the pygmies, or anyone else.'

'Yeah, that's what you said from the beginning. At least I know where you stand.'

They stood glowering at each other for a moment longer, before Bear glanced down at her watch. Without another word, she turned in the direction they were headed and sprinted off. Luca let her run ahead for a few paces then broke into a run himself, following in her foot-steps.

★　★　★

They heard the low roll of thunder as night drew on. Soon came the rain, the droplets beating against the leaves high above their heads before finally reaching them. As the night grew blacker, the rain grew worse, bending the broad leaves of the forest under its weight and turning the ground into grim tar-coloured mud. It oozed over their leather boots, reaching their knees in the deepest places.

Neither Bear nor Luca had said a word to each other since they had resumed running. They stopped when they passed one of the water vines, but even then only rested for a matter of seconds, drinking quickly and without speaking. As every hour passed, each had quickened their pace, progressively trying to outdo the other. Although naturally stronger, Luca had been suffering from what he suspected were two cracked ribs, and as the day dragged on the pain worsened. He tried to block it out, focusing on the next step, then the next, never thinking about how long they had been running or what lay ahead.

The rain intensified, coming down in vertical sheets. White bursts of lightning flashed across the sky followed by rolls of thunder. Both of them were absolutely sodden, their clothes clinging to their bodies while their trousers chafed against the skin on the inside of their thighs, rubbing it raw.

Dipping down into a steep ravine, Bear suddenly cried out, losing her footing on the treacherous ground and sliding a few metres on her back in the mud. Her knee jammed against an exposed tree branch, making her cry out in pain, but Luca simply stepped over her and continued running. She stared up at him, cursing under her breath, before pulling herself back on to her feet and sprinting hard to catch up.

Before long, they came upon a massive fallen tree. Its roots, encrusted with clods of earth, jutted out towards the sky. A huge crater in the ground extended round the trunk in a half-moon shape. Bear pulled up, her chest rising in time with her breath. They had been going for six hours and every muscle in her body ached.

'There might be some cover there,' she panted. Against the main part of the trunk, she could just make out a small area that was sheltered from the rain. It was only a few feet deep, but wide enough to lie down in.

'I'm stopping,' she said. 'I've got to rest. At least for a couple of hours.'

Leaving Luca standing out in the rain, she carefully crawled past the roots and into the dry opening a little deeper inside. With her shoulders pressed against the soft earth, she lay flat on her back, letting out a long, ragged breath. She had never felt exhaustion like it. They had barely eaten in over two days and her stomach was cramping from lack of nourishment. On the last two hours of the run, it had got so bad that she had started to feel dizzy and nauseous. She had had to stop and break out the last of the energy bars, but even then, the sick exhaustion had barely left her for a moment.

Bear exhaled again, sinking deeper into the earth. She was absolutely broken. The knowledge that they would have to do this again and again, day after day, if they ever wanted to make it out of the forest alive, made her whole body go limp. It just seemed so impossible, so hopeless.

Luca remained outside with his hands on his hips. He was breathing heavily, blowing the droplets of water off his nose and out into the night. The rain beat down so hard that his hair was slicked flat against his cheeks, while his T-shirt stretched across the muscles of his lower back.

Turning her head to one side, Bear could just make out the top half of his body beyond the line of the roots. She watched him, the anger and frustration of the morning long since replaced by a desperate tiredness. A ghost of a smile passed across her lips. They were just as stubborn as each other.

'You have to get out of the rain,' she called. 'Even you need to rest at some point.'

Still Luca didn't move.

'Come on. We both need our strength, so let's rest for a couple of hours then be on our way.'

He turned towards her, his expression hidden by the darkness.

'Please, Luca.'

Without a word, he came closer, crawling over the roots and squeezing into the opening beside her. She turned her body sideways, pressing herself back against the earth to make room for him. He pulled off his sodden T-shirt and wrung out the water. Bunching it up to use as a pillow, he lay with his back to her, staring out into the night.

Bear was only a few inches away from his back and could feel the damp heat rising from his skin. She let her eyes blur in the darkness, fighting the pain in her shoulder. It had got worse again, sending a dull throb across her entire back.

For several minutes Bear stayed like that,

staring into the dark as she tried to relax. But memories of the day kept resurfacing. They came in a relentless cycle, until finally one image drowned out the others, settling across her vision like a sunspot. At first it was little more than a hazy outline with no real detail or substance, but then she understood what it was. It was the Polaroid of her son, pinned to the cockpit of the Cessna. She could clearly see Nathan's face now, smiling, as he stared straight at the camera.

Bear swallowed, wincing as she felt her throat tighten. Just to see him one more time, to hold him tight against her chest and bury her nose deep in the curls of his hair, was all she wanted now. Her nostrils flared as she tried to conjure up his smell. She knew it so well, but now she couldn't place it; there was nothing but the damp earthiness all around. Closing her eyes, she tried to picture his face again, but it had warped this time, turning instead to the faces of the pygmy boys.

Bear sniffed loudly, feeling shame well up inside her. Before she even realised what was happening, she found herself trying to stifle sobs. Tears ran down her cheeks, making her eyes burn, and she sniffed again, trying to hold it all back. But no matter what she did, she couldn't stop herself from imagining her own son being ripped to pieces by bullets.

'I'm sorry,' Bear whispered, raising her hand to touch Luca's back. There was no answer, so she held her hand where it was, her fingertips millimetres from his skin.

'You didn't deserve what I said this morning.

You were right. We shouldn't have got those boys involved.'

Luca remained facing outwards, his body rigid. Bear felt herself willing him to respond, to say something to console her. The tiredness and fear had broken her down and now she felt a physical need for Luca's affirmation, for him simply to say that it was going to be all right, and that they would make it through.

'Say something, Luca.'

He turned until he was facing her. She could just make out the profile of his face in the dim light, and the wet strands of his hair.

'There's more,' Bear added, the words so quiet that they caught on her breath. 'More to me, I mean. I do care what happened to those boys, but I just couldn't deal with it then. Couldn't face up to what had happened.'

She waited, trying to read his expression, but it was too dark. She tried to stop herself from feeling this way, to hold back, but already knew that she wanted more from him. Needed it. Inching her body closer, her lips found his in the dark. They pressed together, the kiss filled with uncertainty, and for several seconds, they just lay there, their lips the only point of contact between them. Then Luca slowly moved his arm out across the ground so that Bear's head rested ontop his bicep. She moved in closer, pressing her whole body against his.

Pushing him on to his back, Bear swung herself on top so that her legs straddled his waist. Pulling off her top, she unclipped her bra and flung it to one side, wincing as the strap went over her damaged shoulder.

'Why . . . ' Luca began, but she gently pulled him up towards her and silenced him with another kiss. Luca leaned back on his hands with his chin tilted up towards her. She could feel his hands slowly move down her back, smoothing her skin as far as her hips. They came round to her belt, tugging the leather backwards as he freed the buckle.

In the darkness, Bear received only jumbled impressions, each movement merging into the next as they made love. There was nothing else but where they were right then, and the incredible feeling of longing mixed with pleasure. It went on and on, neither of them wanting the sensation to end, as they escaped from the reality of everything else around them. Finally Bear collapsed down onto him and lay still, her skin shining with sweat. She was breathing hard and as she reached forward to kiss him once again, he could feel a smile on her lips.

For several minutes they lay like that, neither of them wanting to speak or by extension deal with the implications of what had just happened. They just listened to the sound of the rain beating against the leaves, with their legs intertwined and Bear lying flat against Luca's chest. He brought his right hand up, running it slowly down the length of her back, feeling every inch of her supple skin. As he reached her waist, his fingers connected with a thin beaded chain that he hadn't noticed before despite her being naked, and he let his fingers play across it.

'My mother gave it to me,' Bear whispered, not raising her head from his chest. 'It was the last thing she gave me before leaving me on the streets in Bunia.'

'How old were you?'

'I was four.'

Bear sighed heavily, the air blowing out across Luca's chest. 'She came back to Bunia a few years later with this man I'd never seen before. I was there, lice in my hair, living off whatever I could find in the rubbish. So she shaved my head and gave me a huge pink dressing gown and some sandals that were meant for a boy. And that was the last time I ever saw her.'

Luca brought his hand up to her neck, his fingers gently playing with her hair.

'This place is just so screwed up,' she whispered. 'Stories like that happen every single day.'

Luca remained still. 'You know, earlier this morning, you were right. I don't understand any of this and shouldn't have judged you like that. Life is totally different out here. I mean, where I come from, you just don't get mothers abandoning their kids.'

As he said the last words, Bear crossed her arms over her chest, feeling a sudden need to cover up. It was as if she could feel the reality of their situation catching up with them, ripping the moment apart. Everything else in her life came flooding back, the image of Nathan now so clear in her mind, and with it, the desire to be with him suddenly emptied.

Dragging the filthy vest up from the ground,

she pulled it over her shoulders.

'You're going to try for the volcano tomorrow, aren't you?' she said, changing the subject.

'If that is a mine, then I think there's a good chance Joshua's still alive. There isn't any reason to kill him if they are putting men to work. But you don't have to worry, Bear. I won't leave you out here by yourself.'

'*Eh! Je peux prendre soin de moi,*' I can take care of myself, Bear snapped 'I don't need your help in the jungle.'

'I know,' Luca replied, raising his hands defensively. 'Trust me, I know. If we could get around the back of the volcano and somehow find those tunnels that Lanso mentioned, we might be able to get into the mine unseen.'

'This is the LRA, Luca. If we get caught . . . '

'We're not going to get caught. I promise you that.'

Bear exhaled deeply, shutting her eyes in the darkness. 'Don't make promises you can't keep.'

There was a long pause before Luca broke the silence. 'All I know is that for the last two years I have been hiding from the world, and now there is this way for me to make up for it all. I have to see if he is in there, Bear. I *have* to do this. The question is — what are you going to do?'

'Me?'

'Come on, tell me.'

A bitter smile crossed her lips.

'I've just broken the only real promise I ever made to my husband, so what the hell am I supposed to feel?'

Settling back into the earth with her arms

pressed across her chest, she stared out rigidly into the darkness. When she spoke, her voice seemed to be devoid of any emotion.

'I'll finish my job and trace the sample back to the mine. After that, I'm going to get as far as I can from this godforsaken place.'

22

The pilot of the Oryx Mk2 helicopter glanced down at the GPS navigation system on the console before staring out across the trees of the Ituri Forest. He then raised his gloved hand with two fingers outstretched. Xie stared at it blankly before General Jian's voice came in over the headset.

'*We land in two minutes,*' he explained in Mandarin, his voice terse. He was sitting on the opposite side of the open cabin wearing full military uniform, with immaculately polished boots and a pressed green jacket adorned by sparkling epaulettes. At his feet was the metal Pelican case that he had carefully loaded on to the helicopter when they first set out.

Jian stared across at Xie for a moment, his black pupils smouldering with annoyance. Kai's insistence that Xie should fly all the way out from Shanghai to accompany him for the final payment had to mean something. Even if they hadn't gone as far as to connect the dummy satellite launch with the missing funds, Xie's mere presence was significant. That much Jian was sure of. From now on he would have to tighten his grip on the situation, ensure that nothing was left to chance.

Jian's concentration wavered as another stab of pain shot through his temples. The pain was just maddening. Despite already swallowing all the painkillers he was prescribed for one day, he felt as if his skull was about to tear in two with each thud of the rotors. The pain was like nothing he had ever known before, and shutting his eyes, he slowly scratched the dried patch of skin at the side of his collar, willing the flight to end.

Xie sat facing him, with one leg crossed over the other, wearing the same brown linen suit as he had the previous day. The fabric was bunched up under his armpits, gradually darkening from sweat as the flight across the forest dragged on. He stared into the General's face; at his tightly shut eyes and thin, pursed lips. At some point in the recent past, Jian must have shaved off a moustache because the subtle hint of a tan line still remained. His hair also looked different and was now smartly cropped in the military fashion, shaved almost to the skin at the sides. It wasn't Jian's style to look so formal, and Xie wondered about the reason for the change.

He watched the other two helicopters flying in tight formation around them. Higher in the sky he could see another helicopter that looked different, bristling with weaponry and with only two people on board, sitting one behind the other. Suddenly, it pitched up and rolled off behind them in a tight banking turn. Xie reached out to one of the seat straps, expecting them to follow, but instead they continued their course, holding straight and level.

Framed by the silhouette of the GPMG machine gun and the side of the helicopter cabin, he could see the beginnings of a vast

244

volcano slowly come into view. First came a long plume of smoke rising out of the crater, then as they drew closer he could see the immense flanks of black porous rock, spiking up through the forest canopy, hundreds of feet into the air.

The helicopters circled round to the northern side of the volcano, dropping to a hover about fifty feet above the ground. As Xie craned his neck to watch, the entire forest floor seemed to move. Vast camouflage nets were drawn back, suddenly exposing an area the size of a football pitch. With a final whine of the engines, all three helicopters touched down, while the gunner just beside them squeezed off the safety catch with his thumb.

Jian reached inside his trouser pocket and, concealing the little plastic bottle of painkillers in the palm of his hand, surreptitiously swallowed three of the large blue pills. His neck flexed, his Adam's apple rising as he forced them down. He then unbuckled his seat belt and stepped out of the helicopter on to the ground. Stooping to keep his head clear of the rotors, he moved away a few paces before suddenly stopping. Hundreds of soldiers stood all around them, pressed together in a dense circle of black limbs and weaponry that fanned all the way back to the edge of the clearing. No one spoke. They just stared silently, eyes narrowed against the sun.

Jian felt sweat collect at the base of his spine as he slowly took in the piratical crew of adolescent boys and men. They were armed with an assortment of Kalashnikovs, Chinese-made QBZ-95 assault rifles and basic AK-47s.

Most had grenades tied to their webbing straps and long reams of ammunition strung across their glistening chests. They wore faded red berets together with an assortment of military fatigues and worn T-shirts, but the majority were simply bare-chested. Their bodies looked lithe and scrawny, abdomens hardened by the privations of the jungle.

Xie followed, clambering out of the helicopter and blinking unsteadily in the full glare of the sun. He came to a halt beside Jian, standing close by so that their shoulders were almost touching. Xie felt his mind empty. There were so many of them, standing perfectly still, their eyes following every movement, like lions closing in for the kill.

'What happens now?' Xie whispered in Mandarin. His gaze continued to pass over the faces, mesmerised by the dark eyes brimming with hostility. There was an apocalyptical savagery to it all, as if somehow they had stumbled across the last people on earth.

'Jian,' Xie whispered, fighting the urge to move back towards the helicopters. But Jian did not answer. Instead, he stood with his chest puffed out, arms stiff by his sides, almost to attention, as if determined not to lose face in front of the army before them.

Suddenly a movement rippled out across the crowd. The soldiers quickly parted, creating a single line that snaked all the way back to the edge of the clearing. A huge man appeared from behind one of the trees. He was brawny, with thick bands of muscle covering his chest and arms, and a huge bulbous head. He stepped into the light, revealing a face pitted by tribal cutting scars. They ran from the crown of his head right the way across his cheeks and down past his jawline.

As he stood there, arms hanging loose at his sides, another man of equally monstrous proportions followed him out into the clearing. Suddenly, a high-pitched screaming erupted. Every single person in the crowd was shouting and wailing, waving his weapon in the air. It was as if the entire forest had burst into life, and Xie and Jian suddenly found themselves surrounded by a tide of oscillating arms and heads, the pungent smell of the soldiers' skin clogging their nostrils. They smelled of earth and ingrained sweat, the smell of Africa.

The shouting grew louder, reaching a crescendo as Joseph-Désiré Mordecai stepped into the clearing.

He was a tall man, maybe only forty-five years old, with a rangy physique and skin that was lighter in colour than his bodyguards'. He was wearing an immaculate white suit which almost glowed in the sunlight.

Mordecai walked along the line of men with a hand extended. The soldiers pushed to be near him, surging forward with hands outstretched and fingers splayed, as they fought for the slightest touch. Despite it all, Mordecai was somehow left unaffected by all the commotion. He walked slowly, his hand drifting from one person's to the next, barely brushing against their skin. It was as if there was a circle of light around him that no one dared to enter.

Coming to a halt in front of Xie and Jian, Mordecai stared at them in silence. They could clearly see his face now, with its high cheekbones and narrow, sculpted nose. The skin of his forehead was smooth except for a single vertical line running down between his eyebrows. But it was the eyes to which both men found themselves drawn. They were a clear, translucent green and filled with a sense of sympathy and calm, as if Xie and Jian had somehow been responsible for a terrible tragedy but he was already prepared to forgive them.

The monster they had been expecting had vanished. Before them stood a man who was attractive and confident, radiating a sense of serenity.

'My brothers,' Mordecai said, opening his arms. 'We finally meet.'

Jian was the first to react, offering a curt bow before stretching out his hand in greeting. Mordecai simply stared at it, tucking his own hands behind his back, but then gave a warm, magnanimous smile.

'You have done much to help our cause,' he said. 'It is your weapons that have built this army. It is with these weapons that we will strike back at those dogs in Kinshasa.' Mordecai's voice grew louder, playing to the crowd. 'Are you ready for Kinshasa my children? Are you ready for war?'

The soldiers erupted again, hanging on his every word. Mordecai let his eyes close for the briefest of moments, revelling in the hysteria.

248

When they opened once more, they were staring directly at Jian.

'As you can see, we are ready!' he said. Then, tilting his head back and straining from the effort, he shouted, 'The time is now, my brothers! Tomorrow we leave on the long march to Kinshasa and we will scorch the earth as we go. We are the soldiers of light and every one of those cockroach *muzungos* will be crushed under our boots. Are you ready to fight?'

The crowd screamed in response.

'Are you ready to bathe in their blood?'

The crowd surged forward, the clamour deafening.

'Then show me!' Mordecai shouted.

A chant began, low at first but building in strength and pitch. 'Mordecai! Mordecai! Mordecai!' There was something hollow, almost detached, about it, as if the name alone was enough to inflict harm.

Mordecai nodded slowly. He had promised them death and they loved him for it.

23

Signalling to his bodyguards, Mordecai set off towards the edge of the clearing with the Chinese following close behind. As they passed under the canopy, they could see yet more soldiers, their bodies half-concealed by dense undergrowth. What they had seen in the clearing was just the vanguard. Mordecai's army was vast.

A narrow path wound through the trees to the base of the volcano, where rough steps had been hacked into the black rock. These led up to a wide natural balcony. Under an overhanging slab of rock was a cave in which a table and four leather safari chairs were arranged. A few okapi hides were stretched across the floor, and an old fridge-freezer stood next to a metal fan. A low hum filtered out across the balcony as the fan slowly drew from one side to the next, circulating the bone-dry air.

The bodyguards melted deeper into the shadow of the cave, leaving Mordecai at one end of the table, facing Xie and Jian. They had climbed high enough to be above the trees and now before them stretched a panorama of the Ituri Forest, vibrant with every imaginable shade of green.

Mordecai signalled to the back of the cave and an old man approached, carrying a tray with a large wire-mesh cage on top. He banged it down on the table, his skinny arms clumsy and weak. Mordecai smiled up at him, gently grasping his wrist.

'*Vous semblez fatigué, mon oncle. Reposez-vous.*' You look tired, uncle. Get some rest, he whispered.

Mordecai then turned to General Jian, who was already staring through the wire mesh. Inside were two identically coloured butterflies, one slightly larger than the other. They had pink markings running back from the thorax, with the tip of each wing ending in patches of jet black. The wings themselves looked incredibly delicate, as if spun from the gossamer of a spider's web.

'*Salamis parhassus,*' Jian whispered, his eyes unblinking as he stared at the specimens. 'I thought they were extinct.'

'There are many precious things left still in the Congo,' Mordecai replied. 'And think of these as but a small token of our friendship.'

Mordecai inclined his head towards Xie.

'I was not aware that you would be coming, otherwise I would have found you a suitable gift. No one leaves my country empty-handed.'

'Coming to your country is . . . much reward,' Xie said, in broken English with a heavy Chinese accent. 'I am only advisor to General. An administrator.'

Xie gave a polite smile, rubbing his fingers over the skin at the corner of one eye, suddenly appearing extremely tired. With his ruffled hair and cheap linen suit, he looked almost uninterested in the proceedings and, after a moment's reflection, Mordecai seemed to discount him, turning his full attention back to Jian.

'These specimens were found in the far north of the forest. I had my soldiers go there especially.'

'They're perfect,' Jian replied with an appreciative nod. 'They shall have pride of place in my collection.'

'Heaven's bounty is endless,' Mordecai stated, clasping his hands together. 'And you deserve a share in it. You have brought us everything we need to overthrow Kabila's regime. For that you will be richly rewarded.'

Jian raised an eyebrow. 'Rewarded? I think that it is you who are being 'richly rewarded'. We are paying you three billion dollars for this mine. That is not an insignificant amount of money.'

'No, it is not, but the price is justified nonetheless. You've produced millions of handsets using our fire coltan and that is going to make you rich men.' He pointed his finger at Jian directly, and smiled as if sharing a joke. 'You will be a *very* rich man.'

Not a flicker of a reaction passed across Jian's face, but inwardly his suspicions were aroused. Was Mordecai referring to the Guild in general becoming rich, or did he somehow know about Jian's own side dealings in the Lebanon? No, that was impossible. How could he know anything about it, stuck out here in this wretched jungle?

Mordecai shifted in his seat, his eyes draining of humour. 'And tell me, when will the handsets be delivered to the West?'

'They have already left the warehouses,' Jian answered quickly, pleased to have a change of subject. The announcement had been made fourteen hours ago and had triggered a worldwide media storm. Shares for the entire existing telecommunications market were already collapsing. 'Everything is in place. And now we are ready to transfer the fifty per cent down payment and take control of this mine.'

Mordecai nodded vaguely, his eyes moving to the butterflies on the table. The rich effervescent pink of their wings glowed in the light.

'On handover, as agreed,' Jian continued, 'we will transfer a further twenty-five per cent, with the remaining balance payable after the first year of production. A total of three billion dollars.'

Mordecai nodded slowly, appearing almost indifferent to the sums of money being discussed. Instead, he turned to survey the view. Seconds passed, with Mordecai seemingly lost in his own thoughts, then suddenly his expression changed, becoming warm and ingratiating again, as if now dealing with long-lost friends.

'The production of fire coltan will continue for many more years,' he whispered, wetting his lips with his tongue. 'You can rest assured of that. But what if I were to make you a better deal?'

Jian shrugged but Xie remained perfectly still, observing every nuance of Mordecai's expression.

'As before, you will take control of this mine, but I will also grant you all the mining concessions for the entire North and South Kivu provinces.'

253

'But they are not yours to give,' Jian countered.

Mordecai raised his arms up to the heavens. 'You have seen our army. There is nothing to stop us from seizing power; the militias are already defeated and Kabila's army is pathetic and undisciplined.'

'And MONUC?' asked Jian.

'MONUC,' Mordecai repeated, the disgust clear in his voice. 'Those *muzungos* will be the first to die. They are gutless and divided, too scared even to leave their compounds.' He leaned forward in his chair and Xie watched as his eyes suddenly changed, burning with a hateful energy that transformed his entire face. There was a terrible certainty in those eyes, as if something had been put in motion that could never be stopped.

'Every single foreigner who occupies our soil will feel our cleansing fires; every man, woman and child will burn. For over a hundred and fifty years, the West has throttled us, killed and enslaved our people, then spat on us with aid. But now, our time has come and, I promise you, the cleansing will be felt far and wide.'

Standing up from his chair, he moved out from the shadow and into the daylight. The brilliant light made his white suit glow. It looked incongruous against the black rock and muddy greens of the forest. When Mordecai finally turned back to them and spoke, his voice had faded to a monotone, as if recounting events long past.

'Once in Kinshasa, I will carve up the Congo

as I see fit. God has given us riches; from copper to gold, diamonds to uranium. It is all right here, just beneath our feet. Either you come in now or get in line with every other nation soon to be begging at my door.'

Xie looked across at Jian, but the General ignored him.

'What price are you offering?'

'You pay the entire sum for the mine. Everything up front.'

'That's three billion dollars . . . '

'It's nothing,' Mordecai interrupted. 'Nothing when you include all that you steal from my country already. You know what I am talking about, don't you, General?'

Jian remained silent, knowing full well that the Guild backed an entire raft of illegal mining concessions in the Congo, ranging from small-scale open-cast mining to major extractions of tin and diamonds. Already that year, nearly a billion dollars' worth of illegal tin had passed through Lubumbashi in unmarked trucks to be sold out of Zambia, while nearly as much in uncut diamonds had passed the border into Uganda. There were other such schemes too. Many others.

'You pay everything up front and I'll legitimise those claims. If not, I will cut off the hand that steals from my people.'

Jian's expression remained fixed. The current president, Kabila, wasn't strong enough to enforce any regulation, but someone like Mordecai would be able to put a stranglehold on all of the Guild's illegal mining activities, selling off the concessions to the highest bidder and driving prices through the roof.

By signing the deal and getting in early, he could secure an incredible coup for the Guild. And the price was only what they were paying for this single mine already, a fraction of the true value of all those other mining contracts. A deal like this would see his influence in the Guild soar. He would be at the centre of it all, liaising between Mordecai as the new leader of the Congo, and on the other side the mining companies in China, desperate for access to the minerals.

Jian slowly turned towards Xie.

'*Get the extra money immediately,*' he said in Mandarin. '*I want the deal finalised today.*'

Xie looked up, eyebrows arching slightly, but didn't respond. Something was wrong about all of this. He was sure of it. They were being used to serve some other purpose, but what it was exactly he couldn't quite see. And Mordecai had been holding something back about the fire coltan. He had licked his lips every time he even mentioned the words.

'*Did you hear what I said?*' Jian asked, staring at Xie impatiently.

He blinked. '*You will have to refer back to Beijing,*' he said, speaking low and uncharacteristically fast. '*You don't have the authority to make this kind of decision.*'

Jian's whole body went rigid as he tried to control his anger, his eyes darkening to jet black. He slowly massaged his temples, trying to stop himself from lashing out across the table at this infuriating weasel of a man. His pulse beat faster, amplifying the pain in his head, until it felt as if his brain had somehow swollen, pressing unbearably against his skull. The pain! It was endless! He had to get this deal done. Get it finished so he could finally be free from the whole thing.

Jian's voice lowered to a hiss. '*Don't you ever question me again, you little shit. I am running this operation. Not you.*'

A strange, almost pained, smile appeared on Xie's lips.

'*I am quite sure you are not intimidated by me, but remember who I represent.*'

'*You are nothing more than a parasite. I will run this deal as I like. Don't even think you have a voice here.*'

Jian stared at him a moment longer then straightened in his chair. He had been the one to build the Goma Project. And he would be the one to control it.

'You have a deal,' he said to Mordecai, his gaze deliberately excluding Xie. 'We will make the payment as agreed and then wire the second tranche of the money when we return to Beijing.'

Mordecai shook his head, waving his finger slowly. 'We don't have the luxury of time. We leave this camp tomorrow evening and the money needs to be in our hands by then. If not, I will consider the many other options available to me. We already have many requests for delegations.'

'You will have the money by then,' Jian replied curtly. 'You just stick to your side of the bargain.'

'We have trusted each other for this long. I see no reason to change things now.'

Xie remained seated with his arms folded across his chest while he watched Jian reach down to the metal Pelican case at his feet.

'Where do we do this?'

Mordecai raised an arm, indicating that he should follow. Leaving Xie seated, they walked back towards the stairway. At the movement, both bodyguards came out from the back of the cave and positioned themselves between Mordecai and Jian.

The steps led over the top of the cave entrance and further back against the side of the volcano to where a military green hut had been built on to the rockface and covered in a mesh of camouflage netting. Outside, large circular satellite dishes were angled up to the sky, along with a collection of radio antennae, while inside the shack itself two men were sitting in front of a bank of radio equipment and computers.

'The miracle of technology,' Mordecai said. 'I could run a small government from here.'

Both men leaped to their feet at the sound of his voice, saluting as they retreated against the side wall. At Mordecai's gesture they quickly cleared a space for Jian on the low trestle table and he rested his Pelican case on top. Clicking open the latches, he unfolded the two halves to reveal a pristine silver laptop nestling inside a layer of protective foam. As he booted it up, the hard drive whirred softly and came to life with a flicker of its screen. In just a few seconds, Jian was directly connected to the outside world through the BNS satellites already in place. Leaning over the computer, he keyed in the first of the passwords to initiate the fund transfer.

'Track it,' Mordecai ordered the nearest operator. The minutes passed, the dry heat inside the shack insufferable. Jian could feel his military fatigues clinging to his skin, but he stayed absolutely motionless while the transfer took place. This moment signified a vast new tap of resources for the Guild, and through his work here China would have exclusive access to Africa's most abundant country. This was one of the pivotal moments in his life. No time to suffer Xie's lack of vision or courage.

Jian went through the next stage of the security clearances, carefully entering the twelve-digit code from memory. A few seconds later, the video-conferencing icon glowed, indicating an incoming call, and the face of a Chinese man in a smart suit came into view.

'*Code in, please,*' he asked in Mandarin.

'*Red. Alpha. Chongqing. November,*' Jian intoned, his enunciation given with military precision.

'*Confirmed. Thank you, General.*'

The face disappeared and Jian closed the lid of his laptop. A few seconds later, the nearest operator turned back to Mordecai and nodded. The funds had cleared.

'The mine is yours,' Mordecai said with a slight nod of his head.

With that, he led Jian out of the shack. Just as they were about to descend the steps again, Mordecai paused, looking at the collar line of

Jian's shirt. In the full light of day, he could clearly see the flakes of dried skin and where the flesh was starting to swell beneath.

As Jian followed him down the pathway, his fingers wrapped around the leather strap of his necklace. He could feel the natural warmth of the Heart of Fire pressing against his skin and held it between his thumb and forefinger, gently rubbing it back and forth. With so much stress and the maddening headaches he was plagued with, he found the sensation strangely soothing. He was still fingering the stone when they reached the entrance to the cave and found Xie staring out at the view.

Passing the line of trees on their way back to the clearing, they saw that the multitude of LRA soldiers had disappeared, leaving only the mercenaries standing by their helicopters. The last of the fire coltan had already been stowed on board. Xie was the first to clamber inside as the rotors began their slow swoop.

Just before boarding, Jian paused, turning back towards Mordecai.

'The money will be transferred tomorrow. Mark my words.'

'Then you will have the rights to it all,' Mordecai answered, smiling. He raised his arms high as if embracing the whole world.

As Jian went to shake his hand, Mordecai stared, unmoving, at the General's outstretched palm, as if it were some kind of personal affront. Then, quite suddenly, he reached forward, shook it, and gave him a reassuring smile before indicating that Jian should get on board. The helicopters then rose in unison and, with a roar of engines, sped off in formation, skimming low across the tops of the trees.

For several minutes after they had gone, Mordecai stayed still. Just as his bodyguards began to exchange nervous glances, he slowly raised his hand up to his face and sniffed. The smell of the foreigner's hand was still there; the sharp, almost surgical cleanliness mixed with undertones of some expensive cologne.

Muzungos. They all smelled the same — Westerners and Orientals. They were like a cancer across this land but, starting tomorrow, he would rid the Congo of their stench.

Their fires would burn bright indeed.

24

Bear and Luca had been on the move for the entire morning, trudging through the dense undergrowth. The rain from the previous night had dulled to a drizzle, but the clouds still looked heavy and ready to burst, making the humidity soar. It was breathless and hot, and both of them felt weak from it.

They had reached a narrow river and now stood on its bank, staring up at the side of the volcano. They could already feel the heat radiating from it and see where the rock had been stained a dirty yellow by the clouds of sulphur venting off its sides. Higher still, only a handful of stunted, ash-coloured trees managed to cling to the sloping surface, leading their eyes towards the bulging column of smoke rising out of the crater and melting into a low bank of cloud.

Moving closer to the river, they crouched down near a bed of reeds. The water looked so exposed that neither of them wanted to risk going out into the open. They had become so used to the trees and the undergrowth that it felt like the slightest break from cover would bring down the roar of the helicopters.

'There's no other way,' Luca said finally. 'We're going to have to swim for it. You think your shoulder will be OK?'

Bear nodded before glancing up at the sky again.

'We'll be out in the open the whole time. If a chopper passes overhead, it'll pick us up immediately.'

'I know,' Luca said, nodding slowly. 'But we're just going to have to chance it.'

She shook her head. 'This is a bad idea. We should stay this side of the river and keep to the cover of the trees.'

'We've got to get closer if we're to stand a chance of finding those tunnels. And it's either that, or wait for the patrol to catch up with us.'

Bear remained silent, staring out across the water. They had heard the drums again earlier that morning. Despite the rain liquefying the ground and all that they had done to cover their tracks, somehow the LRA had found them again. It was almost impossible to understand how. The soldiers must have kept going the entire night without a single break and were still gaining on them as the morning drew on. It was inhuman.

Finally turning back from the water, Bear shook her head.

'*C'est une vraie mauvaise idée,*' This is a really bad idea, she grumbled to herself, before kneeling down and untying her laces.

As Luca stood up and slung his boots over his shoulder, their eyes met. Neither of them had even acknowledged what had happened the previous night and now the whole thing seemed so out of context, so pathetically inappropriate. What the hell had she been thinking, having sex like that?

'Ready?' Luca asked.

Bear walked past him, wading into the water

and plunging in. They broke into front crawl, trying to keep their heads above the surface. The river was tepid and filthy, the rainwater from the previous evening washing mud from the banks into its main channel.

They had to work hard, gasping in mouthfuls of air as the current pulled them downstream. It was far stronger than either of them had anticipated and when they finally crawled out on to the opposite bank, they had almost rounded the far bend in the river, nearly a hundred metres on from where they had first started.

They slowly worked their way round the volcano's flank and into a vast moraine field filled with huge black boulders. Here, the heat was more intense; the air hot and dry, tinged with the bitter stench of sulphur. They tried to fight the burning in their throats, but a fine black dust covered everything, making them cough almost continuously. It swirled around their ankles in the slow breeze, clinging to their clothes and skin, and blackening the palms of their hands.

They had been going for almost an hour, passing several narrow tunnels that fed back into the rock along the side of the river. Luca had stopped beside each one, crawling a couple of feet inside before reaching a dead end or the tunnel becoming too narrow for him to continue. He was just crouching down near the opening to a small cave, when Bear suddenly stopped. A hundred yards further on, she could see the dim silhouette of a figure lying on the ground.

'It's got to be one of the guards,' she whispered.

Luca nodded. The figure was lying with its head towards the sun and one knee slightly raised. They waited for a couple of minutes, but there wasn't the slightest movement.

'Looks like he's asleep. We could climb higher and get above him.'

Bear stared at him, her skin darkened by the black dust. It made the whites of her eyes appear brighter, while her once-white vest had blackened to such an extent that it was practically indistinguishable from the rest of her body.

'This is crazy. What if he wakes up and sounds the alarm?' she said.

'We'll go high and just pass around the top of him. Don't worry, he won't see us.'

'What the hell was I thinking? We should never have crossed the river.'

Luca raised his finger to his lips, indicating for her to lower her voice.

'Just give me ten minutes.'

He pushed forward, quickly climbing the rocks directly above them. He then worked his way horizontally until he was positioned over the slumbering figure but still hidden behind one of the many boulders. Craning round, he was trying to get a better view when the toe of his right boot dislodged a rock, sending it clattering down the hill. It spun noisily, kicking up puffs of dust with each turn, before plunging into the shallow waters off the riverbank. It had missed the figure by only a few feet.

Breaking cover, Luca skidded downhill until

he was standing only ten feet away. With a rock held in his right hand to use as a weapon, he crept closer, trying to see into the man's face.

'*Putain*,' Shit, Bear breathed, wanting to cry out and stop him. She watched as he came right up to the man, then saw his hand slowly lower as he pitched the rock back on to the ground.

Bear ran over. In front of Luca's feet lay a corpse locked in rigor mortis. The face was turned towards them, with the palm of the right hand outstretched as if clasping at something, while a layer of dust covered the man's open eyes, dimming the dead pupils. Two congealed lines of blood ran down from his nose and the whole left side of his face was hideously deformed. A thick swelling distorted his neck and the side of his cheek, disguising his natural features and making them look somehow twisted and monstrous.

Just to the right of the corpse lay a slab of overhanging rock and beneath it the dark entrance to a tunnel. At some point in the distant past, an old lava flow had burst out of the side of the volcano, leaving a trail of igneous rock that wound down the slope like a dried-up river.

Bear crouched down, staring closer at the man's face. 'He looks like a Bantu. Maybe from one of the villages near here. But if he managed to escape, why didn't he make a break for it? Try and hide out in the jungle or something.'

'Maybe he was too weak to make it any further,' Luca replied. The man's frame looked ravaged from starvation and forced labour. 'Poor bastard.'

'What's that swelling on the side of his face? You ever seen anything like that before?'

Luca shook his head. 'No, but we met a doctor in Goma who said he'd seen swelling on the bodies dumped in the river. It's got to be the same thing.'

'So what the hell is causing it?'

Luca didn't respond. Until that moment, he had only focused on trying to track down Joshua, not sparing a thought for the kind of condition he might be in if they eventually found him.

'I wonder if they're all like that,' he whispered. 'The miners, I mean.'

Bear guessed what he was thinking.

'That doesn't mean your friend is the same. We don't even know what's causing it or what we are dealing with here.'

Luca's eyes turned to the entrance to the tunnel.

'I guess there's only one way to find out.'

He crouched down and peered into the gloom of the tunnel. It was only a couple of feet high at most and so narrow that they would have to squeeze their shoulders through. A sickening draft of air, laced with the smell of sulphur, blew against his face. For a moment he just stared, blinking against the heat.

'You really don't have to go in there,' he said. 'If this is the mine, I could get a sample for you.'

'Yeah, but I can't stay out in the open either. So it looks like I'm screwed either way.'

Luca gave a hollow smile. Drawing the survival knife from its sheath, he untwisted the top. He then pulled off his T-shirt, cutting it into strips from the bottom and carefully winding them around the blade. Taking one of the waterproof matches from the cellophane wrapper, he struck it on the rock and held it under the fabric. The flames licked up, fanning sideways in the draft.

'Stay close,' he said, then slithered forward into the darkness. Bear tried to bring herself to follow him, but instead watched as the flickering light of the torch gradually receded deeper inside. She was well used to enclosed spaces from inspecting mines for the company, but there, they had lights and machinery; it was noisy, with a multitude of workers. Here, there was only the scrape of Luca's boots against the rock and the long, beckoning darkness.

Just as the last glimmer of light faded from view, Bear slid down on to her stomach and shuffled forward. A few feet into the tunnel, the smell of sulphur intensified. It streamed into her nose and eyes. She coughed, feeling herself retch, and tried to cover her mouth with her hand as she leopard-crawled forward. Just ahead of her, she could make out the small bubble of light from Luca's torch with its flames licking up against the low ceiling. She focused on the light, trying to block out everything else.

On they went, the tunnel narrowing so much that Luca had to stop several times, wriggling through with rough jerks of his shoulders. The rock around them grew hotter with each metre. It was a dull, timeless warmth that made them sweat after only a few seconds of being inside. Just ahead, Bear heard Luca curse, then the yellow flames faltered, before plunging them into darkness. Bear stared ahead but there was not the faintest shade of grey or shadow to be seen. It was just black. She reached forward, her fingers feeling out across the rock until they connected with the heel of Luca's boot. She grabbed on to it, gripping it tight.

She felt him shuffle forward again, working his way deeper inside the tunnel. They must have been going for only five or ten minutes but each second dragged, the only sound that of their bodies scraping across the bare rock. Her elbows and knees burned from being pressed against the hot surface, while her neck muscles strained to keep her face clear of the ground. Dust clogged her mouth, congealing with her saliva and forcing her to spit every few seconds to get rid of the terrible taste.

'I see something,' Luca whispered.

Bear squeezed his foot, the knowledge that it would soon be over lending her a quick burst of energy. They both moved faster, relief flooding through them.

They began to hear noise. There was a thud, followed by the low beat of hammering. They heard a shout and the clank of metal chains. Just ahead of them, Luca found a small opening in the ceiling of the tunnel. He swivelled round so that he was facing upwards, then levered his shoulders through, one after the other, before dragging himself up and out of the tunnel.

Bear followed, desperate to free herself from the claustrophobic heat, but the mineshaft they

269

emerged into was little better. An old electric light at the far end illuminated a long line of crooked timber supports feeding back towards a single opening. On either side the black walls were scarred with drill marks, and small piles of rubble were heaped on the ground in long-forgotten piles. A wooden bucket, black with dust, lay to one side of the tunnel opening, along with a small crowbar and a lump hammer that must have belonged to the dead man outside.

Bear walked forward to the nearest pile of rubble, then crouched down, sifting through it. She brought a couple of chunks up to the light before casting them away again. After a moment she stopped, holding a small fragment of rock in front of her face. She peered at it more closely. In the dull electric light, she could just make out the vein of red lacing through it.

'It's the same stuff?' Luca asked, standing over her.

Bear nodded. 'Yeah. We were right about this place. This is where the fire coltan's coming from.'

Crouching low, they edged down the long mineshaft towards the light, moving from the shadow of one timber support to the next. The noise grew louder, hammer blow after hammer blow interspersed with the compacted thud of pneumatic drills. They saw a figure shuffle past the opening in front of them, no more than twenty feet away, but it didn't seem to notice their presence. It was dragging a filthy piece of tarpaulin heaped with black stones to some unseen destination.

They reached the end of the shaft. In front of them stretched a vast cavern with level after level carved into its sides. The levels ran in circular bands around a central atrium, like the contours of a map, before feeding up into a massive domed roof, hundreds of feet above their heads. Natural light poured into the mine through a single hole directly overhead, weakening steadily as it descended lower into the clouds of hanging dust and dark, opaque rock.

There were nine levels in all, each one ringed by a wooden balcony and covered in a mass of metal troughs moving ceaselessly up and down. The troughs were connected by heavy metal chains to a pulley system somewhere further up. Bear and Luca watched as stone from each level was carefully shovelled into the troughs before being hauled away. He could see figures now, tens of them on each level, piling their loads, moving slowly in the suffocating heat.

'Jesus Christ,' Luca breathed. He turned to Bear, but she was staring straight ahead at a couple of figures working just in front of them at the base of the mine. Both were withered to the point of starvation, moving listlessly while they scraped away the rock and gradually piled it on to a waiting tarpaulin. They looked to be on the point of collapse, and as one of them turned in the light, Luca saw that he had the same misshapen features and grotesque cranial swelling as the corpse outside. Blood was seeping out of the man's ears and he shuffled with slow jerking movements, crippled by exhaustion. His unseeing eyes seemed to look

271

right through them.

'Look at these people,' Luca whispered, his voice lost to the sound of the drilling. The air was filled with the noise of splintering rock and the clank of metal chains.

Bear pressed her mouth against his ear.

'Where are the guards? I can't see any.'

Luca's eyes steadily moved from figure to figure and up along the levels. Each person simply shuffled forward, tipping their loads into the waiting troughs before retreating into a network of mineshafts dug back from the central atrium.

'I don't see any guards either. Where the hell are they?'

'Maybe they don't come down here. Would you, if you ended up looking like those miners?'

As Bear said the words, she suddenly realised that the figure of a man was slumped on the ground no more than ten feet away from them. He was resting against the wall, with his knees tucked up to his chest and head lowered. His limbs were angular and wasted, pressed back as if fused to the rock. She was scarcely able to believe that they had been so close without seeing him, but then she started to see others too, half-hidden in the darkness; a single raised limb or the silhouette of a person slumped face down on the ground. The dead were all around them, abandoned and ignored.

Bear felt her stomach cramp. The heat and the stench of sulphur were making her nauseous. Even after all the war-torn hellholes she had been to, she had never seen anywhere more

272

pitiless and desperate.

'We can't stay here, Luca,' she hissed, nudging him with her hand. 'We've got to hurry.'

He nodded hesitantly. 'OK. We have to ask if they've seen Joshua. Someone here must know where he is.'

'Luca, look at them. They're like ghosts. They can barely stand, let alone answer questions.'

'Then we try one of the other levels further up. We've got to keep going until we get an answer.'

Bear grabbed his shoulder.

'If we go higher, we'll be caught. We should go, Luca. Get the hell out of here, while we have the chance.'

'I'm sorry, Bear, but I've got to try.'

She stared into his eyes. Now that she had discovered the origin of the fire coltan, she felt a terrible need to get out of here. The impulse overran any sense of control or composure, and she half-turned back towards the lava tunnel. She had to get away from the claustrophobia and death.

Before she could say anything more, Luca crept out of the opening to the mineshaft, skirting round the edge of the central atrium. The floor of the mine was naturally dark, lit only by the remnants of natural light flooding down from outside and the occasional electric bulb. The whole of Luca's upper body had been smeared black from the dust in the tunnel, greying the sheen of his white skin and helping him melt into the shadows. Bear watched him for a moment, slowly shaking her head as she tried to decide.

A few metres distant, Luca had stopped beside one of the thick-set timber supports, trying to work out how best to climb it. Bear watched him for a moment, cursing under her breath. Then, abruptly, she stepped out from the mine-shaft and swiftly clambered into one of the metal troughs. As Luca scrambled to get in next to her, the trough jolted and was slowly hoisted into the air.

They passed one level, then the next, keeping their backs bent into the metal frame and their heads low. Over the lip of the trough they could see more people now, working in the long lines of shafts which fanned out from the central atrium. Each one silently dug, hammered, or carried. There was an overwhelming air of sadness to them all, as if the rest of their lives had been stripped away along with the last vestiges of hope.

Luca squeezed Bear's arm as they slowly clunked past another level. Both of them leaped from the trough, landing with a thud on the rough wooden decking. They crouched down, terrified that someone had heard, but with all the noise and commotion of the mine, no one had even noticed.

'Keep away from the main area,' Luca warned, grabbing Bear's arm and pulling her down the nearest shaft. They ran further inside, turning one ninety-degree corner and then another, before coming across a man hammering a small metal spike into the rock. He moved slowly, struggling to keep the spike steady. Bear touched

274

his shoulder to attract his attention. As he turned towards her, she saw that his eyes were laced with bloodshot veins and an ugly swelling bulged at his neck.

'*Avez-vous vu un blanc?*' Have you seen a white man, Bear asked, then when his expression didn't alter, tried asking in Hema and then Swahili. The miner just stared, uncomprehendingly.

'Come on, we've got to try someone else,' Luca interrupted, pulling her back along the mineshaft.

Retracing their steps, they waited by the entrance to the main atrium, searching for guards. There was still no sign of them and it looked more and more as though the miners were being left to their own devices. Clambering on board another trough, they moved two levels higher, repeating the same process. Here, they immediately noticed the heat was less severe, while the swelling the miners suffered was also less pronounced. Each man they questioned reacted more quickly, able to focus better and actually understand what Bear was saying.

But despite this, the result was always the same. None of them had ever seen or heard of another white man in the mine.

Eventually, Bear grabbed hold of Luca's arm.

'We've been here too long,' she said. 'We can't keep going like this.'

'Just another . . .'

'*Non! Assez!*' Enough, Bear hissed, trying to control her voice. 'Luca . . .'

'We've got to find Joshua,' Luca pleaded. 'He's
. . . got to be here.'

Bear shook her head. 'Enough, Luca. We're in
the middle of the LRA base, and if we carry on
like this, we're going to get caught.'

'Please,' he said, grabbing her hand. 'Please,
just one more.'

Bear shut her eyes, the situation suddenly
feeling utterly hopeless. What Luca was doing
was sheer insanity. They would never be able to
find Joshua in all this.

They turned back to the central atrium, and
crouched beside the opening as they looked from
one face to the next. As they searched, Bear
suddenly became aware of a man's presence just
behind them. She turned, and before her was a
miner they hadn't seen before, standing with a
crowbar held loosely in his hands. He didn't
move for several seconds, his bloodshot eyes
blinking slowly.

'*Blanc*,' White man, he whispered, his voice
gravelly from disuse. Then he jerked his finger to
the balcony two levels higher on the opposite
side of the atrium.

'*Oui, un blanc*,' Bear repeated. '*Vous avez vu
un blanc là-bas?*' You've seen a white man over
there?

The man nodded slowly, before his eyes
settled on the distant light coming through from
the domed natural roof of the mine. He stayed
like that, eyes drifting in and out of focus as if he
hadn't seen the light in years.

'*Merci, merci*,' Thank you, Bear stammered.
They raced around the side of the wooden

balcony and climbed into a half-full trough moving higher. They lay perfectly still, the seconds dragging as it trundled upwards with the chains clanking from the added strain. Jumping out at the fourth level from the top, they moved into the nearest mineshaft, sprinting down it and hurdling the low piles of rubble as they ran. Some miners there were using pneumatic drills and the nearest of them stopped as they approached, his drill jerking to a standstill in his hands.

'*Où est le blanc?*' Where's the white man? Bear shouted above the din. A man slowly raised his hand, pointing further along the mineshaft. Around the second bend, Luca suddenly stopped, his boots skidding to a halt on the gravel floor. A white man was sitting with his back to them. He was desperately thin, the vertebrae of his spine visible through the soiled and ripped T-shirt he was wearing. His head was bent forward as he sorted through a small pile of rocks.

'Josh,' Luca whispered, edging closer. 'Josh, is that you?'

The man's head slowly turned at the sound, his body twisting as he tried to see behind him. As his face came into the light, Luca immediately recognised the pale blue eyes of his old friend.

Dropping down on his knees, Luca folded him in his arms, almost squeezing the wind out of Joshua's frail body as he hugged him close. Joshua's eyes were blank with shock. He tried to speak, but his cracked lips only parted a little.

'Luca?' he managed.

Luca pulled back, a broad smile breaking through the layers of dirt on his face as he nodded. His eyes shone with happiness as he grasped Joshua by his shoulders, shaking him lightly as if to wake him from a dream.

'What . . . ' Joshua stammered, trying to understand what was happening. 'Don't tell me they got you too?'

Luca's hands gripped his shoulders.

'No, Josh, we got in through a tunnel at the base of the mine. We're here to rescue you.'

Joshua's face twisted in confusion as he stared at his old friend. He motioned for Luca to help him up, and staggered to his feet.

'Rescue?' he asked, gripping on to Luca's forearm. 'There's another way out?'

Luca nodded. 'We found the tunnel from the outside. One of the miners had been drilling down when he must have broken into an old lava flow and followed it out. We've been running through the whole damn' mine looking for you.'

Joshua stood, shaking his head in disbelief.

'You found a way out?' he gasped.

'Yeah, we did,' Luca said, smiling widely. 'And we're getting you the hell out of here.'

Joshua went rigid at the prospect of escape. He glanced past Luca and Bear to where three other miners had followed them down the tunnel. They were staring expectantly, their whole bodies taut with nervous excitement.

'*Dites aux autres, nous partirons d'ici,*' Joshua announced before Luca could stop him. He'd come to rescue only his friend, but it seemed Joshua had other ideas.

25

Two more men arrived at the end of the mineshaft. They were covered in dirt from head to toe, every pore clogged with dust and the palms of their hands charcoal black. They stood in an awkward group, wretched and emaciated, their clothes no more than tatters of old fabric.

Luca turned as Bear came nearer.

'*C'est fou!*' This is madness, she whispered. 'He wants to bring the whole damn' mine. What do you not understand about this? We're going to get caught.'

Luca nodded and grabbed hold of Joshua's arm. 'We've been here too long, Josh. We've got to move.'

Joshua looked around in despair. There were so many others, so many desperate others, he should try to save. Over the last few months, some of them had learned that he was a doctor and had asked him to treat their wounds. More often than not, there was nothing he could do, but they still looked to him as their leader, heaping what remained of their hopes on his shoulders.

'Josh,' Luca pleaded. 'We can't take any more. We have to leave *now!*'

Joshua hesitated for a moment more, then shuffled towards Luca. As he moved, he reached out one arm for balance, leaning his whole weight on his friend's shoulder. His right leg was totally useless, pulling behind him with the toes just dragging across the ground.

'What the hell happened to you?' Luca asked.

'Mordecai,' Joshua replied, in a low voice. 'I got caught trying to escape and he severed my hamstring. Bastard crippled me for life.' He looked into Luca's eyes. 'We are going to make it out this time, aren't we?'

Luca nodded. 'Yeah. This time we're going home.'

'Home,' Joshua repeated, drawing out the word.

'Yeah, but come on. We ain't there yet.'

Joshua went up to one of the miners who had just arrived. The man carefully unfolded a filthy rag. Inside was an old metal compass with the glass face torn off and the dial faded by the sun. Beside it were a box of matches, a small knife with a crude wooden handle, bound together with wire, and a sealed cylindrical cardboard tube with Chinese characters stamped on one side. It was an old military flare left behind by one of the guards.

'Our escape kit,' Joshua said, staring down at the pathetic collection of possessions. It was all that they had been able to scrape together over four months. The miner then handed Joshua a small plastic gourd of water. He drank from it deeply, before giving it to Luca.

'Come on,' Luca said, wiping his mouth with the back of his hand. 'We've got to keep moving.'

The group set off down the mineshaft with one of the miners leading the way and Bear closely tucked in behind. She moved stealthily, with her body pressed flat against the roughly hewn rock and her eyes fixed on the distant light of the atrium. As they drew closer, they heard the noise of the metal chains grow louder; the troughs moving up and down in constant motion.

'Where the hell are all the guards?' Luca whispered.

'They're too scared of the fire coltan to come down here,' panted Joshua, his eyes narrowing in pain as he forced himself forward. 'They've barricaded us in from the outside, leaving only a few of them on the top level to send down the bread and water each day. But every few weeks this evil son-of-a-bitch Captain comes in and they flush everyone down to the next level.'

'So how come you're still up here? You've been missing for months.'

'We managed to dig ourselves a hiding place and they missed us the last three rotations.'

Joshua swallowed, trying to get some moisture into his mouth. He hadn't spoken this much in as long as he could remember.

'Mordecai himself even comes into the mine. He preaches at us, shouting down like some kind of goddamn' Messiah, saying that we have to pass through the nine levels to 'cleanse' our ways before they'll let us out. Some even believe him, but most of us know that down there . . . ' he paused, the lines around his eyes tightening ' . . . down there, there's only death.'

'So what the hell is happening to everyone?' Luca whispered. 'What's going on here?'

'He's got us all down here digging, but

281

something bad happens when this new coltan combines with heat. Tumours start developing, the cancer spreading faster than anything I've ever seen before. And the greater the heat, the worse it gets. Down on the lowest levels, those poor bastards only last a couple of weeks before the swelling gets into their brain.'

Bear and the lead miner reached the entrance to the atrium. The others waited, keeping out of sight in the mine-shaft. Luca could see her crouching down, her face tilted up, searching for guards.

Joshua nodded grimly. 'It's like some sort of sick, fucking merry-go-round. Fresh workers brought in to the top, the dead flushed out from the bottom. Then, they just toss the bodies into the river and let them float off downstream.'

He slumped back against the wall, chest heaving from the effort of moving so fast. Luca could see his collarbones rising up and down above the threadbare neck of his T-shirt, his flesh sunken from malnutrition. Joshua was so weak, he barely had the strength to stand.

'The worst part is, I don't even know what they use it for. Here we all are, dying down here . . . and for what?'

Luca turned back to him, pressing his shoulder under Joshua's arm to prop him up. 'All we know is that it's taken out of here by helicopter and then sold to the Chinese in Goma. We don't know what happens after that, but Bear thinks it's something to do with mobile phones.'

'Mobile phones? We're all dying so that

somebody can make a fucking phone call?'

Luca nodded slowly. 'It looks that way.'

'Jesus,' Joshua whispered. 'What's going to happen if they've started making mobile phones out of this shit? If it's anything like what happens to us down here, then it'll kill anyone that uses them. Don't they get it? This stuff reacts to heat. And computers, phones . . . all those kinds of things generate heat whenever they're switched on. Since I've been here, tons and tons of fire coltan's been shipped out. God only knows how many phones they've made. Millions of people could be affected.'

'Bear was only guessing. It might not be as bad as all that.'

'If it's got anything to do with that bastard Mordecai, then it'll be worse, I promise you.' Joshua shut his eyes. 'We've got to warn someone. Tell them what this stuff does.'

'Whatever happens, we've got to get out of here first,' Luca replied. Bear was still squatting down by the entrance to the atrium. What the hell was taking her so long?

'I guess the only good thing is that there's barely any left,' Joshua said, almost to himself.

'What? But there's hundreds of you still down here.'

'I know, but trust me, the whole mine's running dry. They had us breaking up all the old rocks that were already discarded, trying to scrape enough of it together for the last shipment. Everyone's been terrified about what Mordecai was planning to do with us all when it finally runs out.'

'Well, that's not going to happen now,' Luca said, pulling Joshua's arm up over his shoulder again and dragging him further up the line of waiting miners towards Bear.

'I still can't see any guards,' she whispered.

'Just wait. They're up there,' Joshua replied, dropping down on to his hands and knees and shuffling forward. His face was caught by the silvery light filtering down from the top of the cavern as his eyes scanned the upper balconies. He waited, the seconds passing, each of them growing more and more impatient.

'Look!' he breathed, slowly raising a finger to point. A skinny teenager had moved to the edge of the wooden balcony, briefly peering out over the edge. He wore a bright red bandana tied across his mouth and nose and was naked from the waist up. An AK-47 was slung across his back with a small portable radio clipped into the waistband of his trousers.

'How many are there?' Bear asked.

'I'm not sure. Eight to ten at the most.'

'That's it? How do they keep you all in line?'

Joshua shook his head painfully. 'Just look at us. Most of us barely have the strength to stand, let alone fight.'

Bear tugged him back into the shadows as the soldier came further on to the balcony, turning his back to them as he leaned against the railing, casually speaking to someone out of sight.

'Get everyone into the metal troughs and then aim for that tunnel down there,' she said, pointing at the mineshaft they had surfaced through.

'*Nous devons descendre au niveau le plus bas*,' We have to go down to the lowest level, Joshua whispered. '*Puis, suivez-moi au tunnel.*' Then, follow me to the tunnel.

As soon as he mentioned the lower level, the miners started protesting. They had spent so long trying to avoid being sent down there that the mere thought of it filled them with horror. They shook their heads, murmuring anxiously together, while the miner nearest to Bear slowly shut his eyes, letting a tear run freely down his grimy cheek.

'*Silence!*' Joshua hissed. '*Venez maintenant ou restez ici. Choisissez!*' Either come now or stay here. Your choice.

They fell silent, realising that there was no alternative.

'You and Joshua are the slowest,' Bear whispered to Luca. 'You go first.'

'But what about you?'

'Someone's got to stay and lead these other guys out.'

Luca gently squeezed her left shoulder. 'Bear, that was never part of the deal. You go first. We'll wait until you're clear.'

'No, we'll be moving faster than you and can catch up.' She looked straight into his eyes. 'And listen to me, Luca. In case we get separated, you have to head due south to the MONUC compound. There was this logging road I saw on the map that runs east to west through the forest. It's about fifteen clicks from here. Hit the road, then turn west and it will take you straight to the compound.'

'Bear, listen to me . . . it's not going to come to that. We're all going to get out of here together.'

'I know.' She paused, her eyes fixed on his. 'There's something else. When you get to MONUC, if they won't help, then try somehow to get hold of my father, Jean-Luc Étienne.'

'Your father? What's he got to do with any of this?'

'He's an old merc based in Goma, running a freighting business across the borders. He's a military man and might be able to help if everything else fails.'

Luca stared at her blankly, confused as to why she hadn't mentioned this before, but knew only too well that this wasn't the time for explanations.

'Now, get the hell out of here!'

Luca stared at her a moment longer, then nodded. 'Stay right behind us, OK?'

Bear pushed him forward. '*Allez!*' Go!

Luca shuffled forward so that he was squatting at the entrance to the mineshaft. Joshua came up next to him and together, they waited, watching the guard and the clanking metal troughs moving up and down. One to their right slowly descended past the first level, then the second, the chains swaying and banging against the rickety wooden balcony.

'Ready?' Luca breathed. He could feel the muscles in his thighs tense with anticipation. As the trough passed their level, he surged forward, yanking Joshua on to his feet and pitching him over the low railing. Joshua's body slammed in

286

like a deadweight, the back of his shoulders and head smacking against the beaten metal. With a quick look up to the guard, Luca nimbly swung his legs over the railing and landed at the other side of the trough, his knees flexing under the impact. Both of them stayed absolutely still with their bodies pressed down flat. Only their eyes moved, watching.

Down the trough went, the chains slowly grinding through the distant pulleys as they steadily descended into the belly of the mine. They could feel the air grow hotter, while the natural light slowly faded to a deep grey, lost in the hanging clouds of dust. The dim electric bulbs were all that was left; their orange-yellow light casting little more than shadows against the black walls.

Luca jumped out and pulled Joshua to his feet, skirting round the side of the central well and over to the shaft they had entered by. He looked up, unable to see Bear but knowing that she would be watching their every move.

'Come on,' he whispered under his breath. 'Please, get out of here.'

★　★　★

'*Maintenant!*' Now! Bear hissed, waving her hand forward. First one, then two of the miners moved out on to the wooden balcony, their backs bent as they kept low. Both had their eyes locked on the highest level. The guard had gone, but they were terrified he might suddenly reappear.

'*Vite!* Faster' Bear urged them on as the metal

trough slowly drew level. The first miner awkwardly swung one leg up on to the railing, trying to manoeuvre his body over, but he wasn't quite tall enough. He struggled for a few precious seconds, while his companion waited for him to get clear.

'*Merde!*' Shit! Bear cursed, watching the debacle slowly unfold. She sprang forward, crossing the balcony in only two strides before crashing into the miner, shunting him over the edge and into the trough. She heard a low metallic thud, then grabbed the second miner and manhandled him over the railing, into the open arms of the container below.

As the trough slowly continued downwards, she ran back under cover, crouching in the shadows and waiting for the next trough to pass. She could feel her heart pumping in her chest as she waited, the seconds dragging by. Staring down at her watch in frustration, she realised four minutes already had passed without another trough even coming close. Then, just further to the left, one finally drew level.

'*N'arrêtez pas!*' Don't stop! Bear hissed as the next two miners clambered past her, scrambling over the railing without looking back. They threw themselves over the edge with such abandon that the first nearly missed the trough altogether, only managing to pull himself back inside with the help of the other.

Bear turned towards the last remaining miner, who was crouching next to her. He was a small man, with long hair so dirty that it had matted into thick, fist-sized clumps. As their eyes met, she realised that he was absolutely terrified. Bear reached out and took hold of his hand, feeling his whole body trembling in her grasp.

'*Il sera bien*,' It'll be all right, she whispered, attempting a smile. '*Quel est votre nom?*' What's your name?

The man stared at her as if it was the first time anyone had ever asked him his name.

'Idi,' he said softly. His lips then curled slightly as he tried to return her smile. '*Merci beaucoup de nous aider*.' Thank you for helping us.

Bear gently squeezed his hand in response, then glanced up to where another trough was slowly pulling level.

'OK, Idi,' she said. '*Suivez-moi*.' Follow me.

Letting go of his hand, she bounded across the decking, clearing the railings in a single jump. But as she landed inside the trough, her right ankle buckled from the impact, sending her toppling over and on to her back.

'*Sautez!*' Jump! she mouthed to Idi, raising her arms as if to catch him, while the distance between them yawned wider with each second.

'*Sautez!*' Jump!'

Without looking down, Idi hurled himself forwards, misjudging the distance so badly that only the top half of his body made it into the trough. He came crashing down with a massive thud, his whole body sliding down towards the abyss. His eyes pleaded for help, while his legs kicked out, desperately cycling in mid-air, until finally Bear managed to lunge forward and catch hold of his wrists.

There was the sound of yelling from

somewhere higher up, then a burst of machine-gun fire. It rang out across the mine; the tat-tat-tat of bullets cutting above the heavy thud of the pneumatic drills. They raked across the rock face before smacking into the metal rim of the trough and ricocheting off in a blaze of white sparks.

Bear felt Idi's body suddenly stiffen in her grip. A split second later, his right shoulder exploded in a spray of blood and splintered bone, splattering across her face and into her eyes. She went rigid, holding on to his wrists with her eyes screwed shut against the blood, and temporarily blinded. She waited for the next burst of gunfire, but none came. High above their position, the soldiers were reloading.

Idi's wrists were slipping from her grasp. Then, the trough suddenly smacked into one of the support beams of the mine, pitching them violently to one side and tearing him away. Bear cried out, dragging the back of her hand across her face to wipe the blood from her eyes, but it was already too late to see where he had fallen. He was somewhere beneath her, lost to the darkness of the mine.

There was another burst of gunfire. Bear screamed, pulling back from the edge and curling up into the foetal position with her hands clamped over her ears against the deafening noise. Bullets hammered into the metal and wood all around her, but it was obvious that the soldiers were firing blind and she was too far away for them to be able to aim accurately.

Curling up tighter, Bear lay still, her mind

reeling from fear and shock. There was nothing she could do except wait until she reached the floor of the mine.

Her trough stopped. The chains bounced up and down, flexing under tension as, slowly, they began to bring her back up to the surface once again.

'*Aidez-moi!*' Help! she screamed, looking frantically from side to side across the atrium. But there was nothing for it. She was going to have to jump.

Clutching the rough metal rim of the trough, she crouched down as low as she could. She tried to judge the distance below her, but everything was blurred in the darkness. There was no way of telling how high she still was above the ground. There was only the void, with black clouds of dust hanging in the breathless air.

She just couldn't do it — couldn't let go and fall into nothingness.

There was another burst of gunfire and Bear suddenly lost her grip. She felt a second of weightlessness, then her whole body slammed into the ground. The force of the blow jarred through from her ankles to knees, then up the length of her spine, folding her in half.

She lay there with the wind driven from her lungs, feeling as if her whole spine had somehow been twisted in two. She tried to shout for help again, but the words died on her lips. Staring out, she felt her vision start to tunnel, darkening at the edges until all she could see was a single electric light bulb hanging dimly in the distance.

Hands grabbed her body and arms, lifting her off the ground. It took several seconds before she realised it was Joshua's miners. They were dragging her towards the mine-shaft and the tunnel beyond.

With their shoulders supporting her, Bear stumbled past the long line of timber supports. She saw the miner's crowbar, then the opening to the lava flow. This was it! They were at the tunnel entrance. The miners immediately pressed her down into the tunnel, so that she was lying flat on her stomach on the hard ground. She could hear the pained grunts of one of the other miners already working his way further ahead, but could see nothing in the darkness.

Forcing herself forward, she moaned softly, feeling as if every muscle in her body had been bruised by the fall. But she kept pushing, trying to inch her way out as the heat and smell intensified. It felt as if the tunnel were closing in around her and, as the minutes passed, she could feel herself becoming weaker. The adrenalin was starting to fade, leaving her utterly exhausted. There was nothing left to give. All she wanted to do was lie still and finally let it all end.

She stopped, too drained to continue, but hands pushed against the soles of her feet. One of the miners was just behind her, shoving her on, desperate to get out of the hideous tunnel.

Up ahead, she could see a glimmer of light. The tunnel opening was only fifty feet further on, but instead of feeling elated, she suddenly felt a cold wash of fear. Then she realised why. The light wasn't natural. It was coming from a torch beam.

Somehow the LRA had already found them.

26

Fabrice let himself into the back office of the Soleil Club and bolted the door behind him. It was 6.30 in the morning. He sniffed. The air was heavy with the familiar stench of spilled liquor and overflowing ashtrays.

Tables stood in a semicircle around the bar with half-filled glasses stacked on top. A strip light had shattered over one of the pool tables in the far corner, showering the red felt with splinters of glass and a thin coating of neon powder. Lying just next to the table was one of the pool cues. It had been snapped in half during a brawl, broken into a jagged spike.

Fabrice stared at the carnage, whistling softly to himself. He felt the soles of his tan loafers stick slightly to the concrete floor as he walked over to the bar. He had just showered and was looking fresh in a pair of pressed white slacks and a laundered cream shirt. Picking his way round a fallen bar stool, he found the youngest of his barmen fast asleep, with the side of his head slumped against the counter. Fabrice pulled him up by the neck of his T-shirt.

'What's their tab so far?' he asked without preamble. He glanced across at the group of people sitting in the far corner near the dance floor. They had been drinking hard since early the previous night.

The young barman blinked several times,

trying to galvanise his brain into action. He searched for his notepad, eventually finding it half-soaked in alcohol and lying on the floor next to his feet. His eyes scanned across the smudged pencil scrawls, trying to decipher what he had written.

'I'm not exactly sure, sir,' he stammered, 'but Monsieur Étienne, he gave me this to cover the charges.'

He pulled a sweaty wad of US dollars out of his pocket.

'There's five hundred, sir.'

Fabrice nodded slowly.

'OK,' he said. 'Now get your ass out of here.'

As he made for the exit, Fabrice called after him: 'And tell everyone I want this shit cleaned up by two this afternoon. No later.'

Leaving the notes where they lay, he reached down to a low drawer and pulled out a ten-year-old single malt whisky. Tucking his fingers into four glass tumblers, he slowly approached the group in the far corner.

Eleven men lay slumped in the low chairs together with a few of the club's girls. Of the eleven, only three were still awake. They sat hunched over the low table with cigarette smoke curling up from an overflowing ashtray in the centre. The last of their drinks stood bunched up next to a near-empty bottle of cheap brandy, while on the far side of the table lay a rolled up fifty-franc Congolese note and a discarded credit card. Pressed into the plastic surface of the table were faint smudges of white powder.

As Fabrice approached, the men looked up

with bloodshot eyes.

'One on the house?' he asked, raising the bottle. All of them were mercenaries with faces hardened from years of fighting. Despite their casual clothes and long hair, there was still something military about the way they sat and moved. They had spent the better part of their lives in the cruellest, most war-torn shitholes on the planet. And it showed in everything they did.

Jean-Luc Étienne was one of the three men still awake. He glanced up at Fabrice.

'You're a good man,' he breathed, his voice rough from cigarettes. 'It's another beautiful day in Africa and we thought we'd spend it getting as drunk as shit.'

'Wise man,' Fabrice answered, pouring out a couple of drinks and handing one across. 'This stuff should see you on your way. A little boom-boom never hurt anyone.'

He watched as Jean-Luc collected himself, then sniffed loudly. He grimaced as the remnants of cocaine burned his nostrils, making his nose run again. Wiping it with the back of his hand, he smiled at Fabrice.

'You must be spoiling us,' he said. 'This is the good stuff. I thought you only brought it out for the diplomats.' There was humour in his eyes, but Fabrice didn't relax for a second. He knew that smile all too well and knew how capricious it could be. The drunken merc before him had a quick temper, and even quicker reflexes.

Fabrice raised his glass in a toast before slugging back the whisky. He didn't usually drink this early in the morning, but this time it was worth making an exception.

'Only the good stuff for my man. You been flying recently or those MONUC pricks got you grounded again?'

'You know, Fabrice, you're a fucking class act,' Jean-Luc said, swaying slightly. He raised his glass and Fabrice dutifully refilled it, struggling to stop the whisky from washing over the rim as Jean-Luc's hand shook. 'Anyone gives you any shit, you come speak to me. You hear me, Fabrice? And by the way, I owe you one for letting us stay on in the bar last night.'

'Any time.'

'No, I'm serious. Some of my boys really needed a drink. I owe you one.' Jean-Luc paused, his face draining of any trace of bonhomie. 'And I always pay my debts. You got that?' His cheeks reddened suddenly with anger. 'You hear what I am saying? I pay my fucking debts.'

'*Oui, je vous entends très bien,*' Yes, I hear you very well, Fabrice replied calmly. 'Why don't you guys all have another shot? Get the good stuff while you can.'

He turned to the other two left conscious and sitting at the table, finding them deep in conversation. They were the pilots for the Rooivalk helicopter and since they had returned from their last sortie, the younger of the two, Anton, had done little else but chain smoke cigarettes and down shots. He had come in as the new rear-gunner pilot only five months ago, and at twenty-six years old was still new to the game. With short dark hair and a thin, wiry

297

build, he looked younger than his age, with narrow brown eyes that darted continually from one thing to the next. Despite his tough Israeli heritage, he was always teased for being the sensitive one of the group, usually preferring to sit quietly and watch events unfold. But something had happened to change all that.

On the other side of the table, Fabrice recognised Jean-Luc's right hand man, Laurent. He was talking in a low voice like a protective father, occasionally resting one of his huge arms on Anton's shoulder. At six foot four and over one hundred and twenty kilos, he was a monster of a man with thick, curly black hair, greying at the temples, and pale blue eyes which shone with withering intensity.

Fabrice had got chatting to him once before and soon realised that Laurent was the kind of man who'd tell you his whole life story on a first meeting. He had been raised in the Karoo desert on his family's farm, before being conscripted by the South African military to fight the SWAPO guerrillas on the Angolan border. It was a dirty little war, filled with bloody injustices and complicated politics, yet Laurent talked about it in absolutes; everything to him was black or white. Fabrice had quickly understood that this was the way he approached his whole life. Everything was rigid, mechanised. You got orders. You followed them.

As Fabrice patiently waited for either of the pilots to respond to his offer of a drink, Anton suddenly shouted a string of expletives. Laurent didn't react, but instead stared up towards the ceiling and exhaled heavily, expelling a great cloud of cigarette smoke. He had been dealing with Anton's explosive outbursts all night and was tiring of the bewildering range of emotions the boy seemed to be going through. It had been like that ever since the last sortie.

They had been ordered to peel off in a search and destroy, but as they closed in, had realised that the target was nothing more than a couple of pygmy boys, firing at them with bows and arrows. Anton had radioed in for clarification, but orders were orders. Seconds later, he had opened up with the 20mm cannon.

On the return flight, Laurent had noticed the smell of vomit even before they had touched down in Goma. During the post-flight checks, he had seen it on the side of Anton's overalls and realised just how much of a mess the kid was in. Ten hours of drinking later and Anton was still as worked up as he had been the moment they arrived in the club.

'Hey!' Jean-Luc shouted, clicking his fingers to get their attention. Anton and Laurent fell silent, turning to him in surprise.

'When a man like Fabrice offers you a drink, you drink it,' he growled, his eyes on Anton. 'Anyway, you should know by now . . . drinking's the only way to get through all of this shit.'

They both took the whisky, thanking Fabrice as Jean-Luc settled back into his seat.

'Been meaning to speak to you,' Fabrice said now. 'My man down at the airport was telling me there's some movement going on.'

Jean-Luc's expression didn't change.

'Yeah,' Fabrice continued. 'He said that there's some cargo coming in and out, but it seems that this time no one wants to cut me into the deal.'

Jean-Luc inhaled slowly. 'You should tell your man at the airport it can be dangerous, talking out of turn around here.'

Fabrice gave him a glowing smile. ''You know what it's like. Everyone knows everyone's business. Talking all the time.'

'Such busy little bees,' Jean-Luc whispered.

'Well, since I sorted out those import licences for you, thought you might want to return the favour? I'm not asking much, but you know how it is round here, Jean-Luc. Everything comes through me.'

Jean-Luc's eyes widened as he inhaled deeply through his nose, flaring the nostrils. The drugs had dilated his pupils so much that his eyes looked entirely black.

'Get me decent fuel rates from 'your man' at the airport and I'll cut you in. Ten per cent of my take.'

Fabrice raised his glass. It had been easier than he had expected. Jean-Luc was obviously in an amenable mood.

'Consider it done.'

'Now leave me the fuck alone,' Jean-Luc slurred, the naked aggression deepening his voice.

Fabrice's smile stayed locked in place as he leaned forward and gently placed the rest of the bottle of malt on the table.

'All yours,' he said. Then, when he was halfway out of his seat, he paused 'By the way, word is someone's looking for you. Seems like some Americans want to meet you in person. My boys on the border said they came across last night, asking questions. You need a place to hide out?'

Jean-Luc's jaw clenched as he processed the information.

'Tell them I'm here. I'll be waiting.'

27

Two men came in through the main entrance to the Soleil Club and stopped near the pool table. They waited, letting their eyes grow accustomed to the dark, before the one closest to the door quietly spoke into the radio mic attached to his lapel. A moment later, four more men strode into the bar with Devlin the last in line.

Laurent was the first to see them. With the toe of his boot, he kicked two of the other sleeping mercs awake as Jean-Luc slowly raised his head. The Americans fanned out into the room, taking up covering positions as Devlin drew nearer their table. They all had muscular necks and forearms, and haircuts that looked too short to be anything else but military. They were dressed in lightweight trousers, browns and tans, with an assortment of safari jackets bulging slightly under the left arm. To a man, they were staring at Jean-Luc.

As Devlin stepped further into the light, his lips parted a little, revealing clean white teeth.

'I see you got your mouth fixed up,' Jean-Luc remarked, his voice slow and gravelly. 'But then again, you Yanks always did like big teeth, didn't you? Heard you have to file them down into these little points just to get those glossy caps on. *Mon Dieu, c'est dégueulasse!* How much did those nice, big white teeth cost you, Devlin? Or did the CIA pay for them?'

Devlin didn't react, standing stiffly in the centre of the room.

'We're here for the co-ordinates of the mine,' he said, his Southern accent making the words come out in a low drawl. 'You got your price for the sample of fire coltan. Now I want to know exactly where it's coming from.'

Jean-Luc leaned forward. 'Have we been flying a little too low for your radar to track us? Pity, that.'

'This ain't the time for games, you French son-of-a-bitch. Tell me what I want to know.'

Jean-Luc yawned, stretching his arms up and flexing out his back. In the silence, Devlin shifted his weight in anticipation.

'No,' Jean-Luc said with an air of finality.

'Don't fuck with us, Étienne, or we will make your life a living hell. You know who I work for.'

Jean-Luc stared at him for a moment longer. 'You just don't get it, do you? You're in the Congo now, and there's nothing you can do about anything that goes on here. So, little man, why don't you stop trying to prove you've got balls and get back on your plane?'

'Screw this,' Devlin seethed. 'I warned you. Now, give me those co-ordinates!'

Devlin reached out his hand as if he could snatch the information out of Jean-Luc's grasp. As he moved his men reacted, hands reaching for their guns. Laurent and the rest of Jean-Luc's men were rigid with anticipation. Some already had their hands on their own pistols.

'Now look what you've done,' Jean-Luc tutted. 'Got everyone worked up, and all I wanted to do was get drunk for a couple of days. You know something, Devlin? You're really messing with my chi.'

Devlin glowered, trying to contain his rage but mindful of exactly how carefully he had to play this. There was just too much at stake to let things get out of control. A couple of seconds passed, with the room absolutely silent, before Devlin slowly lowered his hands.

'OK, Étienne. If this is how you want to play it. How much do y'all want to drink yourself into the next year?'

Jean-Luc inhaled deeply. 'I'm not selling. Come back tomorrow.'

Devlin shook his head in disbelief, his cheeks flushing red with anger. But he couldn't lose his temper. He had to hold back and not rise to this son-of-a-bitch's petty games. Ever since Langley had identified the fire coltan as the substance used in the new generation of Chinese satellite phones, the situation had escalated beyond anything he could have imagined. Right now, he needed to keep his head.

Only two days ago, ChinaCell had made their launch public, and since that time US scientists had been working around the clock trying to understand how they could produce a regular handset small enough to communicate with low-orbit satellites. These things were flooding into every high-street store, crippling the West's telecom brands as customers queued around the block for the handsets to come on sale.

It was only when they had discovered that fire coltan was crucial to the capacitors and antennae, enabling the high-frequency bursts to the satellites, that they started to piece it all together. Fire coltan made the circuitry run hotter than normal, but aside from that, the technology was flawless.

Suddenly, Devlin's investigation had escalated from being a minor provincial affair into a matter of national security. The entire Western communications platform was being overrun, and fire coltan was the mineral at the centre of it all. The directive was simple — they had to get their own supply and take control of that mine.

But it was a balancing act. Everyone knew that they could never openly challenge another veto member of the UN Security Council. They couldn't be seen to be interfering with Chinese interests in Africa, and so from the outset this was a war that was going to be fought by proxies.

A task force had already been sent to negotiate with the Mai-Mai south of Bukavu. The rebels there were renowned for their brutality, contravening almost every single rule of engagement during the bloody years of the Congolese civil war, but despite their pariah status, they were the only rebel force left in the Congo who might have a chance of defeating the LRA. Despite the fact that the UN had spent almost a decade trying to disarm them, now all that was going to change.

An American C-130 Hercules had dropped a huge shipment of weaponry at a Mai-Mai outpost near the Rwandese border and by now the rebels were already on the move, heading north towards the Ituri. They knew the mine was somewhere in the forest, but had still to get the exact co-ordinates.

And here Devlin was, right at the centre of it all. Until the main task force arrived from Langley, he was the man on the ground in a situation fast climbing the ranks of importance in US foreign policy. All eyes were turning to the Congo. And for the next eight hours, he was the man in charge.

Devlin stared at Jean-Luc, watching the way his head swayed from the booze. The Frenchman was a belligerent animal with no understanding of the value of the information he possessed. Trying to beat it out of him would take too much time. But there was another way.

'You know, since you boys have been buzzing the skies around here, we've been picking up a bit of chatter. Usual stuff, nothing fancy, then we heard a mayday call from a Cessna 206. Call sign Golf Hotel Juliet. Mean anything to you?'

Jean-Luc stared at Devlin blankly. Casually reaching inside the pocket of his safari jacket, Devlin took out an iPod and a small black speaker. As he set them down on the table, he stared at Jean-Luc.

'Still doesn't ring any bells?'

They all listened as a woman's voice played out softly across the room. She was obviously in distress, running through the protocols of a mayday call, but as she reached the co-ordinates of her crash location, the recording had been deliberately wiped clean. The room was silent for several seconds before Devlin spoke again. This time, he was smiling.

'We did some checking and the plane's registered to one Beatrice Makuru. Damn' shame, but it looks like she was shot down over the Ituri.'

'What the hell was Bear doing up here?' Laurent interupted, his voice barely more than a whisper.

'She and two white men busted her plane out of MONUC quarantine three days ago.'

'Who were they?'

Devlin shrugged. 'Like I give a shit. Now, you listen good Étienne because you're gonna get this deal only once. You give me the co-ordinates of Mordecai's mine and I'll tell you exactly where her plane went down.'

Jean-Luc's eyes glassed over as he felt a flood of emotion hit him. He couldn't quite believe it. Bear had crashed her plane. The news that she might be in pain or hurt filled him with a sense of paternal outrage; something he hadn't even thought existed in him any more. But it was there, visceral and uncontrollable, suddenly making him boil with anger.

The years seemed to peel back and he could hear the same muffled static in her voice from when he had first taught her how to fly, diving low over the savannah. So much time had passed, so many regrets. He had presumed the memories were all but buried. But still he thought back to that night in Cape Town . . . the night he had last seen her, all those years ago.

Laurent followed the direction of Devlin's gaze, knowing just how much Jean-Luc's little girl meant to him. To some degree she had been raised by them all, touring with the squad from mission to mission, country to country. And now Bear was the one thing they never spoke about.

Devlin snapped his fingers in front of Jean-Luc's face.

'Looks like you'll be giving me those co-ordinates after all,' he said, not bothering to hide his glee.

'How do I know she survived the crash?' Jean-Luc whispered. 'What if I give you the information and she turns out to be dead already?'

'You don't. She could be alive or dead, but guess what? You're shit out of options. But do make your mind up quickly, because if she is alive, you'd better pray you get to her before the LRA do.' Devlin's smile widened. 'I saw a photo of your girl on file. Pretty. I bet she's just the LRA's type.'

Laurent shook his head in dismay. Don't toy with Jean-Luc, he wanted to say. Especially not about his daughter.

'So,' Devlin continued. 'We got a deal?'

'You'll get the co-ordinates for the mine,' Jean-Luc said. 'Now, leave.'

Devlin's smile twisted with uncertainty, not wanting to lose the momentum of this encounter. 'I don't think y'all really understand how things work,' he began, but Jean-Luc suddenly jumped off the sofa, seizing Devlin's throat with his right hand. The speed of it took everyone by surprise. There was a delay before the room erupted in a flurry of movement, as both sides reached for their guns.

'Wait!' Devlin screamed, the word coming out in a strangled wheeze. 'Don't . . . shoot!'

Jean-Luc put his face close to the American's. 'You'll have your co-ordinates and you'll get your bloody little war. Now . . . tell me where she crashed before I rip your throat out.'

Devlin struggled in his grip, tilting his chin down to try and relieve the pressure on his windpipe. He could smell the alcohol, rank on Jean-Luc's breath and skin, and stared into his bloodshot eyes, terrified. His mind raced as he desperately tried to keep a handle on the situation.

'OK . . . OK,' he wheezed, signalling to one of his men to hand over a piece of paper. Laurent snatched it from his grasp.

Jean-Luc held on to him for a moment longer before releasing his grip. Devlin staggered back towards his own men, before leaning forward to rest his hands on his knees.

'The Mai-Mai are already marching north,' he wheezed. 'You better hurry . . . because they'll be past that position before daybreak tomorrow. Now, give me those goddamn' co-ordinates.'

Jean-Luc didn't answer, only turning towards Laurent.

'Captain, I want a complete weapons check of the Rooivalk. Lose the ATGMs and take a full complement of MK4s with the cannon set to five-round bursts.' His gaze swooped over the other men. 'Take all you can carry of the 7.62mm rounds and I want each Oryx loaded with a full med kit and rescue gear for ground extraction — two-hundred-metre ropes and the winch systems up and running.'

His men took in the information with quick nods of their head, the drunken lethargy evaporating. They hadn't heard Jean-Luc talk like this since the old days.

'We leave in an hour. And, Captain, I want full thermal imaging on the Rooivalk.'

Laurent nodded smartly. 'Yes, sir.'

'Now, give them what they want.'

Scribbling the co-ordinates of the mine on to the back of a paper serviette, Laurent passed it across to Devlin. Then he led Jean-Luc's men towards the exit.

'This better be right, Étienne,' Devlin warned, waving the serviette in front of him. 'Or I promise you, we'll come for you.'

Jean-Luc returned his gaze.

'Don't worry,' he whispered. 'I'm going to pay you a special visit when I get back.'

28

Luca lay on his back next to Joshua, staring up at the open sky. Sweat ran down his forehead, mingling with the river water soaking his hair. He was too exhausted to move. The swim across the river had been gruelling, with the current pulling them much further downstream than they had anticipated. Now, they lay on their backs, the black mud of the riverbank oozing up around their shoulders, trying to muster the strength to move.

'We've got to wait . . . ' Joshua panted ' . . . wait for the others, I mean.' His voice was little more than a whisper and he looked utterly broken by the swim. On the last section, all he had been able to do was grip on to Luca's shoulders. The extra weight had pulled Luca down almost beneath the surface so that he had had to fight for every lungful of air.

'I know,' Luca replied, too tired to say anything more. He forced himself up on to his knees with a low groan and reached out one hand. The palm was black and Joshua stared at it for several seconds before grabbing it.

'I never thought I would see all this again,' he whispered, his eyes moving from the river to the sky. 'I haven't seen the sky for so long. You forget what it's like. How big it is.'

'Take it all in because once we get into the forest, you're not going to see it again for a long time.'

'I can live with that,' Joshua replied, finally clambering to his feet. 'Just don't ever take me back to that mine again.'

Side by side they slipped across the thick mud, using the long blades of bull grass to pull themselves forward and into the cover of the forest. As they reached the trees they turned left, heading back upstream towards the tunnel entrance. They had been going for nearly ten minutes when Luca suddenly stopped and pulled them both down to the ground.

There in the mud, only three feet away from where they were lying, was the clear imprint of a military boot. It was fresh, possibly minutes old, with trickles of water still collecting in the impression of the heel.

Joshua remained still, his whole being paralysed by an incredible sense of disappointment. What had he been thinking, allowing himself to believe that they would escape? He should have known that they were never going to be free from Mordecai. The mine was all there was. The sum total of existence. Staring at the footprint, he let his eyes slowly close. It was just impossible that they could have been found so quickly.

Luca looked up, checking that no one was nearby, then inched closer to Joshua.

'An LRA patrol was following our trail all the way here,' he whispered. 'This must be one of their tracks.'

Joshua blinked, processing the information, while Luca warily got to his feet. He stood over the footprint, staring out into the bushes, and tried to focus on what to do. But already his mind was thinking ahead to the tunnel. As soon as the others took one step out of it, the patrol would be on them.

Joshua staggered towards him, speaking so quietly that Luca had to hold his breath to hear what he said.

'If it's the patrol and not the guards from the mine, then they might not know about the tunnel. They might have passed further along the riverbank. Out of sight.'

Luca crept forward, his eyes moving between the footprints and the bushes in front. At most, they could see only a couple of metres ahead of them. Following them like this was madness. The LRA could be lying at their feet and they wouldn't even know it.

They continued on towards the riverbank, moving in absolute silence. They stifled their breathing, senses straining for the slightest sound. There were more footprints, then a whole scattering of them from where the patrol had evidently converged into a single group. The footprints led to a patch of high river reeds and Luca parted the foliage to reveal the open water beyond.

There on the opposite bank were LRA soldiers. They were standing in a group with their rifles in their hands, while one of them was crouching down with a torch, shining it into the depths of the tunnel.

'Not this,' Luca groaned, his eyes passing from one soldier to the next. A shout went up as Bear was ripped from the darkness, her long hair spilling in front of her face as she blinked in the harsh light.

Joshua put his hand on Luca's shoulder.

'There's nothing you can do for her now,' he said.

★ ★ ★

Bear stumbled, dropping down on to one knee. She could see the ring of soldiers all around her, their rifles thrusting into the air as they shouted. A few metres in front of her stood the Captain. His back was towards her, huge, hulking shoulders moving as he laughed. The noise was deep and resonant, a cruel sound that rocked his entire body. She could see the sweaty folds of skin running down from his bulbous neck, then, as he turned, his face.

He stared at her, the pleasure in his eyes making them sparkle. With a lick of his lips, he revealed his teeth. Each one had been filed down to a point, leaving only blackened stubs. His tongue ran across them while his gaze moved slowly over Bear's body. As he stepped closer, a cheer went up.

Bear backed away, her back arched like a cat's. Her arms were crossed over her chest defensively, but as she reached the edge of the circle of men she was shunted back towards him. The Captain caught her with one arm while the other ripped down the front of her vest, tearing the fabric in two.

His head slowly tilted downwards, his eyes running over every inch of her breasts. He grabbed one of them, roughly kneading the flesh in the pads of his hand. He smiled, staring into her eyes as if daring her to protest, then, raising one of his broad thighs, he forced it between hers.

'Vous l'aimez,' You like it, he breathed into her face. 'Vous êtes une vraie pute, n'est-ce pas?' You're a real little whore, aren't you?

Bear shut her eyes, her whole body going limp in his grasp. The LRA were famous for raping women and children, and once the Captain had had his way, she knew the others would take their turn. Tears started streaming down her face as she tried to disconnect herself from what was happening, to blank everything out. She squeezed her eyes shut tighter, dimly aware of the Captain forcing his hand past the buckle of her belt, his fingers curling hungrily into her groin.

Suddenly, he stopped. Bear waited, too scared to open her eyes, but in the charged silence, she heard the low hum of a petrol engine. The noise echoed across the expanse of water behind them, drawing closer.

A long dugout pirogue appeared around the bend in the river. It was nearly forty feet long, carved from a single trunk of hardwood and filled with soldiers. The pirogue fought against the river current, engine revving higher as it slowly drew nearer. Seated in the front, set apart from the others, was a man dressed in a white suit. His arms were folded casually across his chest in an attitude of absolute patience.

Bear looked up into the Captain's face. His

315

gaze was fixed on the river, eyes wide with fear.

'Mordecai,' he whispered, the word escaping from him like a breath of foul air.

The Captain suddenly straightened, shunting Bear away from him with such force that she bounced on to the ground, skidding to a halt in the dirt. He shouted for his men to line up, but his voice cracked slightly as he gave the command. She saw him swallow several times, switching his gaze back to the river before repeating the order.

Mordecai was coming.

Everyone watched as the pirogue drove up on to the bank, jolting to a halt in the mud. Mordecai slowly stepped down off the craft into the tar-black mud. It rose up past his ankles, staining the trousers of his perfect white suit, but he didn't seem to notice. Coming to a halt in the centre of the group, he stared at Bear who was lying on the ground clutching the torn fabric of her vest across her chest.

'And you are?' he asked, his voice soft, almost conversational.

Bear just stared up at him, mesmerised by the translucent green of his eyes. It was as if she could look straight through them.

'Beatrice,' she managed, wincing as she pulled herself on to her elbows. 'Beatrice Makuru.'

Mordecai nodded as if he had heard the name somewhere before but couldn't quite place it.

'You know, Beatrice,' he whispered, 'it's not you with whom I am displeased. No, not at all. Who can blame a person for trying to rescue a friend?' He motioned towards the pirogue and his two bodyguards. They stepped down into the mud, pushing three LRA soldiers out in front of them. The soldiers were young, with red bandanas tied around their necks. They had been stripped of their rifles and staggered forward, their legs barely working as they drew closer to their fate.

'These were the guards responsible for the breakout from the mine,' Mordecai explained. He gave a smile that was warm and genuine.

'I believe that such misguided conduct must not go unpunished. Dereliction of duty is a sin. But from now on, they will no longer see, hear or speak such evil again.'

Now, the teenaged soldiers threw themselves down into the mud, begging for mercy with their hands clasped together in front of them. They writhed in the bodyguard's grip, their legs slipping out from under them as they collapsed into the mud.

'Come, my children,' Mordecai said softly, raising his hands as if to embrace them all. 'When you err, you must be cleansed.'

The closest bodyguard pulled the soldier at his feet into the centre of the semicircle of men. Mordecai reached down, cupping the boy's open face in his hands. He smiled again, his eyes blinking with unhurried calm. The boy stammered some kind of apology, but no intelligible words escaped his lips.

'You shall speak no more evil,' Mordecai whispered.

The bodyguard standing behind him pulled out an old blackened knife from his belt and

317

grabbed the boy's head. As his entire arm wrapped around his face, the huge, bulging muscles of his forearm and bicep pressed into his skull. With his other hand, the bodyguard then grabbed on to the boy's lips and sawed through the soft flesh, pulling with his fingers at the same time so that it tore away in chunks. Blood sprayed out over his hand and arm, making the jet-black skin of his forearm glisten in the sunlight, before finally, he straightened, tossing the tattered remains of the lips to one side like giblets from a chicken.

Mordecai nodded with satisfaction, before his eyes turned to the next of the three.

'And you shall hear no evil,' he said.

No one moved or spoke as they witnessed the next soldier's ears being hacked off and the other crudely blinded. There was absolute silence as the work was done, each witness silenced by the horror.

'It saddens me to see such a loss of faith,' Mordecai said at last. 'But only through fire can the Lord forgive.'

He motioned for Bear to be raised up. Mordecai gave a faint smile as he watched her press the heel of her boots into the ground, trying to stop her legs from shaking. His head then tilted to one side, as his eyes ran down from her shoulders, across her arms, to her stomach.

'God has blessed you indeed,' he said. 'Blessed you with such beauty. And yet, here you are, an African woman turning against your own brothers.'

He raised his hand, letting the backs of his

fingers gently brush across her cheek, pausing at her lips.

'I am not a monster,' he whispered. 'Not at all. I am just doing what needs to be done.' The vertical line in his forehead deepened. 'It is what *has* to be done, don't you see?'

Bear's eyes followed his fingers, then moved back towards his eyes. A strange sense of apathy came over her that seemed to dull the choking fear. It was as if she had resigned herself to the fact that she was going to die, and from that single point, realised that there was nothing left to be fearful of. As Mordecai felt her trembling stop, he looked into her eyes.

'You're nothing more than a sick bastard who murders children,' Bear hissed, pulling away from his hand. 'You'll burn in hell.'

Mordecai suddenly raised his arms. 'But this *is* hell!' he shouted, his voice booming out across the deathly silence of the crowd. 'Can't you see? This is hell! And I have to get through it. To do what needs to be done.' He paused, shaking his head as if pained by his own conviction. 'I have to get through it, and I *suffer* day after day. How I *suffer*.'

As Bear stared at him blankly, he suddenly stepped forward, grabbed her shoulder and dug his thumb into the newly closed wound. She screamed in pain, her knees giving way as Mordecai twisted his thumb deeper. Blood seeped out, smearing the cuff of his white suit.

'How many others are there?' he said, mouthing each word slowly.

Bear screamed again. Mordecai's eyes glowed

319

as he turned his thumb again, causing her whole body to jerk as if hit by an electric shock.

'How many are with you?' he repeated.

As Bear's back arched in pain, her fingers curled into a fist. Suddenly, she swung her whole arm up and punched Mordecai straight in the mouth. The blow split the top of his lip and there was a faint crack as the cartilage in his nose snapped. Recoiling in shock, he dropped her from his grasp. He staggered backwards, dabbing at his nose and lips with his fingers.

Mordecai stared at his hand, as if bewildered by the sight of his own blood, while his whole body seemed to convulse in speechless rage. Bear tried to get back on to her feet, but the nearest of the bodyguards leapt forward and cracked his fist into the side of her temple, sending her sprawling on to the ground.

Mordecai's furious gaze turned to the bodyguard.

'I wanted her conscious!' he seethed, his breath showering flecks of his own blood into the air. As the man immediately backed off, Mordecai stared fixedly at the ground. Slowly a smile began to appear on his lips, revealing white teeth splattered with blood.

'This is God's will,' Mordecai whispered. 'He works in ways that are so hard to see. So hard! But I am sure of it now. He wants her to die slowly, so that she can reflect on what she has done. He wants her to suffer.' He paused, turning towards the soldiers. 'Put her inside the mine with all the others. Then blow up the entrance so that no living thing moves in or out, and seal up this tunnel. They will all die of thirst. Die slowly from it, while we complete our glorious march on Kinshasa!'

The soldiers bowed their heads as Mordecai strode back towards the pirogue, signalling to the driver to start the engine.

The Captain moved over to Bear's unconscious body and scooped her off the ground. Her head hung limply over the edge of his arm, with her hair spilling down towards the ground. As he stared down at her naked breasts and the delicate line of her lips, his thickset face grimaced at the lost opportunity. Then, moving across to the bow of the pirogue, he placed her between two bench seats, jamming her body into the well of the canoe.

He turned back to survey the shore with a final glance as the engine revved higher. The pirogue pulled out into the main flow of the current and rapidly moved downstream, leaving only the smell of petrol and the fading vibration of its engine.

29

General Jian watched his reflection in the mirror slowly fade as the old electric lights flickered then went out. He waited, staring into the darkness, as one by one all the lights in the mansion went off. There was silence. As the seconds passed, Jian stayed perfectly still, feeling the darkness close in around him.

Since returning from the mine, they had been staying at one of the old colonial houses on the shores of Lake Kivu. By day, its sweeping colonnades and high, ornate ceilings had seemed almost charming, brimming with a sense of faded grandeur and the sophistication of a bygone era. But by night the house had taken on a far more sinister feel. It wasn't so much the groaning lead pipes or rising damp, more the lingering sense of what had once been. The place reeked of the old days, as if the horrors of Belgian rule were still etched into every single room.

There was a soft buzzing sound before the antique lights started to glow once again. Jian blinked, taking in the image of himself newly revealed in the huge, gilded mirror. He stared into his own eyes, blinking slowly as he tried to focus. They looked duller, the blacks of his pupils somehow faded and less alive. Every day he felt worse, the headaches never leaving him for a second.

What the hell was happening to him?

On the bathroom surface in front of him lay a bottle of single malt whisky and a glass. Scooping a handful of painkillers from his jacket pocket, he broke them up and poured the powder into the glass. He then added a huge measure of whisky and downed the glass's entire contents in a single gulp. Staggering back a pace, he flung the glass to one side, sending it smashing down on to the faded marble floor.

Jian reached up and clutched his head in both hands. He screamed. The sound came out in a long, wretched wail, echoing in the tight confines of the bathroom. Jian scraped his fingernails down the sides of his face, leaving thin trailing red marks, and stared back into the mirror with wild, desperate eyes. The pain! The pain was unbearable!

It was like a vice clamped across his temples, ratcheting tighter with each passing second. Every thought, every feeling, was drowned out by it, robbing him of sleep at night and leaving him absolutely exhausted by day. The painkillers seemed only to dull the harshest spikes, but always there was this crippling undercurrent.

Jian let his eyes slowly trace down one side of his face. A hard swelling was poking out just above his shirt collar. It was getting bigger. He was certain of it. It had to be the reason why he was getting such bad headaches. But what was happening to him?

The Guild. It had to be the Guild. They had

somehow found out about the satellite launch and the money he'd taken. They were trying to poison him.

Jian reached out to steady himself, feeling his vision darken around the edges. He had been drinking the same mixture of whisky and painkillers throughout the day, lacing the last couple with Ritalin to stave off the fatigue. Everything was starting to blur, the light from the flickering bulbs trailing across his vision like sunspots.

It was Xie. That bastard had been sent to poison him. Why else would those gutless bureaucrats at the Guild send him out to the Congo at the last minute? Suddenly it all made sense. They were delaying Jian in Goma, stopping him from reaching any sort of proper medical help, while the poison Xie was administering took hold.

He had to get out of here, had to find some way to get away from them all!

There was the faint sound of a gong echoing out across the house and Jian glanced down at his watch. It was eight o'clock and dinner was about to be served. Splashing deep handfuls of water on to his face, he dabbed it away with a hand towel before finally leaving the bathroom. As he walked down the corridor, he forced himself not to give any outward sign that he was in pain. He wouldn't lose face in front of Xie, or give him the slightest opportunity to see that his poison was working.

The corridor opened up on to a wide veranda with a dining table set at one end. At the other, comfortable chairs were positioned in a semi-circle, facing out over the sloping lawns which led down to the lake's edge. In the moonlight its dark waters were just visible and the surrounding hills rising up towards the night sky.

On a low table in front of the chairs was the cage Mordecai had given him. The butterflies were there, slowly opening and closing their wings, their delicate pink deepened by the dull light. Jian craned his neck closer, watching every movement. They wouldn't last long in captivity like this, maybe a few more days at most. He had to get them back to Beijing quickly and add them to his collection while they were still fresh. Such an incredibly rare butterfly as the *Salamis parhassus* could not be allowed to wither and die in the Congo. He had to get them out of here.

A trace of a smile passed across Jian's face at the irony of the situation. Both he and the butterflies were in equal need of rescue.

Next to the cage was his laptop. As the screen lit up, washing his face in its artificial glow, he connected with the New York Stock Exchange. It had only just opened but already telecom stocks had dropped to a new all-time low. Ever since the announcement of the Chinese satellite phone they had been in freefall, with every one of the existing major brands crippled by share devaluations. He was already $230 million richer from the deal. Now, all that remained to be seen was how much further the stocks could fall.

There was a shuffling sound on the far side of the veranda and Jian turned to see Xie. He had finally changed out of the crumpled linen suit into fresh clothes, but somehow still managed to look tired and unkempt, with dark-ringed eyes and his hair sticking out at unlikely angles.

They sat down at the candlelit table. Jian grabbed the bottle of wine cooling in the centre and poured himself a large glass. The wine tasted vinegary and sharp. Jian stared over the rim of his glass at Xie, not bothering to disguise the venom in his eyes. He knew what this clerk was up to, stalling with the money while the Guild waited for the poison to take effect.

'So we're still ordered to wait,' Jian began, but Xie only shrugged, then smiled slightly as the waiters arrived with their food.

'With each hour that passes, it becomes more likely that Mordecai will back out of the deal. And yet, you do nothing. Tell me, Xie, what's the real reason for your delay?'

Jian spat the words out, the tone of his voice taunting and aggressive, but on the opposite side of the table, Xie seemed oblivious to it all. He was enjoying his food, every now and again politely dabbing at the corners of his mouth with his napkin. Jian suddenly leaned closer to him across the table.

'What? Suddenly you don't talk any more?'

Xie rested his fork and then his knife on the side of the plate. Each movement was unhurried and deliberate.

'Mr Kai specifically stated that such large sums of money should be properly discussed. That we should wait until . . . '

'What the hell does Kai know about any of this?' Jian roared, his words slurring slightly as the painkillers and alcohol started to take hold. 'One billion . . . that's the cost of legitimising all future claims. So, answer me! Why the delay?'

'Mr Kai suggested that it would be prudent to evaluate things more thoroughly,' Xie replied, dabbing his mouth again. 'That perhaps there was more to this than met the eye.'

'Met the eye?' Jian repeated, slamming his fist down on the table. 'What can that old cripple Kai see behind those thick glasses of his anyhow?'

Xie looked up, genuinely surprised by such a brazen insult. 'Perhaps it would be better if you spoke to Mr Kai yourself about this. It may take a little time, of course, but it can be arranged.'

'You'd like that, wouldn't you? You'd like to see me waiting here for as long as possible.'

Xie shrugged. 'What I would *like* is of little significance. I will file my report, and that is all.'

Jian gave a bitter smile, his head swaying slightly. 'You know that Kai isn't the only one. There are others in the Guild who have the money to finance this, and if he won't give me an answer, then maybe I'll look elsewhere. The Governor of Chengdu might be interested to hear what's going on.'

'I would have thought that money wasn't the problem. That you had enough of that already,' Xie said softly, not making eye contact. 'Satellite launches can be such profitable things.'

Jian froze. 'Is that an accusation, or just another of your spineless insinuations?'

Xie kept his gaze averted as Jian inched a little closer to him across the table. The flickering light from the candle shone under his chin, giving his face a ghoulish look.

'You think you've got it all worked out, don't you? Keeping me waiting like this. But you know what's really interesting is how you just upped and left Shanghai, without a single thought for where you were going. This is the blackest heart of the whole damn' planet. Out here bad things happen, as easy as that.' He clicked his fingers together, right in front of Xie's face. 'Especially if you're all alone.'

Jian nodded towards the lake, still visible in the darkness beyond the end of the sloping lawns.

'You know, that over the years countless bodies have been dumped into that water. Thousands upon thousands of them: Tutsis, Hutu, Hema, Lendu. It didn't matter what tribe it was, they just carried on killing each other until the waters ran red. They say that at one point, there were so many corpses floating in the water that the fishing boats couldn't even leave harbour.'

Jian lowered his voice even further. 'Do you think anyone would notice another body or care if just one more were left to rot out there?'

Dragging his chair back from the table, he downed the contents of his wine glass without moving his eyes from Xie.

'Get me my money,' he hissed. 'Or by tomorrow night those niggers won't be the only ones floating in the lake.'

30

Bear jolted awake as an explosion ripped though the mine. The noise was immense, reverberating off the rock walls in a series of rippling aftershocks. There was a low cracking sound as fragments of rock splintered off the main arch of the entrance tunnel before it finally collapsed under its own weight in a mass of rock and rubble. The rock kept on coming, fanning out across the upper reaches of the wooden balconies and tipping over into the central atrium. As it finally ground to a halt, the clouds of dirt blown high by the blast started to settle, coating everything in a thick, noxious dust.

The miners fell silent as the realisation slowly dawned on them all. They were sealed inside.

Bear had her eyes shut when a new sound began to fill the mine. It was a high-pitched, wailing noise which echoed all around her. Clasping her hands over her ears, she tried to blot it out, twisting from one side to the next, but the sound seemed to be coming from every direction. Then she realised what it was. It was the miners. They were screaming.

Mordecai had sealed off the mine. The thought seemed abstract, of little relevance to her, as if it was something to be revisited sometime in the future. She had been unconscious for over two hours in the well of the dugout and now found herself struggling to make sense of it all. A swirling fog of dust surrounded her, clinging to her skin and face and choking her lungs as she tried to breathe. Then, as she reached out to the railings just in front of her, she found her hand missing the wooden bar. She tried again, but still her hand met thin air. What was wrong with her? Why did she keep missing?

Slowly reaching up to the side of her head, she pressed her hand down on to her temple. There was an open cut still weeping blood, while her ear felt swollen and hot. A thin line of blood oozed down from inside the ear itself where the bodyguard had struck her. That was why she couldn't balance. The bastard must have burst her eardrum.

Hand over hand, she dragged her body up the railings and stood, swaying slightly. Folding her arms across her chest, she took in the heaving mass of movement below. The miners were lined up on the balconies, pointing hysterically above her to where the entry tunnel had collapsed.

Only then did she understand the significance. Only then did she feel the same wave of absolute dread as the others. They were all trapped here, with no hope of escape.

Bear didn't move, letting her eyes drift from one face to the next amongst the hordes of people below her. Fights had already begun to break out on the lower levels, with some of the miners grabbing water pouches and hunks of bread as the scrabble for survival began.

On the far side of the atrium, on the level directly below her, she could see two men attacking others. They already had several plastic gourds of water slung over their shoulders and were clambering up the metal chains as if to try and escape from the top level. Bear could see the domed roof stretching high above them. The last of the evening sun was filtering down through the crack, but she already knew that there was no escape. The only two exits had been cut off by thousands of tons of rock. There was nowhere left to go.

As she took in the chaos, she suddenly realised that there was a small wooden cabin only about twenty metres to her right. The whole structure was listing to one side from the force of the explosion, looking as if it might collapse at any moment. Staggering over and pulling back the rickety door, she realised it was the old LRA guardhouse. Inside were a few basic items: a table, chairs, a row of hooks with jackets still hanging from them. But as she moved further inside, she saw a metal bucket three-quarters full of water, with a bar of soap left to one side. The water was scummed by black dust, but it did not matter to her. It was water. She gulped it down, her throat working as her stomach began to bloat.

She kept on drinking, forcing every last sip down until finally she let the bucket fall from her grasp. She felt as if she might vomit and reached out a hand to steady herself while her eyes drifted over the lines of crooked shelving, vaguely registering the assortment of possessions that had belonged to the guards. Everything lay untouched, with no sign of a struggle. They had gone quietly when Mordecai had summoned them.

Then she saw it. Lying to one side, forgotten. The snub nose of a pistol gleamed in the half-light and Bear picked it up, feeling the weight of it in her hand. She had seen this type before — a Norinco. It was standard issue for the Chinese military. Pressing down the release button, she saw the magazine had all nine rounds still neatly clipped inside. Chambering the first, she held the pistol in her right hand while she moved over to the jackets hanging by the door. She pulled one over her ripped vest. It was tight-fitting. The LRA soldier who had owned it could not have been much more than a boy.

Just as she was about to go back into the body of the mine, she stopped. There was nothing but mayhem and confusion out there. A crippling wave of exhaustion washed over her. There was no more adrenalin left in her, no glimmer of hope to ease her through. This was how it would all end — in a mine in the middle of the Congo.

The fire coltan . . . that was why she was here. Her lips curled in a bitter, humourless smile at the futility of it all. She was going to die because of some new mineral that she had been too stubborn to ignore. Everyone from her husband to Fabrice had warned her of the dangers but still she had gone, daring herself to continue each step of the way. And now that same pig-headed tenacity had led her here — to a lonely death, deep in the middle of the jungle.

Bear screwed her eyes shut, feeling a sickening

mixture of self-pity and regret wash over her. Why did she always have to push so hard, to never back down? Why did she always have to be so stupid? Reaching into the thigh pocket of her trousers, she pulled out the Ziploc bag and held up the small lump of fire coltan she had been carrying. She let her eyes rest on the vein of molten red in the centre, while her vision slowly fogged from tears.

This was what they were all looking for. And this was the reason she was going to die.

The door of the shack suddenly burst open and two men appeared. They looked frantic and aggressive, searching for anything they could take. The one on the right jumped at her and in that split second Bear reacted, swinging the pistol round and firing. The gunshot rang out, deafeningly loud in the tiny shack, as the bullet spun the man round from the force of its impact.

His accomplice turned on his heel and sprinted off as fast as he could. Bear watched him go, her ears ringing from the explosion as the door slowly creaked shut again.

She didn't get up, but let her hand fall so that the nose of the pistol scraped across the rough wooden flooring. She felt no remorse or even regret for what had just happened. She knew full well that those men would have killed her in a heartbeat. She could hear a low groan as the wounded man dragged himself away from the door, and sat listening to the sound. It was as if the very last of her emotions had ebbed away and there was nothing left for her to feel.

'Luca,' Bear whispered. Her only hope was that he and Joshua had made it past the LRA patrol and were somehow on their way to the MONUC compound.

'Just get to the road,' Bear murmured.

'Just the road,' she repeated, and let her eyes slowly close.

31

Joshua's fingers raked down Luca's back as he tried to stop himself from falling. Luca turned, but wasn't quick enough to catch him and watched as his friend collapsed into the mud, groaning from exhaustion. It had been like this for the last two hours, their progress getting slower and slower.

'I've got . . . to stop,' Joshua whispered, his throat so dry he could barely say the words.

Luca turned on him.

'Come on, Josh! Get on your feet! We've got to keep moving!'

Joshua stared into his eyes, pleading. His bad leg dragged across the ground, snagging on every root and branch, and continually yanking him off balance. Nearly four hours had passed since leaving the river and the undergrowth seemed endless. The ground was saturated with pools of standing water and for the last hour they had been going painfully slowly. Sinking down to their knees in the mud, they tried to crawl their way across it, with Luca pulling Joshua forward by his shoulders, inch by inch, both of them becoming increasingly desperate and tired.

The ground worsened, becoming one vast quagmire. They were covered in tar-black mud, with their clothes clinging to their bodies and their hair plastered to the sides of their heads.

'No more,' Joshua breathed, but Luca reached out his hand. Joshua stared at it for several seconds before catching hold. As Luca heaved him up once again, he cried out in pain. His leg was already starting to swell and he could feel his vision blackening at the edges. He was only moments from passing out.

Rounding the next in a long line of thickets, Luca tried to keep the compass steady, but their progress was erratic, the needle swinging from side to side across the faded dial. They were heading due south, trying to reach the old logging road Bear had mentioned, but as more time passed with not the slightest break in the forest, Luca had begun to doubt whether the road even existed. The rest of the escape kit was pretty much useless, with the possible exception of the Chinese flare.

A tree branch snapped back, hitting Joshua square in his chest and knocking him down into the mud. He stayed on his hands and knees, chest heaving as he tried to muster the strength to move. His arms shook with strain and a thin line of spittle hung from one corner of his mouth.

'I can't go on,' he managed.

Luca rounded on him, his eyes savage.

'Get up!' he screamed. 'We keep going. One step after the other!'

But he could see the sick exhaustion in Joshua's eyes. In that moment, he already knew it was over. There was just nothing left for his friend to give.

'I can't . . . ' Joshua began, but drifted into

silence. Both of them knew what he was going to say next.

'It's OK,' Luca said, trying to catch his breath. 'We'll just wait it out. We do it by hours; one on, one off. Just keep going until we make it back to MONUC.'

Joshua slowly shook his head. 'We both know that won't work. There isn't enough time.'

'We don't know that. We've got to focus on the here and now, get you out of this damn' jungle.'

'No,' Joshua breathed, 'there's more to this than just you and me. You've got to get help before their water runs out. It's the only way.' He paused, an image coming to him of the miners desperately searching for a way out, knowing that the clock was ticking. 'And, Luca, this is just the tip of it. We've got to get the message out. Tell everyone what this shit does to people.'

Joshua's chin tilted up as he stared at Luca.

'The one thing I know about Mordecai is that he hates foreigners. Hates us like nothing you've ever known.'

Luca returned his gaze, confused.

'Don't you see?' Joshua continued. 'If this stuff is going into mobiles all over the world, then just imagine how many people are going to die. I know what that sick bastard is like. For Mordecai, it would be like some kind of divine retribution; an apocalypse to punish the West for God knows what.'

'We don't know that it is used in phones,' Luca interjected. 'Bear was only guessing.'

'Whatever the hell it's being used for, we know one thing — if it heats up, it kills people. That ought to be enough. We've got to get the message out, Luca. Tell them how dangerous this shit is.'

Luca didn't respond, only letting his head slump forward in the silence. He stayed like that for several seconds, suddenly looking totally defeated. It was the first time Joshua had ever seen him look like that.

'Luca?'

As he glanced up, Joshua could immediately see the pain in his eyes.

'It took me so long to find you,' Luca said. 'To actually get here. And now you're asking me to leave you out in the forest again. I can't do that, Josh. I can't leave someone again.'

'Come on, Luca, don't do this to yourself.'

'It's the same fucking thing. Over and over.'

'No!' Joshua shouted. 'That was about a mountain. This is about saving every goddamn' person inside that mine. Trust me, I don't want be left out here by myself, but you are the only one who can do this.'

Luca stared out towards the bushes.

'I'll be all right. I'll just sit it out and wait for you to come and rescue me again.' Joshua paused, attempting a smile. 'You rescued me from the inside of an LRA mine, for Christ's sake. Out here should be a cinch.'

Joshua stared at the back of Luca's head, waiting for a response. The seconds went by, but Luca stayed where he was, staring out into the haze of undergrowth.

'How the hell did we find ourselves in the middle of all this shit?' he said quietly.

'Don't you remember? Ever since we were

kids, whenever we were together, we got into trouble.' Joshua paused. 'At least this time we don't have your old man chasing us across the field with a golf club because you crashed his car.'

A wheezing laugh escaped Luca's lips.

'I can't believe you let me take the rap for that,' Joshua continued. 'And I never even got laid that night!'

Luca turned to him, a smile creeping across his face.

'Yeah, those girls weren't too impressed with us, were they?'

They both laughed at the memory, then slowly fell silent. Seconds passed with neither of them wanting to admit that their time together was over. Finally Joshua broke the spell. Hauling himself out of the mud, he crawled to the shelter of some nearby bushes. Luca went to help him, crouching down so that their heads were almost level. Without any warning, Joshua grabbed his shoulders, pulling him into a hug.

'Just don't forget about me,' he said jokingly, but his smile quickly faded. Luca could see the fear in his eyes and squeezed him tight, trying to offer some reassurance.

'You've got that red flare,' he said, 'so if you hear anything, you fire it. You hear me?'

Joshua nodded. 'Yeah, I got it.' He stared hard at Luca through the gathering darkness. 'I'll be waiting.'

32

Jean-Luc gazed out of the open door of the Oryx helicopter. The cabin's interior light washed his face with a dull red glow. Only fifty feet below the trees rushed by in a continuous blur, their outlines jet black against the setting sun. All that was left of the day was a faint glow of orange in the west as night quickly came on.

There were no clouds. The sky was clear but dark, with the moon a thin crescent skirting the horizon. Jean-Luc could feel the air temperature steadily drop. Drawing a *Gitanes* pack from his top pocket, he lit a cigarette with a windproof lighter and sucked down on the filter. The smoke went deep into his lungs, filling them with its comforting warmth, and his eyes scanned the vast landscape beneath, taking it all in. A slight smile appeared on his lips. This was the Africa he knew.

Suddenly the helicopter banked right, forcing him to grip on to the door handle to keep his balance. Only thirty feet to their left, the branches of an enormous tree rose up above the jagged outline of the canopy. He had told the pilots to keep low and they were doing just that, using their dual-scope P-15 night vision goggles to skim the treeline.

They had already been to the co-ordinates Devlin had given them, and after nearly an hour searching, had found what remained of the plane. Only the starboard wing of the Cessna 206 still remained above water, with the rest of the plane fully submerged. They winched down one of the men. He had dived into the water with a waterproof torch, searching the tiny cockpit for any trace of Bear. Finally, he had emerged with the remnants of a half-eaten corpse. The crocodiles had got to it first.

But the body wasn't Bear's. It must have been one of the white men Devlin had spoken about. That meant she was either on the run, in which case they would have to try and pick her up using thermal imaging, or the LRA had already tracked her down.

Jean-Luc drew deeply on his cigarette. If the LRA had got to her, there was only one solution. A staggered attack on the volcano, using the MK4 rockets on the Rooivalk with support fire from the Oryx's GPMG guns. As all hell broke out from the air, he would send an extraction team on to the ground to hunt for her amongst the chaos. It was a long shot, but it was all they had. Mordecai was not a man who could be negotiated with.

Pulling on his headset, Jean-Luc half expected to hear the usual chatter between the pilots, but tonight there was silence. He knew the reason why. They all suspected that Bear had already been caught, and although none of them dared admit it, believed an attack on the volcano was inevitable. Now they were silent, steeling themselves for the fight of their lives.

Over the last eight months they had delivered crate after crate of standard AK-47 rifles to the

LRA base. Then, two weeks ago, they had thrown back the tarpaulin covers to see a shipment of Chinese HQ-7 SAM surface-to-air missiles. There were other crates too; W-89 long-range mortars, rocket-propelled grenades, and a whole host of field weaponry. Someone in the Chinese Army was backing the LRA with everything they needed to transform themselves from a provincial rebel group into a proper military force.

But the weapons weren't the worst of it. It was the sheer number of LRA soldiers. There were thousands of them, living in a vast tented city deep within the forest, and each one of them unquestioningly devoted to their leader.

Jean-Luc had seen the growing cult of Mordecai at first hand. New recruits were beaten down until there was nothing left; forced to do unmentionable things time and time again until they were numbed by the horror. It was all designed to destroy any ingrained sense of morality, so that by the time they were ready to be built back up again, they believed everything Mordecai said, no matter how fantastical.

Mordecai had them believing that if they anointed their foreheads with holy water, they would be impervious to bullets, or that they could be healed just by his touch. The cult was a perverse hybrid of Christianity and voodoo magic, becoming ever more distorted by the cocktails of hallucinogens and amphetamines they all used. But of one thing Jean-Luc was certain — the cult worked. Mordecai had built himself an army that was as fearless as it was loyal.

As the thud of the helicopter rotors continued, Jean-Luc stared out, his eyes narrowed against the rush of air. He thought back to all the times he had gone into battle, the journey to the frontline dragging on like the calm before a storm. There had been so many campaigns, so many dirty wars spent crossing from one border to the next. He had been a mercenary his whole life, and now there was nothing else. That was what he was. The sum total of *him*. Like an old smoker being asked to count the years of his addiction, war had always been there, been part of him.

But for the first time in his life, the reason for it had changed. This time he wasn't going in because someone was paying him to. He was going in because his little girl needed him to.

Pulling back from the open door, Jean-Luc gently patted the gunner, Louis, on the shoulder as he moved past him towards the pilot. He nodded with satisfaction, knowing that his men were ready. Each one of them had fingers resting on a trigger, silently scanning the ground through their night-vision goggles for the slightest sign of movement. There was courage in their silence. They had all obeyed his command, boarding the helicopters back in Goma without question. Yet all of them had known that if they didn't track Bear down in the forest, they would be flying on to the volcano and into the biggest shit storm imaginable.

Jean-Luc leaned over the pilot, Thierry. He

343

was a short, stocky man with a bald head and a deeply tanned face.

Looking past him to the GPS on the screen, Jean-Luc glanced down at his watch. They had enough fuel to keep searching for Bear for five hours.

'Major, we've just picked something up on the thermal imaging,' came Laurent's voice over the radio. 'It's a single heat source moving west along the old logging road.'

'You're sure it's human?'

'Negative, sir.'

Jean-Luc nodded, reaching out a hand to steady himself. They were going to follow each and every lead until he found his daughter.

'Proceed.'

All four helicopters banked sharply, maintaining formation as they turned west towards the faint outline of the crooked dirt track. The old logging road had long since become impassable to ground vehicles, with the forest reclaiming almost all of the cleared track, but from the air, it was still visible.

'Target moving off the road, sir. Now heading south.'

'Get in front. I want a four-man team on the deck.'

The lead helicopter slowed, with the pilot pitching up the nose and lowering the collective to reduce the torque on the rotors. Ropes were flung out as four men moved out to the edge, preparing to abseil into the darkness.

The ropes buzzed as the soldiers descended at speed, jerking to a halt only a few feet from the surface of the ground. As they pulled the slack through their harnesses, they swung their M4 carbine rifles off their backs and surged forward across the ground.

'Target has stopped,' came Laurent's voice. 'North. Twenty metres.'

With their rifles tight into their shoulders, the four men advanced. They moved, silently, black combat uniforms melting into the background. Their faces were darkened by camouflage cream. Five metres further on they begun to converge on a single point, but still none of them could see the target. The bush was too thick.

'Target dead ahead. Three metres.'

All the men stopped, their rifles trained on the ground. Then, suddenly, one of them recognised the outline of a man's leg, his back, and finally his head. He was lying absolutely still, curled up into the base of a thick bush.

'*Ne bougez pas!*' Don't move! the soldier shouted. As the three others kept their weapons trained on the target, he swung his rifle across his back and grabbed on to the man's boots, dragging him feet first out of the bush. With a sharp kick, he spun him round, reaching for his weapon in the same movement and jamming the barrel of his rifle into his chest.

'*Qui êtes-vous?*' Who are you? he shouted, staring down at the man's mud-splattered face and his pale blue eyes. The man was half-naked with his hands slightly raised, the blackened palms facing the soldiers as if trying to push them away.

'Don't shoot! Don't shoot!'

'Who are you?' the soldier bellowed, switching into English as he twisted the gun barrel in deeper.

'My name is Luca. We need . . . help.'

The soldier grabbed him by his neck and hoisted him on to his feet.

'Lucky for you the Major wants you alive,' he said, then shunted him forward towards the waiting helicopters.

★   ★   ★

Two of the three Oryx helicopters had touched down on a clearing to either side of the old logging road. They were stationary except for the low swoop of their rotors as the pilots kept the engines powered up and ready to take off at a moment's notice. The white beam of their searchlights swung round, revealing the four soldiers with Luca. He had his hands raised, but nothing more could be seen of his face. The light had bleached out all his features, leaving only a hazy outline.

Jean-Luc was on the ground, dressed in full combat fatigues with his short-barrel G3 rifle slung over his back. His chest bulged with a row of front webbing pouches, each filled with ammunition and grenades, and he had clipped off the lenses of his night-vision goggles, leaving just the strap across his forehead. It pressed down on his tangled mop of hair like a sweatband, bunching up the skin at the corners of his eyes. As the ground team approached, he went out to meet them,

346

flinging his cigarette aside.

'His name is Luca . . . ' began the lead soldier, but as he spoke the Rooivalk swooped low overhead, drowning out the sound of his voice. They all looked up as it passed through the halo of lights. Luca immediately recognised the distinctive stepped cockpit and the fuselage bristling with rockets. There could be no mistake. That was the helicopter that had killed Lanso and Abasi. These were the bastards who had been hunting them down on the inselberg!

He swivelled round and swung a wide punch at the man just behind him. More by luck than any sense of timing, his fist connected, ripping off the soldier's night-vision goggles and snapping his head to one side. As the soldier stumbled sideways, Luca stepped forward, shunting him back with the palms of his hands, so that he went crashing into the man behind.

In the confusion, he ducked out of the glare of the searchlights and sprinted towards the treeline. The other two soldiers gave chase, but their rifles and webbing made them slower. Luca was pulling away. In only ten metres, he would be past the clearing and back into the cover of the trees.

Jean-Luc cursed, raising his rifle and firing. Three bullets smacked into the tree just ahead of Luca in quick succession, stopping him dead in his tracks and missing his body by just a few inches. Luca stared at the splintered tree bark for several seconds before slowly turning back towards the helicopters, eyes narrowed against the light.

Suddenly, he was thrown forward as the nearest of the soldiers crashed into him, pitching them both on to the ground. The man immediately wrestled Luca's arms behind his back, trying to force his hands through a long, plastic cable tie. Luca fought him off, but then a second soldier arrived and, dropping his knees on to Luca's chest, pinned him down. They jammed the cable tight around his wrists, the plastic cutting deep.

Jean-Luc watched as the prisoner was brought to a halt in front of him.

'Why are you here?' he called, his voice raised against the sound of the rotors.

Luca didn't answer.

'I am not a patient man. Tell me, now.'

He waited a few seconds, but Luca remained silent. With his mud-splattered torso and hair stuck to the side of his face, he looked wild and hunted. He was nearly a head taller than Jean-Luc, and stared down at him with undisguised venom.

'I'm going to tire of asking,' Jean-Luc hissed. 'Last time.'

'Screw you.'

Jean-Luc nodded to the soldier just behind. He slammed the butt of his rifle into the back of Luca's knees, felling him to the ground. Luca groaned, wincing as he fought the pain. As the soldier raised his rifle to strike again, the Rooivalk passed overhead. This time, Luca's gaze fixed on it, the hatred clear in his eyes.

'You've seen that helicopter before, haven't

you?' Jean-Luc asked. 'When?'

Luca stared up at him from the ground. 'What kind of coward kills a couple of boys?' he spat. 'They were pygmies, for Christ's sake. With bows and arrows!'

Jean-Luc slowly nodded. 'So you were on the inselberg, running from the LRA. Were you anything to do with the plane crash on the river?'

Luca fell silent again.

'Because we found this guy in there, all chewed up by crocodiles. Nasty business.'

Luca shut his eyes at the image of René.

'So it's true,' Jean-Luc said. 'You are one of the men running with my daughter, Beatrice.'

Luca opened his eyes. 'Beatrice?' he said disbelievingly. 'You're Bear's father? But . . . she told me to try and find you.'

Jean-Luc nodded towards his men. They surrounded Luca, bundling him on board through the open door of the Oryx and slamming him down on the riveted metal bench seat at the back.

'Looks like we got to you first,' Jean-Luc said to himself. Then, with a twirl of his finger, he signalled to the pilots to take off. Putting on his headset, he reached forward and placed the spare set over Luca's ears, before drawing a thin, delicate-looking throwing knife from his belt. A silver line ran down the length of the blade from where it had been ground razor-sharp.

'Now,' Jean-Luc said, pointing the tip of the knife at Luca's chest, 'you're going to help me find my daughter. And if you so much as . . . '

' . . . we're after the same thing!' Luca interupted, jerking his wrists up behind his back. 'Now get these fucking things off me!'

Jean-Luc stared at him for several seconds before grabbing hold of his shoulders and pivoting Luca forward in his seat. He sawed through the plastic cable ties in a couple of strokes.

'If my daughter's harmed in any . . . ' Jean-Luc began, but Luca cut in once again.

'Shut up and listen to me,' he said. 'We don't have time for this bullshit.'

Jean-Luc's eyes narrowed, but he remained silent.

'Bear's being held in a mine not far from here. But the LRA are planning on sealing all the miners inside. We've got to get over there and somehow get her the hell out.'

'When was that?'

Luca shrugged, trying to remember when they had left the river. 'It was late in the afternoon. Four, maybe five o'clock.'

Jean-Luc already knew the time, but still found himself glancing down at his watch. That was nearly four hours ago.

'And what condition was she in?'

Luca hesitated.

'I said, what condition was she in?'

'She was unconscious. That's all I could see from where I was.'

Jean-Luc knew there was more, but forced himself to accept the information for now. They would be over the volcano in just under twenty-two minutes.

'So how was Mordecai planning on sealing it? Just posting his men or did he barricade them inside?'

'We didn't actually see. But when we were on the run, we heard some explosions.'

'Shit!' Jean-Luc hissed, his fist slamming down on the side of the seat. 'If they've collapsed the entry tunnel, there's no way we are going to be able to get inside.'

'No, there's another way. At the top of the mine, I saw this crack that lets in the natural light. But it's got to be at least a hundred metres above where the miners are.'

'We can hover above it and my men will abseil in.'

'Maybe. But even if you're just above it, you're going to need a shitload of rope.'

Jean-Luc turned away from him, tilting the mic closer to his mouth.

'Captain, how much rope do we have?'

There was a pause before Laurent's voice came in over the radio. 'Each Oryx has a seventy-five-metre line attached to the winch, sir. And there's two one-hundred-and-twenty-metre static lines in the hold of your aircraft.'

'Can you rig the winch lines together?'

'It's not going to be easy, sir, because it won't run through if we knot them up.' As Laurent spoke, Luca moved forward and grabbed hold of Jean-Luc's wrist.

'I'm a climber,' he said. 'I can rig it together. Just give me the damn' rope.'

Jean-Luc stared into his eyes. 'OK, climber. You can prep the rope. But after that, you sit still in the back of this helicopter and stay the hell out of our way.'

Luca nodded. 'There's one more thing. I escaped with a friend of mine. He's down there in the forest right now, about four miles due south of the mine. We've got to stop en route and pick him up.'

Jean-Luc's expression didn't change.

'All you've got to do is hover for a few seconds . . . ' Luca added, but Jean-Luc cut him off.

'Every minute we waste is another minute Beatrice is in danger,' he said. 'Your friend stays. With luck, we'll pick him up on the way back.'

Luca went to protest, but Jean-Luc raised a finger in warning.

Slowly turning towards the open door of the helicopter, Luca watched the forest whip past below them.

'Hold on, Josh,' he muttered to himself. 'Just hold on.'

33

Jean-Luc sat hunched over in his seat on the helicopter. His broad forearms were folded across his chest, resting on top of the webbing pouches, while he waited for the minutes to drag by. There was a look of grim determination in his eyes.

'ETA sixteen minutes,' came Laurent's voice over the radio.

At this the gunner, Louis, standing just to the left of Jean-Luc, started fidgeting from one foot to the next, minutely adjusting the focus on his night-vision goggles. He then leaned forward, clipping open the belt feed of 7.62mm ammunition, realigning it slightly.

'Have you checked it already?' came Jean-Luc's voice over the comms. Louis turned towards him and nodded. 'Then leave it alone.'

Reaching up to his top pocket, Jean-Luc took out another cigarette and lit it, with his eyes fixed on Luca.

'So what was Bear doing out here in the first place?' he asked.

Luca's arms were also folded across his chest. Without a T-shirt and half-covered in damp mud, the downdraft from the rotors was making him feel cold, but he was too proud to ask for anything to cover himself. He was also desperately thirsty and had been eyeing the water bottle on the side of the gunner's belt since they had first got on the helicopter.

'She was looking for this new mineral,' he replied flatly. 'This stuff called fire coltan.'

Jean-Luc didn't react, but inwardly he felt his heart sink. If they had been on speaking terms, Bear would only have had to call him. He would have told her everything, even supplied her with some of the damn' stuff if that was what she wanted. He knew now that he would have broken every professional code of conduct and handed over all his contacts, if only she had asked.

'So that's it,' Jean-Luc said, his eyes darkening. 'You two get in a Cessna and start buzzing around the skies looking for coltan. What kind of fucking idiots are you? I've done some reckless shit in my time, *mais putain, ça, c'est fou!* Do you even know who the LRA are?'

Luca's eyes stayed fixed on his. 'Yeah, I know exactly who they are. You're the one who can't tell who the hell he's shooting at.'

'*Peut-être,*' perhaps, Jean-Luc conceded. 'But that still doesn't change the fact that you both went off into the Ituri like a couple of fucking tourists. The LRA is the most dangerous militia group in the whole of the DRC. They've thousands of soldiers. Thousands! And you thought . . . ' He paused, suddenly catching himself on the radio and realising that the other men would be listening to their conversation.

In the silence Luca turned away, attracting the attention of Louis standing over his machine gun. Luca pointed towards his water bottle. 'I need some water.'

Louis looked back to Jean-Luc for approval before handing it over.

'Listen,' Luca said, wiping his mouth with the back of his hand, 'we have sixteen minutes to talk about what is going to happen, not what's happened. I saw the volcano from the southern side and reckon that if you fly up to the crater, the roof opening should be somewhere west of that.'

Jean-Luc forced himself to focus on the planning. 'How far is the opening from the smoke?'

Luca shrugged slightly. 'I'm not sure. I only saw it from the ground, but it's got to be close.'

'Well, if it's too close, the ash will block our intakes. We'll fall out of the sky like a stone.'

'If it's too close, then we think of something else. One way or another, I'm getting into that mine.'

Jean-Luc could see in Luca's face the same hell-bent determination that he had once known, and suddenly felt a stirring of his own senses. It had been too long since he had felt anything but ambivalence and the desire to forget, one mission blurring into the next. In Luca, he could see something else. And as much as he hated to admit it, it felt like an elixir to him.

'Major, we have an issue,' a voice broke in.

Jean-Luc pulled himself round towards the pilots. 'Go ahead.'

There was a pause while Laurent tried to articulate what he was seeing, his finger pressing down on the comms switch several times before he actually spoke.

'I'm getting readings all over the forest, sir,' he managed.

'What is it?'

'I don't know, sir, but there are thousands of them. The whole console's gone yellow with heat sources. It's like the fucking forest has come alive.'

'Reboot the system. Check it's reading correctly.'

'Sir, it's not the system. I am telling you, there are thousands of people in the forest below us.'

Luca suddenly understood. 'Tell your pilots to pull up!' he shouted. 'Mordecai said his army was marching on the MONUC compound before heading on to Kinshasa. That's what the reading is.'

Jean-Luc stared at him for a moment before speaking low and fast into the mic. 'Break formation. Climb to four thousand feet.'

Scouting out ahead, the Rooivalk was the first to react, climbing at an almost vertical pitch. The Oryx were flying in trail formation behind and, as one, they followed, engines straining from the speed of their ascent. Luca was thrown back against the side of the metal cabin, his arms flailing as he tried to get his balance, before he managed to grip on to some cargo netting and steady himself. The engines grew louder, sending reverberations through the entire hull of the helicopter as the pilots pushed them higher and higher.

Jean-Luc's voice came over the radio. It was level and calm.

'Anyone gets locked on by those SAMs, fire

the magnesium in cluster bursts.'

Through the front window, Luca could see the Rooivalk still climbing, while behind them the two other Oryx helicopters had dropped out of sight. Over the radio they suddenly heard the warning siren of a radar spike, then a long, continuous tone. One of the other helicopters had been missile-locked.

There was the sound of the pilot shouting into the mic, but Luca couldn't hear what was being said. Then from somewhere below them the sky lit up in a blaze of white. It fizzed in long, streaking arcs as bright as lightning, leaving thick trails of hanging smoke as the M-206 counter-measure flares went off in sequence.

A few seconds later they reached 4,000 feet, levelling off with a sickening lurch. Luca stayed exactly where he was, staring into Jean-Luc's face while both of them listened for the sound of an explosion. But none came. For some reason, the LRA hadn't fired their surface-to-air missiles.

One by one the helicopters pulled back into formation and the pilots began to ease up on the controls. In only a few seconds, they had passed over the LRA ground troops and were now out of range.

'OK,' Jean-Luc said. 'Show's over for now.'

'Wait a second,' Luca said. 'If that was the LRA, then who the hell is left guarding the mine? That could mean that they've all gone.'

Jean-Luc didn't bother to turn round. 'Don't get too excited,' he said. 'For all we know that could be just a couple of thousand of them and

357

the rest are still in camp.'

Luca stared at him in disbelief. Just a couple of thousand! He knew nothing about weapons and guns, but how could four helicopters be a match for so many soldiers? Jean-Luc glanced back and caught the expression on his face.

'Hey, don't get me wrong,' he said, a sly smile appearing on his lips. 'A few thousand's a good start.'

★   ★   ★

The Rooivalk led the attack. First one, then an entire stream of its MK4 rockets fired off towards the LRA base, leaving their yellow trails blistering across the sky. They impacted in a series of huge, mushrooming explosions that sent tremors all the way up the side of the volcano, like the aftershock of an earthquake.

Then they heard the 20mm cannon open up. It hammered through the trees and undergrowth in a blaze of white sparks. The Rooivalk's pilot, Laurent, was targeting everything manually, flying in a series of low strafing runs, which followed the natural curve of the volcano. They watched as he twisted the helicopter from side to side, the engines screeching, obliterating everything in his path.

The burning trees lit the ground in a dull, orange glow, sending tall plumes of smoke into the air like chimneystacks. Amongst the wreckage of broken wood and charred bushes, Luca could see the dim silhouettes of figures running for cover. Until that moment he had believed that their attack was little more than suicide, but now it seemed as if nothing could stop the Rooivalk from tearing the LRA base apart.

There was the pop of small-arms fire from somewhere on the edge of the treeline as soldiers fired their AK-47s blindly into the air, but it was several minutes before they heard the first bursts of anti-aircraft fire. The noise was lower, a booming thud that sent the 25mm rounds ripping out into the night sky. The attack had obviously caught the LRA completely off-guard and men were scurrying in all directions, desperately trying to regroup and return fire.

The Rooivalk banked steeply, coming in low across the trees as it faced off a gun battery camouflaged deep into the side of the volcano. While the LRA soldiers frantically swivelled the twin muzzles of Type 87 battery, Laurent sent his last remaining MK4 rocket straight into them. It was a direct hit, the entire combination of men and machinery disintegrating in a ball of orange fire.

'Out of rockets . . . running low on the 20mm,' came Laurent's voice over the radio.

'Pull back, Captain. Save some,' ordered Jean-Luc. 'Bravo and Delta team, give suppressing fire to the north. We're going up to the summit to try and winch into the mine.'

As the other two Oryx moved off into position, Jean-Luc's banked round and began climbing the side of the volcano. The black rock beneath them stretched up in one long, continuous slope until finally, far above them, they could see the faint glow of the crater's rim. As the helicopter powered upwards, Luca suddenly saw a small hut perched on a natural lip of rock. It was about a third of the way up and bristling with satellite dishes. Two men were standing by the door, watching as they roared overhead.

They flew higher, the gradient growing steeper with each moment that passed. Just under the summit, the sides of the volcano rose up into a vertical wall of rock, over one hundred metres high and scored with deep-set cracks. These ran down from the summit like claw marks, with the smoke and ash from the crater hanging in between.

The engines changed pitch as the pilots levelled off, unable to get any closer. The evening breeze had pushed the main column of smoke to the west, barring their way and covering any trace of the opening to the mine. There was silence. Everyone waited for Jean-Luc's next order.

'*Merde!*' Shit! he roared, slamming his fist into the metal wall of the cabin. '*Putain de merde!*'

There was nothing more that could be done. They couldn't get high enough to use their winches and their rockets wouldn't be able to penetrate the side of the volcano. With the entrance tunnels collapsed, the only option left was to dig. But that would take weeks.

Jean-Luc's entire frame seemed to radiate anger, the muscles on his right arm bulging as he gripped the strap above the door. He looked like a cornered animal, turning from one direction to the next as he desperately tried to think of a solution. He screwed his eyes shut and swore once again, unable to accept that there was nothing left to do.

Presently, he opened his eyes again, only to see Luca lying down on the floor with the entire top half of his body leaning out of the open door of the helicopter. He had his right hand wound into the cargo netting to steady himself, while his eyes scanned the side of the volcano, taking in every crack and gully.

Jean-Luc leaned forward and followed the direction of his gaze. The slope looked impassable, with solid slabs of rock reaching all the way up into the haze of volcanic smoke.

'You're fucking kidding,' he whispered.

'Just get me those ropes and a couple of abseiling harnesses,' Luca replied without looking back. 'And drop me at that hut we passed. I saw some kind of a route up from there.'

'I am not going to waste my men or put my helicopters at risk . . . '

'I didn't ask for any help,' Luca said, turning back to face him. 'I climb alone.'

Jean-Luc didn't answer for several seconds, just staring into his eyes.

'Come on!' Luca shouted. 'What other option do you have? This is the only way we can get in.'

Jean-Luc knew that Luca was right. He wondered if such a climb was even possible at night, but the fact remained, this was the only way. Reaching out, he pulled Luca to his feet again.

'We'll set up a perimeter lower down the slope and stop the LRA from cutting you off.'

'If they get even halfway up the slope, there's going to be no way for us to get out of here.'

'You let me worry about that,' Jean-Luc said. 'You concentrate on getting in there and getting Bear out.'

The helicopter seemed to drop out of the sky as the pilot brought them down in a steep-angled dive. When they reached the communications hut, the gunner opened up with an aiming burst, then followed with a long, ragged hail of gunfire that tore through the crooked walls of the hut, killing the men inside. The pilot then skilfully crabbed the helicopter in sideways, inching them on to the flat lip of rock as Jean-Luc jumped out.

'I want the perimeter here,' he shouted over his radio. 'Everyone out of the helicopter! Just leave the rotors turning.'

Luca was standing next to the open door as Louis jumped down and unclipped the rear compartment, delving inside for a few seconds. He emerged with two massive coils of black rope which had been looped into a figure of eight and neatly tied off. He handed them over to Luca then sprinted back to the helicopter, pulling the GPMG machine gun off its door pivot and setting up position on the edge of the rock. Seconds later, the pilot, Thierry, joined him, with his M4 carbine angled down towards the trees.

Luca tied off the two ends of the ropes and wrapped them over his shoulder, so that he was carrying them like a rucksack. He did it with fluid, well-practised flips of his wrists, tucking the spare harness into the folds of the rope and readying himself in just a few seconds.

'I'd send someone up there to watch your back,' Jean-Luc said, 'but I get the feeling they'd only slow you down.'

Luca didn't answer, his eyes already turning up towards the rockface. In the dim light, he could see it stretching off in jagged lines, with the upper reaches completely hidden from view. He could feel that the palms of his hands had already dampened in anticipation and his pulse beat steadily at his throat. In the darkness, he would be climbing blind.

Just as he was about to set off, Jean-Luc grabbed his arm.

'Take this,' he said, offering a small black pistol that he had taken from his webbing belt. 'It's going to be like some kind of hell in that mine and everyone will be wanting to get out on that rope.'

Luca stared at the weapon, never even having held one before. Jean-Luc saw his confusion. 'That's the safety. When you aim at someone, point at their chest and squeeze. Whatever happens, you put your man down.'

Luca let his fingers curl around the grip, the weight of the pistol surprisingly heavy. He reached behind him, tucking it into his belt.

'How long to the top?' Jean-Luc asked.

'An hour, maybe less. It all depends on finding a clean route on the last section. The rock's not good.'

'Well, the others have got just under two hours left in their tanks. After that, there's going to be no more air support.'

Luca nodded. 'Just hold those bastards off as

long as you can. I'll get Bear out.'

Pulling his feet through the leg straps of the harness and tightening the buckle, he jogged to the other side of the rock and started scrambling past the first of the boulders and scree, working his way higher in a smooth, unrelenting rhythm. Jean-Luc stood where he was, watching the faint outline of his body snake higher and higher, until finally it disappeared from view.

A long burst of machine-gun fire echoed out across the forest. He couldn't see where it was coming from exactly, but knew that it was one of his GPMG machine guns. The Oryx were firing and that could only mean one thing.

The LRA counter-attacks had begun.

34

Luca reached the beginning of the summit climb and stopped. He let his gaze roam across the unbroken wall of rock, feeling it looming over him like a living, breathing entity. It looked ominous and unforgiving, while the cracks running down from the top were melded together like a maze of dead ends. From the helicopter, he'd thought he had been able to see some kind of workable route. Now, all that had changed.

He turned, facing out from the mountain, and wiped his hand across his forehead to clear away the sweat. As he brought his arm back down again, he realised that his hands were shaking. He stared at them, terrified by the sight. In all his years of climbing, they had never been like this. He had to slow down, had to climb more carefully. From here onwards, without ropes, all it would take was a single slip.

Far below, he saw a glint of movement as the helicopters patrolled along the edge of the volcano with their machine guns blazing. The noise rolled up towards him like distant thunder, followed each time by the sound of the LRA rifles returning fire.

Battle was raging, but for him it felt distant, almost irrelevant. There was none of the blood and hysteria, the fires and explosions, up here. He was detached from it all.

Luca looked up as the smoke trail of a rocket scorched past one of the helicopters, missing its rotors by what seemed like just a few inches. It continued into the sky like a firework before there was a deep booming explosion and then, a split second later, a shock wave reverberated across the sky. Even from where he stood, he could see that the fighting was becoming more intense. There must be hundreds of LRA down there.

Luca swore, chastising himself for wasting so much time. The battle was nothing to do with him. His was right here, and he had to focus.

Stepping up to the cliff, he reached out both hands and gripped on to the rock. It felt warm beneath his fingertips, but so brittle that he could break off entire pieces of it in his hand. He already knew that it would be too unstable for him to climb normally and that he would have to move in constant motion, never putting too much weight on any one hold.

Blowing the dust off his fingertips, Luca started to work his way up, lightly gripping one handhold, then the next, never holding on too tightly or pressing down too much weight. Entire chunks of rock splintered off in his hands and Luca pitched them over his shoulder, listening to the sound of them clatter down the side of the volcano before becoming lost to the darkness somewhere below.

On he went, higher and higher, the minutes passing like seconds as he became completely absorbed in the climb. Time seemed to condense, no longer measured in seconds but by the stretch of his arm or the bend of his leg. He climbed in fluid, precise movements, with his boots pivoting from one side to the next and his hips pressed flat against the cliff. Then, as he stretched past a slight lip, his foothold crumbled like ash, pitching him downwards. Luca cried out. His hands scraped down the rockface as he desperately tried to break his fall.

By chance, his left foot smashed down into a slight indentation in the rockface, and this time it held. He stayed stock-still, not trusting himself to move an inch, and screwed his eyes shut. His breathing came in quick, shallow bursts and, as he slowly uncurled his fingers, tiny fragments of rock slipped from his grasp.

He felt as if he was about to lose his balance at any moment. Fear had tightened his muscles to bursting point and he could feel panic rising within his chest. He had to stop it, had to fight the fear. He tried to shut it all out and switch his thoughts to Bear. He pictured the shape of her face, the smell of her skin, anything. But each time an image formed in his mind, it dissolved. There was nothing but the cliff and the beckoning darkness below.

'Breathe,' he whispered to himself. 'Just breathe . . . '

A few seconds passed before he managed to open his eyes again. He jerked his head up, refusing to look down and staring towards the summit instead. He could see the grey smudge of smoke fanning out into the sky and guessed that he was nearly halfway up already. Halfway, he repeated to himself. Halfway. He just had to keep on pushing.

Shifting the weight of the ropes on his back, he let his fingers play over the rock face for several seconds, trying to find a solid handhold before moving higher. His body felt leaden and unresponsive but he willed himself on, forcing his arms and legs to respond. He was following a fissure that led up unbroken all the way to the summit. Only a few feet higher it widened out, allowing him to press his whole body inside. With his back squeezed against the rock, he felt much more secure. Slowly, his confidence began to return.

There was a bitter smell of sulphur and Luca looked up to see smoke belching over the summit only twenty-five feet above his head. It rose up in an immense column of ash and vapour, deep orange at its core and fading to a nicotine-stained yellow at the edges. There was the summit . . . only a few feet more to go.

Continuing up the very last of the cliff, Luca reached out his right hand and dragged his body on to the flat surface beyond. For several minutes he lay on his back, letting the relief wash over him. He had made it. The climb was over.

Dragging himself to his feet again, he staggered forward. Smoke was everywhere, clouding his vision and making him walk like a blind man with hands outstretched. His eyes moved from one shadow to the next across the uneven ground, as if expecting the opening of the mine suddenly to appear and swallow him whole. He weaved round one boulder and then another, all his senses straining in the fog.

Then, somewhere to his right, he heard a low metallic clanking sound. It was soft, muffled by the smoke, but he could definitely hear something. As he approached, he suddenly saw the opening loom out of the darkness, running in a long, jagged line across the ground. Lying flat, he craned his neck inside and saw the dull pinpricks of electric lighting and the grey outline of the wooden balconies far beneath. This was it! He'd found it!

With a sudden surge of energy, Luca shrugged off the ropes, feeding one of them out on the ground to check for knots. The other he left still coiled. He would use it for abseiling down the cliff he had just climbed.

About three metres from the edge of the opening lay a waist-height boulder and Luca tied the rope off around it. He then dumped the remaining slack into the mine, watching the line pull taut under its own weight. With the spare harness tucked over his shoulder, Luca fed the rope through his 'eight' abseiling device, before moving his feet out to the edge of the opening. He could feel the heat and stale air rising up towards him, and suddenly the reality of what lay beneath struck home.

He was going back into the mine. And all that he had to defend himself with was a pistol that he didn't know how to fire.

★　★　★

Luca dropped in, abseiling with his face turned up towards the massive domed roof. It seemed to close in around him like a shroud, while clouds of black dust hung in the air and the air grew stiflingly hot. Luca felt as if he were descending into the very pit of hell.

Below him, shapes began to emerge. They were only impressions at first, but soon he recognised the lines of the balconies and the arching necks of the cranes used to control the heavy metal troughs. Then, as he reached about thirty feet above the first level, he could see the faint outlines of human beings. They were sitting on the floor with their heads slumped forward, waiting for the time to crawl by. The hope of a miraculous rescue had long since faded. Now they only waited to die.

Luca reached the ground and pulled the remaining slack through his harness. A group of four men stood staring at him. All of them were gaunt and desperate, their faces twisted in confusion as they tried to understand who he was and what he was doing. They moved closer, their eyes cautiously flickering between him and the dangling rope, not daring to believe that it could be true. Suddenly, one of them shouted in excitement, realising that Luca couldn't possibly be LRA. He was a white man.

As one, they surged forward, crowding around him and shouting with joy. Two of them reached up and grabbed on to the rope, as if to check it was real, tugging down on it with all their might. Gradually, the commotion filtered down across the levels of the mine. It was such a different sound from the low groans of despair that it instantly woke the other miners from their apathy.

'Bear!' Luca shouted. He gripped on to the rope, hoisting himself above the gathering crowd, and shouted her name again. More miners had come, and still more were scaling the metal chains between the levels. They climbed as fast as they could, moving like spiders to a fly.

'Bear!'

One of the miners shunted Luca to one side and, curling his fingers into the rope, tried to climb it. His forearms shook with strain for several seconds before slowly he slid back down again. Another man immediately jumped up, frantically grabbing hand over hand, but the rope was just too slippery. He was roughly pulled out of the way as another contender pushed forward and began trying to scale it.

Luca watched, knowing full well that they would never make it more than a few metres. It was a 10.5mm static line rope with a full Teflon coating. It was impossible to climb it without the proper gear, and already the miners were starting to become frustrated.

People were now crowded around the rope, jostling and fighting to get their turn to climb. Fights were already breaking out on the periphery, while in the centre the rope bounced up and down. Three men were trying to climb at the same time, their elbows smashing into each other's face and chests as they vied for position.

Luca pushed his way out from the crowd and ran over to the edge of the balcony. Along the entire length of the mine's grim interior, he saw men climbing, pulling themselves up the chains with desperate abandon. He stared from one to the next, never having dreamed that there could be so many people inside this hell.

Where could Bear be? What had that bastard Mordecai done with her?

Sprinting to the other side of the balcony, he tried to get a better vantage point into the atrium. He passed row upon row of heavy lifting cranes, their chains swinging and clanking as the miners tried to climb up, and then he saw the huge pile of rubble fanning out from where the entrance tunnel had been. Ten metres further on, there was a crooked hut tucked back into the edge of the mine. It was the only structure left on the first level.

As Luca kicked open the door, he immediately saw Bear, slumped on a low chair with one arm trailing to the floor. He rushed forward, a terrible fear growing inside him that she was dead, but as he grabbed her arm, she gave a soft moan. Gently cradling her face in his hands, Luca tried to say something but found the words choking on his lips. An incredible wave of relief and happiness washed over him and he let his forehead drop on to hers as he whispered her name over and over again.

A few seconds passed before Bear opened her eyes. Her pupils were wide from concussion, staring straight at him.

'You came back,' she whispered, barely able to speak, her lips were so cracked and dry.

She looked tired, so deathly tired that it was obvious she was struggling just to stay conscious. Leaning forward, she pressed the weight of her head into his hands and Luca held her close, curling his fingers into her hair.

'I can't believe you're alive,' he whispered. 'The whole time I was running, I thought that I would never see you again.'

Bear's face tilted to one side and he could see the tears welling up in the corners of her eyes. For a long while she didn't speak, but stared into his eyes while she silently cried. Luca squeezed her to him, so that her whole body was resting against his.

'I didn't think anyone was coming,' Bear managed. 'I thought that was it.'

Luca leaned forward and kissed her. He felt her reach up and gently rest the palm of her hand on his cheek.

'Take me away from here,' she whispered.

'Can you walk?' he asked.

'I got . . . hit on the head,' she murmured, the dryness in her mouth making her voice rasp. 'I can't see so well.'

As she said the words, Luca saw the trail of dried blood coming down from one ear. That bastard bodyguard must have burst her eardrum. Swinging her arm over his shoulder, Luca held her tightly against him.

'Just hold on to me. This time, we're getting out of here.'

Emerging into the main body of the mine, they saw that the crowd had grown. All those who were able had climbed up to the top level and now over a hundred people were surrounding the rope. It swayed from side to side as the miners fought to try and climb it. A couple of men had succeeded in getting a few metres off the ground, but they were tiring fast, and now all they could do was to hang on to the rope as it jerked violently in their grip.

Bear and Luca stared at the scene, watching as the miners turned on each other in desperation. They were pulling people out of their way and stepping on the bodies of those who had already fallen.

'My pistol,' Bear said, suddenly realising that she had left it back in the guardhouse.

'Try this one,' Luca offered, pulling it from his belt and handing it across. 'Your father gave it to me.'

'My father? What do you mean?'

Luca could see the sudden hope in her eyes. 'He's outside with a load of helicopters, bombing the shit out of the LRA.'

The look of disbelief on Bear's face slowly gave way to a faint smile.

'I hope he kills every last one of them,' she whispered, and raising the pistol, she suddenly fired two shots into the air. The blast echoed around the closed walls of the mine, silencing the miners.

'*Reculez de la corde!*' Get back from the rope! Bear ordered, but her voice was still weak and barely carried across the crowd. As they approached, her body slumped against Luca's for support, with her one arm raised to aim the pistol.

'*Reculez!*' Get back! She snarled again, and the crowd shuffled back a pace.

'Easy,' Luca whispered. 'All we need is their attention. I need you to translate for me. Tell them that I can show them a way out of here. That I can teach them how to climb the rope.'

Bear tried to steady herself against his shoulder, dropping the pistol to her side. She then shouted out to the crowd as best as she could. They were deathly silent as they listened to what she said. Everyone had seen how pointless it was trying to climb with bare hands. Finally, here was a solution.

'Take off your boots,' Luca said to Bear, crouching down on the ground.

'What?'

'I need your laces. Come on . . . quickly.'

Luca stepped up to the centre of the crowd with his hands raised so that everyone could see. He then took the first of his bootlaces and tied the two ends together in a tight knot. After doing the same for the other, he moved over to the main abseiling rope and attached the two lines, looping them back in on themselves three times each.

'It's called a prussic,' Luca explained over his shoulder. 'We use it in crevasse rescue all the time. The knot slides up the rope, but jams if you put weight on it.'

Making one of the loops longer than the other, he placed the toe of his boot inside.

'You use one of the prussics for your foot and the other attaches to your harness. That way, you can use your legs to step up and climb the rope.'

'But none of these men have harnesses,' Bear objected.

'Yeah, but they can just tie it on to a belt or another line around their waist. That's all it takes. And tell them that when they reach the top, they've got to sit tight and wait for a rescue. It's a war zone out there, but they'll be safe as long as they stay on the summit.'

As Luca finished, there was an excited murmur amongst the crowd, with those who had laces already reaching for them. Others had already left to go in search of rope. Quickly looping the spare harness around Bear's legs, Luca walked her up to the line and attached the prussics.

'You got the strength for this?' he asked, brushing away a strand of hair from her eyes.

'I'll make it. Anything to get out of here.'

Luca helped her fit her right boot into the loop. At first, Bear's movements were laborious and slow, the prussic knots jamming each time she pushed down on her foot. But soon, she was making real progress, with her hands and feet moving in unison. By the time Luca had got ready, she was already thirty metres above their heads, and gaining.

Luca followed, his movements fluid and well practised, and in what seemed like just a few seconds, he was already at the same height. A cheer went up from the crowd as they watched them move up the rope together and soon disappear into the shadows of the mine.

Far below, the miners had already begun to follow.

35

There was movement between the trees. Silhouettes glided from one trunk to the next, no more than blurred outlines in the darkness. The LRA was amassing just beyond the edge of the volcano, and for nearly half an hour Jean-Luc had been watching their numbers steadily increase. He could see only glimpses, but knew that there were hundreds of them out there, silently waiting in the shadows.

The gunner, Louis, shifted his position slightly, pressing the wooden butt of the machine gun tight into his shoulder and taking in the slack on the trigger. Sweat ran freely down his face. Five metres further on from him, the pilot, Thierry, had stacked six magazines of 5.56mm ammunition on the rocks to one side of his M4 carbine. He was staring down the night sight of his rifle, switching from one movement to the next amongst the trees.

'I want short, controlled bursts,' Jean-Luc whispered. 'Don't use your grenades too early.'

He knew both men were veterans and wouldn't fire wildly into the night, but he also knew how his men locked on to the sound of his voice before an attack. It gave them something to focus on, grounding them against the rising panic and helping them keep control.

Jean-Luc looked back towards the helicopter. It was tucked far enough into the side of the volcano to be out of the LRA's direct line of fire, but if they broke out the W-89 mortars, they wouldn't stand a chance of escape. Their only hope was that Mordecai had taken all the main field weaponry with him on the march to Kinshasa.

From somewhere deep in the forest, they heard the low beat of drums. It was slow at first, methodical and unhurried, but soon the tempo built. Others joined, the beats becoming one, blurring into a frenzied crescendo of noise and motion. Then came the smoke. From the edge of the trees, smoke grenades were tossed out into the no-man's-land between them and the LRA, and soon thick acrid clouds drifted up into the air. It formed an impenetrable wall, masking the beginnings of the counter-attack and closing the distance between them.

'Steady,' Jean-Luc whispered. 'Put each man down. One by one.'

He stared at the nearest of the grenades as it lay on the rock thirty feet below him. Smoke belched out in a continuous flow, flooding the entire area in a surreal, blood-red glow. A shrill scream went up as suddenly a wave of LRA soldiers charged. They sprinted through the smoke in a rough line with their heads thrown back and their mouths open wide. They clambered over the first of the rocks with their AK-47s blazing. Most were firing on full automatic with the bullets ricocheting wildly off the rocks far above Jean-Luc's head, while others were simply running, their faces contorted by their screams.

As one, Jean-Luc and his men opened up. They fired in bursts of two rounds, taking down one man, then the next, in quick succession. It was relentless, each man shifting his elbows on the hard rock as he brought his line of fire on to the next soldier. The whole battle became a series of movements, with one soldier reaching up to his neck as a bullet passed straight through his throat while another doubled over as a bullet tore through his insides, the exit wound pulling out a great chunk of flesh by his liver. Everywhere, the macabre silhouette of wounded human figures danced and twisted, backlit by the blood-red smoke.

The carnage continued, with the steady double-tap shots of the mercenaries rising above the wild burst of the LRA guns. As the last few soldiers clambered forward, Louis fired a long, raking burst with the GPMG, swinging the barrel right across the entire field. The bullets cut through every living thing, dropping those still standing and severing the limbs of those already lying on the ground.

A confusion of bodies was left, with few killed outright. Most had their hands clasped over their injuries, screaming in pain.

'Reload,' Jean-Luc shouted, ejecting the magazine on his G3 rifle and smoothly clipping in another. He stared down at the wounded lying on the ground and saw they were barely more than teenagers. The LRA commanders were obviously throwing their most inexperienced troops at them first, saving the hardened fighters until last.

The drum started again and another scream went up as the next wave of LRA attacked. They ran with the same blood-curdling shouts, the same desperate abandon. There was no fear or hesitation, no pause or respite. It was as if each of them had somehow missed the slaughter of their comrades, just seconds before.

The three mercenaries worked swiftly, shifting between targets and squeezing off round after round. The barrels of their rifles smoked in an unbroken stream, while around them hundreds of bullet casings lay spread out on the rocks, the metal still warm to the touch. To the right, a group of four LRA soldiers had made it nearly two-thirds of the way up the slope. They were ducking and weaving between what little natural cover there was. And they were making ground. Thierry levelled the sights of his rifle on to them and fired, but the sweat was dripping into his eyes, making it hard for him to see. He managed to take down only one man. Three of them still remained, getting closer by the second.

Jean-Luc swung round so that he was half resting on his back and fired the 40mm grenade launcher tucked under the barrel of his rifle. It went off with a deep, rolling boom, blowing the men apart in a fine shower of blood.

Just as they were reloading, another wave burst through the smoke. These LRA soldiers were more experienced and attacked in proper military style, with one man advancing as another crouched down, giving covering fire. They jumped over their fallen comrades, gaining ground and coming within range of their grenades.

Explosions went off in clusters all around them. Those that remained were close now, only a few metres further down the slope, almost upon them. Jean-Luc quickly raised himself up, dragging the barrel of his rifle from right to left on full automatic and mowing the men down at waist-height. To his right, he could hear the sound of Thierry's M4 firing, but just beside him Louis had gone silent.

As the last of the LRA soldiers finally fell to the ground, Jean-Luc turned towards his men. Louis's head was resting flat against the rock with his gun tilted into the air. Jean-Luc could see that a lump of shrapnel had staved in the top part of the gunner's head.

'*Désolé, mon ami*,' Sorry, my friend, Jean-Luc whispered, as he turned back towards the forest. Above the wash of red smoke, he could see one of his Oryx helicopters circling. It had been firing in constant bursts, cutting the main body of the LRA army in half and preventing those deeper in the forest from reaching Jean-Luc and his men. As the Oryx banked round for another pass, a rocket was fired from the ground. This time it found its mark and the tailfin of the Oryx disintegrated in a blast of fire and metal.

They watched as the helicopter lurched to one side and the cabin began to swing round on its own axis. Without the stabilising rear rotor, it whipped in a circle, faster and faster, while the machine fell from the sky. As a distant cheer rose up, Jean-Luc watched it crash into the tops of the trees before finally disappearing from view.

'Laurent,' he shouted into his radio as the sound of drums began again. 'Fifty feet below our position. Use the twenty-millimetre.'

The Rooivalk swooped down for one last pass. The cannon under its belly swivelled, spitting out the last of its rounds in a long burst of gunfire that ripped through the forest. Bits of bark splintered off and the ground became alive in the maelstrom, destroying the next wave of the LRA attack before it had even begun. The helicopter roared overhead, then pulled back into a hover on the far edge of the battlefield, just beyond the range of the RPGs.

'You can't do anything else,' Jean-Luc shouted into his radio. 'Now get the hell out of here.'

'Sorry, Major,' came Laurent's voice. 'It's over five hours before I can reload and get back.'

Jean-Luc pressed the earpiece hard against his head, trying to make out what Laurent was saying above the noise of the drums.

'Say again,' he shouted.

'Rotation. Five hours for reload.'

'Copy that. Now get clear.'

As he gave the order, Thierry turned to look at him with doubt in his eyes. Their own helicopter was sitting twenty feet behind them with its rotors still turning. It was their only chance of escape. They had to take it.

'Major,' he shouted. 'Five hours? Even with the last of the 7.62mm rounds, we've only got enough for one more attack, two at most.'

'Man your post. We wait until Luca and Beatrice get back.'

Thierry's jaw clenched.

'Don't you get it, Major? That was an impossible climb! There is no way he would have been able to get into the mine.'

'We maintain this perimeter,' Jean-Luc snarled, reaching out his fist and grabbing the front of Thierry's webbing. 'That's it.'

'But this is suicide,' Thierry whispered, his voice rising in desperation.

Jean-Luc's fist clenched harder. 'You man up! We're not leaving this position.'

Thierry stared rigidly down the sights of his rifle. They had already lost one helicopter, but still the Major couldn't see what had been obvious to them all. No one could have made that climb at night. They were waiting for dead men.

In the distance, they saw two more rockets rise up. The first missed the last Oryx, while the second detonated twenty or so feet to its port side, rocking the entire aircraft. Slowly, it listed over and started to lose altitude, the engines whining under duress, until it fell down into the trees and exploded in a mushrooming ball of smoke and red flame.

'What do we do now?' Thierry screamed. 'What the hell do we do? There's one chopper left against an entire fucking army!'

Laying down his rifle on the rocks, he stared at Jean-Luc, eyes shining with impotent fury. 'Major! We have to leave now! I'm getting on that chopper.'

Jean-Luc didn't turn towards him, but when he spoke his voice came out in a low hiss.

'Pick up that weapon or I will kill you myself.'

Thierry didn't move and slowly Jean-Luc's finger slid up to the trigger guard of his rifle. He was ready to turn round in an instant if Thierry decided to do something stupid and put a bullet in his back. But then, out of the corner of his eye, he saw Thierry slowly pick up the weapon. He chambered the first round, just as the next wave of attacks begun.

Jean-Luc emptied the last of his ammunition in quick controlled bursts, then switched to the 40mm grenades, loading each one into the chamber individually and firing them off. To his right, he could hear Thierry firing on automatic, screaming as he shot at anything that moved.

This was their last stand, and both of them knew it.

As Jean-Luc reached out to grab the last of his grenades, he suddenly caught sight of movement past the Oryx. A small team of LRA had scaled a near-vertical section of the slope and was now trying to outflank them. Pulling back from the edge, he skirted around the tailfin of the helicopter and fired his last remaining grenade. It detonated a few feet in front of the group in a blaze of fire and white smoke, leaving a trail of bodies strewn across the rocks.

Just as he was turning back, he saw one of the bodies slowly clamber to its feet. The man swayed slightly as he fought to regain his balance. Even from the distance, Jean-Luc could see that he was vast, with massive brawny shoulders sloping down into a wide back. He had obviously lost his weapon in the explosion and Jean-Luc waited for him to retreat, but instead he started a slow, lumbering jog towards him.

'What the hell?' Jean-Luc whispered, eyes narrowing in disbelief. He stared for a few seconds more, bewildered by the sheer insanity of the attack. The man was now clearly visible, approaching fast. He was half-naked from the waist up, with bulging muscles knotted across his abdomen and arms. A solid mass of V-shaped cutting scars ran down from the crown of his massive head, giving his features a cruel, inhuman look.

It was the Captain of the LRA patrol. When he was within ten paces, Jean-Luc swiftly reached for his pistol but his fingers encountered the empty leather of the holster. He had given the pistol to Luca! Just as the Captain bore down on him, Jean-Luc yanked out his throwing knife and spun it hard at the man's throat. The blade dug deep into the Captain's breastplate, but did nothing to stop him.

The man roared with pain, reaching out to grab Jean-Luc. As his fingers widened in anticipation, Jean-Luc ducked swiftly out from under him, smashing his fist directly into the Captain's jaw with an audible crack.

Jean-Luc stepped away, retreating in a wide circle and shaking his hand. The Captain slowly turned round to face him. The punch had split the skin over his chin and lip, splattering blood across his mouth, but the man seemed not to have noticed. He smiled, revealing the blackened points of filed teeth. He threw his head back, roaring in defiance as he reached up and ripped the throwing knife out of his own chest.

Jean-Luc had his fists raised like a prize fighter as they came together again and landed a clean one-two on the Captain's face and chest before ducking out from under his reach. He danced round, feigning a left jab, before swooping in low and twisting up with a massive right hook. It slammed into the side of the Captain's face, jarring his whole head to one side.

Backing away again, Jean-Luc watched as the monster before him simply stretched out his jaw and gave a slow shake of his head. That hook was one of the hardest punches Jean-Luc had ever thrown, yet it hadn't stopped his opponent for a second. As the Captain loomed closer, Jean-Luc could see the line of saliva oozing out from between his teeth. His eyes looked glazed from drugs which coursed through his veins, blocking out any sensation of pain or emotion.

Jean-Luc connected with another jab, but as he tried to roll out again, found his whole body being swung off balance as the Captain pulled him closer. He had managed to grab hold of Jean-Luc's front webbing and, with a swing of his gigantic head, butted him on the corner of his eye and lashed out with the knife. Jean-Luc went reeling backwards as the blade flashed past his throat, missing him by an inch.

Collapsing on his knees, Jean-Luc ran his fingers over the deep indentation in his face where his cheekbone had been caved in. The

Captain came in for the kill, with the knife raised high above his head. As he drew level, Jean-Luc suddenly pivoted round, sending the heel of his right boot crashing into the man's kneecap. It snapped, backwards, instantly dropping him him on to the ground.

The Captain bellowed a scream of pure rage as he swung his huge torso round in the dirt. Jean-Luc pulled himself backwards over the ground, trying to get clear, but as he finally stood up, his vision swam from the blow to his head and he fell to the ground again.

The Captain flung himself forward so that his body landed on top of Jean-Luc's. He gripped the knife in his right hand, driving it into Jean-Luc's belly with all his strength. As the blade went in deeper, Jean-Luc's body spasmed and he let out a low gurgling sound. The Captain pulled himself closer, so that his face was right in front of him.

'*Oui*,' he breathed. '*Sentez-le*.' Feel it.

Jean-Luc stared back into those black, gleeful eyes, filled with absolute evil. He couldn't tear his gaze away. It felt as if they were draining the life from him with each second that passed. Then a single gunshot rang out and the Captain's head suddenly slumped down on to Jean-Luc's chest. For a moment he lay there, unable to move, while warm blood soaked into his neck and shoulders.

'Major,' Thierry shouted. 'Are you all right?'

He was standing just to their left with his rifle still raised. After a moment's hesitation, he ran forward and pulled the deadweight of the

387

Captain off Jean-Luc.

Jean-Luc stood up with his legs wide, trying to steady himself. He knew enough about abdominal wounds not to pull the knife from his body, but could feel that the blade had gone deep into his stomach. Too deep. As he stood there, swaying slightly, he knew that now it was only a matter of time.

'Major!' Thierry shouted.

'Yes, I'm OK,' Jean-Luc whispered, resting his arm on Thierry's shoulder. 'Thank you.'

As they staggered back towards the helicopter, Jean-Luc could see the black hilt of the knife protruding above the line of his webbing. It felt surreal, such a small thing, yet there it was. And now, without proper medical attention, there was nothing more that could be done.

Reaching up to his breast pocket, he pulled out a cigarette. The tobacco was crushed flat, but it still lit and he drew down deeply on it.

'Bring the GPMG back from the edge,' Jean-Luc ordered. 'And stack up the last of the ammo.'

As Thierry moved off, Jean-Luc gripped the knife hilt. He had seen many men die of stomach wounds before; watched as they writhed in pain, begging for it to end quickly. Whatever happened, he couldn't let Bear see him that way. After all he had put her through, he was not going to let her see him like that.

Shutting his eyes, he yanked the blade out of his stomach, gasping as blood spurted out, soaking down into the fabric of his trousers. He let the knife drop from his hand and stared at it for several seconds, only looking up again as Thierry returned.

'The attacks have stopped,' he said. 'I saw gunfire farther over to the west, down past the edge of the volcano. What the hell's going on, Major? Why are they retreating?'

'It's the Mai-Mai. Devlin's finally got them here. The LRA are regrouping,' Jean-Luc managed, staring out towards the outline of the forest. They heard the sound of rifle fire intensifying, rattling out in bursts from one side then the next. There was the whoosh of another RPG, followed by an explosion.

Jean-Luc offered Thierry a drag of his cigarette.

'The Mai-Mai should keep them occupied for . . . ' he said, then stopped as behind them they heard a shout from higher up the slope. It was a woman's voice.

They saw two figures clambering down the last of the rocks towards them, then a moment later Bear burst on to the flat ground with Luca trailing behind. She rushed forward with her unlaced boots flapping open, and without breaking stride ran into her father's arms. Jean-Luc wrapped his arms around her body, hugging her to him.

'Papa,' she whispered.

36

Thierry strapped himself into the pilot's seat of the helicopter and immediately began prepping them for take off. His hands moved over the switches in a steady rhythm while behind him Luca clambered on board, listening while the engine changed pitch and the rotors began to quicken. They whipped up dust from the ground in a wide radius. Arm in arm, Jean-Luc and Bear hurried towards the cabin, the tops of their heads pressed together. Jean-Luc was gently pushing her forward with each stride and, as she ducked under the rotors and came into the light, Luca could see that she was crying.

'*Mais je ne comprends pas,*' But I don't understand, she pleaded, turning to face her father straight on. '*Pourquoi tu ne viens pas maintenant?*' Why won't you come now?

Jean-Luc hugged her close, kissing the top of her head and brushing her hair back from her eyes.

'*Je dois rester et attendre les autres mineurs.*' I have to stay and wait for the other miners. 'It's OK, *bébé.* You go and I'll catch up.'

'Please, Papa. Don't do this now,' Bear begged, her forehead creasing in confusion. '*Quelqu'un d'autre peut faire çela. Viens avec moi.*' Someone else can do that. Come with me.

Jean-Luc gave a faint smile. 'But no one else is left,' he said, then raising his right hand, he gently stroked her cheek, knowing that it was the last time he would ever see his daughter. He saw that his fingers had left a thin trail of blood down the side of her face.

'I'm sorry, Beatrice,' he whispered into her ear. 'I am so sorry for everything.'

'Papa!' Bear cried, the tears running freely down her cheeks. 'Please, Papa, stop this! Get on board the helicopter.'

'Not this time,' Jean-Luc said, his voice cracking slightly. '*Je t'ai toujours aimé, ma petite.*' I have always loved you.

Pushing her up into the cabin, he gestured at Luca to take hold of her and stop her from climbing back out.

'Fly low and get to Goma,' he ordered Thierry. 'Contact Dr Samuels from *Médecins Sans Frontières* in Kigali and get them to bring their Sikorsky. It's the only helicopter big enough around here to carry out all the miners. The Mai-Mai should tie up these bastards for a good few hours, and Laurent should be able to cover them during the extraction.'

In the front seat of the helicopter, Thierry twisted round so that he could see Jean-Luc.

'Copy that, Major.'

'Now go!'

Thierry switched back to the cockpit and brought up the throttle. The sound of the engines drowned out Bear's screams as she fought against Luca's grip. Her whole body arched as she tried to break free, while just to one side of the helicopter Jean-Luc stayed stock-still, not attempting to move back or try to shield his eyes from the blast of the rotors, as slowly the helicopter drew up from the ground and started to bank round. It hung there for a split second longer, before the nose dropped forward and Thierry pitched them headlong into the night.

As the sound of the rotors subsided, Jean-Luc continued to stare. He stayed like that long after the helicopter had disappeared from view, until finally his knees gave out from under him and he dropped to the ground. He sank back so that he was sitting with his legs outstretched in front of him, listening while his breath started to slow, coming in heavy, drawn-out gasps. Already, he knew he had done the right thing. Bear should never have to see him like this.

He stared out across the dark silhouettes of the forest. The trees were only just distinguishable in the faint moonlight and he watched as the high branches bent and swayed in the evening breeze, listening to the soft rustle of leaves. The drums had moved off, farther to the west, and the sound of machine-gun fire was lessening.

For the longest time he stayed like that, letting his eyes drift over the endless forest, and marvelling at the sight of it. It stretched on and on, infinite and perfect.

This was the Africa he knew.

★　★　★

'We can't have made more than three miles,' Luca shouted into the mic. 'Head due south from the mine.'

Thierry nodded, his eyes moving across to the GPS on the screen and minutely realigning their course. He stared at the fuel gauge, shocked at just how little was left in their tanks, and dropped their speed a fraction. They would be coming into Goma on the very last of their reserves.

'We have fuel to circle for twelve minutes,' he said into the radio. 'No more. After that, I don't care what happens, we are leaving.'

'Don't worry, he'll hear us,' Luca replied. 'You just look for the red smoke.'

Thierry nodded again, blinking several times as he tried to force himself to stay alert. Now that the battle was over and the last of the adrenalin had ebbed away, he felt absolutely exhausted. As he raised his right hand to rub the skin at the corners of his eyes, he could smell the bitter stench of cordite on his fingers, while his left ear was still ringing from firing so many rounds. From experience, he knew that it would only take a couple of days for him to be back to normal physically, but for the rest it sometimes took weeks.

Behind him in the cabin, Luca turned back to where Bear was sitting with her arms clamped tight across her body. Her hair tumbled around her face, obscuring her eyes, and she was rocking backwards and forwards.

Sitting on the bench next to her, Luca put his arm around her shoulders and gently pulled her against him. He could feel the soft tremors in her body and for several minutes they stayed like that, staring blankly towards the open door and watching the forest move past beneath them. Eventually, Bear turned her face towards him.

'He's not coming back, is he?'

Luca slowly shook his head.

'I'm sorry, Bear,' he whispered.

'Why do I care?' she asked, sniffing loudly. 'I haven't seen him in nine years so why the hell do I care *now*?'

She shut her eyes. Nothing seemed to make sense any more. Why did her father stay behind like that? After going through so much to get her out of the mine, why would he leave her now? Bear closed her eyes, feeling her chest tighten. It was as if a weight were pressing down on her; a massive, immovable weight that she could no longer support.

'I just don't understand.'

'All I know is that he risked everything to get you out of there,' Luca said.

'So why leave me now?'

'I don't know, but I can only guess that he had his reasons.'

As Luca said the words, the helicopter suddenly banked to the right. He looked up to see Thierry craning forward in his seat as he tried to peer down into the forest below.

'Visual on the smoke,' he shouted triumphantly.

Clambering towards the open door, Luca peered out into the darkness. The helicopter started to descend in a wide arc, circling down on a point somewhere beneath them. As they dropped lower, the forest seemed to rise up around them. Luca watched the leaves and branches shake from the downdraft of the rotors, before pulling back from the edge and clipping his abseiling harness into the winch. He was searching for the controls when Bear suddenly stood up and flipped back a small panel on the rear wall of the cabin.

'I'll lower you in,' she said.

'Thanks,' Luca replied. He could still see the pain in her eyes, but with it was a look of steely determination.

'Just make sure you bring me in slow on the last bit,' Luca said, before moving out to the edge of the cabin and sinking his weight into his harness. Just below, he could see a faint column of smoke steadily rising up through the trees.

'Go get him,' Bear said, and pressing the winch button, sent him winding downwards.

Luca raised his hands to protect his face as he ripped down through the branches. Breaking through the upper layers of the canopy, he sped towards the ground before landing heavily in the mud. He unclipped himself from the winch and ran forward, frantically searching for the source of the smoke.

'Luca!'

He could hear his name being called above the sound of the rotors, and crashed headlong through the bush, but it was so hard to see. There was nothing but clouds of red smoke and the twisted silhouettes of the undergrowth.

'Luca!'

Then he saw him. Just ahead was a large, overhanging bush and underneath was Joshua. He was lying on one side with his body propped up on his elbows, and as their eyes met, Joshua's head dropped forward on to his chest in sheer, exhausted relief. Luca scrambled across to him and grabbed him by his shoulders, hugging him tight.

'You son-of-a-bitch,' Luca managed. 'You made it!'

Joshua didn't reply, but an exhausted smile crossed his lips. After all the waiting and doubt, it was finally over and he let his whole body slump against his friend's.

'I didn't think you were coming back,' he whispered. 'I was just waiting . . . '

He stopped, tilting his head up, and Luca watched as his smile slowly faded. He suddenly looked terrified. The hours of waiting had taken their toll and Joshua reached out a hand, gripping on to Luca's wrist.

'It's over, mate,' Luca said, squeezing his hand. 'It's all over.'

The look in Joshua's eyes was scaring him and he forced himself to smile. 'Now get up, because this is the last time I'm rescuing you today.'

A ghost of a smile passed across Joshua's lips. Luca hauled him up and together they shuffled back towards the winch line. With each step, Joshua's right leg scraped across the sodden ground and, as they rounded a clump of bushes, he suddenly turned towards Luca.

'Did you get the others out? The other miners, I mean.'

Luca nodded, grimacing as he slipped down on one knee in the mud.

'I left a static line up to the roof and showed them how to use prussics.'

Just ahead of them, Luca could see the winch line cutting down through the trees, while directly above they heard the steady boom of the helicopter.

'We've got to get hold of MONUC,' Joshua shouted. 'Get them over to the mine.'

'It's all in hand,' Luca shouted. 'Now for once in your life, stop worrying about other people and let's get out of here.'

Joshua nodded, gripping Luca's shoulders as he clicked down on the radio and Bear started the winch. They were effortlessly drawn up into the air, both of them hunching over as the branches raked their backs and faces. Up they went, past the tops of the trees and on towards the dull green fuselage of the helicopter hovering just above. They could see Bear leaning out with her hair streaming wildly around her.

As they reached the top of the winch, she grabbed on to them, swinging them inside the cabin and releasing some slack. They came crashing down on the floor in a heap of arms and legs, with Bear reaching out a hand to steady Joshua. Before she even had time to get him to a seat, Thierry had swung the helicopter round and started for Goma.

'You OK?' Bear shouted, helping Joshua back on to the rear bench and giving him a headset. Joshua nodded, sitting down heavily. Only then did she see how haunted he looked. In the dull lights of the cabin, his face looked ashen, his cheeks hollow and stretched, dazed by fear. It was a look Bear knew only too well.

'It's all over now,' she said, reaching out towards him. Joshua gripped her hand, still trying to come to terms with the fact that the ordeal was over. After so many months held in the mine, it felt impossible that he was finally free from Mordecai, and from the endless forest.

On the other side of the cabin, Luca sat hunched against the side of the cabin, his head in his hands. Now that it was all over, his body seemed to have shut down, and his eyes were already starting to close. He had been strung out for day after day, pushing himself beyond anything he had thought possible, and now there was simply nothing left to give. As his head dropped from his hands, jerking him awake, Joshua called across to him.

'Luca, you said the other miners were OK. What's happening?'

He looked up wearily and pointed towards Thierry. 'The pilot's already put a call into *Médecins Sans Frontières* in Uganda. They're going to get some big helicopter to come and rescue the others.'

'But what about the LRA?'

'The main part of Mordecai's army is marching south and Bear's father pretty much dealt with the ones who remained at the mine. And now the Mai-Mai are also there, finishing them off.'

'The Mai-Mai? What the hell are they doing involved in all this?' Joshua whispered, barely able to believe that the LRA at the mine had been defeated.

'Who the hell knows?'

'And what about the fire coltan? Has anyone got the message out?'

Luca shook his head. 'First, we get you to a hospital. Then, we'll deal with all that.'

'No,' his friend said, fighting the tiredness in his own voice. 'I can wait, but that stuff can't. We need to find out where it was being shipped and warn the people involved. We've got to stop it ever getting out on to the open market.'

'We can trace it through my company,' Bear offered, but as she spoke Thierry's voice cut in on the radio.

'Two days ago, we delivered some Chinese general to the LRA base. The Major said that he was the guy in charge of all the shipments we've been running.'

'So who is he?' Joshua asked.

'I don't know, but I do know that we picked him up from one of the old colonial houses down by the lake.'

'Can you get us there?'

Thierry nodded. The old Belgian residences lined the shores of Lake Kivu and were less than a kilometre from the airport. Even without checking his instruments, he knew they would have enough fuel to make it.

'I can get you there, but by now I reckon those guys must be long gone.'

37

Three Nissan Patrol 4x4s followed the old dirt road beside the shore of Lake Kivu. They drove in tight convoy, their headlights blazing the way as they snaked down the potholed road and past the lines of old mansions tucked into the hillside. The cars drove slowly, taking care not to jostle the passenger sitting in the rear seat of the middle vehicle, surrounded by a handpicked squad of PLA Special Forces.

As they passed the first in the line of mansions, Kai Long Pi turned his gaze out through the window, resting his old head against the glass. Most of the houses visible were little more than shells with broken-down walls and glassless windows, while black-eyed vines had reclaimed the once-cultivated lawns. Farther along, he could see the soft glow of lights from a huge house built on a peninsula jutting out into the lake. It was the only one still inhabited.

Kai adjusted the angle of his right leg. As he moved, the doctor sitting in the passenger seat next to him immediately reached across to do it for him, but Kai slapped his hands away. The movement caused the thin oxygen tube running up to his nostrils to come loose, flapping over his cheek, and Kai jerked to one side testily as he tried to realign it. The tube was only installed when he was travelling and it was the one part of his medical treatment that infuriated him.

Despite arriving in Africa by private jet and his entourage attending to his every need, the journey from Shanghai to Goma had been long and exhausting for him. He did not like damp climates, nor heat, and the Congo was plagued by both. But Xie's message had been emphatic. He must come in person. It seemed that the General was barely in control of himself or the situation, and already he had exceeded his express orders by transferring $2 billion to that local thug Mordecai. And now, after all that, he was insisting on more.

The cars turned off into the mansion's long driveway and slowly pulled to a halt around an old fountain, long since defunct. Standing at the door were four black servants, each dressed in immaculate white uniform, and to one side of them stood Xie. Even in the poor light his modest demeanour was unmistakable. As the car doors opened, he shuffled forward to greet them.

'I am honoured that you should come,' Xie said, bowing low.

Kai's eyes were magnified by his thick-lensed glasses. As he moved forward and into the light, the sagging folds of his skin became visible. The deep lines across his forehead were fixed in a permanent scowl. He made vague tutting noises as the doctor eased him into his wheelchair and tucked a blanket tight across his bone-thin legs. Kai waited, fingers drumming impatiently on the sides of the chair, before his head suddenly snapped round.

'I am extremely displeased to find this situation so out of control,' he said, his voice rasping in the still night air. 'Take me to the General at once.'

Xie bowed again, this time lower, as Kai was pushed through the massive front doorway and into the house. The plain-clothes PLA Special Forces walked either side of him, looking lithe and athletic, and shortening their stride to keep step with Kai's trundling wheelchair. The lead soldier was the Squad Commander and he strode ahead, eyes passing rapidly over the outlines of furniture and doorways lining the dimly lit corridor. Reaching the far end, he was the first to step out on to the veranda. General Jian was standing to one side of it, his arms folded across his chest.

'I am honoured,' he said flatly, giving a perfunctory bow as Kai was wheeled forward.

'Why have *you* brought me here?' the old man said, with a sharp jab of his finger.

'You're mistaken. It wasn't I who requested that you come,' Jian replied, turning his gaze towards Xie.

'No, but it is *your* actions that demanded I did!' Kai spat, his frail old body lurching forward in the wheelchair. Jerking his head to one side, he pulled some extra slack for the oxygen tube before speaking once again. 'Tell me, General, on whose authority did you transfer the entire balance for the mine? A decision of that magnitude is made by the Guild's committee, not on some unilateral whim.'

'We had no time . . . '

'Don't interrupt! You transfer double the

agreed sum and then have the audacity to ask for more?'

Jian didn't respond immediately. Instead, he looked at the eight bodyguards flanking Kai and wondered why there were so many. Was it simply because the Head of the Guild was travelling to a place as inherently dangerous as the Congo, or were they here for another purpose entirely? Perhaps they thought the poison wasn't working fast enough and were here to expedite the process?

Jian slowly switched his gaze back to Kai.

'I have successfully launched the new network and now, in one fell swoop, have legitimised all our mining interests in the Congo.' A tense smile appeared on his lips. 'I would have thought that a matter for congratulation, not recrimination.'

Kai tried to speak, but Jian continued, 'And while I am sure your underling has whispered all sorts of dark stories into your ear, you should understand what an extraordinary deal this is. From this point on, all our mining interests here are protected.'

In the silence, they could hear the slow wheeze of Kai's breath through the oxygen tube.

'We shall see,' he said.

As Kai gestured that he wanted to be brought closer to the table, the Squad Commander standing just to his right stepped forward. He was staring past Jian and out towards the lake, squinting into the darkness. There was the faint sound of rotors, barely audible at first, but as they all listened, the noise became clearer. Kai turned from one person to the next, confused.

'What is it?' he asked. 'What are you all doing?'

'Helicopter, sir,' said the Commander. 'We are near the airport, but even so I'd advise moving back inside.'

As he spoke, the sound of the rotors grew louder and soon they could see the helicopter's landing light flashing white in the night sky. It was coming in low over the lake and heading straight for them. The bodyguards drew closer to Kai, stepping in front of him while they waited for the helicopter to pass overhead, but as it started to slow and pulled up in a hover, they reached for their pistols and pulled him back towards the shelter of the corridor.

'General, are you expecting company?' the Commander shouted.

Jian shook his head, but as he stared at the bulbous shape of the helicopter hovering over the lawn, he recognised it as one of the Oryx he had used on the visit to the mine.

'Wait,' he ordered, raising a hand in the air. 'This is one of the delivery helicopters.'

It touched down, and a few seconds later three figures clambered from the cabin. They walked across the lawn and up to the edge of the veranda. Upon seeing the PLA soldiers, they all raised their hands in the air. Jian saw that there was a woman and two men, and all of them were absolutely filthy. Both men were coated in thick black mud, one of them looking so thin that it seemed as if he were going to collapse at any moment.

'Who are you?' Jian shouted in English.

'We're from the mine,' Luca replied. 'From Mordecai's mine in the forest.'

Jian looked from one person to the next, his eyes finally settling on the woman. She was tall, with matted hair and filthy clothes. And she was staring at him with smouldering animosity.

'You're messengers from Mordecai?' Jian asked incredulously.

'No, we escaped from the mine. We're here to speak to the people buying the fire coltan. A Chinese general was here, at this house, a few days back. You're him, right?'

Jian said nothing.

'Yeah, you're him,' Luca said, taking in Jian's sharp, military haircut and stiff demeanour. 'We've come to tell you that Mordecai's betrayed you. That he's betrayed everyone.'

Jian could feel his mouth go dry and a cold sweat start to prickle across the small of his back.

'The mine's empty,' Luca continued. 'Mordecai sealed the whole thing off and tried to kill everyone inside.'

'That's a lie!' Jian roared, turning his head back to look at Kai. 'I was at the mine two days ago and collected an entire shipment.'

Joshua stepped forward. 'That shipment was scraped together from the very last bits of coltan. Trust me, I know. I was one of the miners who dug it out.'

Jian started shaking his head. He could feel his pulse quickening, sending sharp stabs of pain through his temples. 'I don't know why you're here . . . ' he began, but Joshua stepped closer,

405

causing a ripple of movement among the bodyguards.

'There's more to this than the mine,' he said, eyes directed towards the old Chinese man in the wheelchair, who was listening attentively. 'You need to know something about the fire coltan you've been buying. It reacts with heat, becoming a deadly carcinogen as soon as it gets hot.'

Jian stared at him in confusion. 'What is carsin-gen?'

'Carcinogen. It means cancer!' Joshua shouted. 'As soon as the coltan warms up, it kills you with a virulent brain tumour. It's been happening to all the miners there. Hundreds have already died!'

Jian stared at him, frozen in horror as the seconds passed. Then something clicked and he started clawing at his own throat, his body doubling over, fingers raking across his neck and chest. Everyone stared at him in shock, backing away as if he had suddenly become possessed, while Jian continued to writhe from side to side, ripping his shirt open with both hands. Finally, he got hold of the leather necklace and forced his fingers violently underneath. It broke with a single jerk of his hand and he flung it across the tiles of the veranda. It skidded to a halt about twenty feet away while Jian remained doubled over, eyes locked on the deadly gift.

Between the open folds of his shirt, Joshua could see the black swelling running around the Chinese man's neck and shoulders. He had seen the same marks many times before on the miners he had tried to treat, and knew that from this stage on the cancer would rapidly advance. In just under a week, it would spread up to the side of the man's head, doubling in size every couple of days. The tumour would pressurise the brain, squeezing it against the bone of the man's skull with maddening intensity, until finally it would kill him.

As Jian slowly straightened, pulling his shirt back across his chest, Joshua's expression changed to one of pity. At best, this man had only a fortnight left to live.

'You get headaches?' he asked. Jian nodded, his expression slowly draining of all animosity. There was only bewilderment there as he struggled to believe it could be true.

'What does this mean?' he asked. 'What is happening to me?'

Joshua moved closer. 'You need medical help right now. But you've got to understand that it's far gone. The tumour is visible from the outside and that means . . . ' He paused. 'It means that you don't have much time left.'

Jian's fingers moved up to his neck, scratching at the flaky skin. He had already rubbed it clean off the lump beneath and now a thin trickle of blood seeped out, staining his fingertips. He was shaking his head slowly, eyes looking from one person to the next as his breathing started to quicken. He stumbled towards the corridor.

'I need to get out of here,' he mumbled. 'I need to get out.'

But before he could leave, Kai signalled to his bodyguards. They quickly closed ranks in front of Jian, blocking the way.

'What are you doing?' he said, his voice rising in panic. 'Let me out of here! I need to get some help!'

'*You were responsible for all of this,*' Kai said in Mandarin, his dry voice cutting off Jian's pleas. '*You can wait. Take him back to his room and ensure he stays.*'

'No! Don't do this,' Jian screamed, turning back from the wall of bodyguards and facing Kai. '*Please. I've got to get out of here! You heard what the Westerner said. I don't have much time.*'

For a moment, Kai didn't respond. Then he gave a slow nod of his head and four of his bodyguards reached forward, grabbing Jian under his arms.

'*We will deal with you later,*' he whispered.

'*We can make a deal,*' Jian shouted, as the bodyguards dragged him back to the corridor. '*Just let me see a doctor!*'

The sound of his protests faded. Kai's gaze moved from Luca to Bear before settling on Joshua.

'You need to get that man to a hospital,' Joshua told him. 'I've seen this before and he doesn't have much time.'

Kai waved away his advice.

'We will deal with our own,' he said in English, with only the slightest hint of an accent. 'This carcinogen . . . you said it is triggered by heat. How much heat is required before you see these effects?'

Joshua shrugged. 'We don't know exactly, but it definitely gets worse the hotter it is. As you can

408

see, even a small amount of the really pure stuff can be deadly when it's warmed by body heat.'

Bear stepped forward. 'You're using this for electronics, right?' she asked. 'Some kind of communications device or computer?'

Kai nodded, seeing no reason to conceal the fact.

'All those kinds of things produce heat; usually lots of it. Laptops have to run fans to keep their components cool, and with a mobile all you have to do is press it to your ear to feel the heat coming off it.'

'But are you sure it's *enough* heat to cause physical damage?' Kai asked.

'No, we're not sure at all,' Bear replied. 'But all of us have been into that mine and seen what it can do. It's deadly. So if you're even thinking about releasing it on to the open market, you'd better test it properly. Otherwise you're going to have the death of thousands of innocent people on your hands.'

Kai pulled at the oxygen tube at his nose. He took off his glasses, rubbing his eyes slowly as he thought through what had been said. Everyone waited in silence while his old eyes seemed to rest on a distant part of the lake somewhere behind them.

Kai knew the Guild had billions upon billions of dollars invested in the Goma Project, each family having committed itself deeply. This was a new technology that was taking the world by storm, and any delay in that process, any seeds of doubt about the safety of it all, would send their own stocks crashing. The financial implications of even halting the launch while further testing was completed would be catastrophic, let alone if they found out that there was any validity to these Westerners' claims.

Xie suddenly shuffled forward. He had been lurking in the shadows. Now he moved through the group of people to stand beside Kai.

'If I may, sir,' he said in Mandarin. '*How do we know these Westerners are telling the truth? We need to check their backgrounds, find out if they were sent here to misinform us and delay the launch of the network.*'

Kai raised an eyebrow, then nodded over to where Jian's necklace still lay on the ground. '*All the evidence we need is right before our eyes.*'

'*But, sir, there are many other factors to consider. The investment is unparalleled and we have an obligation to the Guild . . .* '

Kai slowly raised his hand, silencing him. Even in the dull light, his face looked sheet white, the natural colour drained completely from his cheeks. His stern gaze moved across to the Westerners before resting on Xie.

'Obligation,' he said, drawing the word out slowly. 'Where do our obligations lie? To the money or to the millions of people who will use our products? To be sure, we have invested heavily in this project and it is of great significance, but if the Westerners are right, then I am not prepared to become a mass murderer just to save our share price.' Kai nodded slowly to himself, the weight of the decision almost too much for him to bear. 'Halt all shipments with immediate effect until such time as this new

410

substance can be properly tested.'

Xie shut his eyes, the sheer magnitude of the decision making his head spin. He already knew the ramifications of this would ripple out across the Guild and, by extension, the whole of China. It would rupture an already fragmented alliance, causing a new wave of infighting and recriminations, which would inevitably tear the three hundred richest families in China apart.

'I shall send the message out immediately,' he said, bowing low.

Kai turned towards the Westerners. 'If we discover that you have misled us in any way, make no mistake, we shall find you.' He gave them a dismissive wave of his hand. 'Now leave us.'

They departed for the helicopter without another word. Xie returned to stand next to Kai's wheelchair. For several minutes they waited in silence, watching the helicopter slowly rise up and fly off into the night.

'*And the General?*' Xie asked, once the noise had died down.

Kai continued staring out towards the lake. '*He stays here. It would seem his fate has already been decided.*'

★ ★ ★

Jian stared out of the window in his bedroom. He had ripped off his shirt and sat with his elbows resting on the table in front of him, the swelling on his neck a deeper black in the dull light. Without even realising it, he scratched the

411

skin again, prompting another trickle of blood to ooze out and run down as far as his armpit.

Jian's gaze turned back to the table. His laptop lay just in front of the butterfly cage, its screen still displaying the share prices on the New York Stock Exchange. With a sweep of his arm, he sent it crashing down on to the bedroom floor before turning his gaze back to the butterflies. The nearest to him slowly peeled its wings apart, revealing a streak of iridescent pink.

Over the years, Jian had added hundreds upon hundreds of butterflies to his collection, but never before had he seen such beauty. These specimens were flawless, the markings on each wing perfectly symmetrical, and the colour was more beautiful than he could ever have imagined.

Two days ago, Jian had given his servants instruction to have everything made ready for his return. A special case had already been made, with 'Salamis parhassus' neatly embossed beneath the framing mount in gold leaf. Everything was ready.

Opening the cage door, Jian reached inside. As he expertly slid his hand closer to the nearest butterfly, his fingers parted to the exact width of the creature's thorax. He held his breath, black eyes widening in concentration as he suddenly reached out, taking hold. The movement was precise, his fingers sliding beneath the fluttering wings. A single touch would be all it took . . .

Jian's mouth opened as he felt the infinitesimal movement of the butterfly in his grasp, before slowly he drew it from the cage and relaxed his grip. The butterfly's wings opened in a burst of colour as it flew upwards, battling against the night breeze flooding in through the open window before disappearing into the night.

Jian watched it go.

'Beautiful,' he whispered. 'Just beautiful.'

38

Luca quietly slid out from between the clean linen sheets and padded over to the bathroom. He splashed some water over his face and quickly pulled on a fresh white T-shirt and his brown, lightweight jungle trousers. Laundry had done the best they could, but still hairline rips ran across the thighs and ankles, while the knees were permanently stained black from mud.

Sneaking out to the door, he paused and glanced over at the bed. Bear was still there, fast asleep with her head buried face down in the heavy folds of the pillows. The sheets were wrapped around her legs, leaving only the soles of her feet visible at the far end, while from the waist up she was naked. Luca stood still for a moment, marvelling at how beautiful she was, even while sleeping.

Shutting the door quietly behind him, he walked towards the main foyer. The hotel was a maze of pleasant, nondescript corridors, all finished in the same decor, while covers of popular music played on pan pipes repeated on an endless soundtrack.

The corridor opened up into a bustling lobby with people crowded into every part of it. Tourist season had just started in Rwanda and the Safari Lodge was the most popular hotel in town. It was brimming with locals and foreigners all going about their business. To one side, Luca could see a suited delegation being herded into the conference centre, while a group of Western tourists were crowded into the curio gift shop, waiting for their tour guide to arrive for the start of the gorilla trek. Each one of them had a long-lens camera and a nose glistening with sunblock.

Everywhere around him people were going about their normal lives. They were eating, working, arguing and laughing; and it made his sense of separation feel all the more acute. He felt utterly detached from these people, as if even their basic needs were somehow different from his own. This was *their* version of normality, not his, yet from all his climbing expeditions, Luca already knew that it was something he needed to come to terms with, and quickly, if he was ever going to fit back into 'normal' society.

This was now his life. And he was going to have to accept it.

'Mr Matthews.'

It took the receptionist several more attempts to get his attention.

'You have a message, sir.' She smiled, somehow looking attractive despite the garish colours of her hotel uniform. 'It arrived this morning.'

'Thanks. And is breakfast still going? I'm starving.'

'They're packing away the last of the buffet, but I am sure you can still get something.'

Luca thanked her and moved out on to the balcony. A huge swimming pool stretched out below him. Tables and sunloungers were neatly arranged to either side, with tourists already busily tanning and ordering their drinks from the passing waiters. Opening the note, Luca read it then slowly folded the paper in two.

It was from Joshua at the hospital. The doctor had cleared him to travel and he had booked them on to the evening flight back to the UK. In only nine hours' time, Luca would be boarding a plane.

He had tried to remind himself that this time with Bear would have to end, but for three days now they had been closeted in their bedroom, only venturing out when hungry. Time had become irrelevant for them, as if reality had been carefully placed to one side and all the days and nights had merged into one. Sometimes they made love in the early hours of the afternoon; other times they talked long into the night. It didn't matter. Nothing that the rest of the world did mattered any more. Their existence centred around each other, and both of them had become lost in it all.

From the moment they had checked into the hotel, Luca had realised that Bear was the kind of person who, when she gave herself to someone, gave herself completely. It was just her nature to be that way; no reticence or prevarication, just her, laid open. As they switched off the light on that first night, she whispered '*Je t'aime*' into his ear. Love. Luca had repeated the words over and over in his head. It somehow seemed so simple, more like a statement of fact than any complicated emotion.

And by the next morning, he had found himself saying the same thing back to her.

With this note from Joshua, all that had suddenly changed. The world that Bear and he had created for themselves would soon come crashing down and there were only a few hours left for them.

Luca turned to see the breakfast hall slowly emptying of diners. Moving across it and grabbing a large plate, he piled what remained of the buffet on to it, quickly reclaiming some of the dried-up scrambled eggs and layers of streaky bacon before the waiters took the large metal trays out from under the heat lamps. There was a pot of coffee to one side and, scooping it all up, he quickly hurried back.

Bear woke as Luca placed the plate down on the bedside table and climbed on to the other side of the bed. He watched her slowly stretch and yawn, unhurriedly drawing her body towards his until she was lying on top of him, with her elbows folded across his chest. She stared into his eyes for a moment, before leaning forward and kissing him.

'You're always hungry,' she whispered. Luca smiled, but she sensed his hesitation.

'What is it?' she asked.

'I just got a message from Josh. The doctors say he's well enough to travel.'

'But what about the chemo and radiotherapy?'

'He still has all that to come, but he wants to get back to England and do it there. The tumour's right at the early stages and he said they have a really good chance of beating it if they start straight away.'

Bear slowly shut her eyes. 'But this means you're leaving.'

'Tonight. The eight o'clock flight.'

Luca leaned forward and kissed her, feeling the words hanging between them. He felt Bear respond to his kiss, but as they parted he could see the sadness in her eyes. There was resignation there too, as if this was something she had been expecting at any moment.

'I was thinking,' he said. 'I could just change my ticket and stay a bit longer. You know, we don't have to do this now.'

'That's not the point,' she whispered. 'It's about where we go from here.'

She placed both her hands on his shoulders and stared into his eyes. 'I meant what I said, Luca. *Je t'aime.*'

'I know. But how do we know this is real?' he asked. 'How do we know this feeling will last? That it isn't just right here and now?'

Bear frowned. 'Because I grew up in Africa, and I can feel it in my heart when I love someone.' She raised his hand, pressing it against her chest. 'I can *feel* it here when I love someone. Even if they can't.'

Luca embraced her, pushing her head back slightly with the force of his kiss. 'I do,' he whispered. 'I do love you.'

After a moment she blinked, staring blankly ahead as Luca curled his fingers into her hair. Already, she was shaking her head.

'I have a son,' she said, her voice so soft it was barely audible. 'Nathan's back in Cape Town, waiting for me. I have a whole family back there, Luca. A life.'

She looked into his eyes. 'I can't just ignore that.'

He stared at her, realising what had to be done, but the very idea of it ran counter to everything he felt right then. He wanted to wrap his arms around her and stay where they were, put everything on hold and be together. But already he knew that this wasn't the basis for any lasting relationship. They were too wrapped up in the horror of the last week, too blinded by the strength of shared experience, to know what was real and what was not.

For several seconds he stared at her. Finally, he spoke.

'We have to leave each other for a while,' he said. 'You have to go back to your family and try to make it work. Properly try. And forget about me.'

Bear's frown deepened. '*Mais comment je peux faire cela?*' But how am I supposed to do that? she pleaded. 'After everything we've been through, you're asking me to leave? Like I can just ignore my own heart!' A tear ran down the side of her nose. 'I can't live like that, Luca! I can't go on pretending that I don't feel a certain way. That you don't exist.'

He reached out, gently pulling her closer to him. 'You will go on, and you will pretend, because you owe it to your son. If you still feel the same way about me a year from now, then come and find me. I'll be waiting.'

There was a pause. 'Why is it that I can't be

with the people that I love?' she whispered. 'First my father, and now you.'

Luca didn't answer, knowing that there was nothing he could say that would suffice. For the longest time they lay in each other's arms, listening to the low hum of the air conditioning and feeling the soft draft of air wash across them. There was the faint rumble of cars going past on the main road beyond the hotel's carefully manicured gardens, and they listened to each sound from the outside world, feeling it draw closer with each minute that passed.

Eventually, Bear looked up and glanced down at her watch. She kissed him once again, but this time, as she pulled back, Luca saw a faint smile on her lips.

'If we only have a few hours left,' she said, 'we'd better make the most of it.'

39

The sun rose above the sprawling city of Kinshasa. It filtered past the high-rise buildings of downtown and the Boulevard de 30 Juin, before beaming down across the mass of tin-shack slums crowding the river. Hundreds of small boats and pirogues were anchored along the water's edge, with rubbish littered high on each bank. Here, the Congo River was wide, as if gathering itself before spilling out into the Atlantic Ocean as its thousand-mile journey finally came to an end.

On the side of Mont Ngaliema, the first light of day crept past the curtains of the presidential palace. It threw into relief the silhouettes of the Louis XV furniture and the high, ornately crafted ceiling of the master bedroom. Lying on the bed, a man was fast asleep, but every few seconds his body jerked involuntarily and he twisted from side to side, knotting the sheets around him. Sweat prickled across his forehead, while his cheeks twitched in spasm. He was starting to wake, and as the daylight crept a little further into the room, his eyes jolted open.

Joseph-Désiré Mordecai slowly raised himself off the bed and sat with his head in his hands. Sweat dampened his palms. As he slowly pulled his hands back from his face, he could see they were trembling. The nightmares had started again.

Since they had reached Kinshasa and his LRA forces had easily overthrown Kabila's ill-disciplined government troops, Mordecai had locked himself in the presidential apartment with orders not to be disturbed. He had left instructions to change the LRA's name, founding instead *Le Mouvement Démocratique du Congo* or MDC, and already every sycophantic minister from the old regime had switched sides and was pledging allegiance. What was left of the MONUC forces were hurriedly dismantling their compounds, while the Mai-Mai rebellion in the east had been swiftly crushed. It had taken a sizeable part of his army to do it, but now every last Mai-Mai village had been razed to the ground. Despite the Americans' money, barely a single man, woman or child from that tribe was now left alive.

Already, the delegations from the West had arrived to start negotiating for mineral rights.

He had learned that the French had tabled a motion in the UN Security Council to downgrade the level of criminal status of the LRA, wiping any notion of genocide from their files, while stories had been circulated in the press that the newly formed MDC was in fact nothing to do with the murderous LRA rebel group formerly led by Joseph Kony. The whitewash had begun, and Western governments were experts at it.

Mordecai heard a gentle knock at the door.

'I said I was not to be disturbed!' he roared, wiping the sweat off his forehead. He stared down at his trembling hands. The nightmares

. . . They were getting worse. He was starting to get them during the day as well, his vision fogging as the images flashed before his eyes. The days and nights were blurring into one; becoming an endless halflight filled with the tortured faces of his victims. But there was one face that kept coming back to him, no matter what he did. That woman by the river. The one that had split his lip and broken his nose. She had been the first to stand up to him, the first without fear, and now, every morning, he would wake seeing her hateful eyes.

Something had switched that day. It made him feel naked and unsure, his confidence diminishing with each new morning, and each new vision. He felt crippled by the very thought of going to sleep and knowing that she would be there when he woke, with those eyes burning into him.

There was another gentle knock at the door.

'Sir, the American delegation has arrived,' a voice said nervously through the door. 'And you mentioned, sir, that . . . that you wanted to speak to them. They have now been waiting for over two hours.'

'Let them wait!' Mordecai screamed. After a pause, he raised himself from the bed and slowly turned away from the door. He paced across to the window and slid his fingers around the edge of the curtain, cautiously drawing it back. From where the palace was situated, high up on the hillside, he could see right across the city. The fires had finally stopped and the war was over. For over a week now, he had been the ruler of all the Congo.

Moving into an antechamber, he went to the beautiful bathroom and swiftly got dressed. His clothes had been laid out for him: a sombre, charcoal suit with a discreet pale blue tie. Hanging in the cupboard just next to him, he could see one of his old white suits, now freshly laundered but still grey stains remained on the cuffs and ankles. He reached forward, gently rubbing his thumb and forefingers across the fabric. How had it come to this so quickly? He was already starting to dress like one of them.

As he finished getting ready and moved back to the bedroom door, he paused, his hand just resting on the handle. He stayed like that for several seconds, with his forehead pressed up against the hard wood, and exhaled deeply, feeling the same trepidation he had felt on waking back in the jungle, he had always found it so easy to face the light, to find the truth. Now everything seemed so unclear.

Pulling the doors back, Mordecai suddenly stepped out into the light. His bodyguards were there, flanked by two private secretaries, waiting.

'Take me to them,' he said, making his voice seem casual and unhurried.

The secretaries quickly led him down one flight of red-carpeted stairs and then another, winding through the interior of the palace to where a crowd of waiting diplomats were assembled in the great hall. There were hundreds of them, grouped by nationality and mutual interest. As Mordecai approached the entire room fell silent, each one of them staring expectantly towards the new leader of the Congo.

'Muzongos,' Mordecai said to himself as a smile appeared on his lips. 'They never learn.'

Acknowledgements

I am always amazed at how selfless people can be. Time, knowledge and energy were offered to me in abundance on this book and I am indebted to a long list of people, from those that accompanied me on the adventure itself to those that inspired me, even unwittingly.

For Oli Steads agreeing to come with me to the Democratic Republic of Congo and guiding me through the process. Then, to those who helped so much along the way; Tom Mills for advice in London, Rosemary Ruf for taking us in at the Okapi Reserve, Mbake Shiva through Thalia Liokatis, who was just so kind and caring. To Luis, our fixer in Goma, and Jon Cadd the Cessna pilot who got us in.

Thanks to Adam Pletts for that evening discussing Kony in Beirut, and Cirine El Husseini for proofing every draft and doing the Arabic translations. To Jeff Willner and his help with the Swahili translations and Charlie Scott for the military know-how which saved the book from my Rambo clichés. To Simon and Chika for their corrections, and for Mike for being a sounding board over pints at the Windsor castle.

Then to Tim Glister at Jankow and Nesbit for such unfailing support. Kate Weinberg, the source of so many ideas and structure for this book. Like the first, I really couldn't have done it without you. Thank you. The same goes for

Rosie de Courcy who went through the manuscript time after time, beating it into shape. It gives me such confidence to know you are there.

Thanks must go to Rick and Margie Garratt in Cape Town for suffering my tired moods and giving up various parts of their house to becoming offices. Oscar and Electra, for spending so little time with you this time round in South Africa. But finally, my thanks go to Robyn. Always there, always patient. We got through it together.

We do hope that you have enjoyed reading this large print book.

Did you know that all of our titles are available for purchase?

We publish a wide range of high quality large print books including:
Romances, Mysteries, Classics
General Fiction
Non Fiction and Westerns

Special interest titles available in large print are:
The Little Oxford Dictionary
Music Book
Song Book
Hymn Book
Service Book

Also available from us courtesy of Oxford University Press:
Young Readers' Dictionary
(large print edition)
Young Readers' Thesaurus
(large print edition)

For further information or a free brochure, please contact us at:
Ulverscroft Large Print Books Ltd.,
The Green, Bradgate Road, Anstey,
Leicester, LE7 7FU, England.
Tel: (00 44) 0116 236 4325
Fax: (00 44) 0116 234 0205

Other titles published by
The House of Ulverscroft:

THE FORBIDDEN TEMPLE

Patrick Woodhead

Climber Luca Matthews thrives on the dangers of the high mountain peaks, sacrificing anything to pursue his goals. And when he glimpses an unmapped, virgin peak in the Himalayas, he wants to be the first to climb it. Together with Bill Taylor, his climbing partner, they set off to a region of Tibet, restricted by the Chinese. But when an accident endangers the life of one of the team, a local Tibetan girl leads them to Geltang, a monastery. They discover that since the Chinese Cultural Revolution, Geltang has remained hidden from the outside world . . . However, Luca and Bill are being tailed by the Chinese secret police and become embroiled in a struggle to protect Geltang's precious secret — and the legacy of Tibet itself.

FORTRESS OF SPEARS

Anthony Riches

The Romans have vanquished the rebel alliance, leaving Calgus, Lord of the Northern Tribes, a prisoner of the chieftains he once led. But there's no rest. The new Roman leader's plan is to capture Dinpaladyr, the Selgovae fortress of spears, and return it to a trusted ally. In a select group of the infantry going north with the Petriana cavalry, Marcus Aquila burns for revenge on an enemy army that killed his best friend. They take the fort before the rebel army arrives. However, whilst disguised as Centurion Corvus of the 2nd Tungrians, he's only days ahead of two of the emperor's agents sent from Rome to kill him. And they are pitiless assassins. They know his real name, and too much about his friends.

DEEP BLACK: DEATH WAVE

Stephen Coonts with William H. Keith

The theft of nuclear artillery shells spells disaster for America's National Security Agency. Its crack undercover team, Deep Black's Desk Three, is sent to investigate and neutralise the threat. Led by Charlie Dean, a top field operative, the team discovers that the plot is headed by an Islamic terrorist codenamed 'the Jackal'. He aims to destroy the West by detonating the shells deep inside the Cumbre Vieja volcano on La Palma in Gran Canaria. And this would send a tsunami across the Atlantic Ocean that would strike the East Coast of America with waves of up to one thousand feet high. Charlie and his team have just days to prevent the devastation of the Western world. Can they stop the Jackal's plan in time?

THE TENTH CHAMBER

Glenn Cooper

Abbey of Ruac, rural France: A medieval script is discovered, and sent to Paris for restoration. There, literary historian Hugo Pineau finds therein a description of a painted cave with the secrets it contains — and a map showing its position close to the abbey. Hugo, aided by archaeologist Luc Simard, goes exploring. They discover a vast network of prehistoric caves deep within the cliffs. At the core of the labyrinth lies the most astonishing chamber of all — as the manuscript chronicled. They set up camp with a team of experts to bring their find to the world. But they are drawn into a dangerous game as one 'accidental' death leads to another. Someone will stop at nothing to protect the enigma of the tenth chamber . . .